Praise for *The Washashore*

"A quiet but engrossing…crime thriller with vibrant details and memorable characters…. Mirabile's prose is clean and clear and lovingly paints an eclectic, vibrant community…. a fine edition to any mystery-thriller collection."

—Kirkus Reviews

"A thoroughly entertaining and suspenseful debut, from a writer to watch. *The Washashore* has action, terrific dialogue, and a charming cast of characters that will keep you hooked on this promising new series."

—William Landay,
New York Times bestselling author of Defending Jacob.

"A main character with guts and heart, a warm love story-a smart, satisfying mystery read."

—Cheryl Richardson,
#1 New York Times bestselling author

"*The Washashore*…pulled me in right away with its moody, coastal atmosphere and a mystery that feels quietly unsettling…a thoughtful, well-paced mystery that leans just as much on character and atmosphere as it does on plot. If you enjoy mysteries that are a little more reflective, with a strong sense of place and a detective who actually thinks things through, this is definitely one worth picking up."

—Seattle Book Review

"[A] clash of iconic American imagery perfectly launches the [Silas] Lopez series. Mirabile's debut mystery … establishes the detective as stoic, principled, and carrying the kind of damage that surfaces at inconvenient moments. [The] pacing is patient and relentless…"

—Publishers Weekly/Booklife

"A gripping, addictive page turner. Atmospheric, character-driven, and relentlessly suspenseful."

—Mary J. Cronin, international bestselling author, entrepreneur, & podcaster

"Mirabile's portrayal of Provincetown is textured and atmospheric, grounding the mystery in a vividly drawn community. Readers who enjoy character-driven crime fiction with a strong sense of place and careful attention to investigative detail will find much to appreciate in *The Washashore*."

—Readers' Favorite, 5 stars

"Good crime writing should draw you right in, and *The Washashore* does just that, serving up a solid police procedural with some subtle coastal noir touches."

—Reader Views, 5 stars

THE WASHASHORE

A SILAS LOPEZ MYSTERY

CHRISTOPHER MIRABILE

A Seaside Mystery Thriller

The Washashore
Copyright © 2026 by Christopher Mirabile
All rights reserved.

Editing, design, and distribution by Bublish.

ISBN: 979-8-89989-115-1 (paperback)
ISBN: 979-8-89989-122-9 (hardcover)
ISBN: 979-8-89989-114-4 (eBook)

To Liz, Charlie, and Grace, *sine qua non*.

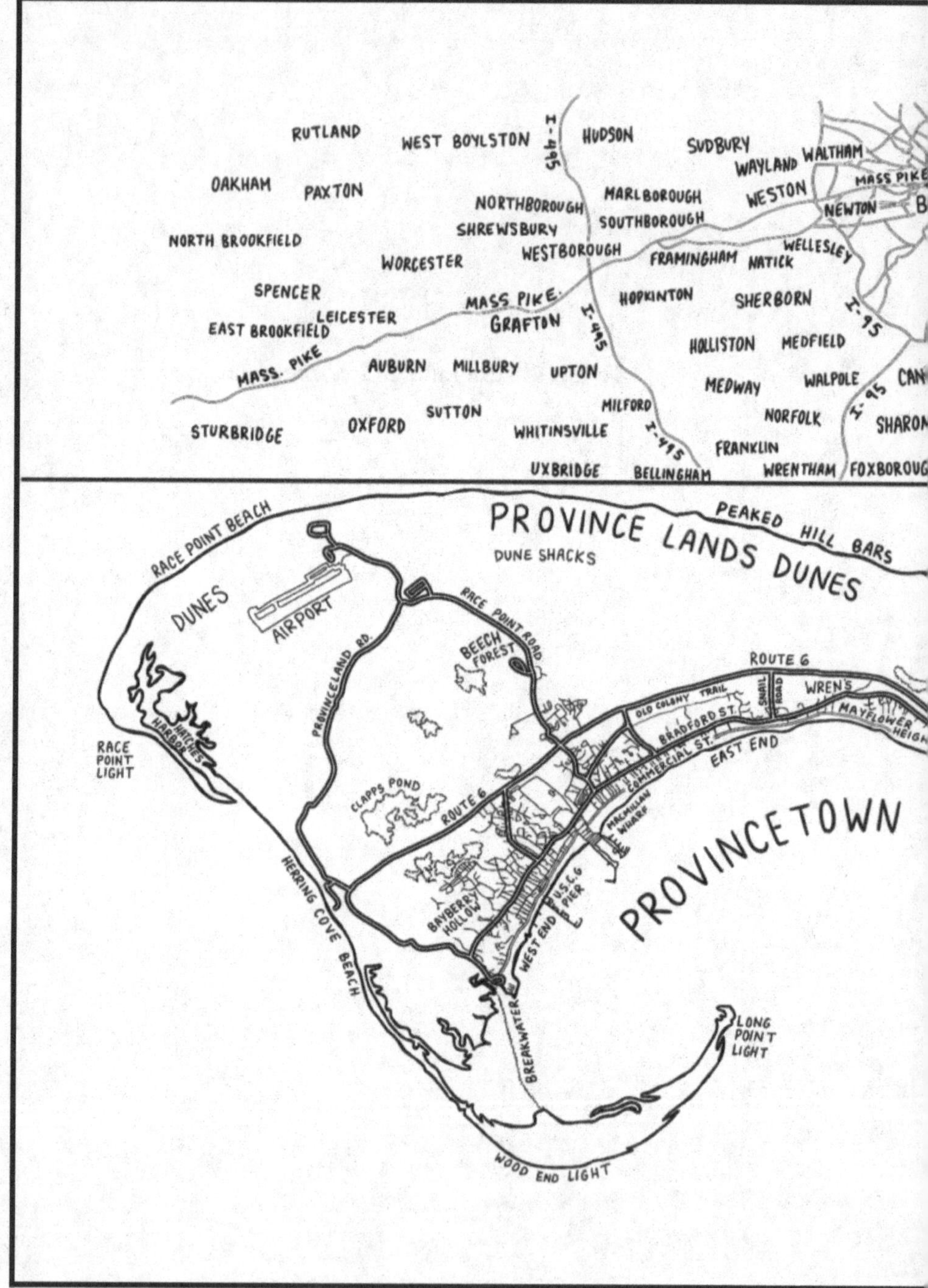

RUTLAND
WEST BOYLSTON
I-495
HUDSON
SUDBURY
WAYLAND
WALTHAM
OAKHAM
PAXTON
WESTON
MASS PIKE
NORTHBOROUGH
MARLBOROUGH
NEWTON
B
SOUTHBOROUGH
NORTH BROOKFIELD
SHREWSBURY
WESTBOROUGH
FRAMINGHAM
NATICK
WELLESLEY
WORCESTER
SPENCER
MASS PIKE
HOPKINTON
SHERBORN
I-95
LEICESTER
GRAFTON
EAST BROOKFIELD
HOLLISTON
MEDFIELD
MASS. PIKE
I-495
AUBURN
MILLBURY
UPTON
MEDWAY
WALPOLE
I-95
CAN
MILFORD
NORFOLK
SHARON
STURBRIDGE
OXFORD
SUTTON
WHITINSVILLE
I-495
FRANKLIN
UXBRIDGE
BELLINGHAM
WRENTHAM
FOXBOROUG

RACE POINT BEACH
PROVINCE LANDS DUNES
PEAKED HILL BARS
DUNE SHACKS
DUNES
AIRPORT
RACE POINT ROAD
BEECH FOREST
ROUTE 6
PROVINCELAND RD.
OLD COLONY TRAIL
SNAIL ROAD
WREN'S
RACE POINT LIGHT
HATCHES HARBORS
BRADFORD ST.
MAYFLOWER HEIGH
COMMERCIAL ST.
EAST END
CLAPPS POND
ROUTE 6
MACMILLAN WHARF
PROVINCETOWN
HERRING COVE BEACH
BAYBERRY HOLLOW
WEST END
U.S. 6 PIER
BREAKWATER
LONG POINT LIGHT
WOOD END LIGHT

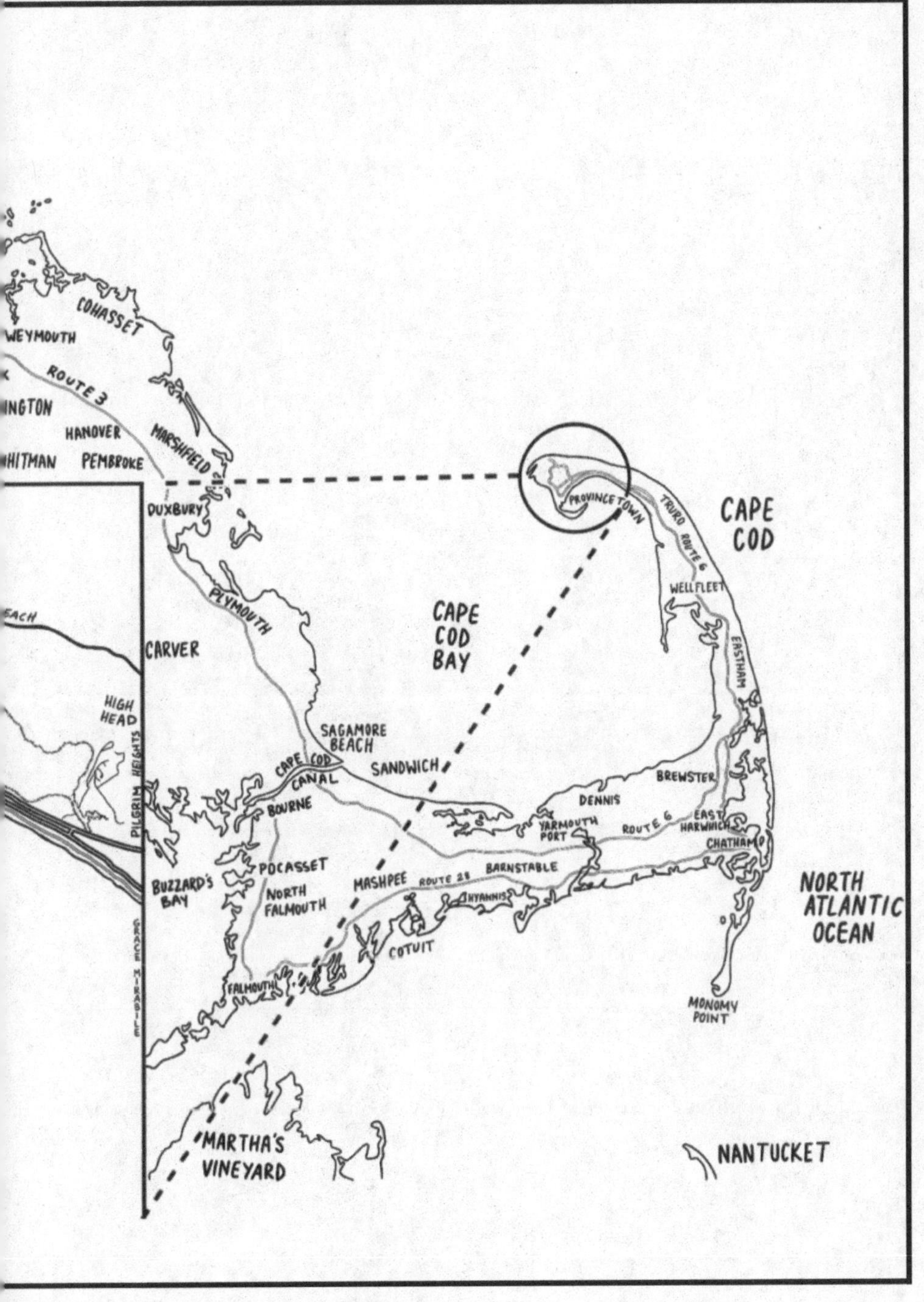
WEYMOUTH
COHASSET
ROUTE 3
HANOVER
WHITMAN
PEMBROKE
MARSHFIELD
DUXBURY
PLYMOUTH
CARVER
HIGH HEAD
PILGRIM HEIGHTS
GRACE M. MOBILE
BEACH
SAGAMORE BEACH
CAPE COD CANAL
BOURNE
POCASSET
BUZZARD'S BAY
NORTH FALMOUTH
MASHPEE
ROUTE 28
FALMOUTH
COTUIT
HYANNIS
BARNSTABLE
YARMOUTH PORT
DENNIS
ROUTE 6
SANDWICH
CAPE COD BAY
PROVINCE TOWN
TRURO
ROUTE 6
CAPE COD
WELLFLEET
EASTHAM
BREWSTER
EAST HARWICH
CHATHAM
MONOMY POINT
NORTH ATLANTIC OCEAN
MARTHA'S VINEYARD
NANTUCKET

CHAPTER 1
Tuesday, September 2

Some mornings start soft, like a dog stretching in sunlight.

This wasn't one of them.

Howling wind, storm tide, a foundered boat—that was how Silas Lopez's day had cracked open.

It'd gone mean from there.

The first call from Provincetown Police Dispatch had come before dawn. Silas was already up, walking around his apartment in an old, mended pair of socks, so he took it himself. Let his team sleep.

"Chief Lopez responding," he'd said.

"Boat in travel lane, Shore Road."

Before setting off in the cruiser, Silas had stared at the dispatch log on the screen, trying to picture it. *Boat where now?*

What was he even doing out here? The phrase *remote outpost* didn't begin to cover it. He'd signed up to be the chief of police—not warden of a glorified sand dune. Maybe this had been a mistake. Probably was. But the milk had been spilled, and he'd made a commitment.

He reached for his keys. "I'm on it."

Silas pulled onto the sandy shoulder of a two-lane road at the edge of town. A line of seaweed and driftwood littered the edge of the cracked asphalt. In the wash of his headlights, a sign for Route 6A flexed back and forth against the wind. Next to it was a town sign that read East End with an arrow pointing directly west.

"Stay here, Bandit," Silas said to the curious blue heeler beside him.

He pushed his cruiser's door open; his nose met with the sharp slap of brine, and wind-driven rain stung his cheeks. A particularly violent gust nearly swept away his wide-brimmed oilskin hat. He cinched its stampede string, keeping it in place.

He took a few steps out into the weather. Dispatch was right. The boat—an upside-down skiff—was halfway into the travel lane. It had recently hit some rocks. Bright shiny gashes of freshly exposed aluminum covered its dull, weathered surface. Silas pulled at the rope tied to the bow—fraying, bright green, and slippery.

He dropped it, wiping his slick palms on his jeans.

A busted mooring line. No mischief. Just broken in the night by the storm's feverish tossing. The boat would have been blown over here from the harbor. Foundered in the surf, and when a gust got under it, pushed up into the road.

Ophelia was Silas's first hurricane. A lifetime in the high-mountain West hadn't prepared him for this sort of damp ferociousness. When he'd heard they would be getting hit with a hurricane, he'd privately felt some apprehension. To his surprise, no one else in town seemed concerned.

In fact, as he'd told his mother on the phone, "Near as I can tell, sixty-mile-an-hour winds don't make the horses blink out here."

Silas looked at the boat. He was uncertain about what to do—a familiar feeling lately—and was too proud to ask the highway department for help. *Haven't met anyone over there yet anyway, so wouldn't know who to call.*

Again, he looked at the boat. *How heavy could it be?*

He grabbed the boat's gunwale and, with an easy heave, righted it, keel-side down. He dragged it back to the grass on the upper beach, thankful for the cover of darkness. *What the hell am I doing? This apparently counts as police work.*

Rather than jotting on his notepad in the wind and rain, he snapped a picture of the registration number on the bow. He'd use that for his report. Then he flipped the boat upside down on the sand, bundled back into his cruiser, and radioed to update Dispatch.

The car might be warm, but something about this day—the churn of the dark, roiling water, the chaotic gusts of wind making birds fly sideways, and the foreboding slash of dawn—felt ominous and unsettling. Like anything could happen. Like he was already chasing something he couldn't see.

Every so often, the wipers swept. He felt a million miles from home. Next to him, turbid surf pounded, unusually strong for the Cape Cod Bay side of the peninsula. He shrugged his wet shoulders to warm up. In the distance, he could see the pitching navigation lights of a rocking container ship temporarily anchored in the bay for shelter. The faint smell of its diesel generators hung in the wind.

Bandit slept on the seat beside him, soft ears back, a warm spot where his chin rested on Silas's leg. Coffee steam rose from a dented steel travel mug sitting in the cupholder. A peachy smudge of dawn was wedging itself, as if by force, under the heavy clouds in his rearview mirror.

A second call from Dispatch punched through the quiet.

A body.

On the sidewalk, right downtown.

By the time Silas radioed Dispatch he was responding, the rain was already reflecting his blue lights back at him.

CHAPTER 2

"Seen highway roadkill in better shape," Silas said to his sergeant, Kevin Clark. "Looks like a pack a wolves got after him. You first on scene?"

Clark nodded.

"Check for pulse? Move him at all?"

Clark shook his head. He was a pale-skinned guy, with full, flushed cheeks and a normally jolly face who carried himself solid—a little on the broad side. He looked more serious and reserved than normal this morning.

"I didn't move him, Chief," Clark said. "I just touched his neck with one gloved finger. No pulse. Felt cold to the touch. I did remove his wallet from his right hip to check for ID."

Silas looked around the dark, wet street corner. They were next to Provincetown Town Hall and their police department, which was located in its basement. The roadway was littered with branches and green leaves, glistening in the rain. There was no traffic, no lights in windows, no pedestrians, save for one runner—the one who'd found the body and called it in.

"Where's the police tape?" Silas said with a grunt. "Let's get it up around the scene. Morning light's comin' up fast."

"I was just about to start working on the crime scene tape," Clark said. "I haven't even been into the office yet. I parked my personal ride at the office and walked over."

"Witnesses?"

"Just him, so far," Clark said, pointing to the wiry man in drenched running shoes, shorts, and a thin long-sleeve running shirt, jogging in place. "I'm guessing he's going to be skipping breakfast."

Ignoring the bravado, Silas asked, "You get a preliminary statement? Anything useful?"

"No, don't think he knows anything. He said he'd just come across the body while out running."

"Get his contact details, and ask him to come down to the station to give a formal statement by noon, while it's still fresh." Silas looked over at the man, then up at the dark rain clouds. "Meantime, cut him loose before he gets stiff as a board in this damp."

"Yes, sir," Clark replied, moving to go, only to be stopped by Silas's sharp look.

"Your assessment?" he prompted. "Of how it got up here on the sidewalk, half on the grass?"

Clark snorted. "Thrown by vehicular impact, no doubt. What else?"

"That right?" Silas asked, turning up the collar of his waxed canvas ranch coat to shield himself against the rain. "This is no bump and bounce. How do you account for pavement smears, deep cuts, signs of dragging on the body? Seen any broken headlight glass around here?"

"Well, no, but any fool can see he got hit. Looking at the roadside location, you'd have to assume a vehicle. How are any of those details going to change the cause of death? The ME will give us what we need, confirm the victim was hit," Clark said.

"Cause of death's important, sure. But scene details matter, Sergeant. They tell us what we're dealing with. Light tap on a victim? Could be accidental. Driver might not even know, depending on the situation—time, weather, vehicle. But with a typical passenger car, a body hit hard enough to be thrown or dragged any distance, driver's gonna know it happened." He paused, giving Clark a pointed look before spelling it out for him. "Means they left the scene knowingly."

"Okay," Clark said.

His tone's turned petulant—impressive, considering it's barely sunrise.

"Look here," Silas said, pointing to the mangled body. "Busted limbs every which way. Lotta blood, deep lacerations. Part of the scalp missing. Torn clothing—shirt's almost off. This victim's been tumbled, dragged hard. Think we're looking for a distracted driver? Texting teen? No, we aren't."

This wasn't just a traffic crash. He could feel it. Something was off. That kind of damage doesn't come from a sleepy tourist drifting off the road.

He didn't want to get ahead of himself, but his gut told him to dig deeper.

"Odds are, we're looking for someone who knows precisely what they did." There was more emotion in his voice than he intended. "Goddamn airbag exploded in their face, Clark, if nothing else." He cleared his throat. "Do you have an ETA on the ME? You say you got an ID on the vic?"

Clark's color came up, and he exhaled hard through his nose. He didn't make eye contact with Silas. "ME's an hour out. She's coming straight from her place in Sandwich. Name's Tammy Reynolds. The victim is Timothy Perkins. Thirty-six." His tone was flat, clipped.

"Kin?" Silas asked.

"He has a husband by the name of Blake Stevenson. The two of them lived in a condo in the development called Gale Force Village, located on Spinnaker Lane—unit seven. I looked the husband up," Clark said, gesturing to his phone. "Husband's two years older and works as a local real estate agent. Our victim apparently worked in IT."

"Contacted yet?"

"No, sir," Clark said, though he sounded uncertain.

"That's good. Prefer to head up there myself so I can get eyes on when I inform him." Then, looking around the scene, he added, "You stay here, control this scene. Until the ME has a tent up, get a couple of cruisers angled 'round this body. Close enough to block the view of this from the street, but far enough not to disturb trace forensics."

Clark nodded, face expressionless.

"Get a patrol officer down here. Make sure they keep traffic flowin' through, move along any looky-loos. You control this scene the whole time, Sergeant—until the ME's finished, removes the victim, cleans up, releases her hold on the area." He paused, eyeing Clark. "But let's be clear: *control* means if a picture of this buzzard's breakfast ends up online somewhere, *Sergeant Clark* didn't follow instructions. Understand?"

Clark's face went as sour as the weather. *But he's paying attention.*

"And get Public Works goin' on cleanin' up this scene as soon as the ME and Forensics are done. They'll need to bring in a licensed outfit to handle what's left of it—disinfect and such. Meantime, update me hourly, or sooner, on any developments down here."

Silas took another look at the grim scene. That bad feeling was sticking with him, and it didn't fade, even as he headed out to speak to the victim's husband. On his way to Spinnaker Lane, he dialed the town manager and was met with a groggy but familiar voice: "Hello. This is Flood."

"Mr. Flood, this is Chief Lopez. Sorry to call before the roosters. Need to update you on a situation downtown."

"You know you can call me Patrick, Silas." Then, sleepily, he added, "What could possibly be going on at this time of the morning?"

"Believe it or not," Silas began, glancing at the notepad in the passenger's seat, "this one's not even my first call of the day. First was a damn boat in the road. This one's a Mr. Timothy Perkins, age thirty-six, town resident. Been killed." He returned the pad to his shirt pocket. "Pedestrian. Vehicle likely involved. Corner of Bradford and Ryder. On my way to his West End residence to inform the husband, a Mr. Blake Stevenson, also a town resident."

"Oh, hell. That's terrible. I don't know either of them. Bradford and Ryder is right outside our office windows. What happened?" Patrick asked.

"Don't know yet. ME is on the way from Sandwich. If you're askin' me to speculate, hit by a vehicle, cut up real bad, maybe dragged some." Silas paused for a beat, then added, "Hit like that, unlikely the driver wouldn't know it. You can imagine for yourself what that implies."

"I can't . . . That's just . . . well, awful. Not a great advertisement for our public safety, either. Can you keep me updated regularly in case the papers or members of the town board want information from me?"

"'Course," Silas said.

Meantime, I need to get eyes on the husband. Sooner, the better.

CHAPTER 3

By the time Silas reached Spinnaker Lane, dawn began creeping in, cool and gray. He pulled into the parking lot of a wood-frame condominium building. Wasn't anything special—an older development with weathered trim and a convenient location.

Silas parked his cruiser, strolling up to unit seven. The bell was weak, so he knocked.

A few moments later, Stevenson opened the door, leaning-on-the-doorknob tired—bags under his bloodshot eyes, face pale, jeans with one pocket still turned inside out, untucked shirt, hair rumpled like he'd just woken up.

"Officer, how can I help you? Here, come in out of the rain." He stood out of the way as he opened the door fully.

Dread already in his voice. Like he knows why I'm here.

Silas stomped his feet and shook his coat. "You're Blake Stevenson, husband of a Mr. Timothy Perkins?" he asked, removing his oilskin hat and holding it to his side to drip.

"Yes, is something wrong? Where is Timothy? Is he all right?"

Panic's rising. He's piecing it together—if he doesn't already know.

"Let's sit down, Mr. Stevenson," Silas said, guiding him toward one of two modern-looking couches. He sat opposite the victim's husband, hat in hand. Stale cigarette smoke still hung in the air, and last night's dishes still sat out on the counter.

Mr. Stevenson's eyes were wide. "Is Timothy all right?" he repeated again.

Silas looked at the floor for a second before looking Stevenson in the eye.

"No, sir, he's not. I'm sorry to tell you this, but Mr. Perkins was killed—looks like a hit-and-run."

Stevenson gasped with shock, hand covering his mouth, eyes darting around as adrenaline obliterated the last of his drowsiness.

Never gets easier, no matter how many times you do it. Doesn't matter who it is—grief always looks the same. Like a trapdoor opened and dropped 'em right out of their own life.

Silas's first impression was that Stevenson's grief and shock looked genuine. *But statistics don't lie. Guy's in the frame until we rule him out.*

"Oh my God! Timothy!" he wailed. "Where? What happened?"

"Sir, our investigation is just gettin' underway, but what we know so far is that it happened down by Town Hall at Bradford and Ryder. Looks like he was hit by a motor vehicle. Probably early this morning."

Stevenson moaned. "He was walking back. My stupid pride! I should have taken him home!"

Silas kept his voice steady. "Sir, walking back from where? When was the last time you spoke to Mr. Perkins?"

"Ah . . . he was out late. At a friend's." He put a hand horizontally across his forehead, like he was trying to concentrate. "Alex Bernardi. I was here . . . at the apartment. I last spoke to him when he left here."

Somethin' about his eye movements just now don't sit right.

"And you think he would have been walking home from the Bernardi residence?"

"Yes." His voice cracked on the single syllable. "I should have given him a ride. Where is he now? Can I . . . Can I see him?"

Silas's mind leaped to the sight of Timothy's body. He kept his expression neutral. "He'll be with the medical examiner for a while yet— but then he'll be released to you, so you can make your arrangements."

"Oh, God!" Stevenson pressed his knuckles to his mouth, shoulders seemingly curling inward under the weight of the mere idea. The finality of never seeing Timothy again, of having to pick out a casket, write an obituary.

Silas gave him a moment before continuing. "One more thing, sir. Can I take a look at your car?"

"My car? Why?" The realization hit midthought. His face twisted, and he let out a low groan before rising to fetch the keys with a halting gait.

They went to the garage. Silas had been expecting shared parking out front, but the apartment complex offered individual garages built into the slope behind the living quarters. He did a quick walk-around of the white BMW. Nothing was out of the ordinary. The car looked pristine—no bumps, scratches, broken headlights. It wasn't damp from the storm.

Silas wanted to leave Stevenson to his grief, so he wrapped it up with just a once-over and said they would have more questions later. "Is there someone I can call for you, sir?" Silas added. "I know this is difficult, and it can be hard to be alone."

Stevenson's hand lingered on the closed garage door. He was already slipping into shock.

"Right. I'll call someone. My sister, probably."

Silas saw him back up to the apartment, no strength left in his posture.

Loss, grief, pain. Tough to watch.

Seemed real.

Doesn't mean he didn't do it, though. Remorse can look awful similar. Meantime, need to speak to this Bernardi right quick.

CHAPTER 4
Wednesday, September 3

The last of the storm had moved out to sea overnight, and morning broke bright and calm.

The police department was in the basement of the large Victorian-era Town Hall, its offices adjacent to other town administrative functions. The department's main briefing room had a drop ceiling hanging a hair lower than eight feet in height. Silas, who stood six foot six barefoot, felt it pressing down on him. Maybe not literally, but enough to notice.

Silas gathered his team in the main briefing room for a case conference. Everyone looked around with uncertainty, milling about and settling into chairs. He waved them along impatiently. If his gut was right, they were dealing with a crime, not an accident. That meant the clock was ticking.

He'd left his life in Salt Lake City behind a couple of months ago, but he was just a week into this job. This was the first full team case conference he'd convened. Normally, he kept routine meetings—roll calls, briefings— very short, but these case conferences were a chance to get everyone up to speed, pool ideas, and learn from each other. All eyes were on him now. Before the team arrived, he'd sent Genny, his administrative assistant, to the Portuguese bakery for some *mornin' grub*—a little somethin' to help folks settle in.

It'd been a vague ask, but Genny had come through. Now, two white pastry boxes filled with traditional *broa, massa sovada,* and *bolo levedo* filled the room with the warm scents of butter, cornmeal, yeast, and vanilla.

Provincetown had a small police department, especially with recent departures, so everyone, including Silas, was expected to put in an oar on police work. Since he was the chief and the only department member with serious experience as a detective, Silas was the natural lead and primary owner on a case like this.

Standing at the head of the table, Silas cut through the chatter. "Let's round up, establish a baseline of facts on Mr. Perkins's death. Till some driver walks in that door and says, 'Dang it, that one's on me,' we're going to treat this like the crime it most likely is. Sergeant Clark, start us off— brief the team on the basics."

Clark had just finished rolling his eyes at Sergeant Travis Evans when Silas called on him. He straightened like a kid caught passing notes, his face made gaunt by the unflattering purple-green cast of the fluorescent lights overhead.

Silas clocked the reaction, annoyance tightening his hands.

With Silas being new to the team, Clark wasn't sure how much detail or opinion to include in his report. So, Clark shrugged, puffed up his chest just a little, and delivered a sloppy, off-the-cuff recitation of the basic facts. He concluded by noting that Silas had visited and informed the victim's husband, Blake Stevenson.

"Thanks, Sergeant," Silas said unenthusiastically. He'd pick his battles. "It's still early, at this point. Husband's a question mark. The shock looked genuine. He asked the questions you'd expect. Seemed a bit off, but shock can do that. Roped him into a preliminary story on whereabouts, timeline, so forth. Said he was at home all night—not sure I liked the look of his eyes when he said it, though. Decided to circle back later before calling him on it. Identified his car, a midsize white BMW sedan, in the garage. Glanced at it; showed no obvious damage."

Done with his report on the husband, Silas shuffled over and leaned against the wall, hands behind his back. The concrete floor was covered from wall to wall with a blue-gray industrial carpet that was as hard as a stove lid. The room's worn chairs mostly matched. When he'd been hired as chief, Silas had insisted on a cleanup of the cramped office space, so the place had a tidy, professional air. Nothing he could do about the dank feel. That came with basement spaces and life by the ocean.

He didn't want to spoon-feed this team, but it was clear they needed some steering.

"Okay, time to get our bearings, pick a direction, and ride. Sergeant Clark," Silas said, nodding at the sergeant. "You were first on scene. What's your initial theory on what went down?"

Clark blinked, caught off guard again. "H-hit-and-run would be my guess," he stammered.

What kind of unprofessional answer is that?

Silas didn't react right away. He let the silence work. But he couldn't leave the word *guess* out there dangling forever. He raised his hand and said to Clark, "Guesswork's not police work. We work with observations and facts."

First big one as a team. First fatality. He understood it was his job to lay out his expectations plain as a paved road, and only then hold his team accountable. *Set the tone; hold the standard.*

He asked if anyone else wanted to add to Clark's theory before continuing. No one did.

"Here's all we know," he began, only to shout, "Bandit, down! Offa there!"

Of course, Bandit would go for that pastry box. Stupid not to see that coming.

Genny moved the boxes toward the center of the table. Bandit abandoned his attempt to steal a pastry and returned to his curled-up position at Silas's feet.

"What I was saying is," Silas went on again, "statistically, when you're looking at a hit-and-run, an ordinary passenger vehicle's most often involved. And when you are looking at an unexplained death, what do the statistics say?" Nobody responded. He sighed. *This is Homicide 101.* "You look at the spouse, significant other, close relatives, business partners."

A few heads nodded.

"With a pedestrian this banged up, we can assume the driver knew they hit something. That means the driver either *meant* to hit the victim in the first place or hit them and didn't stick around."

He let that sit. No need to finish the rest out loud. They'd get there.

Silas paused to look around the table. "So, based on odds, what are we lookin' for?"

Silence. *Figures,* he thought. *Nobody wants to be wrong in front of the new chief.* But no room for being timid around him, so he waited.

Laura Burig, a young patrol officer with ice-blue eyes, the muscular build of a competitive swimmer, and long blonde braids so pale and bright, they caught the light like fresh straw, spoke up and said, "Motive?"

Someone snickered.

"That's one," Silas said, giving Burig the win. He'd ignore the snicker for now. "Fact is, we're looking for two things: first, the vehicle that hit Mr. Perkins; second, driver with reason to hit him, reason to flee, or both. As Burig correctly pointed out, lookin' at motive can help narrow the search. So can eyewitnesses and video."

Silas paused, noticing some officers taking notes. *Good, not everything has to be said twice.*

"Speaking of witnesses, which of you patrol officers handled the scene?" *Time to start trimmin' this down to pieces we can actually work.*

A patrol officer named Gavin Byrne raised his hand. Silas looked at him. The newest member of the team, he had permanent stubble on a strong square jaw, dark hair, hazel-blue eyes. The "black Irish" look of someone with ancestors in Galway. "I was on the scene all morning, Chief."

Nodding, Silas said, "Did our runner witness say he saw anyone else around?"

"Uh, no?" Byrne answered. *Too slow. Too vague.* Silas filed it. Either the witness hadn't been asked, or Byrne wasn't sure he'd asked the right way.

"Byrne, you take his statement when he comes in. Double-check no one else was around. Now, any rubberneckers come by while the ME was there?" he asked, moving on. "Any of 'em seem like they might've been there earlier, returnin' to the scene?"

"No, sir, Chief," said Byrne.

That answer was too fast. This new kid's so eager to please, he's getting in the way of himself. Let it slide for now—they're stressed, unsure.

"Good work, Byrne." *Praise in public . . .* Then, scanning the group, he said, "Cameras?"

Blank stares greeted him. "Genny, I should know, but does this town maintain any official traffic cams or the like?"

"Unfortunately not, Chief."

Turning back to the team, he added, "Now, anybody canvas the immediate area for video doorbells, security cams, webcams, parked cars with dashcams yet?"

The team looked down, and one stopped chewing.

"Listen up. Byrne, canvas east and west of the site down here"—he pointed at the wall map with a finger—"along Bradford. Look everywhere. Eaves, windows, sides of buildings, car dashboards. Any video doorbell, security camera, webcam, dashcam, or possible eyewitnesses. Burig, same for you, but south of Bradford onto this area, along Ryder, Commercial. Couple of blocks' radius."

He studied the map again. *What's left here?*

"Clark, check that train-car-elevator thing and its booth in the park across the street. Marsh, I want you on public records online. Figure out if this guy or the husband had any business disputes, personal disputes, lawsuits."

Silas looked at Officer Anna Marsh. She had dark, curious eyes. Self-possessed—no vanity. Tidy light-brown hair always in a loose bun, often held there with a yellow Ticonderoga No. 2. Inquisitive attitude. Young, very good with computers. *Gotta hunch tells me this task will be a fit for her.*

"Evans, you're coordinating those efforts, supporting these officers," he concluded, pinning Evans in place with his stare. "Compile anything useful your officers bring back. Want an inventory documenting what we got by end of day."

He said it flat. Didn't need to bark it. *Be interesting to see if Evans has natural leadership instincts, organization skills. Seems like a straight shooter so far.* Youthful-looking Black skin, chiseled face with a huge natural grin, warm brown eyes. Hair shaved close on the sides, bit longer on top. *Got a little maturity—a family man, seems pretty even-tempered, solid, but not flashy. Seems dependable, but early days. We'll see about that.*

"Sergeant Clark, you're covering any unrelated routine police matters, so work your elevator canvas in the best you can."

Sergeant Clark nodded, and Silas noted a sour look on his face. Among the rest of the team, there were murmurs and exchanged glances.

"Genny, schedule a follow-up interview with Stevenson, the husband, for end of day. Want to meet at his home, not work, and make sure Marsh knows the timing; she's coming with me."

Genny's eyebrows jolted up a fraction at that, and she wore a small smile as she exchanged glances with a stunned-looking Marsh. *Huh. Guess the old bosses wouldn't have taken anybody with them.*

Then, looking around the room, he asked, "Questions?" Slightly disappointed to see no one raise their hand, he barked, "What you waitin' for? Burnin' daylight, people! Let's get after it!"

CHAPTER 5

Morning had brought clear skies, but there was a slight chill in the air. After grabbing a coat, Silas went to interview the victim's neighbors. He walked up the flagstone path leading to the condominium downstairs from Stevenson. There was a scrubby little garden around the path—still, a lot greener than home. It was a cheap-looking building, not attractive, but the condo association seemed to be trying to keep it in good repair.

He knocked on the aluminum storm door. *That rattle could wake the neighborhood's dogs.* It took her a while to answer. He could hear voices in the unit as she shuffled closer and cracked open the door.

He held up his badge and ID. "Mrs. Ascher?"

"Yes?" she said, blinking back at him. She looked to be in her late seventies. Cardigan with bulging pockets, silver hair in curlers under a sheer scarf. *This is going to take patience.* Still, the only way to learn anything was to ask.

"Morning. Chief of Police Silas Lopez. I'd like to ask some questions in connection with an incident last night."

Again, she blinked like an owl. He felt a flicker of amusement but kept his face straight. From somewhere inside, an elderly male voice called out for her, though Silas couldn't understand what the man was saying.

"A policeman, Mort! He needs to talk to us!" she called over her shoulder. She turned her owl eyes back to Silas. "You'd better come in. I'm Bethany Ascher. I'll fix us cookies and coffee."

She moved back, motioning for him to enter. He stepped into the dim apartment. It was the same floor plan as Stevenson's apartment, but the worn surfaces and furniture had been forgotten by time. Thick curtains had been drawn across the windows. The air inside was still. *Bet they pay their own utilities.*

"No need for cookies and coffee, ma'am. It's just a few questions."

"It's no bother. Sit down," she ordered, pointing to a floral-print sofa pushed against the wall.

An elderly man entered the room. *Has to be her husband, Mort Ascher.* The man moved across the worn carpet and eased himself into a glider rocker with sagging cushions. Silas detected a trace of the scent of Listerine.

Mort squinted at him. "Is this about those two?" he said, his thumb gesturing up toward the ceiling.

Those two? Silas felt a tinge of bewilderment. Somehow, he'd already lost control of the interview and hadn't asked a single question. The slam of the microwave door saved him. Mrs. Ascher bustled in, tray loaded with store-bought cookies, a sugar bowl, a little pot of milk, and a green-colored mug with instant coffee still swirling, white foam clinging to the rim, stained in spots with brown coffee crystals.

"Thank you, kindly, ma'am—and yes, sir, I'm here about your upstairs neighbors," he replied, nodding at the ceiling. "Been an incident. Have a couple of routine questions."

The Aschers exchanged glances. He could tell they had some grievances to air.

"How long have you been neighbors?"

They looked at each other. They clearly didn't know exactly, but Bethany guessed. "It's been at least several years."

"You know of any troubles between them?"

"Oh yes," Bethany said, while Mort nodded vigorously.

"What kinda trouble?"

"They fight all the time!" Mort said. Now it was Bethany's turn to nod vigorously.

"What kinda fights? How do you know they fight?"

"Well," Bethany said, "we frequently hear them shouting at each other through these paper-thin walls."

"That right?" Silas jotted down a note. "Physical? Things bumping or crashing?"

"It never sounds violent or physical, but . . ." Bethany shook her head. "There's been lots of door slamming, shouting, and so forth. It's distressing. It gives me indigestion. Some nights I can't get back to sleep at all, even after two Tums."

"Sorry, ma'am. Now, turning to last evening . . . Did you hear anything during the night?"

"Oh yes, I thought that was why you were here," Bethany said, and Silas sat a little straighter.

"There was a terrible fight last night," Mort said, right as Bethany added, "We were afraid someone was going to get hurt. One of them left in a huff."

"Approximately what time might that've been?"

"I know exactly what time it was because we had just finished *CSI* on CBS, so it was ten p.m."

Silas jotted that down. *TV always makes for a solid time stamp.*

"Thank you. So, one of them went out. Now, Mr. Stevenson said he stayed in for the rest of the night. Lookin' to have you confirm that, if you can . . ."

Bethany's immediate frown caught him off guard. "What? No," she said, glancing at Mort for some backup. "No, he didn't, Officer. Someone went out later that night."

Silas's eyes darted over to Mort, who said nothing.

"Are you sure, ma'am? It's important I have the right day, right timeline."

"Oh yes, of course. I take the diuretic medicine, so I'm up and down. The garages for all these units are on this side," she said, pointing to the downhill side of the building. "Theirs is directly under our bathroom."

These people might be old, but they're still sharp. Good witnesses.

"The opener hums, and the door squeaks and clatters very loudly in its track every time it opens or closes." She pointed toward the floor in the hallway. "I've asked both of them to look into it, but they never do. So I know I definitely heard it open during the night."

"You're certain, ma'am?"

"I remember because I thought, *Who goes out in the middle of the night?* I even told Mort this morning, when he was having his marmalade toast—didn't I, Mort?"

Mort nodded sheepishly, and Silas wondered if maybe he'd been paying more attention to his marmalade toast than his wife's chitchat.

"What time would have that been, ma'am?"

"I don't know exactly, but it was very late." Then after a moment, she added, "The pills usually wake me up around three a.m., if that helps?"

That helped. Silas thanked them, handed over his card in case they thought of anything else.

Outside, he got in the cruiser and scratched Bandit behind the ears.

"Walk soon, partner," he murmured. "Let's go back to the office."

CHAPTER 6

Bandit hopped out of the car and jumped up, placing his front paws on Silas, reminding him about the much-needed walk. Commercial Street was crowded, but the air had not grown hot yet in the late-morning shadows. Silas knew it was a stretch, but he preferred to think of this walk as "foot patrol." Either way, it was a chance for him to think. Bandit tolerated the leash, but just barely. He seemed to think he should be released under his own recognizance, since he was neither a flight risk nor a danger to the community, but Silas knew better. He needed to observe the rules downtown, especially when the street was busy.

He passed through throngs of sunburned tourists, lost in thought. Tourists window-shopped before lunch, ducking into galleries, boutiques, and T-shirt shops. Theater performers called out to passersby, trying to recruit the evening's audience members with flyers. Two tired, sweaty kids on a bench dipped into a box of saltwater taffy with a cellophane window, removing twisted wax paper from the pastel-colored bites. Buskers claimed their spots and set up for the day.

As they stepped out of an alleyway Bandit had wanted to sniff, the dog darted right, distracting Silas just as a woman stepped in front of him. He stopped, pulling Bandit up short. The near collision put him on his back foot. Already surprised by the sudden encounter, he was knocked off-balance because this woman was striking. Striking enough to fluster him.

She was smiling and looking up to make eye contact with him.

She had blazing reddish-brown hair, fair skin with freckles all over. He was noticing the details, as was his habit, when the slanted morning rays hit her eyes. Green, deep green—lit up like glass. Tall and willowy, which appealed, given his height. Looked to be in her early thirties, so just a little younger than his thirty-seven. Elegant, even dressed casually—jeans, loose blouse open at the throat, sleeves rolled back. No makeup, almost no jewelry—didn't need any of that. Confidence. And poise. No, more like effortless grace. Her face looked kind. And something about her felt familiar.

Pointing at Bandit, she gestured with her camera and said, "Would you mind?"

"No."

"No, you wouldn't mind?" she clarified with a smile as warm as melted honey butter.

He nodded once. *Find your words, Silas.*

They stepped over into an eddy in the flow of pedestrians, and she crouched—more freckles visible on the skin showing through soft, pale denim torn at her knee. She extended the back of her hand to Bandit. Silas was about to manage her expectations, but to his surprise, Bandit assessed her with a look and then a sniff before licking her hand.

That was unexpected. *Bandit doesn't usually cut any slack—he needs a reason to trust. This one he likes at first sight.*

"Huh. Bandit doesn't usually warm that much, that fast, to strangers."

She smiled up at Silas. "I've always had luck with dogs. Maybe they sense I'm a dog person."

She was down on one knee, the other leg jutting straight out to the side. She positioned herself, framing a portrait of Bandit with a view down Commercial Street behind him. Silas watched her work the camera with fascination, though there were distractions. *Those jeans fit like a glove—no help to my concentration. Real hard not to notice.*

"Or my scent could be familiar," she added, taking a few stills. The camera clicked, and Bandit seemed to love the attention. "I've seen him around Town Hall. I work there too."

She works there too? That could be where he'd seen her.

"I'm Wren. Wren Bradford. I work for the town. Human Services."

Why did his face feel hot? "Name's Silas Lopez."

She nodded to acknowledge him. He liked that she avoided the formality of a handshake. Instead, shaking Bandit's paw, she exclaimed in a baby voice, "Ooh! I *cannot* get enough of this adorable black spot over his eye like a pirate mask and this gray speckled fur!" Adjusting her camera settings, she said, "Pure Australian cattle dog, I presume?"

Nodding, Silas said, "Yes. When they're this color, people call 'em blue heelers." Then, seized with an inexplicable impulse to overshare with this appealing stranger, he added, "From a line of workin' dogs out West. Way he eats, maybe a little extra dingo mixed in."

Laughing as she worked, she captured a few more shots and stood. She moved in close to show him the stills she'd taken. The way she stood there, only inches away from him, one would think they knew each other well. The soft gold hair on her freckled arm brushed his where the shirtsleeve was rolled back. She smelled better than honeysuckle. He stooped to look, but with the glare, the angles, the dim screen, Silas couldn't make anything out on the camera display. Not that it mattered. He was too scattered to focus on photos.

"I post them on my @ptownpups Insta—he'll be famous."

"Your what now?"

"Instagram. You know, social media?" she said. "I have a page where I post pictures I take of dogs in town. In case you haven't noticed, this town is heaven for dog lovers. There are so many great dogs." Without pausing for breath, she said, "They're a favorite subject of mine because they wear their emotions so plainly."

Wren paused.

She looks self-conscious, like she's worried she's babbling. She wouldn't be wrong, but I don't mind it.

"With dogs, what you see is what you get . . ." she said bashfully.

He looked at her with undivided attention, saying nothing. It was comforting to know he wasn't the only one feeling a little off-balance.

"I enjoy photography. I do it as a side gig. The Instagram posting is a way to bring attention to my more serious photography work."

A second passed. He noticed a blush creeping into her cheeks.

You're staring, Silas. Get a hold of yourself. Do something friendly. Maybe toss her a line, ease the moment some?

"Noticed the dedicated camera. Often phones nowadays."

"Yes," she said. She held up her expensive-looking camera. There was a strip of shiny black electrical tape on its front that caught Silas's eye. "Lavish gift from an indulgent aunt who always pushes me to go into photography full-time. It's an old-school range-finder type of camera, and the brand is a bit ostentatious, so I keep black tape over the brand name and the red dot."

That was a stampede of information. Not sure what to do with all that.

He hadn't suppressed his quizzical look in time—he hoped she didn't see it. Truth was, he found her chitchat charming—actually, her whole presence was charming. He could listen to her all day. So, he nodded and smiled contentedly before acknowledging her point.

"Attracts less attention that way," he said.

"Right!" She paused, looking down at Bandit. When she turned to meet his eyes, she held them a second—enough for him to notice—then she regrouped and stepped back.

"Well, I'll leave you guys to your walk," she said. "Thanks for the pictures. If I see you around, I'll show you the posted final shots. His name's Bandit, right? And for the caption—how old is he?"

Silas was surprised to feel disappointment at how suddenly the moment was ending. But she was already backing into the crowd.

So he gave her a nod. "Two years," he said.

He stood there, motionless, and watched the crowd as she disappeared. What had just happened? And why was he so jittery all of a sudden? Bandit's pressure on the leash brought him back to the present. He shook his head, then turned back to their walk.

CHAPTER 7

Sergeant Evans knocked, entering before Silas could give him the go-ahead. He strode toward Silas's sturdy, worn desk, moving with the smooth, economic confidence of an athlete perfectly aware of the position of each limb.

"The canvas for cameras and witnesses has been a complete bust so far, Chief," he said, as if unsure whether the idea had been foolish from the start. "At least in the area right around the scene of the incident."

Silas frowned.

"The body was found in front of a small niche art gallery—rarely open, no cameras or security. Town Hall is just to the west, but the floodlight camera above its side door is pointed too far down to have caught anything useful."

Silas made a mental note to check the reason for that angle himself.

"The park across the street has no cameras, either. Neither do the buildings to the east."

What kind of town is this? Finding this car might be trickier than I reckoned.

"One witness said they thought they may have heard a truck rumble during the wee hours of the morning," Evans said, giving Silas a little hope—only to dash it. "But he didn't get up, didn't see anything, and didn't make a note of the specific time. So, all we've got from him is an unsubstantiated claim that he'd possibly heard a truck rumbling."

Silas grunted a quick, "Thank you, Evans," dismissing the sergeant—leaving him in peace and quiet to process everything he'd just learned.

He wasn't surprised by this lack of eyewitness information, given the hour of the incident, but not to have any video evidence in this day and age was unbelievable. He'd spoken with the medical examiner's office that morning. It had placed the time of death at around 3:00 to 5:00 a.m., with injuries consistent with a severe vehicular impact—all as he'd already expected.

Genny's voice in his doorway pulled Silas back from thought. "The second interview with Mr. Stevenson, the victim's spouse, has been arranged for five forty-five p.m. You'll need to leave soon."

"Right, Genny. Thanks."

Marsh filled Silas in on their drive over. "Overall, Stevenson and Perkins are clean," she said, reporting that she hadn't come across any lawsuits, Better Business Bureau complaints, or negative Google or Yelp reviews about Stevenson's real estate business, and nothing about the company where Perkins worked as a remote home-based IT professional. No interesting footprints anywhere. "The IT company confirmed his employment; the company appears totally legit and uncontroversial. They said he was liked at work, liked by clients, will be missed. They seem like normal people. Apart from their very ordinary social media accounts, I could find absolutely nothing about them on the internet. I even checked their marriage license and credit history—both have good credit."

Silas nodded slowly. *Could mean nothing. But still, a little unusual nowadays to see so few breadcrumbs.*

"What about Bernardi? We got a meeting lined up yet?" Silas asked.

"I've left him two messages telling him we need to speak with him. No word back yet."

"Door knock him if we haven't heard back by ten in the mornin' tomorrow. Set it up for end of day, at his home."

He parked in the shade across from the same cheap-looking building he'd visited twice in the last two days. He cracked the windows for Bandit, then turned toward Marsh. "I'll take the lead, but get some careful notes so you can give me a second opinion about Stevenson and why he might have lied about staying in."

Marsh blinked at him but then nodded her agreement.

They walked up the flagstone path, entered, and went up a flight of stairs. When Stevenson opened the door, he seemed exhausted, leaning on the doorknob for support. Bags under the eyes, face pale. He motioned them to come in and stepped out of the way.

"Again, sorry for your loss, Mr. Stevenson," Silas began, removing his hat. "Wondering if we could trouble you for a few minutes? Got a few more questions for you, clear up some details." That sounded plain enough. He braced himself for what came next, which wasn't plain at all: "And we'll need to take a closer look at the underside of your car."

Stevenson sighed audibly. "Sure, questions are fine." Instead of the usual comment about how they should come in and sit down, he added, "And I am happy to show you the car, but I don't have it at the moment."

Silas's head swiveled toward him, his feet rearranging to follow. "Where's the car, sir?"

"It's at the detailing place down by Beech Forest and the transfer station."

Silas glanced at Marsh before turning back to Stevenson. The room suddenly felt low and small.

His head was swimming, but he kept his voice neutral as he said, "Your spouse was killed last night by a vehicle, and you're tellin' me you went to get your car professionally cleaned today?"

Stevenson's eyes went wide. What little color he had drained from his face.

"Well, when you put it that way, it does sound off, but it's not like that."

He sounded sincere, but Silas couldn't hide his skepticism. A flush of anger rose up inside him. Did this guy think he was a dumb hayseed?

"Then help me understand what it is like," Silas said, tone icy.

"I'm a real estate agent," Stevenson began, not realizing Silas already knew that. "I try to keep my car clean because I take clients around to properties. There's no parking in this town, as you know, so it makes sense to carpool to a showing whenever possible. I have a standing monthly appointment with the detailers—you can check—and it's hard to reschedule."

Silas's eyebrows went up involuntarily. *This guy is good. Or telling the truth.*

"I already had the gap in my work schedule to drop it off." Stevenson waved a hand, shaking his head. "And . . . well, I needed something to keep me busy. They say you're supposed to keep yourself going through the motions at times like this."

"Do they now?" Silas said, nodding his head and making a mental note to speak to the detailing place next. He glanced at Marsh. "Well, that'll take some running down."

"Mr. Stevenson, let's have a seat," Silas said, gesturing toward the living room. "I'm hoping you can clear something up for me. This'll be quick."

Stevenson nodded, then collapsed into a slump on the couch, inviting them to sit opposite him, which they did. Silas hadn't caught Marsh's eye, but he knew she had been taking detailed notes, as requested.

"Last we talked, you said you were home alone all night—since Mr. Perkins left during the evening, that right?"

Stevenson's answer came tentatively, after just enough of a delay to be noticeable. "Yes . . . that's what I said."

Silas let a pause stretch.

Then, he softened his voice, let just a hint of innocent-sounding confusion creep in.

"So, help me out here. We've got an eyewitness who says you went out in this car of yours in the middle of the night. Which was it? You stay in, or you go out?"

Stevenson's face flushed immediately. Eyes wide, like a man caught in a lie. Silas felt a rush of adrenaline at the reaction. Now, they were getting somewhere.

"I can explain," he said, holding up a palm.

"Explain what, exactly?" Silas said, stealing a glance at Marsh to be sure she was paying attention.

"I was embarrassed. I got flustered with the emotion, the shock. I meant to say I was alone all night, which I was, and at home most of the night, which I was, but it came out together, and I said I was home alone all night. After it happened, it felt like it was just semantics. Now, of course, I realize the specifics matter. I freely admit, I did go out. I went out looking for Timothy, because it wasn't like him to not come home."

"And that's embarrassing?" Silas said, glancing at Marsh to emphasize his skepticism.

"No. Well, yes, it's embarrassing that I misspoke, but what I meant was that I went to look in somebody's windows, and I saw Timothy," he added, face red. "*That* was embarrassing."

"Whose windows?" *This story's unfolding into a funny shape.*

"Our friend Alexander—Alexander Bernardi. He's Timothy's ex, and they're . . . they were still close friends. Closer than I liked, if I'm honest."

Well, that's a hell of a thing to admit. This guy's either pretty good at spinning a yarn, or he's innocent.

"What time was this, and where's Mr. Bernardi live?"

"It would have been sometime around, maybe a little after, three a.m. I tossed and turned until about then. Then I got up, threw on some sweats, and went out to see if I could find him."

"What'd you see, and what'd you do next?"

"I saw through the window—Alexander has a place over on Standish near the cemetery. They were just talking. Drinking wine together, slumped in chairs with their feet on the coffee table. There was nothing going on. I felt like a fool for making assumptions and looking in windows like a Peeping Tom. So I just drove home and went back to bed."

"That right?" Silas kept the edge in his voice, but something about this rang true in his gut—messy, shameful, human. "Anything else?"

"I'm sorry I didn't say so before. This is all so surreal."

Silas stood, and Marsh followed his lead. "Like I said, our condolences on your loss. Let us go do some more fact-finding. But how about you call me right away next time you remember any other embarrassing things?"

Maybe too sharp. But he left a hole you could drive a truck through. And I'm not here to soothe feelings. I need the truth.

They let themselves out. Silas stayed quiet until they reached the car, thoughts crowding in, none of them settled yet.

CHAPTER 8

Silas dropped Marsh off at the department, planning to stop by the auto shop before going home. Bandit looked hungry enough to eat a toad, and Silas felt bad for making him wait longer for dinner. Still, worth a shot to check, and it was now or never. Maybe the guy hadn't touched Stevenson's car yet. Maybe he'd catch a break.

A hollow opened in his gut as they crested the first hill on Race Point Road and saw the trim, gray-shingled shop. Silas could see an immaculate white BMW parked right in front, gleaming in the evening light. That was a blow.

At least the bay door to the shop was still open, and the lights were on.

Silas pulled up under the big tree out front and parked. A guy, probably midthirties, was sweeping the main garage bay.

Silas got out and approached him. "Evening. Chief Lopez, Provincetown Police. You work on that car today?" he said, gesturing with a thumb over his shoulder toward the BMW behind him.

"Yeah, why? What's up, Chief?" asked the young man.

Wiry, not tall—had to be fourteen inches between us. Accent—hard to place—but probably somewhere like the Middle East? He was the only person around, and he had the tired, rumpled look of a small business owner cleaning up after a long day. The smell of detergents, waxes, and sprays wafted in a fog through the open bay. Silas felt a headache blooming behind his eyes. The chemical smell wasn't helping. Neither was the disappointment.

"Pedestrian hit by a vehicle," he said, and the young man's eyes widened. "Possibly the vehicle out front, which you just cleaned. Can we take a look?"

"You think *that* vehicle was involved in a hit-and-run? Really?" The young man waved Silas to the pristine BMW. "There's not a scratch on it. It barely needed to be cleaned."

Silas didn't argue. He crouched down at the front fender. Nothing. Not a nick, not a smudge, not a dent or a scratch. He craned his neck to check the wheel well and along under the rocker panel, and still, there wasn't evidence of anything unusual.

This was already feeling like a dry well, but he'd see it through. "Notice anything outta the ordinary when you cleaned this car?"

"No, sir. I do it every month; Mr. Stevenson says he uses it for clients. It's always clean when it comes in. I can't imagine, based on the shape it was in this morning, that it hit a bird, let alone a pedestrian. Look. See, this grill, this hood, this fender? It's all like new."

So, that checks out. Monthly appointment, like Stevenson claimed. Doesn't mean he wasn't lying, but it nudges things toward believable.

"You have it on a lift, get a look at the underside?" Silas asked.

"I didn't do it in the lift bay today, no. Yosef had a car on the lift already—but I did get under it from the floor pit in the other bay to power wash the undercarriage."

"Any new scrapes, dents, marks? Blood smears, bits of fabric, human tissue?" Silas asked.

The detailer looked queasy at the thought, and Silas was reminded of how thick your skin got on this job. But the detailer rallied. "I've never worked on a car that hit somebody, but I've worked on cars that have hit deer, so I know what you're getting at. Stuff gets all over."

Silas nodded. *It sure does.*

"There was nothing unusual on that car. And I'm not messing with you, Chief. If there were crap on that car, I would tell you. We run an honest business here, and I'm not looking for any trouble. That car was normal, no different than any other month."

This guy reminded him of the entrepreneurs he'd bumped into so many times. Same wary eagerness. Anything to help. Anything to avoid interruptions to the business. Silas had seen that look before. He squinted. Still hadn't quite made up his mind on whether he could trust this guy.

"Even the rinse water coming off the underside was clean. Our floors are white—see?" He pointed to the gleaming wash bay. "If there had been blood under there, I would have seen pink going down the drain. But I just saw the usual brownish-gray runoff."

That detail clicked for Silas. He made up his mind this guy was telling the truth, and the slightly unusual energy he was sensing boiled down to just an accent and some shyness. The weariness piled in on top of his hunger, and he realized he was done here.

He nodded and said, "Last question, for now. You say he comes in every month. Does he call and make an appointment each time? When did you know he was coming in today?"

"No, it's a standing appointment, so it is always in our calendar unless he calls to cancel or move it."

Silas gave the barest nod. Enough for now. *This isn't our vehicle.*

"Thanks. Been helpful. Appreciate it."

He walked back to the car, and he and Bandit headed home.

CHAPTER 9
Thursday, September 4

Silas was going over the car situation in his head as he put his key in the door. He'd have to find another vehicle if this was going to hang around Blake Stevenson's neck. But even this second-car theory didn't make sense. Stevenson would have had to move impossibly quickly to get his hands on a second vehicle, smash it up hitting a pedestrian, get rid of it in a place no one would find it, and get home in time for Silas to knock on his door. *That's the kind of nonsense timeline that gets you laughed out of a courtroom.*

He dropped his bag on the eat-in kitchen table and hung his hat and holster on the rack by the door. His apartment contained a few cheap, worn pieces of furniture—what you'd expect of things left in an apartment by vacating tenants, although he'd picked up a couple of them at the thrift shop at the Methodist church. There was a bed frame, and the mattress was new. The mother hen in Genny had insisted on replacing it after the previous tenant. As the department administrator responsible for setting up an out-of-town chief with a basic place to live, she'd pulled a few strings. Silas wasn't keen on all the fuss, but he had to admit the new mattress was pretty comfortable.

It had been a long day. He'd been at it for hours. His mind was jumbled. He recognized the fog of exhaustion. *You can't beat yourself up or figure a case proper—what's possible, what's not—when your tank is running low. It always looks better after a bit of grub and some shut-eye.*

Grub before anything else. The steak in his fridge would work. But Bandit first. He kicked off his shoes and put out a meal for the dog. He rinsed and refilled Bandit's water too. Then he started warming two large tortillas for himself and sliced some leftover steak into long, thin strips. It was a good, sharp knife. The clean cuts against a solid cutting block felt like the first satisfying thing all day.

He seared the strips quickly in a hot skillet to remove the chill, then arranged the steak onto the tortillas. He had some leftover cold black beans he could use. He'd made them the way he always did—with cumin, garlic, olive oil, and lime. He tore off a handful of cilantro leaves from the bunch he had standing in a glass of water in the fridge. He sprinkled the cilantro over the beans and steak strips, rolled up both tortillas, and wolfed them down. He was lost in thought as he waited for the food to ease the gnawing feeling in his gut.

After cleaning up the dinner dishes, Silas read for a little while before drifting off to sleep, thinking about the clean white BMW. He'd been out cold for a couple of hours when he was startled from deep sleep by chatter on the police radio sitting on a chair by his bed. It woke Bandit up, and between the disembodied voice and Bandit's excited whimpers, it took Silas a moment to orient himself in the dark room. *Right. This isn't Salt Lake City anymore. These guys? They're my team now.* He recognized Byrne's voice on the radio, calling for backup.

"This is Patrol Officer Byrne. Again, I need assistance. Is anyone in a position to respond?"

Silas sat up, noting the precise time—1:17 a.m.—out of habit. He picked up the corded mike on the radio next to his bed. He hovered his thumb over the transmitter key and listened a moment before transmitting. He sighed. *What are these guys up to now?*

"I'm at the convenience store on Shank Painter, and I think we've got a robbery in progress. Store is closed, but I have a suspect in the store going through the shelves with a duffel bag, removing merchandise. It's not any clerk I recognize. Can't tell if he's armed."

Silas listened with a mixture of amusement and mild annoyance.

"Repeat, I'm on Shank Painter at the convenience store, robbery in progress—one suspect. Don't know if he's armed. I need backup so I can go in the front, and someone can cover the rear."

"This is Sergeant Clark; I copy you. I'm coming to give you backup—need a minute to get dressed, but I'll be there shortly."

Silas was frowning but tried to keep it light. Byrne was still new. "Evenin', boys. Chief Lopez here. Officer Byrne, hold your horses. Don't approach. Repeat, do not approach. Sergeant Clark, please stand by. Repeat, stand by."

"Chief, the guy is grabbing stuff and sticking it in a bag right this second!"

Patience, he thought. *Remember, it's early days.*

"Understand. Officer, you're man on scene. Whyn't you gimme a sitrep? Some lights on in the store, overhead lights, or he workin' by flashlight?"

"Lights, Chief? Yeah, there are lights. Some overhead lights. Not as bright as when the store is open, though. And none of the outdoor lights are on."

"You see the suspect's hands?"

"Can see shoulders, arms. Hands sometimes when he puts things in the bag."

One step at a time. They needed to learn to break it down. "How fast is he movin'?"

"How fast, Chief? Not sure what you mean."

He felt the irritation rise but kept his voice steady. They needed to learn, and that meant staying calm—even if it was after one in the damn morning. "He smackin' stuff around, makin' a mess, movin' like there's a house on fire, or he pickin' items out calmly?"

"He's picking items. Looking at them. He may be after more expensive merchandise or the stuff you can fence, like laundry detergent or baby food."

Okay, so this guy at least knows something about smash-and-grabs.

"There a getaway car running out front, or is his car switched off, parked down at the end of the row, with dew on the windshield?"

"Besides mine, there's one car here, Chief, parked down at the end of the row."

Yep, just as he thought. *Time to call off the dogs.*

"Officer Byrne. Stand down. Secure your service weapon. He's an employee. He's pulling expired stock off shelves, taking inventory, maybe restocking. Approach to confirm—if nothing else, it's good practice. But do it in a casual, friendly manner so you don't startle him. Might as well run it to ground as an exercise in community relations. You can check his ID"—*or look at his damn employee name tag*—to confirm he works there, then let him finish his graveyard shift in peace."

"Chief, you sure? This guy looks suspicious to me."

"I'm sure as the foot of a mule. Seen this before, Officer. Pretty common practice with bigger chains—keep the night shift on after closing, freshen up shelves, set up shop for the next day. Lemme know if you learn anything different." Then, after a pause, he added, "Sergeant Clark, go to bed."

Woke me up for a night-shift shelf rustler?

Silas punched some thickness back into his pillow and put a hand on Bandit's warm flank.

Work to do here, Bandit. We sleep first.

CHAPTER 10
Two Weeks Earlier

Silas and Bandit had rolled into Provincetown for the first time on a late-August afternoon.

He hadn't carefully planned the trip east from Salt Lake City, so he'd felt some relief making it to the East Coast with a little time to spare. Enough to feel his way along the cape and let himself be charmed by the historic coastal New England towns.

He'd gotten his first glimpse of the dunes of Provincetown as he'd driven off the pine-forested plateau that marked the end of Truro. The bluffs simply stopped, giving way to a wisp of low-lying coastal flats ringed by sand dunes and surrounded completely by dark-blue sea.

The outermost reaches of the cape—as he'd learned to call Cape Cod—were just a skinny peninsula tip, thirty miles off the mainland as the crow flies, nothing much more than a few low sand dunes. Just like on the map, the town had seemed skinnier than a needle, clinging to the edge of the coast inside the hook of the peninsula. In town, the main roads had seemed to him like the two sides of a long ladder with little cross lanes and alleyways as the ladder's rungs. The historic houses and buildings were packed tight as a ball of twine.

To Silas's unaccustomed eyes, it felt almost too beautiful to be real. First impressions of the place hadn't been bad. Kinda crooked and old, as you'd expect for a spot first settled four hundred years ago—but crooked and old in a charming, antique way.

He'd had to spend a little time cruising around before they lucked out with a modest room on the ground floor of a historic inn. Silas had learned that the inn was formerly the home of a sea captain. It had been the first time he'd stayed in a hotel room that was over two hundred years old, and the first time he'd parked in a lot paved with crushed white seashells. *Don't see that out West.*

The town had smelled different from what he was used to, the ocean all around. The smell of hot pine pitch also hung in the wind. These were different pines around here. Sweeter, like vanilla and cork and the earthiness of moss. The town had sounded different too: gulls constantly squawking along the water; crows cawing from pine tops; bike bells jingling; street musicians playing; and people eating, drinking, laughing at outdoor tables everywhere.

Been some strange twists and turns lately. No idea about this job, what I'm getting myself into, or if they even want me. Even less of an idea what to do if they don't. Too late to worry about any of that right now. Ride a little farther first, see where this trail leads.

The day of Silas's job interview started warm and hazy with a marine layer of fog off the water—typical for August, he'd learned. As soon as the sun came up, the fog burned off, and it began to warm up and turn into a perfectly beautiful day, which was also typical for August.

The town manager's office had looked nice when he was shown in at nine o'clock sharp the following morning. It wasn't large or extravagant, which was a good sign. *Down-to-earth is good.* But it wasn't without its charms—beautiful original woodwork and tall Victorian windows with enormous panes of glass. One window was already open a crack, and Silas caught the smell of cut grass being carried in on the breeze off the harbor. It was a comfort to him.

As he was ushered in and Town Manager Patrick Flood looked up, Silas clocked him doing a double take, but Flood didn't comment on Silas's unusual height or appearance.

He'd put on the one clean shirt and pair of jeans he'd set aside during the trip, and because he wanted to look professional, he'd dug out his leather bolo tie with the turquoise stone on its silver slide. *Too much? Nah. Never hurts to make a little effort.* He was clean-shaven and combed, and he'd even taken a moment to run his wood-handled boot brush back and forth.

Flood looked younger than Silas had expected. Glasses, clean haircut, khakis, button-down with no tie and sleeves rolled, wedding ring. He offered Silas a warm smile. Confident, with no-nonsense energy. Silas was reminded of why he liked Flood when they'd first spoken on the phone. Something mature, pragmatic, and unfussy about the guy. Silas felt comfortable and sensed his shoulders relaxing.

"Welcome, Mr. Lopez. Good trip? Any trouble finding the place? Traffic okay coming over the bridge?"

How many questions was that? Sitting down after their handshake, he said, "Trip was fine."

The chair was snug for his big frame. Upholstered seat and back, polished wood arms, and legs that curled like they'd been carved with a plan in mind. *Old. Nice for a town office but not overly nice.*

The town manager gathered his thoughts.

Not someone who felt rushed to start blabbing. Another good sign.

"Okay. Let's see. Chief of police. Where do I start?" After a long beat, during which he looked out the window at the busy street below, he said, "Look, I might as well be straight with you. This is a very unusual town, with a young, inexperienced department close to crisis due to unexpected departures at the top. I personally love this town and appreciate the things that make it unusual, but . . . well, let's just say that not every law officer would want to run this department, even with a full roster of experienced talent. I know because I've talked to quite a few this summer. I've got to get that on the table."

Silas tipped his chin. *Points to this guy for honesty.*

"We have thirty-eight hundred brave souls in the winter, sixty thousand not-always-perfectly-behaved ones in summer. Even more during the week of carnival. We admit to our crippling affordable housing crisis, gentrification issues, budget challenges, cultural differences—but we boast about our eclectic mix of tourists, artists, fishermen, writers, vibrant LGBTQ+ scene, chamber of commerce, and our world-class beaches."

Flood paused to take a breath as Silas contended with the verbal traffic building up in his brain. He'd been alone on the road for the last two months, talking only to Bandit and the occasional diner waitress. This conversation was like jumping back in at the deep end, and all these words were stringing together and stacking up fast. He knew he'd readjust to civilization soon enough, so he pushed the feeling aside and redoubled his focus.

After the shortest of pauses, Flood continued, "This town is home to artists of every variety—actors, writers, theater performers, musicians. And of course, we have all sorts of other perspectives, from property developers to environmentalists and social activists. Even different cultures. The Portuguese have been here for centuries. We have a community of Jamaicans who have been here for fifty years, and every summer, numerous seasonal workers arrive. In recent years, they've been coming from Eastern Europe, mostly Bulgaria."

Silas was fighting to catch up with the backlog again. *What's this guy on about Bulgaria for? Focus, Silas. You can do this. He's just trying to explain the place is a bit unusual. It's hardly needed—any fool could see that.*

Flood was on a roll, making his case for the quirkiness of the town. "We have a coast guard post and dock in town. And of course, there's the warm embrace of the Cape Cod National Seashore, which, as you can see from any map, controls every single square inch out here that's not grandfathered as town land. Naturally, getting on well with the park service rangers, not to mention pretty much every other variety of humanity, is a critical facet of the job."

Flood took a breath, as if to see whether Silas would interrupt him with questions. Silas was still a sentence or two behind and said nothing, which was what he probably would have said anyway if he'd been given a chance to respond.

"Beyond the budget for police payroll and basic equipment, we have no big-force resources for our department, like you'd be used to in Salt Lake City. That means with anything complicated, you're going to the state police or bigger communities up the cape—forensics, toxicology, special computer work, or God forbid, search teams, dive teams, and the like."

None of this was surprising. If anything, this setup seemed spiffier than he'd feared. The guy should stop apologizing and get on with it. *Already got over three thousand miles on my ass this summer, and this chair's none too comfortable.*

Silas shifted slightly in his chair, the wood frame creaking under him, but said nothing.

"In addition to the unexpected passing of the chief, the department has lost its two lieutenants. One to long-term disability after falling down a two-story fire escape on the job. The other left for a big-city job in Portland, Maine." Silas winced at the thought of the injury and opened his mouth to respond, but Flood kept going. "I'm not finished getting the issues on the table."

Silas nodded silently as Flood continued.

"I'll be frank: the former chief and his two lieutenants were something of a clique. I was developing concerns about the way they were running things, and in particular, I didn't like the way they hired and developed talent— or rather, didn't develop it."

Silas eyed him quizzically.

"They seemed to favor young hires who wouldn't challenge them and didn't appear to put much effort into training or letting people gain experience. Part of the reason I've been keen to meet with you is that when we talked on the phone, you mentioned mentorship as core to your style."

Silas nodded, holding Flood's gaze. He wasn't sure if he was supposed to respond, but Flood continued. *Guy's got a lot to get off his chest.*

"So it's a young, incomplete team that lacks development and experience, has lost its senior leadership, has been overly reliant on seasonal community service officers to get through this busy season, and has been suffering through oversight by a town manager who knows nothing about policing."

Flood exhaled as he held two hands out, palms up. To Silas, the expression on his face looked apologetic, even desperate. Then something else occurred to Flood. "Oh, and the local talent pool for young people looking to get into police work is basically nonexistent, so you're going to need to be good at developing what you have, or get creative in finding replacements and bringing them here."

Silas gave a slow, noncommittal nod, fingers drumming once against his knee.

Flood paused for a moment, as if checking to see whether he'd succeeded in scaring Silas away, as he apparently had all the other promising candidates he'd interviewed this summer. But Silas continued to sit there stone-faced and placid.

After a moment's pause to scrutinize Silas's face, Flood continued. "Finding the right fit," he said, tone shifting to a softer, nuanced register, "meeting my expectations, and meeting the town board's expectations is critical."

Now he's getting to the nub of things. I can build and develop a team, but I can't work for people I don't respect. Who don't respect me. This is the important stuff.

"I'm speaking in terms of sensitivity—a commitment to progressive community policing, and calibrating to the way things are out here. I'll repeat myself: this isn't a job for just anyone."

Flood halted so pointedly that Silas felt he had no choice but to acknowledge what he'd said. He guessed he needed to give this guy something, so he gave a slight shrug and said, "Expect not."

Flood looked at him, tilting his head in a way he probably wasn't aware of.

Maybe this guy's wondering why I don't seem more worked up about these issues. Maybe I should be wondering that myself.

Getting no read at all, Flood plowed ahead. "Therefore, whoever I hire is going to start with a one-year probationary period, four full seasons, to try things out. If it feels like a fit on both sides, we can make it permanent. The official title in the paperwork would be *Acting Chief of Police* during that probationary period, but in public-facing contexts, we'd refer to the role as simply *Chief of Police.*"

Silas nodded. *Give things a try before locking it all in. No harm in that.*

"Almost finished with my overview of the key issues—then, I want to talk about you," Flood added, waving his hand toward Silas. "The department is very busy in the summer. Crowd control, parking, keeping speeds down out on the highway, you name it.

"But we're lucky overall. While we have plenty of minor infractions—such as illegal bicycle parking, disorderly bridesmaid parties, parents who have lost their kids, noise complaints, and numerous other small things—we're blessed to have relatively few serious issues. For the most part, this is a happy place, with happy people and a low crime rate. I'd very much like to keep it that way."

Flood exhaled and adjusted the stack of papers in front of him, clearly signaling the end of his pitch. Silas remained still, allowing the moment to settle. Eventually, Flood put two hands together in a praying motion and brought them to his mouth. He looked Silas in the eye and said, "So, with that table-setting done, assuming you're still interested, tell me what I need to know about you, Mr. Lopez."

Showtime.

"Got personal questions not covered in the CV I sent, feel free to ask 'em. Otherwise, I'll talk 'bout how I work." Silas looked at Flood to make sure he was on board with that approach, and the expression on his face indicated he was.

"Way I see it, effective policing—policing that feels okay to the community—takes on-the-fly judgment. That discretion, judgment, the responsibility that comes with it only works well when it's vested in the officers on the street, interacting directly with community members."

Flood's head tilted to the side again. Silas was pleased that he seemed to be interested.

Silas felt himself warming to the task, a surge of energy inspiring him to sit up straighter and lean forward as he added, "Problem is, pushing discretion down and out to the edges of a team, empowering 'em to do good work, means more opportunity for mistakes, errors in judgment."

Flood acknowledged the point by nodding.

Silas let it sink in, then continued. "Keeping mistakes to a minimum takes building a strong culture on the force. Culture of integrity, respect, professionalism, commitment to the highest levels of service, learning mentality, pride in your work."

That's the crux of it, and it's why larger departments are hard. Again, he waited for a nod indicating Flood comprehended. He liked the idea of a smaller department, where he wouldn't get stabbed in the back and dragged into bullshit by higher-ups.

"Strong cultures, they don't happen by accident. Takes deliberate building by a leader. Leader working with intention. Leader committed to training, developing, inspiring. Leader clear as blue sky about his high expectations. Leader uncompromising in holding people accountable to those standards."

Flood was sitting up and paying close attention now. He said, "And are you that kind of leader, Mr. Lopez?"

"I am, sir," Silas said. After reflection, he added, "A person can't break mustangs well as me, if they aren't born with natural leadership instincts. Horse can tell a leader when they see one. Won't come to heel for anything less."

"Yes, I'm aware of your background in ranching. Tell me more about your leadership in this specific context. Give me your, ah . . ." He wiggled his hand in a rolling motion. "Philosophy of policing, as it were."

Right. Silas felt the slightest twinge of flush come up. *Wasn't trying to go off topic, just explainin' myself.*

"Sum it up with one word: humility," Silas said, and Flood's eyebrows shot up in surprise. "Police are just like everybody else. Not special, not better. Got specialized training, sure, but that doesn't make them any smarter, any better than the citizens they work for. Lotta officers, police forces, make the fool's mistake of thinking they gotta project power, project authority to do their jobs. That's wronger than a three-legged plow horse."

He could tell he was coming across as passionate, but he didn't care. Hell, he *was* passionate. This was an important point, and whether Flood understood it would go a long way toward deciding if Silas could work with him. He blew out a calming breath.

"Projecting power doesn't make cops effective," he said, putting it plainly. "Just challenges citizens, community. Provokes resentment in the strong ones, intimidates the weak ones, isolatin' you from those who need you most."

Flood had both elbows on his desk, his chin on his fists. His face was neutral but engaged. He seemed to be tracking what Silas was saying. *That's a good sign.*

"Seen plenty of bullies in my day. Don't like 'em. When I was younger, called a lot of 'em out, had my share of fightin' and scrapes. Been trying to put my fistfighting days behind me, but doesn't mean I'll tolerate a bully—or any single instance of bullying behavior—on my force. And through training, mentorship, and settin' a good example, I'll teach 'em how to handle bullies in our community as well."

Flood's head was bobbing in agreement. He gestured for Silas to continue, saying, "How does that play out in a complex town like ours, though, with an extremely diverse and progressive population?"

Lemme finish here. Not one for speech-making, but this needs to be covered.

Silas held up a single finger. "Now, regarding sensitivity. I know this town's unique, has special aspects to its culture. Appreciate that. Obviously, there's a lotta groups here I'm not a member of, or even especially familiar with. I get my limitations—I know better than to wade into water I can't see through—but I got a philosophy about people. Generally allows me to get along in a lotta situations."

He cringed thinking about the mess in Salt Lake, but he hadn't said *all* situations. And anyone would agree he'd been provoked in that one.

Flood's eyebrows went up slowly in apparent curiosity. "Tell me about that philosophy."

"Way I see it, a community's not so different from a herd of cattle. Some are wild, some are steady, some are lame, some got a mean streak, but you don't get to pick and choose which ones you look after. You keep 'em all moving in the right direction, make sure none get trampled, and don't play favorites. My job isn't about pushing folks into pens they don't belong in—it's to keep the peace and make sure everyone's got a fair shake at the water trough."

"Okay . . . but help me relate that to Provincetown," Flood said, his face betraying the slightest trace of impatience.

Silas nodded. "Being able to do that takes a philosophy about people that lets you look at 'em the right way. Guess you could say I believe in judging folks by their actions, not by who they are or who they love. On the ranch, we didn't care much about labels or what folks did on their own time. You like square-dancing, don't like square-dancing, it don't matter. What mattered was how they did their job, how they treated others, and whether they pulled their weight."

"We're not talking about ranchers managing cattle here, though, are we?" Flood said, again seeming ever so slightly impatient.

Silas felt a cold stab of doubt.

I'm being as plain as the nose on your face. Am I not getting through to this guy?

His palms felt a little clammy, and he was aware of his armpits in the warm office. Was it him, or was this guy just unable to see ranching as a metaphor for life?

Silas nodded emphatically. "Of course. I know Provincetown's got more colors than a rainbow after a spring shower. Doesn't bother me none. Might not have walked a mile in every moccasin, but I don't have to. Just have to make sure they get the same fair treatment as anybody else. Understand Provincetown's different from a cattle ranch, but I reckon same principles apply. I'm just sayin', if you'll have me, I'm here to serve the whole community, not just part of it."

Now that Silas had brought it all full circle, Flood's brows lifted, and he gave a slow, impressed nod, smiling at first until his lips slowly bent down into a thoughtful, frown-like expression.

Silas had said what he'd come to say and then some. The heaviest talking was behind him. The contemplative look on Flood's face seemed positive—Silas felt like a weight was lifting. He still felt pricks of sweat on his scalp and upper lip, but maybe that wasn't nervousness anymore. Maybe it was excitement. *Maybe I got through to this guy after all, and he was just testing me. For the second job interview of my life, it's possible this wasn't so bad.*

A long moment of silence passed between them. "Huh," the town manager said, sitting back in his chair, studying Silas the way one might an abstract sculpture. "That obviously came from the heart, and I would be lying if I said it didn't inspire me a little bit."

"Sorry," Silas said, feeling the stress ebb out of him with each exhale. Was that a sense of optimism pushing into its place? Maybe he wanted this position more than he realized. "Got to runnin' my mouth there. Not usually one for speeches or hearin' the sound of my own voice, but once I start down a trail, gotta follow to the end."

"There's absolutely no need to apologize. I like what I'm hearing." Flood nodded with vigor, drumming his fingers against his chin, thinking, "I like it a lot. In fact, I'll be candid. I've looked at enough candidates to know what I'm looking for. I feel a good fit here, and I'm thinking of calling an audible, if you'll pardon the football metaphor."

Silas waited. *What the hell is an audible?*

"I'm overwhelmed trying to supervise this force myself since the previous chief's abrupt passing. It's still our busy season. I'm a pretty good judge of character, and I tend to be decisive. I've talked to almost a dozen candidates for this job, and I either didn't like or scared away every single one of them."

Seems like a red flag.

"I know, red flag," Flood admitted. *Least he's bein' honest.* "But you, I like. And you don't seem to scare easily, so I haven't scared you off." He tapped his fingers on the desk, giving Silas a nervous laugh. "I mean, I haven't scared you off, have I?"

I'm still sittin' here. "No, sir."

"Great. Well, then—let me ask you a couple of final questions."

Silas shrugged. "Shoot."

"I know you traveled here for this interview. Could you stay a little longer? A couple more days?"

"Hotel don't throw us out, we can stay long as you need," Silas said. *I ain't got nowhere else to be.*

"We?" Flood said.

"Me and my dog, Bandit."

"Ah, okay. Second, and this is awkward, but I need to know this before I stick my neck out and do something irregular." He seemed to search for the phrasing. "If, hypothetically, this job were to be offered to you at the salary and benefits in the listing, would you take it?"

Silas thought. He liked this man, and he had a good feeling about this place growing on him. He didn't care what the salary was. But an alarm bell started up somewhere, faint but familiar. *Need to lay out some nonnegotiable ground rules and boundaries before agreeing to anything.*

"Got questions of my own first," Silas said.

"Shoot," Flood said with a grin. *See what you did there, Patrick. Nice.*

"Need trust, space to do my job. Happy to keep you informed every step of the way, but it'll be me runnin' things—not you, not us. I'll seek input when I need to. I'll follow all the town's rules, budgets, procedures. But you gotta give me a length of rope to work with, and don't always be pullin' it in. I need flexibility, how I do the job. If you can do that, you're never gonna have a better partner. Two partners, actually—Bandit rides with me. We're a package deal."

"Okay, that sounds reasonable," Flood said.

"Not done."

"Ah, sorry, please go on," he said with a surprised look on his face.

"Minute I walked in here, opened my mouth, you could tell I'm not the typical fella for the job. Folks'll say I'm doin' stuff unorthodox. People'll think I'm some hayseed blown into town like tumbleweed. Well, that's the way I like it. As my partner in Salt Lake used to say, 'Having people misunderestimate me has worked out pretty smart.'"

Flood gave the knowing smile of someone in on the joke. That was the effect he was going for—it emboldened him to be blunt and direct. The urge he was feeling was to talk from the heart, put it on the line.

"I know exactly what I'm doin' and what I need. I'm looking to find a community I can care about, that can care about me. Been mentored by some great people. Now's time to pay it back. Given a chance and the space to work, I can build a tight, effective police force that'll make a positive impact on this community. An impact several times the size of its budget. It ain't gonna happen overnight, but you give me a shot, you won't regret it." Silas looked Flood in the eye. "Sounds acceptable to you, be honored to be your chief."

Flood's grin was broad—he was not even trying to hide his pleasure.

Silas felt some emotion choking him up a bit too, and the feeling made a slight flush of embarrassment creep up his throat. *Talked a whole year's worth in this one meeting.*

Flood started nodding. "Okay, here's what I'm going to do. I'm going to tell the town board we've found our man, then ask them to juggle their schedules and get a majority of them to meet with you—or at least be offered the opportunity to—as quickly as they can. Probably take a few days if that's okay?

"Yep," Silas said. *This went better than I ever could've hoped.*

"If they have no problem, my town administrator's office will get you that probationary contract, and you can start the minute it's signed. The administrative assistant to the chief already has a line on a temporary apartment you could start out in."

Silas stood with a nod. He looked Patrick Flood hard in the eye and, after a moment, stuck out his hand. Flood stood as well, and they shook on it.

Two minutes later, Silas stepped out into the sunlight downstairs. He looked around him, appraising the place as his probable home for the first time. *Get through those town board meetings without shooting myself in the boot, and it looks like this is gonna be home for a spell.*

He felt satisfied. And maybe a little bit happy too, for the first time in a while.

CHAPTER 11
Thursday, September 4

Silas walked into the basement break room to fill his water bottle before the second all-hands case conference and was caught short. Wren was standing at the speckled Formica counter and looked up at him with a surprised expression that gave him a jolt.

She recovered quicker than he did. "Hi. No tea bags upstairs, so I thought I'd raid your coffee station. You caught me." She smiled. Her eyes looked mischievous as she put her wrists together and jutted them up toward him as if for handcuffs. "I surrender."

It was a joke he'd heard before, but this time, it made him grin. *She's a funny one. And cute too. No, not cute. Stunning. And staring at you, fool.*

She added, "Nice to see you again. It's Wren, by the way."

"I know," Silas said with a courtly nod.

"And you're Silas, right?"

"Uh-huh." *Best to rustle up some words before too long, Silas.*

A silence blossomed. After a beat, Wren busied herself fixing some tea. She stole a glance. If she was uncomfortable, he couldn't tell. Then, she chanced a cheeky question. "You don't say much, do you?"

This one's direct. Like that.

"I say what's necessary." It came out much too matter-of-factly. Looking at her face, he felt a stab of worry. Was he already blowing this? The feeling became a little grip of panic, so he smiled and added,

"Something you'd like me to say? Not gonna press charges for the tea, if that's your concern."

She laughed. "That's a relief. Being a convicted felon would complicate my work. How's the pup? Bandit, right?"

"Last seen under my desk, presumed armed and dangerous. Likely chewin' my badge, a box of live ammo, or some food he stole from somewhere in the building. But he won't stay put long."

"Is that right? He wanders?"

"Already identified building regulars too weak to stand up to begging. Stares them down until they buckle under the pressure, fold like a cheap lawn chair, and surrender their food to him." *If only the dog situation were as funny as he's making it out to be.*

"That's adorable, like a mascot. Everyone loves him, I'm sure."

"Patrick Flood's, ah, still warmin' to him."

"Uh-oh . . ." Her face became mock serious. "Well, with that much cuteness, the black fur eye patch, those soft, pointy ears at his disposal— I'm sure it's only a matter of time until he wins Mr. Flood over."

Silas chuckled uneasily.

"Oh! That reminds me," she said, fishing her phone out of a pocket. "Speaking of cute, here's Bandit's very first Instagram post."

She handed Silas an ordinary smartphone, but it was tiny in his large, calloused hands. He cradled it in his palm and stared at the picture. He felt a ringing rush of blood in his ears and the heat of her gaze.

She watched him, and after a moment, she said, "What do you see?"

Trying to figure that out myself.

"This area's the thing that's tuggin' on me."

"What do you mean?" she asked.

After another long contemplation, he said, "Guess the softness."

"Show me," she said, moving closer.

Whoa, Nelly. Silas felt electric prickles from the closeness. The scent of her hair was bringing him right back to the moment she took this very photograph. And he could sense that moving closer to him had made her pulse points warm. He inhaled the scent of her skin. Momentarily transfixed, he needed to snap out of it and pull himself together. He had to explain what he was focusing on.

"The background here. And here. The light. Softness of things." He pointed at areas in the photo. "Not like crime scene photos."

"Well, I'd hope not!" she said, surprising him with the ready laugh and jabbing him on the upper arm with an index finger.

"What you're looking at is called a shallow depth of field. It's a lens thing. The lens aperture—or size of the lens's opening, specifically. The lens is like the pupil of an eye. The more dilated it is, the more light it lets in, but the shallower the focal plane. Anyway, it's cool. I promise I'll explain it to you sometime if you want," she said, nodding to encourage him.

Silas returned the nod with a grin he hoped wasn't stupid.

"For now, I need this back." She tapped her phone with an index finger. Silas handed it to her, and she picked up her tea. "I've got to get back upstairs for a meeting starting in two minutes."

"Right," Silas said, snapping out of it. He was mortified to feel himself blushing. "Me too."

Wren turned and headed toward the old building's grand staircase with a little wave.

Silas watched her whisk away for a second time.

Hell. This one blew right in like a storm, scattered me like porch furniture. How in the hell? He could feel the dumb smile still on his face.

CHAPTER 12

The team was buzzing with cross-chatter—less nervous and self-conscious than during their first all-hands case conference. Silas rolled the backs of his shoulders to relax them before walking into the main briefing room.

"Listen up," he began, wasting no time. "Don't want this meeting longer than it needs to be. Put our heads together, take stock of where we're at. Couple of folks not here. That's okay. We can't all work on the case all the time, but we can all learn from it. Take a minute here, minute there for briefings, and y'all can learn from following bigger cases. It's why I round the team up. Invest time because this here is . . ." He paused to emphasize the last words. "A learning organization."

Even with the pause, he wasn't sure the point had landed hard enough, though.

Spell it out for 'em, Silas.

"Each of you needs to commit to learning all the time, every day. Understood?" This time, he got a few nods out of them. "Plus, I like having people know what's goin' on so they can cover each other. Small team. Need everybody familiar with major cases so I can grab anybody, go do something, and they're already up to speed."

Again, a few nods, but mostly blank stares. He debated making it clearer that he intended to—without warning, sometimes—take whoever was on duty as support for various cases, but he no longer cared to elaborate. *They've been warned. Only time will tell who's gonna be reliable.*

"High level," he went on, voice booming, "I still like the husband for it but don't like his car. Not at all. Had a few interviews. ME's report, we can update y'all on. Marsh, whyn't you go first?"

Given this wild card of a new boss, Marsh shouldn't have been surprised, but Silas could tell from the look of horror on her face that she was. He took no pleasure in it. *Sooner they figure out how I work, easier it's gonna be for them.*

She collected herself. Her voice was tentative. "Chief Lopez and I went to the home of Mr. Blake Stevenson at Gale Force Village, unit seven, at approximately—"

Sounds a little like we are back at the academy.

"Precision where needed, Marsh," he interrupted softly, "avoided where it's not. Yesterday, Marsh and I talked to the husband again. What'd we learn, Marsh?"

She consulted her notepad. "We learned that Mr. Stevenson actually did go out during the night, after he'd claimed originally that he'd stayed in."

Soft exclamations could be heard as team members exchanged glances.

"So, he lied to the police in the first interview?" Silas asked rhetorically, figuring it was okay to be leading her along a little bit this time.

"Yes, he told you he was home alone all evening, but when confronted with eyewitness testimony to the contrary, he admitted he'd been out," Marsh said.

"And what reason he give for the omission, Marsh?"

"He said . . ." She paused, consulting her notes. "He said he was flustered and in shock and misspoke and was embarrassed."

"Which was it, really—in your estimation, Marsh?"

"Why did he lie?" she asked, glancing at Silas, who nodded. "I think he was embarrassed and a bit flustered, and that led him to, ah, misspeak."

"Embarrassed about what?" Silas asked.

"He left the house to spy on his husband—I mean, the victim—through the window of a friend's home . . ." She paused again, checking her notes. "The home of a Mr. Alexander Bernardi. The victim was at the

Bernardi residence, talking to Mr. Bernardi. Stevenson admitted to having some jealousy issues around Perkins and Bernardi. He said that after he saw nothing inappropriate was going on, he'd felt foolish for spying."

"Was he telling the truth?" Silas asked.

Marsh looked at him blankly, as if she couldn't believe she was being asked the question. He found her dumbstruck reaction a little bit funny, but he needed to choke it down and act like his was the most obvious, reasonable question in the world if he was going to land his point.

"You got a gut instinct. You're as plain capable as anyone of answering the question, Marsh. People, listen up. Judging credibility is a core skill we all need, you hear? And a muscle we exercise once we got it. So, you think he was telling truth or not?"

Marsh's mouth was open, and she had a bewildered expression.

"He look at you or look into the distance? Blink or steady? Show increased mental load of someone makin' up a story, or did it roll off the tongue?" Silas asked.

"I might have missed some of those specific cues, Chief, sorry. But to me, he did seem like he was telling the truth," she said.

It was a bit tentative, but good enough.

"Agreed. He's either telling the truth or got natural talent for lying. Now, how about the car? He tell us anything about the car? You get a good look at it?"

"No, he had taken the car to the detailing shop to be cleaned before we got there."

Audible gasps could be heard around the table.

"That's right. So, I asked him why in hell he'd do that, didn't I?" Silas said. "You find his answer credible, Marsh?"

"What he said about using the car for clients made sense, and we could easily verify that he made the appointment in advance like he claimed—so, he'd be reckless to lie about that."

She's brave. Knocked off-balance, but doesn't back down. She's an officer to watch.

Silas nodded. "Thank you, Marsh. Like the reasoning. Done good. Thank you for your help with the interview. Write up a summary, get it to me for review 'fore you get scarce for the day."

Marsh nodded, visibly relieved to be out of the hot seat.

Then, Silas looked around the room. "Now, other things we've turned up. Spoke to the downstairs neighbors, an elderly couple, the Aschers. Live below the Stevenson and Perkins unit but above their garage. I learned two things: First, victim and husband fight, argue a lot. Aschers hear fights at home regularly. Door slammin', shoutin'. In fact, they had a big dustup the evening of the incident, front door slammed around ten p.m. when Perkins left."

The team nodded, interested. *Good.*

"Second, Stevenson opened the garage, went out to spy on the victim around three a.m. Admitted as much to Marsh and me when we confronted him." He sensed people understood the weight of the implication. "Yep. What we learned from the Aschers ain't a good look for Stevenson. Combine fighting with the jealousy, add in the three a.m. walkabout—that's facts so ugly, even the tide wouldn't take 'em out."

A couple of people grinned, seemingly warming to his odd manner of speaking.

"But before you get your handcuffs out, I also talked to the car detailing shop."

He was in his element. Weight on the balls of his feet. Case energy in his legs. Still, he measured his tone to match the somberness of the next bit.

"Fact is, there's no way Stevenson's car was involved in any sorta crash. There wasn't even a scratch on it. In simple terms, the white BMW ain't our car, and it's the only car they own. That's why Perkins thought nothing of walkin' home that night. He's used to hoofin' it around town. And the timeline for gettin'—and gettin' rid of—another vehicle is tight. So, we need to find out what the fight was about, if we can. Plan to speak with Bernardi, the friend, see if he knows, can confirm basic times and places. More on that later."

Turning to Genny, who was giving bits of her breakfast to Bandit, he said rather firmly, "You feed him, you'll only encourage him. At least make him sit, shake a paw, lie down before he gets a snack. Gotta train him the way you're trainin' me."

Dog's a hardened con artist. Ought to throw him in jail right now.

Silas picked up a report from the table and flicked it hard with a finger. The loud snapping sound refocused the team's attention, just as he'd hoped.

"Final item: report from the medical examiner's office." Everyone perked up a bit. "They place time of death late, between three and five a.m. Cause of death, blunt-force trauma—almost certainly from a vehicle, given circumstances, injuries, location of body. Victim was otherwise in good health. Medical records and lab tests say normal hearing and vision. Some alcohol in the blood and red wine in the stomach but not impaired, not over the limit. No signs of recent sexual activity, no defensive wounds, no weapons. Wallet, nice watch, some cash, all found with the body."

Keep the pace up. Keep these case conferences tight. Long meetings make people stupid.

"ME says something interesting, though. On the surface, this case looks like the classic mistake of wearing dark clothes, walking with no light, reflectors. But . . ."

Need to get them focused on details. Clearly, no kind of a habit yet.

"ME states it's unlikely to be an accidental hit. Report says the body was definitely dragged and hit by more than one wheel. Her report speculates it was most likely either an intentional hit or at least a knowing hit-and-run. The driver of an ordinary vehicle would know they ran over something that big, tumbled it around, and dragged it that much."

Clark and the other officers exchanged surprised glances. He could tell they understood the gravity of this development. *Good to see Clark taking it in, given the flippant attitude he's had so far.*

"But it gets more complicated. The body had a few deep lacerations, like something rough and sharp and rusty cut into it. Something with nonautomotive black spray paint on it. We're talking about bigger, sharper, deeper gashes than you'd get from the smooth underside of a modern passenger vehicle.

"Tread prints on the body, but inconclusive," Silas went on. "ME's forensic examiner says could be any one of a few different heavy-duty truck or utility-type tires. Putting it together, ME and forensic examiner suggest we could be looking for something a little different than usual, like a lifted beater pickup truck. Maybe the owner touched up some rust with spray paint around the wheel arches, rocker panels."

The team sat in thought. *Time to convert this meeting into action.*

"Unfortunately, that describes a whole lotta vehicles. Basically, back where we started. No point in tryin' to look up old trucks—too many of 'em. Might be worth checkin' auto body shops, tow companies in case a vehicle took a hit hard enough to crack a radiator, need a tow. Or— long shot—got taken to the shop because this old thing with spray paint is somehow worth fixing. 'Cept the fix is more work than this amateur mechanic can do at home."

Silas looked at the team. He knew what came next was not going to be popular.

"Means we need to find video, eyewitnesses. Need it bad enough to make it hurt if we don't. Evans, you and Byrne, call body shops. Focus on the radius you would drive an old truck if you were lookin' to get it fixed out of this immediate area. Long shot—so don't give yourself a hernia doin' it—but see if anybody brought in a spray-paint special, claiming a deer hit or the like.

"Genny, before I forget, can you grab a small Provincetown thank-you deal? Like fudge, some of that taffy, a small art doohickey, whatever, and send it to the ME's office with a card that says it's comin' from the grateful newcomer at Provincetown PD or some such?" He hoped this example was being noticed. "Can't hurt to build relationships, people."

Genny's got good instincts and understands what I'm getting at, even if I'm not spelling it out. Might have stumbled over a four-leaf clover with that one.

Turning to Clark, he said, "Sergeant, you and Marsh get back out, find me a witness or some video if it kills you. Burig, you're comin' with me on the interview with Bernardi when it's set."

Upon hearing his assignment, Clark made a disgusted face. Silas clocked it. *Fine—handle that next.*

"Move, people. Meeting's over." Then, with a stern look, he added, "Clark, my office—now."

CHAPTER 13
One Week Earlier

Silas had first been introduced to Sergeant Kevin Clark on his first day by Town Manager Patrick Flood in the police department. The more senior of the force's two sergeants, Clark had been serving as Flood's point of contact and interim lead on the force.

"Silas, this is Genevieve Moreau, administrative assistant to the chief and all-around brains of this operation. People call her *Genny*, with a *G*."

Genny looked to be early fifties, maybe midfifties, and stood more than a head shorter than Silas. She somehow managed to project authority, anyway. Neat gray hair, all one length, somewhere between chin and shoulder; tidy blazer; not a thing out of place. Pleasant face, warm brown eyes behind horn-rimmed glasses, and a steady, assessing gaze that told him she missed nothing. There was a hint of lavender in the air around her— old-fashioned, but it somehow suited her. She carried herself with the confidence of somebody who kept a thousand threads straight without breaking a sweat.

"Pleased to meet you, Genny." *Let's pray she's as good as she seems. Person in her position can make or break a department like this.*

"And this is Sergeant Kevin Clark," Flood went on. "It's truly my pleasure to introduce you to Chief Silas Lopez. Chief Lopez and I have spent some time together, as has the town board, and we've been impressed. I feel his philosophy and approach to running a team and a police force, along with his commitment to the town's community policing priorities, will make him a very strong addition to our town."

Hmmm. Flood is selling a bit hard. This oughta be interesting.

Clark said, "So, wait, you're telling me he's already been hired?"

Bingo. Silas's hackles came to attention.

"Yes, it's official, as of nine a.m. this morning."

"So, you won't be needing our input?" Clark said. "I figured you'd want us to maybe interview Mr., uh . . . Mr. Lopez?"

Yeah, it's "Lopez," like the man said, pal.

Silas stood quietly and watched the exchange unfold with interest, betraying no concern.

He noticed Genny didn't make eye contact with him. She looked like she wanted to crawl under her desk. He could feel the discomfort radiating off her. When she chanced a look, he winked, and her eyes grew large.

Is she worried I can't handle a bucking bronco like this one? She'll see.

"Well, he's an acting chief for the time being," Flood clarified. "As you can appreciate, we needed to move decisively because we're still in our busy season. This process has been ongoing for two months now, and we've finally found our candidate. You and the force deserve the support that comes with a full team. This department needs leadership to organize things, an experienced officer to backfill the vacancy left by Chief Maddox's unexpected passing."

"Can we speak in private, sir?" Clark said to Flood.

Gotta hand it to him, this kid has cojones. Guess we'll see how that works out for him.

Flood said, "Chief Lopez, if you'll excuse us momentarily," and turned left into the nearest office, just a few feet down the hallway. Clark followed. The door shut behind them with a muted click, and Flood's expression as it closed suggested he wasn't thrilled about this sidebar.

Silas didn't move. From where he stood, the office was close enough he could have reached out and knocked. They had to be standing right up against the door—maybe it was thin, maybe just badly sealed—because clear as a rung bell, Silas and Genny heard Clark say, "We were doing just fine and don't need any help. Especially not from some guy who's not from around here and, even worse, from some big-city force, hired in above us."

Genny cringed and turned beet red, an apologetic look on her face. Silas was completely calm. *Temper's not useful in situations like this, and Clark's not holding the cards, anyway. Just let it play out, Silas.*

Flood's tone was curt. Silas could hear the icy sharpness even through the door. "Let me remind you, Sergeant Clark, that the police department reports to the town manager. It's my job, not yours, to determine what the department needs and to make any decisions regarding whom the department hires. I suggest you give this arrangement a chance."

You'd have thought Clark would have wanted to, anyway. Why not observe a little, get the lay of the land, keep your options open? Not too impressed so far on the thinking with this one.

They emerged from the side office. Flood's jaw was tight, his mouth a hard, flat line. His face said he'd had about enough.

"Sorry about that, Chief. Anyway, like I said, it's a pleasure to introduce you two."

Silas held out a hand, offered a warm grin, and said, "Sergeant Clark, delighted to meet you. Lookin' forward to workin' with you, learning all you can teach me about this force, this town, and this area. As you may have heard, I'm new in these parts, and so I look to experts who've been around here their whole lives."

Let the kid dig his grave on his own if he's of a mind to.

"Yes, very good," Flood said promptly, as if ready to cut his losses. "Well, gentlemen, I'll need to head upstairs, but Sergeant, why don't you give Chief Lopez an overview of open matters?"

Clark shrugged and said, "Not much to tell."

"Really?" Flood said, turning quickly enough to be noticeable. His brows were raised, and his tone carried frustration and anger.

Unbelievable. Thinking mechanism's definitely out of whack with this one.

Silas said, "Nothin's goin' on, town this size, tail end of the busy season?"

"Nothing that would interest someone used to big-city crimes," Clark remarked. "It should be fine for you to head into your office and get your desk blotter set up. Me and the team can take care of the open stuff and keep you posted."

Silas felt heat in his cheeks. He couldn't stop his eyes from narrowing, but he gave Clark a cool look and said in an even tone, "Not much of a desk guy. Prefer to hear what the team's workin' on."

Clark still hesitated, so Silas figured, *Why not see how much game Genny's got?*

"Genny, you seem like someone whose finger is on the pulse. Since cat's got Clark's tongue, why don't you try and give us an overview?" Silas shot Flood a glance. *What are you dumping on me, Flood?*

Genny didn't hesitate. "Well, in the summertime, parking is always an issue, and we're having to supplement the parking enforcement team with community service officers, as usual." Genny thought for a second. "Since it has been really hot, we've been dealing with some late-night crowd control, especially in places where the busiest bars and restaurants are closest to residential areas."

She's doing well.

"The department is in the middle of a campaign to crack down on speeding out on the main road—speeds always creep up in the summer. We're looking into some graffiti that may have been a slur about sexual orientation. Oh, and two cars were broken into in the Alden Street lot in the last forty-eight hours, which is quite unusual."

"Knew we could get a proper overview once we found the right person. Thank you, Genny. That's a big mix of police work—look forward to supporting everyone on those matters."

Later in the day, Silas received a phone call from Patrick Flood.

"Silas, I wanted to apologize for Kevin Clark. I'll take responsibility for perhaps not handling the hiring situation as well as I could have."

Silas appreciated the humility. "Got nothing to apologize for, Mr. Flood. And nothing to worry about."

"As you know, the former chief—Alan Maddox—died suddenly earlier in the summer. I'd just lost one lieutenant to another job and the other to long-term disability. I didn't have my ducks in a row on succession, and I just needed a short-term point person. Clark happened to be the most senior. I hadn't had much direct contact with him before the chief's passing and the lieutenants' leaving, and I didn't realize how green Clark was when I'd made him the department's temporary point. By the time I realized Clark was inept and likely to misread the situation completely, it was too late."

Yep, that tracks. Can see how that could happen.

"Add the bad attitude to the other deficits, and I have to admit, I am now not sure if Clark can be turned around. I am really sorry to leave you in that situation," Flood said.

Silas wasn't convinced he was DOA.

"Appreciate you sayin' all that, but I'm not the least bit concerned," Silas said. "Brought mustangs to heel that were more spirited, ornery than him. He's the type that only responds to a strong hand."

"You really think you can whip him into shape?" Flood asked, his surprise clear, even on the phone.

"Don't worry. With a little time, some teaching, I'll get him there. Before too long, he's gonna learn you don't wanna mud wrestle with a hog. You both get muddy . . ." Silas paused, a big grin on his face. "But the hog likes it. Keep you posted on his progress, Mr. Flood."

With a hearty chuckle, Flood said, "Glad to hear it. And please, Silas, call me Patrick."

CHAPTER 14
Thursday, September 4

Once the rest of the team had filed out of the briefing room after the second all-hands case conference, a sour-looking Clark joined Silas in his office, as requested.

This Clark situation has festered long enough. Time to drag it into daylight.

Neither of them sat before Silas said, "Follow me, Sergeant."

"Where are we going?" Clark asked.

"Foot patrol."

They left the building, walking together in silence through the busiest section of Commercial Street, heading toward the West End. The pavement was still cool enough that Silas had brought Bandit, but he kept him on a leash. He nodded and smiled at the pedestrians who acknowledged them, like he didn't have a care in the world.

The crowds thinned, and they left the restaurant food smells behind as they walked away from the town center. When they arrived in a pool of quiet shade, Silas figured it was as good a spot as anywhere and sat on an old rock wall. Its weathered stones were dotted with bright patches of honey-yellow lichen. He motioned for Clark to do the same.

"Ain't been likin' the way you been carrying yourself, Sergeant Clark. How about you tell me what's on your mind?"

Any fool would see this for the entrapment it was, but Clark didn't hesitate to speak his mind freely. "Well, Chief, no disrespect meant, but this is a small town. Me and the team are locals and have spent our lives here. Not clear why Flood felt it was necessary to go outside the department, let alone the region, to replace the chief."

Suppose that's one way you could look at it. Not the right way, but one way.

"Uh-huh," Silas said, thinking. "Well, I can't say he felt it was necessary. Way I understand it, Flood had an opening, I applied, we talked, found common ground, and he thought me the best man for the job, so he hired me. Ain't that complicated."

Clark looked like he was sucking on a lemon wedge. "Flood didn't discuss the opening or the final decision with me, or the needs of the department."

"Have concerns about Flood's selection, Clark?" Silas asked, forcing himself to swallow—keep it even and calm.

"Like I said, this is a small town with a long history. Unique seaside tourism challenges. What does a big-city guy from a big-city force from the other end of the country know about any of that?"

A sea breeze rustled the leaves above them. *No need to answer yet. Let him get to the nub of it.*

"Flood disrespected me," Clark said.

There it is.

"How so?" Silas asked. "Feel you were supposed to be consulted? Or you really sayin' you feel you earned this job and were entitled to it?"

"I was entitled to it—to some respect. I should have at least been consulted," Clark said.

"How old are you, Clark?"

"Twenty-eight. I got out of the academy when I was twenty-two. Six years on the job, with an unblemished record."

Uh-huh. Still wet behind the ears.

"Clark, surprise you to learn I'm a small-town guy too?"

"You're from Salt Lake City. You spent sixteen years on their force," he said.

"I'm a fifteenth-generation ranch hand from outside an outta-the-way place called Cortez, Colorado. Ranching since I was big enough to close my hand around a lead rope and walk a horse. At it full-time by fourteen, schooled at home by my mama. I was just passing through Salt Lake and happened to pick up some policing experience, learn a few tricks along the way," Silas said. "Because'a that small-town background we got in common, think you and me have the potential to get along just fine."

Clark didn't reply.

Silas looked out at the harbor between two houses and felt the seething rigidity of Clark's posture on the stones next to him. "Instead, you're saddle sour. I can see the trail you're blazin' here, and it don't go where you think it goes. Not sure how you like to communicate, so I'll be as blunt as the back of a knife." He gave Clark a steady eye. "Where this relationship's headed, that's up to you. Want to stay an angry, incompetent shit-heel your whole life? Well, that's your right."

From the look of shock on Clark's face, he could see his choice of words might have been a bit too strong. *Well, can't unsay them, so might as well get use out of 'em.*

"And assuming you keep your attitude to yourself, I can tolerate it a little while until I have an opportunity to replace you with someone who can pull their weight," he went on, applying even more pressure. Clark's eyes got bigger. "Go or stay, don't matter much to me. Either way, won't change how my coffee tastes."

A few seconds passed in silence. Clark looked like a teenager on the verge of throwing a fit.

The gulls squawked while flapping by, silhouetted against a white overcast sky. With every tick of the clock, it became clearer to Silas that Clark wasn't going to respond. So, he figured he'd go ahead and finish his monologue unfettered. "I know you're used to feelin' like you're top dog around here—havin' all the local knowledge and bein' the temporary point person, and all. You held the department together, worked with Flood this summer. That's nothin' to turn your nose up at, but shit, son— even civilians like Flood can tell you're a greenhorn."

Silas paused before continuing. Clark was stone-faced. *Maybe I need to be plainer.*

"I didn't take your job. I took a job. You want it next? Gonna need to start actin' like it. You stick around, keep your head down, and learn something—you might end up in my chair one day with this very job as chief. But if you keep resenting me, I promise you, someone else will be chief after I'm through with it, and it won't be you."

Finally, Clark sighed. It was petulant, but it was a reaction, which was better than nothing.

"So, what?" he began, clapping his hands on his thighs. "I'm supposed just to sit back and watch you take over and run the show?"

A headache was forming between Silas's eyes.

"No, I don't want you to sit back. I want you to learn. Watch how I do things, why I make the decisions I do. Ask questions. But most importantly, do your job. Carry your weight." Silas turned his head and looked Clark in the eye. "And with a big fat smile on your face. Show what you're capable of. Do that, and who knows what the future holds?"

All that's left is to put some healthy fear into this bronco.

"But you've been warned your coat's already hangin' on a wobbly peg with me, Clark. You're not careful, you could knock out what little relationship seed corn you have left," Silas said.

Silas stood, looking down the street. "But lucky for you, I don't see the point in holding grudges. I go by how folks ride, not by the dust they kick up."

Silas turned and gathered Bandit's leash, signaling he was almost done. *Not much more to say or do but kick this kid loose to go work it out for himself.*

"Feel free to go have a think on it. Take as much time as you need. But in the meantime, if I catch another smirk on your face in one of my meetings, I'll make it disappear faster than a door slams in a storm and march you right out of this department by the scruff of your neck. Used up some of my patience, son. Thing you need to be clear as a full moon on: testing Silas Lopez is a mistake you don't want to make. Long as you understand that, you and me ain't gonna have a single problem we can't get past. Sound good, Sergeant?"

Clark stood without answering, eyes cast downward. Silas couldn't say for sure, but he thought some color was missing from Clark's face. *Good. Means some of this landed. Isn't trust yet. But maybe a start.*

CHAPTER 15

After the walk with Clark was done, Silas spent the rest of the afternoon at his desk, poring over minor local police issues, as well as the Perkins case. When he'd had just about enough of sitting, he went to the bullpen—an open area with eight pairs of desks with low surrounds pushed together, occupants facing one another, each desk pair serviced by a beige power conduit dropping down from the ceiling—to see Patrol Officer Laura Burig.

"Is the interview with Bernardi set up, Burig?" Silas asked, once again taken aback by Burig's fair complexion and ice-blue eyes.

"Affirmative, Chief," she said. "We'll need to leave in about five minutes. Funny thing—when I reached out to set it up, Bernardi said, 'That was fast.' Apparently, he'd just called the main number after hearing about the incident and said he wanted to help. The reason he hadn't heard his messages or returned my call was that he had to run to New York City for a work meeting."

"What'd you make of that, Burig?"

"Well, Genny spoke to him, not me . . . but I've thought about it." She smiled to acknowledge she knew he'd ask. *They're catching on. Slower than I'd like, maybe, but steady progress.* "And it could mean one of two things. It might be a genuine expression of concern and offer of help, or it could be an attempt to buy some time and try to help Stevenson spin a story."

"Sounds 'bout right," Silas said. "Though, considering jealousy issues—and the fact he was closer friends with the victim than the surviving husband—I'm not sure what motive there'd be to lie on behalf of Stevenson. Find out soon enough, guess. Lemme grab Bandit, and we can head out."

They went just a single block before turning onto Standish Street, where Alexander Bernardi's colonial-era, single-story home ran parallel to the road. A street-facing gable added some character at one end. Like many in town, the house had been updated during the late 1800s with a smattering of ornate Victorian-era trim around the front door and the portico supports. Looked pretty good to Silas.

It was a modest building, but he could see it had been painstakingly maintained—slate-blue stain on the tight shingles, thick cedar shakes on the roof, white trim, black window frames, and a bright-red front door. There was a white picket fence with a low-trimmed privet hedge inside it. Even from the car, Silas could see it would be easy to peer into the house through its low first-floor windows.

Story's checking out so far.

There was no delay between the knock and the door opening. *Either eager or just expecting us.*

Bernardi was tall and skinny as a rail. Tan. Flat-fronted khakis, loafers with no socks, white button-down shirt, cuffs rolled back, two buttons open at the top. Chunky gold aviator's watch on a dark leather band. Brown hair with silver mixed in, cut in a close buzz. Professional-looking, even stylish. Composed, calm. Economical with his movements. *This guy is put-together.*

"Afternoon, Mr. Bernardi. I'm Chief Lopez. This is Officer Burig. Appreciate your offer to help with our investigation into the death of Mr. Perkins. Mind if we come in?"

"Please, yes, come in. Have a seat," he said, gesturing to a charming living room with wide pine-board floors, held in place with the original square-head nails. *Beautiful home. There's wealth here.*

There were tasteful modern couches, but everything else in the room was antique. A patterned area rug filled the center of the room, and a large model of a schooner sat next to a brass captain's clock on the mantel over the fireplace. The house was hot and stuffy, as if it had been closed up all day. *Can tell from the smell there's some of those dried, perfumed flower crumbles in a bowl on a toilet somewhere.*

"Understand you were friends with Mr. Perkins," Silas said, taking a seat. Mr. Bernardi began opening windows for a cross-draft. *Nervous energy is to be expected.* "Sorry for your loss."

"Yes, Timothy and Blake were good friends of mine." Bernardi took a seat in a plump chair across from Silas and Burig. He clutched an embroidered pillow. "It's terrible what happened. I'm sick about it. Do you have any idea who did this?"

"That's why we're here. It's our understanding Mr. Perkins was at your house on the evening of the incident. That correct?" Silas asked.

"Yes, he was here. He was very upset. He and Blake had a disagreement. They're going through a difficult patch right now, I'm afraid. Or rather, were . . ."

"Mr. Perkins tell you what the fight was about?" Silas pressed. When Bernardi gave him a look of reluctance, he added, "You're probably the last person to speak to him, see him alive, so it would be helpful if you could tell us 'bout his state of mind."

Bernardi gave an involuntary shudder at that thought, and Silas felt a wave of empathy sweep over him like a cold draft. *This never gets easier.*

"Well, like I said, he was upset. It was the same issue Blake and Timothy have been having for a while now. Timothy is—was—younger, around my age, and Blake worried about him, worried about the choices he made, wanted him to take better care of himself."

"Choices?" Silas asked. *Careful word. Avoiding some kind of issue.*

"Well, about lifestyle stuff, his social life. Partying, mostly, but healthy eating and getting to bed at a decent time instead of clubbing with friends until all hours. Blake wanted him to quit smoking entirely, cut back on drinking, and, well . . ." Bernardi paused. "Sometimes recreational drug use," he said softly, raising his palms as he added, emphatically, "Nothing heavy, mind you, but Timothy was young and carefree, and Blake wanted him to slow down, not take his health for granted, and stop acting like he was invincible."

"So, they fought because Mr. Stevenson worried 'bout Mr. Perkins," Silas clarified. "He wanted Mr. Perkins to be, ah, healthier . . . In other words, they didn't fight because of jealousy or insecurity issues, money worries, those types of things?"

"Oh no. Their relationship was solid." Bernardi leaned forward slightly. "You're not thinking Blake had anything to do with this, are you? There's absolutely no way!"

Interesting. Ignore that for now, though, and keep pressing.

"No jealousy issues?" Silas prompted, pushing him a bit.

"Well, I do think that Blake was sometimes threatened by me because Timothy and I are both younger and dated at one point a million years ago, but it was never a big deal. We socialized all the time together. They really loved each other, which is why this is so tragic."

Silas felt his bullshit antennae tingling. *Is this guy just trying to take himself out of the frame? Convenient way to do it.*

"So, Mr. Perkins came to speak with you because he was fed up with being nagged?" Silas asked, deliberately trying to provoke a response.

Bernardi's head jerked back slightly, and his mouth gaped. "No, no . . . not that. The opposite, really. He has been trying to work through why he has such a negative reaction to Blake's attempts to 'mother' him. He worried maybe he could have self-destructive patterns that were undermining his health and his relationship. I've ended up as something of an unofficial therapist because we've always been so close. He loved Blake and wanted to get out of the cycle of bickering about it."

"What else did you talk 'bout?" Silas asked.

"Not a lot, really. Just sat, sipped wine, talked about where the patterns might be coming from, childhood, parents, high school—wide-ranging, introspective stuff."

Silas looked around the room for any other clocks besides the one on the mantel.

"What time did he arrive? What time did he leave?" he asked.

"I was still up, so before eleven p.m. He stayed a long time, and it was a good talk. But eventually, I said I'd better head to bed because I had work in the morning."

"Time?" Silas asked.

"That was around three forty-five a.m. I only know because I glanced at the clock, thinking how few hours there were before I had to be up again," he said, nodding toward the mantel. "I offered him the couch a bunch of times. But he said he'd prefer to walk home because he wanted to clear his head and didn't want Blake to wake up to an empty bed. That would just fan the flames and make talking through things more difficult."

Cohesive. Guy hasn't had much time to plan an elaborate story. Tilts in favor of true.

"Very helpful," Silas said, nodding to himself as he scootched forward on the couch and jotted a note. "So, let me recap. Mr. Perkins and Mr. Stevenson loved each other, good relationship, except when they fought because Mr. Stevenson worried about Mr. Perkins. Mr. Perkins was trying to work on his negative reactions and make better choices, keep the relationship even-keeled. Have I got that right?"

"Yes, that's right. Two people finally find each other in this mad world, they fall in love, they build a good life together, and this happens. It's almost too sad to bear."

Pullin' at the heartstrings now. This is either true or about as slick a cover story as I've ever seen.

Silas turned to Burig. "Officer Burig, do you have any questions for Mr. Bernardi?"

"Mr. Bernardi, can you think of any reason anyone would want to hurt Mr. Perkins?" Burig said.

Nailed it. Mighty fine to see her good instincts in play.

"No!" Bernardi did the backward head jerk again, with a look of distaste in his eyes. "I really can't. He was well liked, had a lot of friends."

"Are there any disputes, any friction with anyone, or any enemies you can think of?"

"Timothy? No, definitely not," Bernardi said.

Burig stood up, and Silas followed suit. "Mr. Bernardi, this has been very instructive." She paused and turned to Silas. "Chief, can I have your card?"

Nice touch, thinking to use mine.

Handing the card to Bernardi, she said, "Thank you for your time and the details you were able to fill in. Once again, we are deeply sorry for your loss. This is the chief's number. If you think of anything else that might be helpful, can you let him know right away?"

When they got back to the car, Bandit was asleep in the driver's seat. Silas felt a little surge of affection for him. And there was some departmental pride mixed into his warm feelings too.

"Nice work in there, Burig," Silas said.

"You sure? It wasn't too much? Why didn't you ask those basic questions?"

"I started to have an overwhelming sense this car hit wasn't 'bout a grudge. Figured if I ask it, makes the cops look stupid, like the boss is steerin' 'em down blind alleys. But glad you asked; that's perfect because, coming from a junior partner, it just makes us look thorough. Understand the difference?" Silas asked.

Burig nodded. *She's quick.* "Makes sense," she said with a smile, looking pleased. *No doubt she likes to be considered a junior partner. Happy to give her that win. She earned it.*

And Bernardi earned some trust. This is feeling less and less like spouse-on-spouse violence. So, what the hell is it?

Silas let the silence linger while he drove and thought.

CHAPTER 16
Friday, September 5

Silas sat in his office, tapping a pen against a pad of paper, deep in thought, facing a blank wall. Things weren't adding up. It felt like every twist and turn only led to another dead end.

The department was hushed. The last twenty-four hours had not been fruitful, except in terms of eliminating theories. Process of elimination was still progress, Silas told himself, but he couldn't deny that things had started to feel stagnant.

This frustrated him. His stomach felt sour. Walls felt tight, cramped.

He heard Evans outside his door, talking to Genny.

"Don't go in when the lights are off like that," Genny said softly. "The chief sometimes needs a quiet moment to think or to recharge after an interaction. Give it a minute."

How has she figured that out so quickly? It's like she knows me better than I know myself.

He got up, put the pocketknife and the chunk of elk antler he was carving back in his pocket, and turned on his light, then returned to his chair, facing the desk. He waited for a break in their conversation.

"It's okay, Genny. Sergeant Evans, what've you got for me on auto body shops?"

Evans stepped into his office but didn't sit down. "Chief, I wish I had something. I even expanded the radius and borrowed Genny for an hour to help make some extra calls so I didn't have to come back empty-handed."

Silas gave him a brusque "tell me" wave of the hand. *Smart to draft Genny, though.*

"No reports of deer strikes or other wildlife in the last few days. Nobody has worked on a lifted high-clearance truck or had a banged-up spray-paint special come in. You know these shops. They handle mostly insurance jobs, fender benders on newer cars."

Silas nodded. *Yep, figured as much.*

Evans shifted his weight and continued. "Nothing on any type of vehicle in the last week that looks like front clip damage from a hard animal or pedestrian collision. Not even any possibles worth going to look at. We know our vehicle is out there, but it hasn't been brought to an auto body shop in the eastern half of the state. Did tell them all to call if anything that fits comes in the next couple of weeks or so."

That's good work. Sometimes you have to burn resources just to take an avenue of investigation off the board. They've done a thorough job and done it quickly.

"That's a kick in the teeth. But good effort, you and the team. Well done—moved fast, helped narrow avenues. If you haven't, last thing you'll wanna check is car fires. If Genny has time, she could probably do it. I were that driver, I'd have been mighty tempted to put some gas and a match to the car that'd been in a suspicious hit as bad as that.

"Meantime, do me a favor, round folks up. We can get Clark's canvasing update with the team."

Everyone filed into the briefing room in what was becoming a familiar pattern. A few team members carried their lunches in plastic containers. *Good. Plenty of time to be seen out getting lunch around town, being approachable, when the department's less busy. Case like this? We work it hard and fast as we can.*

Over soft murmuring, Silas said, "Team, I just learned from Sergeant Evans's body-shop squad that auto body shops were a bust. Team did good work—thorough and fast. Our vehicle hasn't been brought in anywhere yet. Gonna check for car fires next. Sergeant Clark, how's the search? Any witnesses, video?"

"No, sir, I'm afraid not."

Silas concealed a smile. *Was that respect in his tone, or was I imagining it?* "All right," he said. "Go ahead and fill us in."

"At that time of night," Clark said, "even the partying crowd is in bed, and the extremely early risers are still scarce. And it was a wet, stormy night. Plus, in my experience, most people who exercise first thing do it on Commercial Street, since it's more sheltered. Me and Marsh knocked on a lot of doors, rousted people, talked to shopkeepers. Couldn't find any cameras covering that spot, any people who had seen or heard anything, or even anyone who could think of possible witnesses who might have. Sorry, Chief."

Sorry is right. Where are all the cameras around here?

"Folks, I know it's temptin' to feel lower than a snake's belly at this point," Silas said, leaning against a nearby table. "Truth is, I've seen tumbleweed on a still day with more forward momentum than what we've got goin' on now. Add to it, Burig and I talked to Bernardi, the friend, then surprised the husband with a third interview. At this point, gotta admit, I'm no longer likin' husband or marital issues as a theory here. Stories are checkin' out. Burig and I also haven't found any rope we can tug on in terms of grudges, enemies, the like. This moment, looks like we're up a blind canyon, with no way through."

He looked at the officers around him. They blinked back in a demoralized sorta way.

Grim. Maybe too grim. "You'll hit low spots like this with every case, though." *Better.*

Then after a brief pause to mark the change of subject, he said, "Unless anyone's got a smarter idea, I'm afraid we're goin' to have to go upstream, expand our radius for cameras in a bigger circle around the site."

He slapped a wall map of the town with a flat hand.

Gesturing toward the map, he added, "Houses, hotels, shops, apartments, dashcams, security cams. That vehicle moved through this town before mowing one of our townspeople down. Means we're goin' to find *any* video there is around that site between three and five in the morning. Canvasin' is a damn chore, I know. Not any happier about this than you are, but it don't change the facts."

The team groaned.

Silas nodded to acknowledge it. *Maybe a change-up would be good, get a jolt into Clark and Evans.*

"Clark, Evans—put your heads together, figure out block-by-block assignments, dole 'em out to officers who've done the least of the canvasin' so far. Meanwhile, I need to go tell Mr. Flood we're still pumpin' a dry well. Not for lack of tryin', though. Thanks, everyone—good work."

Flood isn't going to be thrilled, but that fire can smolder till day's end.

CHAPTER 17

Silas asked Patrick Flood's assistant if he was in. Late in a long, dispiriting week, the air on the second floor felt thick and used up. *Was hoping to have more to show him for the amount of time and resources funneled into the case.* Silas's mood was bleak. It felt like he was suffocating under a heavy blanket.

"Silas, what can I do for you?" Flood asked. He sat in late-afternoon shadows. The office got no western light, so it was cool and dim, the desk covered in tall but orderly stacks of paper. It smelled of old dust, maybe traces of mildew in the air coming from the floor vent. Flood looked busy and not especially chipper himself.

"Mind?" Silas said, pointing to one of the cramped antique chairs.

"No, sit down. I imagine you're here to update me on this hit-and-run, and I've got something to talk to you about too."

"Want me to go first?" Silas asked. Flood nodded. "Well, we've got a pretty good idea who *didn't* run over the victim, but still workin' on who did."

Flood put down the pen he was holding and leaned back. "That doesn't exactly sound solved. Tell me more."

Silas took Flood through the progression of the case.

Flood's eyebrows raised with interest, but Silas knew the town manager wouldn't stay impressed for long.

"But deeper we dug," he concluded, "the less Stevenson fit as a suspect. Solid marriage."

"So, where does that leave us, Silas?" Flood asked with a sigh. "The board and the newspapers are breathing down my neck for answers."

Might not be in Salt Lake anymore, but some things are the same everywhere.

"Well, so far, the search for the vehicle has been a dead end too." He paused to zoom out a little and try to impart some perspective. *Flood might not understand how cases like this work.* "Case like this, dead of night, with no eyewitnesses, no ballistics, no evidence beyond the body itself, gonna come down to luck or video. Team's looked under every stone for witnesses. On video, got teams out for a third sweep, this one wider, to find clips of any vehicle moving anywhere in this town late that night."

Honesty's the best policy. Might not make him happy, but at least it'll build trust for the future.

"That don't work, we're graspin' at straws, lookin' at mobile phones moving from towers in town to towers down the cape. Obviously, that'll require more resources and a lotta time. That's needle-in-haystack work. Hope we don't have to go down that trail. Keep you posted how we go, regardless. We'll get there on this case. Tracks always show if you keep lookin'."

Flood looked frustrated, cross. He set his pen down with a sigh and gave Silas a long look. "Silas, there's something else we need to talk about."

"What's that?" Silas asked.

"The dog, Silas," he said, tone dry as paper, like the day had already used him up.

Christ. Not this. What'd he do now?

"It's not professional, having him wander all over Town Hall, following you everywhere. This isn't a bring-your-dog-to-work job."

"Respectfully, sir, it is. Think I was about as plain as tracks in fresh snow with you about that. As you may recall, that's the job you and me shook hands on."

"I might not have understood what you meant. That dog wanders this building, barks when people are trying to talk on the phone, has been seen taking food off the table in a break room and off the counter at a coffee station. He begs in every office. He follows you everywhere, goes to every police meeting, goes on patrol with you, rides in the car with you . . ."

"Dog-friendly town, sir."

"Silas, it's about impressions, professionalism. I get that you're from the Wild West, and I've been biting my tongue about the way you dress. Jeans, Western shirts, boots, cowboy hat some days—these aren't how police officers in the Commonwealth of Massachusetts, let alone *police leaders*, dress."

What about that stuff was a surprise? Tin I came in was clearly labeled, wasn't it?

"I understand you are who you are, and I like who you are. I'm trying with all my might to let the way you dress pass—but to have your four-legged sidekick stuck to you like a barnacle is just too much. It's going to make the department a laughingstock, if it hasn't already. I cannot have the chief of police being a canine Pied Piper."

"Even if he's a police dog?" Silas asked.

"He's *not* a police dog, Silas."

"He is to this police officer," Silas said, thumbing his chest. "Look, if nothin' else, Bandit humanizes this force, makes a lot of witnesses more comfortable, makes the department approachable. Kids in town love him. One of your citizens put a string of beads 'round his neck the other day. Letter carrier gives him biscuits. You should see the waves and smiles he gets."

Laying it on a little thick, but this dog does more good than harm.

"Seems to me, humanizing, approachability, friendliness—those are the guts of the community policing you're lookin' for," Silas concluded.

Flood pinched the bridge of his nose, still for a moment before shaking his head. "Look, Silas, I'm not trying to pick a fight here. But that's not a police dog. I'm not kidding around."

I can see that, but what's the big deal here? It's just a dog. My dog—and he's sticking around, or I'm not.

"I'm up for reappointment next year, and you were an important, visible hire," Flood went on. "I stuck my neck out for you. How you act is a reflection on me too."

"Okay," Silas said.

"Okay, you'll fix it?" Flood asked, surprised.

"Okay, heard what you said." Then, to be clearer, Silas added, "I understand you don't like it."

"So, you'll fix it, then?" Flood said.

"Didn't say that."

Flood did a double take. "You heard me say I don't like something, and that I want you to change it, but you're declining?"

"Correct," Silas said, nodding.

"I just said we're both being judged. And I pointed out that I hired you—as in, *I am your boss*, Silas."

"True," Silas said.

After a lavish sigh, Flood asked, "Is this job important to you at all?"

"Dog's important too, and he's been in my life a lot longer than you have. Listen, we had an understanding on the matter when I was hired. Feels like you're changin' the rules. Slippery slope, my opinion."

"Dammit, Silas, you confound me!" Flood threw up his hands. "I just don't understand why a person in your position would take a stand like this."

"Guess you don't know me all that well," Silas said. "Like I explained on day one, we're a package deal, like a cow with her calf. He's an exceptional animal and good companion, smart as hell. And has a staggering capacity for hard work, comes by it naturally. Genetics."

Judging by the steam coming out of his ears, best get to the point.

"And I know a little bit 'bout such traits. Bandit keeps me centered and focused. I don't leave work by six p.m. to go home to my family. He's my family. And he and I put in more hours here than any two people combined on this force."

"Your point, Silas?" Flood exploded with a derisive tone.

"Gettin' there. Look, how 'bout this? I'll curb his wandering around the building and find a way for him to contribute. What, in your estimation, would it take for him to be a police dog?"

"Do something useful! Help me get reappointed when my term's up! Don't embarrass me with this 'cowboy cop and his sidekick Bandit' show, for heaven's sake. I need behavior that reflects well on the force, not some kind of mascot traipsing all over the building like a raccoon on garbage cans!" Flood shouted.

That's the rub, isn't it? He wants polish. I was hired for effectiveness. Gonna take a spell to prove the value of that. Need to buy myself a little time.

"Okay," Silas said.

"Okay, what?" Flood asked, exasperated. "Let me guess—you understand but aren't going to change?"

"I can do that," Silas said. "I can reflect well on the force."

And then he stood with a smile, nodded, and retraced his steps. *Time for some quick thinking, Silas.*

When he got back down to the basement, he said in a quiet voice, "Genny, got an emergency assignment to put on you. I'm sorry. I need you to get me some kind of a K-9 vest—most official-looking thing the rules will allow—that will fit Bandit, and I need it real fast."

Then he gathered Bandit and went home for the weekend to lick his wounds and put this beating of a week behind him. *Don't know if the vest will keep Flood from buckin' so hard, but it's a start, a change with some weight to it that Flood can grab onto. Bandit deserves the title, anyway.*

CHAPTER 18
Monday, September 8

As first light was rising Monday morning, Silas and Bandit walked most of the slender four-mile center of town. Silas held a folded leash in his hand, but Bandit didn't need it. He stuck close to Silas, zigzagging across the pavement, stopping to sniff noteworthy spots on the street.

The colors of dawn were intensifying, and the cool still air felt good on Silas's face. Bandit alerted to a fox, its rust-red fur glowing warm in the shadows as it slinked home to its den after a predawn hunt. Bandit knew better than to give chase. He was all about the smells this morning, anyway.

It had been a long, busy, tourist-filled weekend in town, and the various private garbage services had come through Saturday morning. Near an alley between two restaurants, the pavement was slick with grease and other stains. Silas wrinkled his nose. Stink was sharp, undeniable. He could imagine the crumbs, spilled ice cream cones, fried dough, French fries, animal scents, and garbage seepage Bandit was cataloging.

His mood had improved, despite Flood's complaints about Bandit and the stall in the Perkins case. He felt an involuntary smile spread as he watched Bandit work.

Usually the first one into the office, Silas was surprised to see lights on.

As he fished out his keys, he was met at the door by an excited-looking Evans.

Wouldn't have been my first guess, havin' young ones at home, but points for work ethic.

"Sergeant Evans, what brings you in so early this mornin'? Coffee on yet?"

"Chief, I didn't want to bother you last night," Evans said enthusiastically, following Silas as he made his way toward his desk. "But I think I have a lead on some possible video."

Silas dropped his shoulder bag on his office chair. "You got my attention." He motioned for Evans to follow him to the department's break room. "Sounds like no coffee yet. I'll get that going so it can run while we talk. So, what's this lead?"

Silas led them to the break room and grabbed the empty carafe. He opened the cabinet above, pulling down the coffee tin. As he started spooning grounds into the filter, Evans launched in.

"Well, Chief, I'm not one hundred percent sure I've got something that will pan out," Evans said as he leaned his athletic frame against the counter, "but here's the situation. Our older one, Tessa, is part of that kids' sailing club that runs out of the sail loft barn down in the middle of the West End."

Silas nodded, fairly sure he knew where Evans meant. He clicked the machine on. The low hiss and pop of the drip starting filled the space. He turned to lean against the counter, arms folded.

"They do an end-of-the-season potluck dinner, and in recent years, it has been held in that Knights of Columbus Hall upstairs on the corner of Ryder and Commercial, across from the sweets shops." Evans pointed south. "Since the place is up on the second story, and so rarely used, it's locked up all the time, lights out. You could easily forget it's even there."

Okay. Promising location, at least—smack-dab on top of our crime scene.

Silas raised an eyebrow. "Uh-huh. Hunch this is leadin' somewhere. Hopin', anyway."

Evans nodded to acknowledge Silas's impatience.

"So, Friday night, my family and I are at the annual potluck. I was at loose ends during the second half of the evening, not really having anyone left to talk to. So I wandered off to look out the window. I saw some janky thing taped to the pane of glass. Had a power cord on it and so forth."

"And?" Silas said.

"From the look of it, it occurred to me it might be a webcam that didn't show up in our canvasing since the place is never open and no one is there to answer the door. So, in the morning, I made some calls and found someone who could let me into the place that afternoon."

Good initiative, especially for a Saturday.

"When I got in Saturday evening, I went to the contraption stuck to the window. I didn't disturb it, but I checked, and it was still plugged in. I could see, clearly reflected in the window, that it had a green light glowing on the front of it." Evans's eyes were lit with excitement now.

"Sounds promising," Silas said, pouring some of the now-ready coffee into a mug he'd grabbed from the cupboard. He held the pot up, silently offering some to Evans.

"No, I'm good—got some from home at my desk, thanks," he said with a dismissive wave. "I asked the elderly gentleman who let me in about it, and he didn't know anything, so I asked him who might. Again, he had no idea, but he said someone in the chapter leadership could know. He gave me the names, and I started calling."

Dogged. Nice. Dogged is good.

"On the fourth call, I hit some pay dirt," Evans said excitedly, pushing off and following Silas back toward his office. "The treasurer of the club said he thought it was set up by one of the members who enjoys tinkering with electronic projects, such as weather stations, fixing old items, and setting up camera bird feeders—things like that. Guy's name is Richard Weissbourd."

Silas sat in his chair, gesturing for Evans to sit in a guest chair on the other side of his desk. He did as requested but perched at the edge of his seat. "But Chief, hang on, because here's where things get a little dicey. He died earlier in the year."

Silas felt the pang of disappointment and groaned audibly. "Killin' me, Evans." *Every lead lately feels like it comes with a catch. Or in this case, a headstone. Gotta be a break comin' at some point.*

"Well, Chief, his wife, Evelyn Weissbourd, is still alive and still in town. That camera has to stream somewhere, and I checked around the place and saw no computer equipment, so it's possible it goes to a cloud account the wife can help us access. Or it could send the footage to a laptop or PC that Weissbourd's wife still uses. It's a long shot, I know, but that camera feed has to go somewhere."

"Can't count those chickens yet," Silas said, leaning back with his coffee. "But we might have something. Every case needs a stroke of luck . . . This might be ours. When folks get in, at a more reasonable hour, let's figure out who's most skilled with computer stuff, and we'll get over to see Mrs. Weissbourd."

Change of luck? Hard to say. False hope's a near-constant companion in this kind of case. One foot in front of the other's all you can do.

CHAPTER 19

It was midday. Silas felt a little stab and realized he was hungry. He was tired of being at his desk and was at a breaking point, anyway, because Bandit was restless. The dog had been patient through the morning's meetings and calls but had started to get fidgety. *Can tell from the motionless stare alone, he's more than ready for a walk. Maybe take him to the park across the street for some lunch and a game of fetch?*

"Okay, okay. Let's go, Bandit. Walk?"

Intense eyes wide, Bandit gave a soft yip, but there was enough enthusiasm to lift all four paws an inch off the floor. Then he went and tugged the leash off the knob on the back of Silas's office door. Silas bent and clipped it to Bandit's harness-like vest. He grabbed his leftovers from the office fridge and filled a bottle with tap water.

Stepping out into the sunlight of the front steps, he saw Wren standing near the building. She was holding something too.

"Oh, hey," she said and pointed. "Lunch?"

Silas held up his container and break room fork, nodding.

"Me too," she said, gesturing with hers. "Hello, Bandit, aren't you a good boy!" She paused, doing nothing to fill the silence.

Take the bait, Silas. Regret it if you don't.

"Walkin' him. Planned to eat on a bench in the park," Silas said, jerking his head to indicate where. *Need more here, Silas. Tell her she's invited.* "Nothin' excitin', but you could join us."

She looked at her food, then up at him. *Was she still learning to decode his plainspokenness? Most people took a while to adjust. Best to encourage her.*

He looked at her with a cocked head and added, "We'd like it."

That's more like it, cowboy—no sense beatin' around the bush.

A smile spread across her face. Nodding her head, she studied him, and he looked right back at her with warmth—*and hopefully no discernible yearning*—in his eyes. Shyness caught up and swamped him, and he broke eye contact to look at the ground.

She said, "Okay, then, I will," and they started across the lawn at the side of the building.

Silas felt giddy, like a kid carrying someone's schoolbooks home. He made an "after you" gesture, and they set out with Wren in the lead. From the crosswalk on Bradford, Silas managed to take his eyes off her elegant stride for long enough to see the town's tourist railcar at the base of its hillside track. It sat idle, as usual.

"Odd contraption," he said.

"That thing?" she said, pointing. "Yes. People think it's called a funicular, but it's an inclined elevator, and it's a story."

"Yeah?" he said, settling on a bench.

"Do you really want to hear it, or are you being polite?"

"Polite's not exactly where I shine."

She'll figure it out soon enough, so might as well be plain about it.

Laughing, she sat, dropping her lunch between them. She explained, "A few years back, the town made big plans for the four-hundredth anniversary of the Pilgrims' arrival. The inclined elevator was part of it— the Bradford Street Access Project plan for the museum and monument," she said, pointing up the hill toward the massive stone monument towering above them. "They wanted to tie the monument into the rest of town, so the nonprofit that runs the monument and museum planned this contraption."

He could listen to her talk—that voice, the town history—all day.

But his reverie was interrupted. Bandit fussed at Silas's jacket pocket.

"You'd think I got a ripe squirrel in here," he said.

Standing, Silas removed the object of fixation and unclipped the leash. Bandit spun in a loop, overflowing with surplus energy. With a sidearm snap, Silas sent the ball and Bandit scrambling to the far end of the park.

"Funicular?" he said, glad for the moment of peace and quiet.

Watching Bandit career into the distance, Wren continued, "Yeah. I don't know? It's kind of a cross between a train and an elevator. Anyway, the pandemic hit, and the celebration was suspended, postponed, and ultimately shelved. When the public health situation improved, the museum and monument's nonprofit still had the plans and permission, so they went ahead and built it, anyway. The hope was that the increased access would eventually pay for the project with improved foot traffic."

"Not workin', be my guess," Silas said.

Urban planners. Someone should explain to that lot that hope is not a strategy. Must be the same everywhere.

"I'm not sure what the projections or expectations were," she said, taking a bite of a Middle Eastern wrap. The scent of its mint leaves, lemon, and chickpeas hit his nostrils, and he felt a little jealous. "It's only open during museum hours, but it doesn't appear to get a lot of use outside of the busiest times."

Silas nodded. "Man plans, God laughs."

"Indeed," Wren agreed. Silas threw one more long one, then sat back down, and they ate. Bandit wasn't done, so Silas alternated between sharing his lunch with Bandit and throwing the slimy ball for him from a seated position. It was the first moment of contentment—other than a few times by himself at home—that he'd felt in a very long time.

"You know a lot about this town. Appreciate you sharing it, seein' as I'm still getting the lay of the land 'round here," Silas said.

"My pleasure." She sighed. It sounded contented. "The sun feels good. This is nice."

It is nice. Very nice.

"Stuck indoors more hours than out—no way to live," Silas said, leaning back and taking a breath.

"I meant the *company* is nice too," she said, grinning and giving him a shove with her shoulder.

She doesn't mince words. Could do with a fair sight more people like this in the world.

"Ah. You mean Bandit?" Silas said with a smile. He dropped his gaze. "No complaints about the company, either." He was trying to wipe dog saliva from his hand onto the leg of his khaki jeans without being detected, but—

Wren noticed.

She smiled, shaking her head but saying nothing.

Foamy tongue to the side, Bandit interrupted them again, dancing and spinning for his next throw. "My goodness, that dog has focus!" she exclaimed. "He's determined! Does he ever wind down? Please tell me you at least considered naming him *Badger*."

"Would suit him," Silas said, hurling the ball.

"You guys work, though. I like the way you are together," Wren said.

"Lotta dog," Silas agreed. "But a good one."

"Why a cattle dog?" Wren asked.

Silas shrugged. "Known the breed my whole life. Worked 'em on livestock. They're special dogs. About as close to a feral animal as any breed there is." He checked with a glance, and Wren seemed interested, so he expanded. "Seen 'em go after big, mean steer to move it into a pen or trailer, get scooped by it, thrown clear over a stock pen fence, and come running straight back and challenge that bull again."

"Thrown over a fence by a bull?" Wren exclaimed.

You have no idea, he thought. "Yep. Also seen 'em run up to the front of a wayward flock of sheep across the backs of the animals if that's what it takes to get back in front of 'em, turn the flock around."

"What? They'll run across the backs of sheep?"

He laughed. People who had not seen these dogs work just didn't get it. "Couple of other herdin' breeds will too. Way these animals work together will make your heart sing, though not many ranchers use this breed of dog for sheep. Truth is, they can be a bit too aggressive for sheep unless they're raised to it—s'pose that's why they call 'em *cattle* dogs, not sheep dogs."

"I have no trouble at all believing that!" Wren's head shook in amazement, and Silas felt himself swimming in memories of amazing dogs he'd had the honor of working with.

"Lotta courage, dedication, these dogs. Lots to admire about 'em." He paused in thought. "It's a shame breeders and ranchers put training effort into only two or three dogs in a litter showin' the earliest, most aggressive herding drive. Others get tossed aside, regardless of potential they'd show just a few days later." *Pisses me off is the truth of it. Cryin' shame.*

"Is that how you got Bandit?" she asked, and Silas nodded. "I'm glad you saved him."

"We both needed it." Looking away, he sighed and said, "But Flood's raisin' a stink. Now I need to make him useful before I got a real problem. You know, I asked Genny to get him a working dog vest he can wear."

"I'm guessing the vest is an attempt to make him fit in and look the part?"

"Yep. From now on, your man Bandit will be tryin' to project a more professional image. I might be tryin' to do the same thing myself," Silas said, and it came out more glumly than he'd wanted.

He doubted she'd missed it, but thankfully, she did not stop to dig into what he'd meant.

"He's certainly smart and driven enough to be trained. Bandit, I mean. Not Flood!" Wren laughed.

"Reckon so. Bit more experience trainin' horses, though."

"I bet you could do it if you set your mind to it," Wren said.

"Time allowed, believe I could," Silas said. "Just need to catch a break on this case, and I can turn to other pressing things—like dog trainin'." *This case may be throwing up disappointments and dead ends at every turn, but on the bright side, this is about the best lunch break I've ever had.*

CHAPTER 20

The team had conferred and reached a consensus that Anna Marsh and Gavin Byrne were the most technically adept people on the force. Silas agreed. He'd already noticed Marsh was savvy with tech, good at fixing things around the department. She'd impressed him with her smarts, not just tech smarts. Practical problem-solver. *Seems like a go-getter. Good attitude. Professional.* And Silas had learned that Byrne had started as a computer science major before switching to criminal justice. He still wrote software and built websites for friends in his free time.

With that decided, Marsh and Byrne were on point to meet with Mrs. Weissbourd at her home at 2:00 p.m.

Mrs. Weissbourd's home address was nearby, so Silas, Marsh, and Byrne walked the short distance to the large old house. In time, Silas expected not to have to attend every interview, but until he had the measure of things, it was for the best that he oversaw this.

Mrs. Weissbourd was wary, sliding the door's lace curtain across its brass rod to see who was knocking. Once she saw their three badges, she opened right up. They stepped into the high-ceilinged entryway alongside an ornate, dark-wood staircase. A rush of the scent of lemon furniture polish enveloped Silas as she started introducing them to her cats. She walked them into the living room, and Silas let Marsh take the lead, as he'd warned her he was going to do. She'd work well with this witness, and it'd be interesting to see how she did.

His instincts paid off. Marsh was patient, and by being very clear and plainspoken, she was able to explain the situation.

"Yes, Richard loved computers," Mrs. Weissbourd said. "He'd collect old ones from the transfer station, you know, the swap shop they have there, and fix them up to donate to the thrift shop at the Methodist and the senior center so they could use them for running their tax program."

"How exceptional!" Marsh said. "Now, Mrs. Weissbourd, do you happen to know if he set up a camera down at the Knights of Columbus Hall for some reason?"

"Oh yes, I remember he set it up for his friend Carl Young to see the parade during carnival last year. They had fun with that project. Carl has emphysema and can't get out without his oxygen tank. He was in the military, so he always loved a good parade. Richard set up a camera for him and showed him how to watch it on his computer, just like he was looking out from the window of the Knights Hall downtown himself. Carl moved to a wheelchair not long after, and it really cheered him up to look at the camera, see the weather, and watch the people. So Richard left it up and running around the clock for him."

A wave of nostalgia enveloped Silas. *So many human stories. All you need to do is look around and pay attention. This guy sounds like a local hero.*

Marsh pounced on the revelation that the camera had been left running nonstop. "So, ma'am, you said your late husband left the camera running? Do you know where the video from the camera went, or how his friend Carl accessed it?"

"Oh, dear, I've no idea about things like that. Last I knew—before poor Richard got sick last winter," she said, crossing herself, "may God bless his soul—was Carl liked to look at the camera."

Marsh was patient. "Mrs. Weissbourd, this is very important. We need to see if there are any recordings from that camera. It could be helpful for an ongoing police investigation. Did your husband leave you any computers, or lists of online accounts, or a list of passwords before he died?"

Mrs. Weissbourd's eyes widened. "Our son, Frank, helped with computer things. He wanted us to keep all our passwords written down and safe, so we keep them in a little notebook locked in the desk where Richard paid the bills."

"How about a computer, Mrs. Weissbourd? Do you have your husband's computer? Or have one of your own?" Marsh asked.

"Oh no, I don't use a computer. I have one of those—what do you call them? Apple Pads, or something, which I use for calls with the grandkids. Frank set it up for me, but Richard's computers are all in the back bedroom upstairs. He called it his project room. It's a terrible mess. I always told him he needed to clean up all that stuff. I can't even get in there to dust anymore. And now I keep asking Frank to come here and go through it and clean it out, but I'm still waiting."

This drip-by-drip process was always tedious, and Silas felt his frustration level rising. *Gotta be patient and listen carefully. Never know which lead will play out. Just need to put the work in. Chase each lead down. At least this woman is being cheerful and cooperative. And Marsh is good. Clear she's got loads of potential.*

"Can you show us, Mrs. Weissbourd? We don't mind a mess," Marsh said.

Silas ducked to clear the top edge of the ceiling as they creaked up the stairs to the back bedroom. It was, as warned, in shambles. A twin bed with a thin bedspread was pushed into a corner and covered with what appeared to be manuals and other technical materials.

Silas smelled dust in the still air. He felt sad for the old man and the wife he'd left behind to deal with this mess.

The rest of the room was wall to wall with mismatched old desks and tables. At its center was a folding table and a chair that looked like the main workstation. There was a soldering iron and, next to a gooseneck lamp, a parts holder with alligator clips at the ends of flexible arms and a large, suspended magnifying glass for use when doing fine soldering work. Every furniture surface and much of the floor was strewn with partially assembled desktop PCs, outdated cathode-ray-tube monitors, and related peripherals and spare parts.

Silas also became aware of the scent of ozone from warm electronics. *Smells like a machine is running somewhere in the mess.*

Marsh and Byrne got to work inspecting the equipment to see if there might be an operational machine among the pieces. Before long, from a spot at the end of the bed, Marsh said, "This one with the dust caked on the fan grille is warm to the touch and has lights blinking on it. It's running. And it's connected to a monitor."

Byrne stepped over to look. "It's plugged into an Ethernet cable too. Fingers crossed."

Silas didn't catch all of those details, but he could read body language, and he could tell his team had found something they thought was important.

"Mrs. Weissbourd," Marsh said, leaning over Byrne's shoulder as he kneeled in front of the monitor on top of the PC's case and woke up the machine. "Do you happen to know the password to this machine? We could take it back to the department to crack into it, but these old machines can be fragile and temperamental. If we shut it down and jostle it around, we might not be able to get it up and running again. It would be safest if we could take a look at your house here. It could really help us out."

"I don't know the password to that machine specifically, but I know the password Richard always used, even without looking in Frank's little book. He used the same password for everything because he always said it would be easier for me when he was gone, God rest his soul."

Silas felt a little surge of affection for this plucky old gal. *Still sharp as a tack.*

"I remember because it is the name of his favorite saint." She sighed. "Saint Isidore, the saint who preserved classical knowledge, Richard used to say. The same way Richard saved these old machines."

"Mrs. Weissbourd, could you spell that?" Marsh was excited, impatient. But Silas liked how she kept it in check, gentle with the witness.

"*I-s-i-d-o-r-e.*"

"Saint too? Do I spell the full word *saint*?" Byrne asked as he handled the old mechanical keyboard.

"No, dear, just *s-t* at the beginning, so it's *s-t-i-s-i-d-o-r-e*."

Keys clacked, and a moment later, Byrne said, "There we go." He clicked and rooted around the machine's desktop for what felt to Silas like an eternity. At least he'd inherited some good skills on the team for this type of digital work, which was becoming increasingly prevalent in investigations.

Byrne said, "There are definitely AVI files on here, some with recent date stamps. I'll need to dig around and figure out how it's being recorded and where they're all stored, but from a quick file search, I can see there are a large number of small files. And from the looks of this one, it does capture the near part of Ryder Street."

Silas figured AVI must mean videos. But he didn't interrupt to clarify; best to let them work.

"Before you get your hopes up," Byrne said, "take a look—it's horrible quality. And it appears to be motion-activated, so we'd need motion to trigger any useful recording. I don't know if motion on Ryder is enough to trigger it or whether it has to be motion on Commercial Street."

Byrne squinted at a window with a list of files in it. "The oldest AVI files are about a year old, so it must be set to purge files beyond a maximum amount of space or a maximum number of files. Should be enough here to cover the last week easily."

Silas stood breathless off to the side, making sure he was out of the way. Not easy with a frame his size.

After what felt like a long wait, Byrne said, "Marsh, grab that portable SSD we brought. We can bag this PC for evidence later, but I'm going to grab a copy of the last one hundred twenty days of files onto it so we can get started and take a look at what we've got."

Finally. Could they be collecting actual evidence? Feels like the first bit of progress in days.

They made the copies, thanked Mrs. Weissbourd, and asked her to keep the back bedroom closed until someone came to retrieve the computer.

"Your help—and your husband's machines—may help us crack a real tough case, ma'am," Silas said. "Don't know about saint, but your husband was a quiet hero." *They're around. Find 'em if you keep your eyes peeled.*

Pleasantries taken care of, they hustled back to the office.

With luck, Silas thought, they were carrying the keys to this case with them. His steps felt lighter at just the thought.

CHAPTER 21
Tuesday, September 9

From his desk, Silas noticed Genny walk into work the following morning carrying a gift-wrapped package and a big smile. She came right in to see Silas and Bandit.

"I have something special for you guys." She held it out for him, beaming. "Here, go ahead and open it."

"What's this fuss?" Silas asked, untying the bow and rolling up the ribbon with the fastidiousness of someone who had worked with ropes his whole life. He shredded the paper apart and grinned. Inside was a black ballistic nylon dog vest. It had big white rubber letters molded into a thick black rubber patch on each side that read: "Working Dog. Do Not Pet."

Silas beamed as Genny got to work holding up the vest and adjusting the straps for an approximate fit. He was tickled. It was perfect. He felt a swell of gratitude.

Genny leaned down and tried it on Bandit while feeding him his favorite dried salmon bits to keep him still. With some adjustment, she got it sitting on him perfectly. By the time Bandit was done shaking to settle it onto him, he looked like an official member of the department.

Silas took stock of Bandit's new vest. Rugged. Professional-looking. And there was a sturdy handle grip running down the top to lift him to safety if needed.

"The wording on the vest is the best we can do," Genny said apologetically. "I played around with different things, but this was the most I thought we could get away with due to the strict rules about labeling officially certified service dogs and police dogs. But I think this works to give Bandit some much-needed gravitas."

"Genny, you hit the bull's-eye. He's gonna wear it every day. In fact, send off for another one at my expense so we have a spare. Allow me to wash 'em. That dog's hard on gear. Burns through a collar in under a year, so havin' two 'uniforms' will let us spread out wear and tear."

He smiled at her. He felt a surge of appreciation and affection.

"Not much for huggin', but maybe just this once? Really can't explain how much this means to me and Bandit." He stepped toward her and gave her a big bear hug, taking in her scent of lavender. "Truth is, I've been ruminating a little since meeting with Flood, and your help just lightened that load. Thank you."

Genny chuckled with delight and returned the hug firmly. Silas knew she would be thrilled to be appreciated. It was obvious from her expression and body language that she was pleased she had been able to do this for him. He was a little overwhelmed. The strong sense of relief caught him off guard. *Hope Flood sees it for what it is—me givin' a little. He's a good guy. Worth meetin' halfway.*

"Let me get settled in, and then I will take him around to show off his new vest," Genny said.

"Perfect. Let me know if Marsh and Byrne are in, and I can check on their progress."

The previous day, Marsh and Byrne had set up a pair of computers in the main briefing room and connected them to the department's largest monitors. They divvied up the video files and spent the afternoon and evening trying to make sense of the footage they'd recovered.

"The recording time stamps seem incorrect, Chief," said Marsh when Silas entered the room, "but they appear to be offset by a consistent number of hours. By cross-referencing with the dates and times of various known events, we've been able to verify that at least the date stamps on the files are correct."

Sounds like some progress, but also picking up some hedging from these two.

"The camera has a wide-angle lens, but it's been pointing down," Byrne explained. "Which means it's mostly Commercial Street in the frame. You can see here a bit of the Ryder Street crime scene in the distorted upper corner of the frame."

Silas stood back and quietly watched them work for a moment.

They had found and copied over a thousand short video files, but each clip was almost random in terms of subject matter, as the recording process was motion-activated. That meant clips of traffic, birds building a nest on the ledge above, and spiders crawling over the lens at night. What was worse was, regardless of the clip's contents, the video quality was always poor—especially when it was dark outside.

When Silas pressed them again a few hours later, they had to admit their hopes were sinking. Despite Silas trying to keep his optimism in check, this news felt like a punch to the gut.

They hadn't seen any videos that weren't triggered by motion in the near part of the frame covering Commercial Street. Motion on Ryder Street, which was all they cared about, didn't seem to be enough to trigger a recording at all.

If that's the case, this goose chase is over.

Silas could feel his spirits ebbing, but he hid it. He told them to keep the faith and stay at it.

His boots were on his desk, and his thoughts were everywhere. The department was silent, save for the hushed voices of Byrne and Marsh in the conference room. Silas was thinking about mobile phone tracing as the next logical step when he heard Marsh call out.

"Hey, Chief, I think we've got something! This clip is from the correct night, and I think we have a vehicle coming up Ryder from the town wharf."

Here we go.

"How'd ya find it? Why'd it record?" Silas asked, stepping into the warm, stuffy room.

"I'd seen a few clips where a coyote was the movement that triggered the camera. Mostly in the predawn hours we need," Marsh said. "And so I doubled down on trying to find any late-night footage right around our date. It was worth the effort. See here? There's the coyote cutting across the lawn of Town Hall toward Commercial, and I think that's what triggered this recording. And you can see a vehicle moving down Ryder. We may have caught our perp on camera."

Silas moved in. "Coyotes usually just a chicken-stealin' nuisance, but this one might be a hero. Lemme see."

Marsh and Byrne walked him through the grainy video and showed him how they knew from the time and date stamps that this was the accurate date. In the video, after the coyote left the bottom of the frame, Silas could see in the opposite corner a light-colored, full-size pickup truck—white or silver, maybe a Chevy or GMC—pulling a long flatbed trailer with what looked like some sort of storage box or half-length shipping container on it.

Trailer's interesting. Could fit some pieces together.

They watched the clip multiple times. The truck was moving fast—certainly faster than the ten-miles-per-hour limit—and slipped along with no headlights or running lights. It ran the stop sign crossing Commercial and continued up Ryder. Then, it blew through the stop sign at Bradford, taking the corner quickly.

The truck itself fit their suspected vehicle profile, but it was the erratic driving that really began to set off alarm bells in Silas's mind. He drew closer, watching as the truck peeled around the corner. The trailer naturally traced a tighter radius, cutting up over the curb and across the corner of the sidewalk just as it passed out of the frame.

For a few breaths, everybody sat there in silence.

That trailer's what did it. Bet my last silver dollar. Fits facts of the crime scene well.

"Show it again, slower if you can," Silas said. After watching it several times, he said, "Believe we now know how our pedestrian got hit."

Marsh and Byrne swiveled to look at him.

"Dark trailer came out of nowhere, movin' fast, cut a tighter turn on that corner, clipped our victim, and took him down before he even knew he needed to move out of the way," Silas elaborated, thinking through the logistics. *Right time. Right place. Right vehicle, with an erratic driver . . . It checked out.*

Byrne and Marsh nodded in agreement.

"This explains how Perkins got cut an' tumbled so bad. Looks like a heavy, two-axle trailer, with a low ramp tail. If the angle and positions are right, both wheels and fender, maybe taillight bracket would have roughed and cut him up—and that drop end would have dragged him, finishin' him off. Body would have rolled rest of the way."

"Could explain the black nonautomotive paint too!" said Marsh.

Now we're on stride.

"Also explains why we can't find a damaged vehicle, because there isn't one," Silas added with a shake of his head. "It was a trailer we should have been lookin' for. Human body wouldn't even scuff a heavy-duty steel trailer like that." He thought some more. "In fact, I think it's possible— not certain, but possible—our driver never even saw Perkins, didn't even know he'd hit 'im. Trailer that heavy, already bangin' up over curb at a corner, truck already straining to pull a hard load, might not have even felt the body."

Still doesn't explain what he was doing at that hour, drivin' without headlights and blowin' through stop signs. Got more questions than answers here.

Dampening the excitement, Silas added, "Only trouble now is, we can't make out plates on the truck or the trailer, the color of the truck, or the make and model. From the side view, looks like a Chevy or GMC—at least, that'd be my guess. White, maybe silver. Either of you?"

Both shook their heads.

Still, hard not to feel a little momentum from this find. Good police work. Team found that camera, tracked down footage, extracted it, analyzed it, found our truck. Make a police force outta this crew yet.

Silas woke up feeling revitalized. Finally, they now had a decent lead on how Perkins had been hit.

He woke up to an apartment that was dark and quiet, with lights from the street casting pale rectangles on his floor. He sat on the edge of the bed, eager for the day to begin. He got up and began making breakfast.

It was still too early to feel real confidence. *Made that mistake too many times before.* He absentmindedly put a hand on Bandit's warm, soft rib cage and stroked. *Fact is, the video doesn't tell us much.* But it would be a mercy to be able to reassure Blake Stevenson that what happened to his husband most likely didn't involve malice. *Doesn't mean we know what it did involve.*

Silas scrambled eggs with pepper jack cheese, deep in thought. Simplest explanation was a hurried driver, Perkins in dark colors, trailer unexpectedly veered into his path before he could react. Arresting a suspect would be better comfort to Stevenson, but at least he could begin the long process of coming to terms with some kind of freak accident.

He cranked open a small can of diced roasted green chiles, loaded the eggs into a tortilla, used a fork to spread the chiles on top, then rolled it up and ate standing at his counter. It was good to be feeling slightly upbeat for a change.

Unfortunately, the upbeat frame of mind didn't last long. It burned away like a morning fog in July as Silas pondered what he could do with this video on his walk to work. He was frustrated he'd had this break in finding the video, but it just wasn't especially useful. By the time he'd arrived at the office, he was still trying to think of some way to leverage it, even if it took thinking out of the box.

We've been searching everywhere, and we're still short any other video of the scene or the vehicle. Painful to admit it, but it's time to open a parallel line of investigation. Gotta get this crew educated and workin' on cell phone data as well. Gonna need to go to a judge to get a warrant to look for phones in town during our time window that left town and started hitting towers goin' up the cape.

Lacking any local contacts whatsoever, he felt the pang of someone far from home.

How to do it, though? Since his victim was already dead, and the perpetrator had been at large for days, an exigent circumstances argument wouldn't fly. What he needed were tower dumps of historical cell site location data.

Time to gather the team for a case conference and take them through it. *A job shared is a job halved.*

Everyone settled in quickly, and a hush fell.

"Folks, I didn't want this day to come because of the pain involved," Silas said, leaning on his hands behind him on the wall. "But we owe it to Stevenson. And to his husband, who died alone in the street . . . What am I talking about? The day's arrived where we've got no other choice but to push the mobile phone angle."

He paused, looking at their faces. *No groaning. That's a good sign.* He went into the details he'd thought over that morning while scrambling his eggs.

Understanding the teaching potential of the moment, Silas leaned his hip against the edge of the table and gestured with an open hand. "What we're lookin' for is called *tower dumps*. We're tryin' to find what they call *CSLI*. Means *cell site location information*—tells us which towers a given phone pinged over time. And that's where obstacles start stackin' up."

He scanned the room. Byrne was fidgeting with his pen, Marsh already scribbling something down. *Good.* He made a lesson out of it, counting off with a flick of each finger. "First, need a warrant from a judge. Lotta innocent people get swept up in any tower dump; they got rights need protectin'. Judges are usually very touchy about dumps, even if they know the requesting officer well."

He drew a quick sketch of the peninsula on the nearest whiteboard and circled a wide area. "Towers all along here's what we're gonna need. This brings us to our second problem: time of year. Summer season? Towers are lit up like a county fair on Saturday night—locals, tourists, even phones on boats pinging them up and down the coast. Needle in a haystack for sure. Gonna require real fine-tooth sifting."

He paused to make eye contact with Marsh and Byrne, then Evans. They sat attentively toward the front, making notes of everything he'd just said. Let them have another moment to shine.

"If we get the data," Silas went on, "Byrne and Marsh might be able to help us find some software to help sort it, if it don't bust the budget."

But they need to appreciate the human factors too. People are squirrelly. Don't always do what you think.

"Next problem is, we don't even know for sure our driver left the area immediately. If he didn't, all that sequential tower work isn't gonna turn him up. Could be hidin' in plain sight, in the shadow of just a couple of towers. And lastly, we don't know if the driver even carried a phone, or if he did, whether the phone was switched on in the middle of the night."

He picked up the dry-erase marker again and began to pull its cap off and click it back on.

He hated to let all the air out of the balloon he'd just blown so hard to fill, but no point in sugarcoating this. "And finally, you need to understand—and this one'll sting—it might be a prepaid burner phone." He paused to let that depressing fact hang for a moment.

When he spoke again, his voice was a little quieter. "This point, you're thinkin' we're blowing a lotta resources on a long shot. And you'd be right. Well . . ." He shrugged. "That's policin'. This gutless horse thief came into our town and hit and dragged one of our people to death. He's out there somewhere, and we're gonna run him to ground."

A moment of silence passed. A chair creaked. Someone exhaled slowly.

It's what we do. It's why we're here. Don't feel the tug of that pulling at you, you're probably in the wrong job.

He caught their eyes one by one, letting the moment settle. Some looked anxious. Some locked in. A few looked like they were already chasing the scent—*good*.

"Clark, you're with me. Teach you how to get a warrant so you can teach the others," he said with a nod at Clark, who perked right up. "Byrne, Marsh," he added, "see if you can find software we can afford. Evans, divvy up the rest of the team between covering day-to-day stuff here and using spare time to, first, locate all cell towers and, second, some phone company law enforcement contact information, and everything else you think you'll need. When Clark and I hand you a warrant, you need to know who you're calling, how you're contacting them, and what you're askin' for. Gotta hit the ground runnin'."

He was pushing them hard, and he knew it, but damned if he didn't detect small sparks of excitement, determination in their eyes. Some of them would catch the bug and develop an obsession. *Some always do.*

"Let's go, people!" he said, stepping away from the board and clapping his hands once. Their group disbanded, everything now in motion.

CHAPTER 23
Monday, September 15

Days were slipping by. Silas was spending too much time in the office at this desk, sitting in the dark, looking at the wall, and thinking through every angle he could. But this case was like pushing a big steer into a small pen. Been a long time since he'd felt this stuck. Giving up wasn't in his playbook, so he'd have to think harder.

The search for video around the scene of the collision was still yielding nothing, and they had only a few remaining buildings to check. The cell phone data process was grinding. Without prior relationships with any of the local judges and the trust that comes with familiarity, Silas had to do some wheedling.

Given the breadth of the requested data, the mobile phone warrant had taken forever to issue and had required multiple rounds of back-and-forth communication. The cell providers whined and had taken their time complying with the requests for numerous tower dumps. Marsh and Byrne found some acceptable software, but there was a learning curve, and each cell provider's data came in a different format.

As Silas had grown accustomed, they continued to have glimmers of hope, only to have them dashed. Early on, they had identified one possible phone fitting their timeline and movement pattern, but as Silas feared, it was a prepaid device with no known subscriber information. So they chased it to ground just to be thorough, learning it had been purchased for cash at a kiosk in New York City—no video on the kiosk—and it had been activated months later in Philadelphia.

At this point, Silas had to be realistic. They'd sunk considerable time and energy into searching the cell phone haystack. He could let the search continue on the side for a little while, but unless something turned up in the next day or so, he would be forced to conclude there was no needle to turn up.

He began to plan for that contingency.

At least it's a chance to teach 'em the value of backing up and coming at things a different way.

After thinking for an hour or so while bouncing Bandit's ball against the exterior foundation wall of his office, Silas got up suddenly and walked out into the department's main bullpen area.

"Gather up, people. Let's go."

People followed him into the briefing room and sat in what were becoming their customary places around the table, coffees and notepads at the ready.

"Noisy as a henhouse. Settle down, or I'll turn my herdin' dog loose on you."

After it got quiet, Silas began.

"Look, I know we're stretching the rope to the breakin' point here. Know you're tired, saddle sore from riding hard. Top of this case, it's still our busy season, and weather's been hot. But we don't have this rattlesnake in our sights yet. Not gettin' lucky on the mobile phones, a bit more checking to do, but looks like his phone was home, off, or dead. Some wells come up dry, but gotta drill 'em, anyway. Video footage from the scene has turned up only a distant glimpse. Fact is, we're gonna need to find another way to crack this nut."

The team looked apprehensive. They blinked back at him silently.

"Been thinkin' about how to do just that, and need your help to riddle it out." Silas paused to make sure everyone was engaged. "Collision site has no more video. We've checked every possibility and got nothing. But video is the key to cases like this—dead of night, no eyewitnesses, no forensics."

He looked around to make sure everyone was listening.

"Means one thing: we need to search for video somewhere besides the scene itself." Silas heard some sighs but continued. "Look, we got the likely vehicle, and given the flow of streets in this crazy town"—he slapped the map on the wall—"and the direction he was goin', we got a small number of most likely routes. Chances are very high he was coming from this bus parking and access road area near the wharf."

Heads nodded. *Pleased to see the team looking intrigued and engaged rather than frustrated and tired. They're using new muscles, but the only way to build 'em up is to use 'em.*

"Where I need your help is we need to expand the scope of the search for footage of the truck into different areas." People groaned. "Now, quit your bellyachin', and hear me out. Search's gonna be real targeted this time. We're gonna focus on the one or maybe two minutes before the incident in exactly the spots where this truck coulda been," he said, slapping the wall map again, this time more for emphasis than illustration.

Without further prompting from him, the team began brainstorming where the truck might have been coming from. Given the long, narrow layout of the town, it didn't take long to tighten the scope. Clark pointed out that due to the one-way flow of traffic in the center of town, it could have come down only through Lopes Square and around past the parking lot, then onto Ryder. In terms of getting to Lopes Square, there were only two options. One possibility was it had come down Commercial Street.

"That wouldn't make sense," Evans insisted. "No one would take a big trailer down narrow Commercial Street. It's a one-way, and wall-to-wall parking this time of year. Too tight for a truck and trailer of that size, and if you hit a pinch point, it wouldn't even be possible to back up and out."

This was the path he'd wanted them to go down. "Okay, that means the driver would have been on Bradford," Silas said with an approving nod to Evans.

"But why would a driver who's already on Bradford," Clark interrupted, "drop down into the tight, crowded streets around Lopes Square with a long, wide trailer, only to circle through the one-way streets and right back up to Bradford just one block down?"

That, Silas thought, was the $1 million question. He'd be interested to see what they came up with, but in his mind, there was only one possible explanation.

Burig nodded. "Right. It wouldn't make any sense. Unless . . ." She pinched her bottom lip with two fingers, thinking it through. "Unless you were going to and from the wharf."

Bingo.

"Onto something there, Burig," Silas said. "Let's think about what flows from that."

In Silas's mind, the wharf area was key. This was a new zone, lying just outside of their previous search grid around the site of the collision. Once he'd gotten them all to absorb this, he put an investigational plan into action.

"Marsh and Byrne, I want you to get to work locating every single business along the path the truck could have traveled immediately before the route segment we've got on camera. Any business you can't reach on the phone, you need to go visit in person. Not that many in just a few blocks, so it's manageable."

He was pleased to see that instead of groans, the team was excited by having a new thread to pull. Against his better judgment, he felt a little spark of hope too.

"Meanwhile, Burig, you're gonna help me web search for old-style live-feed webcams around town." Quizzical looks greeted him. "Yeah, I know outdoor live cams aren't as popular as they were back in the day, but I also know from a case in Salt Lake there's still plenty of 'em out there. Some hobby rigs like that Weissbourd camera, but also commercial. Especially in outdoor recreation destinations like this town."

Silas held an index finger above his shoulder to wave a circle like a little helicopter blade, and everyone stood and gathered their things to head out. There was a steady murmur of voices, less a conversation than a buzzing energy. Case energy. Just what he'd hoped to accomplish with the case meeting, Silas thought with more than a little satisfaction.

CHAPTER 24

It wasn't the soft knocking on his front door that woke Silas but Bandit's short, sharp warning barks. He'd been in a deep sleep, even though it was only 9:00 p.m. Sprawled on the couch, his head and torso were illuminated by warm light from a single reading lamp. There was a copy of *Land's End: A Walk in Provincetown* open face down on the end table.

"Hold your horses!" Silas muttered, sitting up.

He drowsily ran a hand through his dark hair and stood—the shirt he'd been mending earlier dropped to the floor, the needle making a barely audible *tink*. His feet were bare, and a bit of the worn, gray long-sleeve T-shirt was still tucked into his beltless jeans. In Salt Lake City, he might have grabbed and carried his service weapon with him.

Not on the streets of Salt Lake anymore. Likely can get to the door and back without needing the gun.

Swinging the door open, he said, "Wren, well, I'll be." She stood on the apartment's tiny stoop, looking agitated and awkward, like she was embarrassed.

Uh-oh, Silas thought. He was feeling an uncomfortable mix of emotions. Pleased to see her, but worried that she looked so upset.

"Here, come in. It's nice to see you. What's up?"

"Sorry to bother you so late," she said. "I was on my way home from seeing a client. I didn't want to call you after nine p.m., but when I saw your light on . . . Silas, I need your help."

Without admitting he'd just been out cold on the couch like a felled tree, he shook off the last of the mental fog and said, "How'd you know where to find us?"

"A while back, Genny mentioned the temporary apartment you were renting." She forced a cursory attempt at humor. "Love what you've done with the place, by the way."

He looked around the nearly empty apartment. With the slightest shrug, he said, "Nothin' to unpack. Place is just for now, anyway. What can I do for you?"

"Unfortunately, this isn't a social call. I'm so sorry to impose, but I didn't know where else to go," she said, the concern returning to her voice.

"Go on, then. And you're not imposin'—always got time for you."

"Well, I guess what I need is advice, Silas. I don't want to overreact and make this police business if it doesn't need to be, so I guess I'm here for unofficial guidance?"

"Sit." He gestured at the couch. "Start at the beginning," he instructed from over his shoulder as he padded into the kitchen to fetch her a glass of water.

She sat facing his end, one long leg tucked under her. Her words tumbled out quickly. "I have a case, a single mom, five-year-old son. There's a boyfriend, but from the way she talks about him, I can tell he's sketchy. I've never met him. He has always made himself scarce anytime I was scheduled to come by. But a couple of months ago, I came by without an appointment to give her first dibs on some boy's clothes that had been donated. I had to knock forever."

Silas turned toward her, offering her the glass of water and giving her his full attention. He nodded, encouraging her to keep going, but he already knew exactly where this story was headed. *Hopefully, this is something that can be nipped in the bud,* he thought.

Wren let out a sigh and continued. "When she came to the door, she had the beginnings of a bad black eye and red marks and bruises on her forearms from fingers squeezing them. The place was a mess. I could see a curtain rod was askew and a glass of milk tipped over on the table. I just got a terrible feeling. Per protocol, I immediately scanned the place for the boy. He was present and appeared physically unharmed, but he was clearly agitated."

"Guy there?" Silas asked, concerned.

Please tell me she is not putting herself in situations of conflict like that.

Wren gave him a reassuring hand wave. "No, no. I asked. I wouldn't have stayed if he were."

Good.

Silas was caught off guard by the depth of relief he felt.

"Anyway, my client said, 'Please don't start with me . . . I know what you're going to say . . . I already sent him on his way . . . I screamed at him and told him never to come back . . . You can save your lecture . . .'"

"What're your obligations 'round here, that kinda situation?"

Wren nodded and started counting off her fingers. "Make sure she's out of imminent danger. Make sure the boy's safe. Try to understand the full context without jumping to conclusions. Make sure she feels secure in the home and feels safe to talk. See if she wants to press charges, et cetera."

"Okay. Did that. What happened next?" Silas asked.

"She said it was the first time he'd ever done anything violent; she made sure it was going to be the last by ending things. She knew he was a mistake but said it was over—didn't want to press charges or have any more involvement with him." Wren squeezed her eyes shut briefly and grimaced, seemingly uncomfortable with the recollection.

Silas gave a knowing nod. Same old story. He'd seen it in police work many times, but what really made it sting, really dug into him, was having seen this dynamic play out with his own mother. The thought made him shudder, but he shook it off; he needed to pay attention to Wren.

"Since he didn't live there and had no legal entitlement to be there—like marriage or a lease—and she said he was gone forever, this makes it a gray area, allowing me some discretion. Ultimately, I acquiesced to her wish to put the incident behind her and try to get things back to normal." Wren paused and held up an index finger for emphasis. "But I told her I was going to need to step up my unannounced visits, keep a close eye on things, and was going to be proactive if I felt she or her son were in any danger."

"Tough situation," he said. *Sounds like she handled it about as well as she could. Gotta put the victim in charge, respect their wishes.* "Agree there was probably no upside in pokin' the bear by going after the guy, though. Tough call."

"Very tough. But, well . . ." She shrugged. "It seemed to be blowing over. I stopped by frequently. She seemed to be getting back on her feet and was being completely open and transparent with me, showing signs of moving forward."

"Another shoe to drop here, I'm suspecting," Silas said, making a rolling motion with his index finger.

"Exactly. Tonight, I stopped by unannounced on my way home, and the place was empty. The door was unlocked, but she and the boy were gone." Her voice breathy and urgent, she continued. "There were toothbrushes on the bathroom sink, Legos on his bed, and the bathroom light was on. Silas, her phone was right on the kitchen table. I didn't know what to do. I sat there for a long time thinking maybe she'd just walk in the door."

Silas felt the urge to comfort her—and before he'd even processed it, he'd already reached across the space between them and put a hand on her shoulder. Wren turned her head to face him, concern, anxiety, urgency written all over her.

"I don't know where she and her son are. She's never mentioned going anywhere. She's living hand to mouth, so it's not like she's flown off to Disney World. And the old car she owns probably couldn't make it off the cape. I can't tell for sure from the apartment whether she's running or merely traveling, but who leaves their phone behind? I don't even know how long she's been gone."

He nodded, understanding. *Not a great set of facts, truth be told.*

"I don't know if I'm making a mountain out of a molehill, or if I should trust my instincts," she said, placing a fist over her heart. "I'm not sure what to do, and I'd appreciate some advice."

"For starters, slow down. Take a breath." He gave her a worried look. "Lemme look into it," he said.

"Wait, Silas. I don't want you to open a police matter or make a missing person report," she said, sitting upright as if to emphasize her concern. "That's not what I'm asking you to do. I am worried about her physical safety, but at the same time, I don't want to embarrass her or undermine her autonomy if this is just a big overreaction."

"No, no. I understand what you mean," Silas said, holding up a hand. "Just talkin' about some off-the-books diggin'. Get some specifics. You need to understand that most of the cases concerning missing persons don't really turn up with lost folks. I'm sure this is one of them. Need her name and address. That a problem to share them with me?"

Wren thought for a second. "No, no," she decided, and pulled out a scrap of paper and a pen from the bag on the floor next to her foot. "Under the circumstances, I think I can entrust a law enforcement officer with those."

"Okay, then. Help's on the way. You've done what you can."

Mercy, Wren's a mess.

"Best to go home. Get some rest. Come by my office in the mornin'. Hopefully, we'll have it handled, and probably will, if experience is any guide."

"What's your plan, Silas?"

"Not gonna kick any hornets' nests, promise. Just a little digging. Leave it with me. I can see you're upset, but trust me. Most likely, it's gonna be fine."

He stood and offered her a hand up.

She got up and took a deep, unsteady breath. Silas sensed it might actually be his calm she was uneasy with. It was having the opposite of the effect he wanted. Did she think he wasn't taking it seriously? He scrounged for some words of reassurance.

"You did the right thing," he reiterated. "Gonna be all right. Go home, get some rest, and let me do this for you. I want to do it for you. I'll run it to ground. Get you some facts. Okay? You gonna be okay?"

She nodded, gathering her jacket. Bandit rubbed against her leg, and she scratched behind one of his soft ears without looking at him. *That's something, at least.*

Silas walked her to the door, palm lightly resting on her lower back. She turned, and he took her hand and gave it a quick, reassuring squeeze. He looked her in the eyes and gave a comforting nod.

Before he let her out, he said, "Wanna be sure you understand I'm not dismissing your concern. Just sayin' this is what I do. Lemme do it. Seen a lot of these. Odds are, get you some comfort quickly. Hate to see you upset, but I've got this."

He looked her in the eyes again for a long moment to see if he could get a read. She blew out a slow exhale, nodding. She turned and grabbed the door handle. He let her go after one last squeeze of her hand.

As soon as the door closed, he texted Genny and Evans, giving them the overview, asking them to be in early, if possible. He was awake now. He had the elevated pulse to prove it. *But this is a chance to be there for Wren. You can be damn sure I will be.*

CHAPTER 25
Tuesday, September 16

Silas beat the roosters to the office the next morning. Genny and Evans showed up at 7:30 a.m. Genny brought a square box of four large muffins with her, and Silas asked if she'd used the coffee petty cash to pay for them. She hadn't, of course, but upon his insistence, she promised to reimburse herself.

After a quick coordination huddle at Genny's desk, everyone got to work on tracking Wren's client, Tonya Holloway. By ten minutes after nine, they had a most likely location and a phone number to reach her.

Silas dialed it, and a woman's voice answered. "Hello?"

"Good morning," Silas began. "I'm hoping to speak to Tonya Holloway."

In a shocked tone, the woman blurted, "How do you know she's here?"

"Didn't—till now," Silas said.

Oops. That was maybe a little too much of a jerk on the lasso. This woman's not a suspect being interrogated, for heaven's sake. But at least I got a rock-solid confirmation.

Possibly realizing what she'd done, the woman said, "Who are you, and what do you want with Tonya?"

Okay, this isn't going quite as smooth as it was supposed to. But we can reel it in.

"Silas Lopez, chief of the Provincetown Police. Sorry if I alarmed you, ma'am. Don't need anything from you except to verify that Tonya—I'm assumin' she's your sister—that she and her boy are safe."

Over the soft hum and static of the connection, he could sense the tense suspicion.

Understandable. Fact is, he'd yet to meet a member of the public who didn't get at least a little flustered dealing with police.

"I imagine they are, since they're with you," he added, jumping back in. "And if so, I can relay the news to her friend, Wren Bradford, out here in Provincetown. It's Wren who's worried."

"Tonya's fine, but what is this all about, mister—ah, Officer?"

"Glad Tonya's good. Like I said, the social worker assigned to her case, Wren Bradford, was concerned by her unexpected absence. I can let Ms. Bradford know, but before I do, if Tonya's there, I'd like to hear her voice for myself to confirm she's good."

Silas heard some muffled shouting.

When Tonya came to the phone, she was wary but reassured to know Silas was from the police and a friend of Wren's. Unsure how much privacy the situation called for, Silas acknowledged only a surface-level understanding of her problem and expressed his support. She told him a bit about what had happened with the unplanned departure.

Silas liked her. She sounded like she had a good head on her shoulders. She told him she was probably being overly cautious, but she didn't want her son exposed to any more drama.

"No, no. Handled it well. Keep your boy safe. Till things settle down, likely better to take too many precautions than too few. Tell you what—we can help keep an eye out if you want to come by the station sometime and give a description of the guy and his vehicle."

"Yeah, maybe. No harm in it . . . I might do that, Officer."

"Meantime, lemme give you a number you can call us at—anytime, day or night—if you feel unsafe."

Tonya was very grateful and apologetic for the false alarm.

Silas ended up feeling that, on balance, it probably did more good than harm for her to know she had people in her corner, looking out for her and her boy. It felt to him like he'd walked the tightrope successfully, and it had come out okay. *Good that she's safe.* Nice to have something go his way for a change.

CHAPTER 26

Wren stopped by his office at 10:00 a.m.

He heard her voice talking to Genny before he saw her, so his head was up when she appeared in his doorway.

"Mornin', Wren," he said, standing up. He raised two palms toward her. "Everything's okay. Tonya's safe. At her sister's up in Duxbury."

"What?" Wren's shoulders sagged with relief. "Wow, that was fast! How do you know?"

"Spoke to her," he said, coming around the desk.

"You've spoken to her? How did you find her?"

"Be sure to thank Genny and Travis Evans. They did all the work. Had 'em come in early. Looked at her credit card, public records on family, some guesswork, some calls, and got her on the phone."

Silas hoped the pride and satisfaction he felt weren't painted all over his face like he was a dopey kid.

"Oh my gosh. That's such a relief. So, she's okay? What happened?"

"They got lucky. Her sister was visiting her in Provincetown. Tonya got a text from the jerk ex-boyfriend out of the blue—one of those late-night 'You up?' texts." He felt himself blush more than a little at the talk of booty calls with Wren, so he hastened the story along. "She threw the boy and the sister into the sister's car, and they took off to lie low for a couple of days."

"Why didn't she tell me?" Wren asked, brows furrowing.

"She asked me to say sorry, tell you she bolted without her phone and hadn't thought to let you know."

"Oh, Silas, that's a huge relief. I can't thank you enough!"

Out of nowhere, Wren surged forward and hugged him. He stiffened just a hair, caught between instinct and office decorum. Her head on his chest wasn't how he'd expected to start the day, but he wasn't complaining.

With her face still buried, she continued, "And I can't believe how quickly you guys did that. I'm genuinely impressed."

She let go. He could still feel the warmth of her against his shirt. He was unsure how to meld the hug with the professional context. *Glad we're not out at Genny's desk, or everyone would be staring at us now.*

He shrugged and said, "Day's work. Like I said, Evans and Genny did the legwork."

"Well, I'm so grateful. Thank you."

"De nada," he said with a warm smile.

He was just glad this was one of the rare ones with a good outcome. If he was honest with himself, he was also grateful for the chance to flex a bit for Wren.

CHAPTER 27

As Silas had requested, the canvasing team was out talking to business owners along the likely routes they had identified the day before in the Perkins case. Silas and Burig were at their respective computers, working the web for possible camera feeds. Silas, however, was chasing a hunch by looking into the businesses on the wharf. He started with the weather angle. *Who cares about weather conditions? Those charter fishing operators, that's who. If anybody's still got a live feed, it's gonna be one of them.*

When he'd finished with one whale-watching tour business, he stopped to scour the website of a big charter fishing outfit. He found a promising reference to a weather conditions webcam and drilled down to find what appeared to be an active live stream showing weather in the harbor.

He felt a gambler's high. The camera was aimed to capture sky and sea conditions, but it had a wide-angle lens, and the scope of the frame covered a section of the wharf around the charter company's boat slip. Silas felt his pulse quicken when he saw that the main roadway down the middle of the wharf was captured in the edge of the frame.

"Burig—have a look here. Got video feed of the wharf. Can't place the exact spot," Silas said.

Burig came over and peered at the screen. "That looks like it's on a flagpole over one of those little retail huts along the wharf. You know, those ones with all the flags? I think this charter company's boat slips are about halfway out the wharf; it's probably on top of their hut."

Silas glanced at the time and said, "Not five o'clock yet, so it should be open. Do me a favor and grab Marsh and Byrne."

When Marsh and Byrne joined them, Silas showed them the feed and asked if the existence of a live feed guaranteed there would be recordings. They both grimaced and shook their heads. *Oh, not again. This fucking case! There's more good video in a single block of Salt Lake City than this entire damn town.*

"Chief, a live feed, in most cases, is just that—a broadcast of what the camera is seeing in real time," Marsh explained.

Byrne said, "She's right, but technically, it is possible. Some of them do make recordings simply to have recent footage to loop on the website if communication with the camera goes down briefly. Sometimes they keep some just because the default setting on the software was to record, and nobody ever changed it. But I do have to agree with Marsh—it's unlikely, but there's a chance."

Only one way to find out, people. Let's get movin'.

"You two comfortable goin' over there yourselves, or want me to come with?" Silas asked. "Officer Bandit's always up for a walk, show off his new vest."

Marsh and Byrne looked at each other with surprise on their faces at his confidence.

"Yes, Chief," Byrne said in his bravest voice. "Officer Marsh and I should be just fine." He stole a side-eye glance at her, and she took the hint and nodded. "We could always call you for backup if we have an issue?"

Silas suppressed his amusement.

"Yep. Meanwhile, I'll update Flood that we've made some progress. Lord willin' and the creeks don't rise, find some video stored somewhere. If there is, snatch us a copy, secure any equipment involved, and let's get a look at it."

"Do the same if it's stored in a cloud account?" Marsh asked.

What is it now? There's always one more hitch. He needed to get a crash course in the world of digital information.

Silas gave her a blank face. "Do I look like a cloud expert to you? Don't matter how; just get me video. If it's up in the clouds or whatnot, make sure it's backed up safe. Make sure it's admissible by gettin' consent, logging your collection process, and gettin' owner details so we can use them to authenticate it. Let's go!"

Finally, something with potential I can show Flood. Probably smarter to wait, but Flood's been watching me grind my gears. Maybe showing a little hope is worth more than another wait and see. Heck with it—I'm going to go see Flood.

The team gathered for a case conference again the following morning. Silas took a measure of comfort from the growing sense of routine they were developing.

He got right down to business. *Short meeting's a good meeting.*

He reported the town manager was pleased to hear they were making a little progress. Then, leaning toward Genny, he cupped his hand around his mouth and, in a stage whisper, said, "Mr. Flood noticed Officer Bandit's new vest. Didn't comment about it, but be damned if I didn't see his brows knock up one click."

Genny beamed, and the other officers smiled. Silas had noticed people growing fond of Bandit. He noticed they were keeping their lunches and snacks away from the edges of tables too, but he could tell they were warming to their four-legged colleague.

"Okay, Marsh, Byrne, lemme turn it over to you two to get us started. Got your text last night sayin' you thought there's gonna be video. Tell me and the team where we're at."

They looked at each other, and Marsh indicated that Byrne should lead. Silas noted that a female officer was deferring to a male officer and hoped that did not reveal any friction within his force. *Probably not— Byrne had been the one to examine the machine and do the copying.*

"The video was being recorded locally, and the charter company's website was pulling from those recorded files," he began. "Looks hopeful we might find something useful, but we're going to need a few more hours to sort through it all. It's an old PC, and the battery soldered onto the logic board is dead. The computer can run fine without it, but those CMOS batteries are how the computer keeps track of time when it's shut down." He clocked people's puzzled responses and added, "Why do we care?"

Right. Had that same question.

"Because every time this machine is shut down, or the power is cut, the next time it comes on, the system clock restarts itself to January 1, 1990."

Silas felt a surge of panic but kept it in check. "So, we don't know when any of the video was recorded? Can't find our day?"

"Kind of. We have a series of sequentially recorded and time-stamped files, one every ten minutes, each approximately twenty seconds long. However, each string of recordings starts with the earliest file, dated January 1, 1990. They're small, low-resolution files. From what we can see, it retains about six months of footage—or more precisely, one hundred eighty days' worth. At six recording files per hour, twenty-four hours per day, one hundred eighty days' worth is just under twenty-six thousand files."

Great, we've got a forklift's worth of video, but we don't know what any of it is. Next thing out of Byrne's mouth better be some clever solution, or these officers might see their chief break down and cry.

"But it's not as bad as it sounds," Byrne went on, as if reading Silas's mind. "We've been able to knock out a couple of big strings of files just based on the season being wrong. We can roughly determine when a string is recorded based on weather cues, people's seasonal clothing, ferry passenger arrivals, and so forth. We're hoping that the power hasn't been knocked out in a while, and our incident is preceded by a relatively long string of sequential clips. If we can locate our string, we should be able to navigate through it fairly quickly. Between the fireworks on July Fourth and other factors, maybe time of sunset, sunrise, we should be able to pinpoint our day and time."

Smart thinking. These officers got some brains on display today. Like to see it.

"Well, team, you heard 'em. Questions? Anything we can do, support you two?" Silas asked.

Evans had his hand up. Silas nodded.

"Mind if we refer to them as *the Geek Squad*, Chief?" Evans asked, to some giggling.

"Well, reckon that's up to them. As you sort it out, best remember they're armed."

Marsh and Byrne were all business, shrugging at the nickname and saying they would circle back either way.

The team filed out of the room, but Silas didn't go straight to his desk. He was in too good of a mood to be at a desk right this minute. He'd go see Genny, thank her again for the extra effort she'd made yesterday. *Might as well pass a little of this good feelin' along.*

CHAPTER 29

Silas sat on the corner of Genny's desk, which was a first. He could tell she was wondering what was up. Shame this case hit so hard and fast right after he'd arrived. Almost no time to get to know her, and he wanted to. *Seen enough to know she's a keeper.*

"Feels like we might finally be making some progress on this hit-and-run. Meanwhile, thanks for comin' in early yesterday, helping Wren track her missing client."

"Happy to do it. Poor Wren. She's a dear," Genny said.

"Dedicated." Then, after a beat, he added, "Both of you are, tell you the truth. Thank you for that."

With a smile, Genny deflected the subject back to Wren. "She's very good at what she does. The people in this town are blessed to have her."

"Caring helps," Silas said. "Could tell she cared about Tonya being okay."

"Yes, she loves this community. Her family has a long history here, summer people for generations."

"Yeah? Good people? Down from the Boston area?"

"Oh yes. Not to gossip, Silas, but they're Old New England–type people." She peered up at him through raised brows. He didn't know what she was getting at, and his face must have given him away because she added, "You know, seriously wealthy. Old money. Old family. Have you ever heard the phrase *Boston Brahmins*?"

"Brahmin?"

"No? Okay, well, I love historical fiction—make sure you keep that in mind for the holiday Yankee swap—so you have come to the right person to educate you."

Silas chuckled. *Hell's a Yankee swap?*

"*Brahmin* is an old word from the 1800s. Back then, the oldest, most politically influential, most educated, wealthiest, and cultured families in the city were referred to as *Boston's Brahmins.*

"I'm not sure exactly what the origin of that word is beyond the fact that it comes from the Hindu caste system, if you can believe it," she said, sitting back in her chair.

Silas scoffed, smiling. "You could put what I know about the Hindu caste system in your eye and still see. But I'm gettin' a kick out of talking with you about it."

Genny laughed and didn't let Silas's reaction deflate her. "Anyway, nowadays it basically means posh people. And that's my point—that's the kind of family Wren comes from."

Silas nodded, eyes toward the ceiling, making a mental note. He wasn't sure how to take this new information beyond apprehensively. Wren, a posh person, wasn't likely to see eye to eye with a country guy who spent his childhood wrangling calves and branding cattle.

"From what I understand," Genny continued, "she always came in the summers as a kid. The last few summers, when she was in college, she worked in a photography studio and gallery out here."

"That right?" Silas said. "She mentioned it's an interest when we first met."

"Yes, she once told me she was studying photography, and she wanted to learn from a pro. Well, the poor young thing ended up effectively running the studio and gallery for her boss. She only laid eyes on him a handful of times her last summer there. Not much of an internship in actual photography, but a decent wage and a foot in the door at a well-respected gallery. The owner's not a bad guy, though I think he knew he was taking advantage. There's still a corner of the gallery space somewhat permanently reserved for her work," Genny said.

Silas's eyebrows rose, but he tried for a very casual tone when he said, "Yeah? Which gallery's that?"

"Salt Light Studio near the Johnson Street lot," she said. "Armand Deschamps's place. He's a much-admired international photographer. He keeps to himself, for the most part . . . He's a bit of an enigma, truth be told. He just turned up in Provincetown one winter years ago and stayed. No one seems to know his backstory, but I get the sense there might be an interesting one."

"And you say some of her pictures are still there?" Silas asked, still trying to sound casual while bringing the focus back to Wren.

Genny's face wore a "gotcha" smile. She sat back in her chair, smirking. "Aha! I mentioned it because I thought it might interest you."

So much for fooling this woman. She's reading me like one of her historical novels.

"You can tell me to mind my own business," Genny said evenly, raising her palms, "but I've got the sense that one's caught your eye."

"Got a sense, huh?" Silas said, trying to come off dry but looking a tinge embarrassed. Yep, she had his number. "My eye, you say? Supposing she *had* caught it . . . You seem to know everything there is to know, so . . ." He grinned. "What else can you tell me?"

"About Wren?" Genny asked. Silas reflexively looked over his shoulder to make sure they were alone before nodding and making a "keep your voice down" gesture with both hands.

"Well, let's see," she began, voice hushed. "I know that when she finished college, she earned her master's degree in social work at Harvard, then completed the required internships, obtained her social work license, and after a couple of years in Boston, she moved out here full-time. I've never asked her why, and she has never offered. The town didn't have an opening in social services right away, but Roger Chandler, who runs Human Services, knows a good thing when he sees it, so they eventually snapped her up. I'm guessing the proceeds from her gallery work and sales of her pieces more than kept the lights on in the meantime."

Silas paid attention, making mental notes. He let Genny keep going. This was good intel, and Genny was clearly in her element.

"For the last few years, Wren has split her time between running the town's Human Services grant program and administering a privately donated trust fund that provides financial assistance to Provincetown families with children. The rest of the time, she serves as a case manager, assisting local families with their finances, housing, SNAP benefits, health care, and disability benefits. She has a lot on her plate and always seems willing to pile on more."

Gal's built outta good timber. Knew she had some grit. Didn't realize how much.

"Huh. How'd you come to know all this?"

"Just good old-fashioned police work." She winked at him. "Since I knew Wren was a"—she held up air quotations with a grin—"'person of interest' to the chief."

"That so?" he said with a burst of laughter he wouldn't have been able to suppress, even if he'd wanted to.

Genny straightened some piles on her desk. "Yes, she worked at Salt Light part-time until the town position opened up, and she's been making a huge difference here ever since." She hesitated and made a deliberative face. There was a twinkle of mischief in her eyes. Silas sensed she was pondering whether to stick her neck out further. Having decided to press the issue, she said, "Silas, I'm not sure it's necessary to tell you, but that one is special. You could do a lot worse than Wren Bradford."

"Based on the findings of your investigation?" he said with a smile.

"Yes, my *extensive* investigation," Genny said, looking relieved Silas didn't appear to mind her matchmaking.

"Hunch tells me so too." Silas winked, turning toward his office. *That was productive. Went to share a little joy with Genny and stubbed my toe on some learnin' with real weight to it. Lots to process there. And how about that Genny? Still waters run deep.*

CHAPTER 30

"Oh, shit," Silas said as Bandit strolled into his office smelling strongly of imitation vanilla. He had whipped cream on the underside of his chin and neck and the sides of his muzzle.

This is not good. There's bound to be a break room cake missing from somewhere in the building. This repeat offender's lookin' at a slam-dunk conviction if there's frosting footprints on the floor.

"C'mon, let's get you into the men's room to tidy up, lickety-split," he said, sighing as he took off for the restroom, Bandit trotting loyally behind him. As he cleaned up Bandit, he could only hope the cake had been mostly gone before Bandit discovered it. If so, maybe no one would think much of the remainder being gone . . .

Pray Bandit didn't leave any telltale forensics. Hair, paw marks, and other kinds of evidence that'll tie him to the crime. Best wipe you down and get you the hell outta here.

It had been a long day of working on other matters while waiting for the video team to find a hit. Feeling impatient and not wanting to hover and distract his team, Silas had decided to burn off some tension by walking Bandit up to Blake Stevenson's office to give Stevenson a courtesy update. Now, the walk was not just case business. It was also calculated to give Silas a chance to get Bandit out of the building before anyone suspected him of theft, or worse, Bandit had an accident on the floor.

Time to walk the perp, establish an alibi, and pray there's no frosting trail. It'll give Bandit a chance to fix whatever trouble's churnin' in there, if his eyes were bigger than his stomach.

Silas didn't feel great about being an accessory after the fact for this crime, especially for a hardened criminal who was indisputably guilty, but sometimes you had to stick your neck out for the ones you loved. *Get through this without getting busted, and I promise we'll figure out a way to get this dog under better control.*

They found Blake Stevenson in his office. Stevenson looked nervously at Bandit, and Silas moved him to his far side, keeping him out of the way. As he anticipated, Stevenson took comfort in knowing his husband had not been targeted or the victim of malicious intent but rather just caught in the crosshairs of one of life's tragic freak accidents.

"That makes much more sense, Chief," Stevenson said, bags still under his eyes. "I have tried and tried to think of anyone who would want to do Timothy harm, but just couldn't."

"Glad to be able to offer that small comfort, sir," Silas said before offering his continued sympathies and assurances that the search for the driver had not slowed down even a little. *These talks'll always sting—don't matter how many you do. Job is to show up honest and not leave a man standin' alone in it.*

On their walk back to the office, Silas called the coroner to square up his trailer theory with her impressions of the injuries. When he described the video and the trailer, it seemed to click for her right away.

"In fact, Chief, the more I think about it," she said, noodling it out loud, "the more confident I am that the trailer theory matches the injuries and forensic evidence precisely. I'll need you to find me that trailer to be sure, but at a bare minimum, at this point, I'd be willing to testify the injuries were consistent with a hit from a trailer like that."

Not an unexpected conclusion, but a welcome one. This medical examiner was good. She was plenty deep on the science and forensic theory, but she knew what cops needed and how to get it out in the most helpful way. *Lucky draw. Seen medical examiners a lot worse than her.*

After arriving back at the department, Silas spent the first half of the afternoon at his desk opposite Evans. He had brought a laptop into Silas's office, and they lost a couple of hours trying to figure out how many trailers like the one in the video were registered in Massachusetts and whether there might be any productive angle to be found there. The desk was tight—with two computers and two large guys, plus the growing piles of files and case materials stacked up. Wedged between a filing cabinet and the corner was a dry-erase board that hadn't been updated in weeks. The hum of the overhead fluorescent light didn't help the mounting sense of futility.

The Massachusetts Registry of Motor Vehicles kept a lot of data on each registered trailer: VIN, make, model, type or class, length, width, gross vehicle weight rating, number of axles, tire size and load rating, braking system, and type of coupling. But none of it narrowed their search.

"None of this data can be used to narrow things down for us, Evans," Silas said, speaking his concerns out loud while pushing back from the desk. "All we know from watching the clip is we're dealing with a large, two-axle flatbed trailer."

"And this state has far too many of those registered," Evans said. "To sort through them all would be tedious at best, impossible at worst. We can't even be sure our trailer was registered in Massachusetts."

Silas exhaled hard through his nose and gave the monitor one last glance before holding up one index finger and leaving the office. He headed down the hall toward the kitchen for a refill of lukewarm coffee, then stepped back into his office, where Bandit lifted his head expectantly.

Silas tried to content himself with catching up on paperwork while the day ticked by. Before too long, his restlessness—and Bandit's not-so-subtle whining—spurred him to get up and take another walk.

"Cake starting to catch up with you, Houdini?" he said, stooping to scratch behind Bandit's ears. "Well, it's your lucky day, because I need another walk too. Let's go."

He walked Bandit out to the front of the station, where Genny sat behind the reception desk, organizing mail.

"Be back soon, Genny. Walking around the block. I have the rover if you need me."

"Roger that, Chief," Genny said, sounding pleased to be told where he was going for once.

Silas was trying not to get underfoot as the team searched the charter fishing footage. With the worst of the summer crowds finally thinning, things were starting to quiet down. Since his curiosity about Wren's photographs had been simmering, and he'd completely skipped lunch, he figured he'd walk in the direction of the gallery, rustle some midafternoon grub on the way, and have a look at her work.

He stumbled upon a couple of nice places he'd never noticed because they were below street level in a sunken courtyard. He went down the wide brick ramp and chose a big roll-up sandwich from a shop specializing in them. It was late and there was no line, so he got his food right away. Bandit climbed up next to him on a shady bench in the tiny, enclosed courtyard, and they worked on eating the sandwich together.

Silas noticed he was next door to a place called ScottCakes that sold only one thing—cupcakes with pink frosting. They smelled and looked incredible, even to someone like Silas, who didn't normally eat that kind of thing. *To get by selling only one thing means they've gotta be good. Need to find an excuse to bring a box of those to the office sometime. Maybe get one for Wren too. Unlike Bandit, she'd be cute with some pink frosting on her nose.*

His target was just one block farther. He'd never been in an upscale art gallery. Already self-conscious, Silas tied Bandit up and ducked inside. The host instantly made it worse.

"Howdy, partner! How can I help you?" he said while eyeing Silas head to toe.

Silas cleared his throat. "Here to see Wren Bradford's pict—, ah, photographs."

The host wore a pale-gray linen suit with a blue shirt open at the neck. Light flooded in the large front windows, and Silas noticed he wore subtle eye makeup. He stood and came around the desk. Not used to being touched by strangers, Silas startled when the host patted the fabric of his red checkered shirtsleeve.

"I love this!" he said, waving his hand with a sweeping motion that took in the enormity of Silas, top to bottom.

"Pardon?" Silas said.

"This outfit. It's working for you. The hat and boots are perfect too. Vintage denim! Pearl-snap shirt. I love it! Are these genuine mother-of-pearl? Delicious!" he said in a teasing way.

Silas stood there, unsure how to respond. His discomfort was intense. This wasn't like any conversation he'd ever had. The man was being funny and kind, but Silas was already so far out of his element in a fine-art gallery, let alone being flirted with so brazenly, that he froze like a jackrabbit staring down a coyote.

The man held one arm across his middle, with the other resting on it, his chin on his fist. After evaluating Silas for a moment longer, he cast his eyes downward from Silas's face to his belt. "Wait, is that a real badge? Oh, my! You're not wearing this getup ironically, are you? You're the new chief of police from out West, am I right?" His voice rose with excitement.

Still struggling to catch up and join the conversation, Silas nodded and said, "Suppose I *was* wearing my cowboy shirt ironically—probably want the badge pinned above this here authentic sawtooth pocket?"

"Right! That would be perfect! Well, I'm thrilled to meet you, Chief." It was said in such a genuine way that Silas couldn't help but take an instant liking to this guy. Holding out a hand, the host said, "I'm Rafael. Let me take you back to Ms. Bradford's collection."

Please, Lord, yes, let's do that.

They walked to the back of the gallery to a collection concealed behind partitions that blocked out the natural light. Above each photograph was an intense overhead spotlight.

Silas could smell traces of dust cooking on the spotlight bulbs and the scent of heavy stock paper and spray mounting adhesive from the framing room in back. In Wren's section of the gallery, large and small prints were hung together in a mix of monochrome and color images. Each was set behind a thick, textured mat surround and showcased in a shiny black frame. There was a mix of street scenes and landscapes. Silas stood in front of them, so transfixed he didn't notice Rafael walk away.

He'd never had the chance to learn about art, but these made him wish he had.

He took his time, closely examining each photograph, trying to figure out why they evoked a response. *Ordinary things, mostly, so what is it that's transforming them? The way she's framing them up in the picture? More than one picture only captures half the subject. Don't think it's just me. These pictures have something artsy about 'em.*

He saw more of the effect Wren had explained with Bandit's pictures—*depth of field*, as she'd called it—as well as images with sharp, fine details. Some were soaked in light, featuring soft, sun-bleached colors, while others were rich and saturated. There were a few dark, moody, monochrome portraits. Taking them all in together, it was overwhelming for Silas to think Wren had gone to all these places, been in all these moments, and somehow managed to capture the light, the feeling, her personal experience in each one. *Feels like she's gathering the whole moment—not just what it looked like, but how it must have felt to stand in it.*

As he stood there captivated by her images, he tried to imagine creating photographs like these. They were different from the memories he could bring to his mind's eye. There was something elevated and essential in the way each fleeting moment had been framed, captured, and preserved. Silas realized that to recognize the potential of these small details, the simplicity of these sweeping landscapes, took a different way of looking at the world—maybe a different way of being.

After taking his time with the last of the pictures, Silas stepped back to think. He struggled to organize his thoughts. *Need to get this straight before we talk. Wanna discuss these with her but need to figure out what it is about these that's chokin' me up.*

His main realization—the one that unlocked it for him—was that, unlike Wren, he felt like he lived in a moving world. A world of interacting objects bouncing off one another, affecting each other's course. A gigantic system of cause and effect. Actions, consequences. Motion, motive, plans. He had strong powers of observation and noticed the smallest details but always in the context of a larger frame of reference—never in isolation, for their own sake, and never neutrally.

For him, details were always a piece of a puzzle. For Wren, the details were the whole point.

Near as he could tell, Wren could key into a different visual plane, a motionless one. A world of just being. A place of just existing in light and dark, color and shadow, minute textures and details. He was blown away by her ability to stop time and grab a sliver of it.

Silas placed himself in front of a large color portrait of an old man. Sunlight drenched the scene. Soft, out-of-focus shapes of ship rigging were visible in the background. Bits of the street scene filled the middle ground. Silas realized if he saw a man like that on the street corner, he'd wonder about his story, what he might be up to, whether he was suspicious, whether anyone might be worried about him, whether he might need help.

The light on his face made his deep wrinkles stand out, along with the white stubble on his chin. The angle of the bright sunlight made the shaded parts of his old flannel work shirt pop with color while the sunlit patches washed out. Silas could practically smell the brine off the water, hear the clunk of the rigging and the rasp of the old man's voice.

Wren had put him there—with that man, in that moment.

Silas thought about Wren's social work. He sensed she had a tremendous capacity for empathy with her clients. He wondered how a camera made it possible for her to separate a subject from their humanness enough to capture just a split second of their story. Maybe he had it wrong.

Perhaps she could capture their moment because she had the empathy, not in spite of it.

Eventually, he became aware of Rafael shuffling things on his desk and heard the gallery door jingle. Silas realized with a shock he'd been lost in Wren's work for over an hour. Rafael was probably wondering what he was up to, so Silas pulled himself away and headed back to the front.

"She's talented, isn't she?" Rafael said. "Are there any pieces you want me to hold for you?"

"Hold?" Silas said, then realized his meaning with a flush of embarrassment. "Uh, no, thank you, not yet. Appreciate your help, Rafael. Thank you."

Silas stepped out onto the street. He blinked as his eyes transitioned to the bright afternoon light. *Gonna need to learn more about Wren and this magic she creates. Lots more. And soon.*

CHAPTER 32

Silas collected Bandit, who had been sleeping in the shade in front of the gallery with his leash loosely knotted to a post, and eased back into reality. Stepping back outside into the sunlight left him blind and blinking, as if awoken from a dream.

Even so, he was in a good mood, still lost in thought about Wren's art. He decided to mix it up and walk back to Town Hall along the beach. The town parking lot next to the gallery ended right on the sand. It would give Bandit a chance to sniff a stretch of beach they hadn't yet explored.

They walked down toward the water and turned along the hard, flat, low-tide sand behind the buildings lining Commercial Street. Other dogs were out and about, so after some waves and hand signals to confirm it was okay with the other owners, Silas let Bandit off his leash to mingle.

"Don't make me regret this, buddy," he said, rolling up Bandit's leash like a lasso. "No herding, nipping, or harassing anything, hear me?"

Bandit tore off. Silas turned left and took in the town's main wharf complex. The scale of the commercial fishing fleet was more impressive from this surface-level perspective, the rusty trawlers looking bigger, more laden with rigging, and more battle-scarred than he'd appreciated.

The tide was almost dead low, so the beach was wide. Bandit and a youthful-looking Labrador retriever ran in circles. Of course, to Silas's chagrin, Bandit aggressively herded the black dog, nipping at him and occasionally mouthing one of the dog's rear legs.

Silas was inclined to intervene but watched for a moment first. The dog spun each time and gave Bandit a good-natured feint to the scruff of his neck before they ran and chased some more. The dog didn't mind Bandit's lack of social skills. Silas suspected he knew why. He noticed the water-loving dog had figured out he could dash out into the shallows anytime he got tired of Bandit's badgering. Bandit liked to chase, but he was certainly not about to do it in water.

With the tide out so far, walking clear under the wharf would have been possible, but Silas just glanced between the sturdy pilings. They were slick with rich green seaweed and pebbled with black mussels and white barnacles. They smelled wet and earthy. He turned up toward the ramp connecting the beach to the base of the wharf where it jutted out from Lopes Square.

After recalling Bandit to his side, Silas bent over to clip the leash to Bandit's new vest when a lit cigarette butt dropped from the wharf above. After painfully singeing the back of Silas's neck, it bounced off Bandit's vest and onto the ramp.

He looked up to find a group of older teens hanging out, and the sight made that old familiar sensation creep up on him: clenched jaw and fists; muscles tensing across the back of his shoulders; time slowing, vision narrowing. *Keep it together, Silas. Keep it proportional.*

Two teens straddled their bikes, and two—including one with a pack of cigarettes in his hand—sat on the raised wooden edge of the wharf directly above him. Silas went up the ramp, turned, and walked up to them, holding the still-burning butt with his index finger and thumb. They stood as he approached.

"Found somethin' of yours," Silas said, holding the butt up and looking pointedly down at the teen who flicked it.

The teenager put on his best tough-guy act for his friends. "Nah, I don't think so. I haven't lost anything. Move along, boomer."

Before the kid knew it, Silas had deposited the lit cigarette butt into his shirt's front pocket.

"Hey! What the fuck, man?" the kid said, swatting to extinguish the butt that was smoldering against the fabric of his shirt pocket. *Too slow, buddy,* thought Silas as a clear burn mark appeared in the light-colored fabric.

"See, I'm certain it's yours, because gravity only works in the down direction," Silas said. "Realizing it came from you left me wonderin' where you got the idea you could just throw your burnin' trash anywhere you want, like, say, on my neck. Started askin' myself, what kind of shit-for-brains pissant thinks that's remotely acceptable behavior?"

The teen looked at Bandit, with his working dog vest, and then at the badge on Silas's belt.

With a cocky smile, he said in a mocking tone, "Ooh. Guys, look, this circus freak is from the police! Am I under arrest, Officer? Are you going to give me a ticket? You definitely shouldn't because I'm telling you, you've got the wrong man."

His friends snickered.

Before he knew he'd done it, Silas's right arm had swung out from his hip, grabbed the front of the kid's shirt, and lifted him off the ground, pulling him nose to nose. The kid had a look of shocked horror on his face and had to be uncomfortable with his shirt gouging his armpits.

"I'm not talkin' about our ordinance against littering, which we enforce, and you just violated," Silas said in a low, grumbling voice through clenched teeth.

The kid's dangling feet jerked spastically. His arms hung at his sides.

"Put me down, you crazy psycho! This is police brutality! Guys, get a video of this!"

The word *video* galvanized Silas's attention like a crack of lightning. Realizing he'd gone overboard, and angry with himself for it, Silas immediately dropped the kid, who fell to the ground and rolled backward.

He was chastened, but he wasn't done. Without skipping a beat, Silas bent onto one knee next to the kid, loomed over him, and said, "Instead of that ordinance, what I'm talkin' about is minimum acceptable standards to be considered a human being and a member in good standing of human society."

Face still painted with shock, the teen scooted back a little from his intimidating figure.

"Son, in case you don't understand what I'm sayin', lemme make it plain for you. This ain't your world," he said, making a sweeping gesture with one arm, and the kid stared at him, mouth agape. "You don't have the right to toss your shit wherever you want. This world belongs to the people around you. It's what's called a shared space: this town, this state, this planet."

Silas paused to look at the other teens.

"Belongs to all of us," he went on. "And if I catch you or these other mold spores you hang with flickin' another cigarette butt *anywhere* other than a proper receptacle, I'm gonna impose a fine that'll make your papa's wallet cry like a baby. Then we'll have a conversation about you cleaning this entire beach with a trash bag and tweezers as your community service. That'll be just the beginning of our rocky relationship. Making myself understood?"

Lying on his back on the ground, the teen emitted an obsequious, "*Yessir.*"

"Pleased to hear it." Standing and looking around, Silas said, "Now, why don't y'all get yourselves out of my damn sight before the very fine mood I'm in starts to sour?"

The teens gathered their bikes and walked away swiftly and silently.

"Let's go, Bandit," he said, and they continued their walk back to Town Hall. It was a long walk. Silas was shaken, angry at himself. How many times had he reminded himself he couldn't afford to lose control like that? And all for a dumb kid whose parents probably never taught him right. *Just be grateful they weren't recording or things didn't spool out worse.*

Silas, you need to do better.

Silas was settling back in at the office when, at twenty past four, his patience with the video search was rewarded.

Marsh's voice called out from the converted briefing room. "Chief, I think we've got it!"

Silas stepped inside, met at once with the smell of stale coffee and unopened windows—the Geek Squad, as it were, having been too deep in thought to care about much else. Marsh and Byrne, sitting side by side in front of the same computer, waved him over.

As he approached, Marsh began filling him in. "We started just looking at nighttime footage, but there's too much of it, too many vehicles," she said, pointing to the monitor. "So, we decided to switch strategies and pivot. It just so turns out this camera caught the Fourth of July fireworks. That gave us an irrefutable date to go off, and we worked from there."

"Smart. Real smart. What'd you find?" Silas asked.

"When we thought we'd located our day, we double- and triple-checked our math to make sure it was the right one. We're confident it is, but we can likely locate some eyewitnesses from that day to definitively verify the date. Anyway, we think we isolated our truck and trailer."

Silas was grateful to have something to think about besides those teens on the wharf—that one was sticking in his craw, circling back into his thoughts like a boomerang.

On the monitor, Silas could see the still image of a pale truck-shaped object in the darkness. It had no headlights. *That lines up.*

"Go ahead and play it," he said.

Marsh said, "It gets clearer when he comes under the light from the hut."

The truck on the screen grew larger as it moved toward the camera's position. When it went through the pool of light cast by the charter fishing hut's outdoor fixture, it was possible to recognize the shape of a blurry license plate, plain-looking in color and design, and the big chrome letters *GMC* reflecting from the grille. Silas could even make out a male driver with dark hair before the reflection of the hut's light on the truck's window glass obscured him again. A split second later, a trailer with a large, corrugated-steel shipping container passed through the frame. Then, the image returned to darkness, dotted with a few distant lights.

"Does look like our truck," Silas said. "If the timing lines up, we may have our guy. Plate's tough to read, though. Can we sharpen it? Or maybe kick it out for enhancement?"

Byrne said, "The angle isn't great. By the time it's close enough to the light to be readable, it's at a sharp angle to the camera. I plan to review it one frame at a time to identify the least fuzzy frames, and then I'll use photo software to sharpen them as much as possible. No promises. It doesn't work the way it appears on TV. But let me see what I can do."

CHAPTER 33
Friday, September 19

By the next morning, Byrne had zoomed-in images of a light-colored license plate with a low-contrast design. Only the first two characters were legible.

After passing it around the table in the briefing room, the consensus was that it began with the characters *GS* or *G5*. The remaining digits were illegible.

Silas asked again, but in Byrne's opinion, what they had on the other digits wasn't worth the cost of sending them out for enhancement. *He'd know better than me. Let's hope two digits are enough—a shallow fingerhold, but maybe just enough to keep us on the rock face.*

"Just drove across the country, so I can tell y'all with some authority that there's a lot of states around here with white, low-contrast license plate designs," Silas said. "Massachusetts, Rhode Island, Maryland, old New Hampshire plates—not to mention other places: California, Illinois, Washington, Nevada . . ."

After a pause to formulate his next thought, Silas added, "Byrne, Marsh—you've both been flat-out. Knock off for the day, recharge. Rest of you, looks like we got us a fresh trail. If you're not on something urgent, start digging into vehicle registries. We're looking for white or silver-colored GMC pickups with plates starting *GS* or *G5*. Probabilities say begin close by. Divvy up the nearby states, and start hitting 'em. This is policing, people. Let's get after it!"

Silas hoped the team felt more energized than they looked as they walked out of the briefing room. Everyone had reason to be tired, but for the first time in this whole case, they had something real to chase after now. *Two letters and a make surely aren't much, but it's something. Something concrete. Something I can work with.*

Even with most of the team working on the license plate search, Silas was resigned to the fact that it would take a few days to cover the amount of ground necessary. They had to search multiple state motor vehicle registries in an ever-expanding radius—and if the perpetrator ended up being from another state, and now perhaps back in that state, that'd complicate everything further.

With only the vehicle's make and the first letter of the plate, plus one of two possible second characters, they had to run two separate searches in each registry, both of which mainly contained wildcard characters. The unfortunate fact that GMC pickup trucks were a dime a dozen was further compounded by the lack of model, year, and exact color information.

Silas walked to the center of the bullpen among the team members' desks. He looked at them all hunched over their computers, searching.

In a voice loud enough that everyone could hear, he said, "Take it slow and steady, folks. Be like Johnny Cash—man sang a song, it stayed sung. Point is: do it right the first time. You sure won't find time to do it over."

He'd seen enough painful mistakes with this kind of search to know that missing something on the first pass and having to start over was death—a disaster for momentum and morale. *Instead of standing around like a midwife, I can use this time to work on my teachin'.*

"Clark, let me know when you're heading out for your highway rotation," Silas said, taking Sergeant Clark quite off guard. "Keep you company."

Clark's attitude had been trending if not toward affability, then at least away from sourness. But the prospect of being cooped up with Silas and Bandit in the car for several hours obviously didn't appeal. The grimace gave him away.

"Ah," Clark said, stammering. "Okay, well . . . I had a couple of reports of rolling stops lately, so I figured I would focus on that."

"Good thinking," Silas said.

Twenty minutes later, their patrol vehicle was backed into a shady spot on the grassy median between the east and westbound sides of Route 6, where the north end of Snail Road intersected the highway.

Gotta hand it to him. Spot's good. First gentle curve off a long straightaway. Drivers heading toward town tend to carry too much speed. The intersection with Snail Road is busy, but only one stop sign and one white stop line control it. This'll work just fine.

It had been a long time since Silas had done any traffic enforcement work, but that didn't mean he thought he was above it. And even if Clark wasn't talking much, it was time spent together, growing more comfortable in each other's company. Silas left Clark to operate the department's laser speed gun while also keeping an eye out for violations at the stop signs. The smell of cut grass drifted in from all around them.

Silas watched for a little while. Clark had a pretty good eye, only bothering to raise the gun for cars Silas also judged to be speeding. Didn't take long before Silas grew bored and stiff. His legs were way too long to slouch down comfortably in the seat.

"Tight as teeth in here. Startin' to feel like a longhorn in a phone booth," he said, inclining the backrest and pulling his hat down toward his eyes. Clark had closed the windows to turn on the air-conditioning in the idling vehicle, but it could barely keep up with the sun now angling beneath the tree branches and pounding through the west-facing glass. Silas felt his jeans and sweaty shirt sticking to the vinyl seats.

Still hot. Summer doesn't give up easy out here. But been in far more uncomfortable situations than this, so no need for bellyachin'.

Clark was quiet, mostly still. He hadn't ticketed anyone—none were that far over the speed limit, if at all. Silas slumped back, drifting into that liminal space between sleep and thought, wondering how they might streamline the license plate search.

Clark's voice startled him from his trance. "Guy just rolled both stops, broad daylight. Gonna need to light him up, Chief."

After flicking on the blue lights, he pulled from their spot in an aggressive U-turn—a turn that, to Silas's annoyance, left angry wheel-spin marks in the median grass.

Easy does it, hotshot.

It was an old pickup. Rolling slow in the right lane, coasting down the last long stretch before town. Clark came up on him aggressively and was able to pull the truck over quickly enough, though the driver took time coasting to a stop. Silas adjusted his seat back to its upright position and watched Clark run the plate through the onboard terminal, checking stolen vehicle reports, outstanding warrants, and any alerts tied to the truck.

Kid knows this part of the job. I'll give him that.

Satisfied there were no additional concerns, Clark grabbed his ticket book and hat, then stepped out. Silas watched him approach. Had to admit—it was textbook technique. Clark spoke to the driver.

Lotta back-and-forth. Clark's body language looks wrong. Too amped up. Gettin' a bad feeling.

Clark stepped back abruptly, edging closer to the truck's side. His tone grew more heated.

When Silas saw Clark move his hand over the handle of his service weapon, he'd seen enough.

He jumped out of the car, shouted, "Officer!" to Clark, and walked toward the rear of the truck on the passenger side. Speaking across the empty bed of the old truck, he said, "What seems to be the problem here, Officer Clark?"

"Driver's not following instructions, Chief. I've asked him multiple times to roll down the window and then to put his hands on the wheel. He won't open up and keeps reaching for something across the seat. Refuses to obey my directives."

The tension and adrenaline were radiating off Clark, and to Silas's eye, the situation had all the hallmarks of a potential escalation.

"Do you see a weapon, Clark? Can you see his hands? Is it safe for me to approach from the passenger side?" Silas asked.

"No weapon visible. Can see both hands in his lap. At the moment, it's safe to approach." Clark leaned forward toward the driver's window from his position, tight against the bed of the truck. "Sir, my partner's approaching the vehicle."

Silas looked in the passenger window. He saw an elderly gentleman who was flustered.

Old khaki pants several inches too large for his skinny waist. Belt loops all bunched up under an old leather belt. *Warm day, but he's wearing a long-sleeved shirt buttoned at the cuffs and the neck. Moving slowly, signs of confusion.* Silas could see a blocky, flesh-colored hearing aid tucked behind his ear over the temple of his thick eyeglasses. This man couldn't hear or understand Clark. He was terrified and agitated.

Before Clark had a chance to mess this up any further, Silas said, "Clark, come back here. Switch positions with me."

Clark came back, and Silas went up to the driver's window. He bent at the waist and waved at the man in a friendly manner, then made an old-fashioned window-cranking gesture with one hand while pointing his other index finger downward. The man figured out what Silas wanted, leaned forward, and began slowly cranking down the old window.

As the powerful scent of menthol rub reached his nose, Silas said in a thunderous and cheerful voice, "Good afternoon, sir. How are you today?"

Still looking alarmed, the old man said, "Well, I'm okay, Officer. But is there a problem?"

Silas shouted, "Truck's a beauty! Looks all original. Can I ask how brakes are workin' for you lately?"

"They're okay," the driver shouted. "It's a 1973 F-100. I've had it since new. Brakes were never great to start with, but now I have to use all my strength to press them."

"Wondered about that, sir," Silas thundered, leaning in—each a strategy to compensate for the man's loss of hearing. "And it doesn't get easier as we get up there in years, right? Do you happen to know the last time you had these brakes looked at?"

"Can't say for sure," the man replied.

"Well, the reason we pulled you over was we were concerned for your safety. You didn't come to a full stop at either stop point as you were getting onto the highway. You can't roll through 'em."

"Yes, sir," the man said.

"If that's too hard for you to do every time, sir, we gotta get these brakes checked and maybe look at alternate transportation arrangements," Silas hollered with as much empathy and patience as he could project. He continued to stoop and lean close to the window. "You think you're able to bring your truck to a full stop at the signs, even if you need to go in and get those brakes looked at?"

"Yes, Officer, I can do that. I promise I will," the man said.

"Tell you what," Silas roared with a big grin to lighten the mood. "Our jail's all filled up at the moment, and our gallows is plum outta order . . ." The man laughed nervously. "But we've got two traffic lights up ahead. We'll follow behind you. Show me two nice, clean full stops in a row, and we'll let you go with just this verbal warning, on account of our jail situation. That sound fair to you?"

"Yessir!" he said brightly.

"Off you go, then," Silas said, giving the door two firm thumps to punctuate the conversation.

They returned to their cruiser and pulled out behind the truck, which was now proceeding at a speed well below the limit. The old man crept up to two painfully slow full stops in a row.

Clark shook his head in frustration and said, "Sir, I don't know if this guy should be driving."

"Got my doubts too," Silas admitted. "That's why you're goin' to look into whether he has family, kids, grandkids, and go have a pleasant, informal, community-relations-building conversation about Grampa's safety."

Clark glanced sideways, meeting his eyes. He didn't look angry—more intrigued, perhaps even a tad enthusiastic about the proposed softer approach, as if clouds were parting in his mind. "All right," he said, nodding.

"Maybe it's gettin' to be time for him to come out from behind the wheel for good," Silas added, eyes still on Clark. "You prepared to work with the family to figure that out?"

"Yes, sir."

Silas mulled their near disaster over in his mind.

"Human beings, Clark," Silas said. "It helps to remember they've got problems, hopes, dreams, flaws, virtues. Our job is to figure out how to help them, occasionally keep 'em from killing each other. They are not to be feared; they need our help. One way or another, I'm going to get you to see that."

CHAPTER 34
Tuesday, September 23

Tuesday morning, Marsh and Byrne were still hard at work on their search.

They'd put in a big first day. Marsh had made it through the New Hampshire registry of motor vehicles with no hits for their combination of plate letters and make. Byrne had eliminated possibles in Rhode Island, and as afternoon turned to evening, they had started on the much-larger Massachusetts database. Silas had to chase them out of the office at 7:30 p.m. and make them promise to take a break until morning.

Despite their dedication, they still had nothing to show for it. But they were undaunted and still optimistic.

Let 'em be. Stay focused. Need to talk to Clark, anyway. Be curious to see if he's ready to talk about Friday's traffic stop with the old man. Time for another ride.

After giving the Geek Squad a nod of approval, Silas approached Clark's desk. "Clark, let's saddle up, get back out there. I'ma ride with you again today."

Clark's color rose, and he looked queasy, but he didn't argue.

Fifteen minutes later, Clark had taken the wheel. As they climbed the narrow, twisty section of Bradford, they had to stop often. Since arriving, Silas had counted thirty painted crosswalks just on Bradford Street alone. This time of year, there was at least one dog on a leash and two people in every single one of them. *Pedestrians in this town are a whole 'nother level of bold.*

When the road dead-ended at the vast flat salt marsh locally known as the Moors, Clark turned right and headed north toward Herring Cove Beach. The road wound past a tidal salt pond where Silas knew bald eagles were sometimes spotted, then ducked under a low hollow of scrub forest before breaking out of the woods, the road surrounded by dunes on both sides. Blown sand encroached on the road along both shoulders, bigger licks of it pockmarked by the footfalls of morning runners. Silas surveyed the sand, imagining a change of season.

Winter wind hits these dunes, bet it turns into some wind-bit hard country. Need heavy equipment to clear this sand.

Clark took a left past the park rangers' hut at the beach parking lot. Just as the road started to turn away from the water, Clark abruptly slowed and pulled up behind a Chevy Blazer parked on the shoulder. There was a flat sandy pullout carved into the pine and oak scrub, but it was marked No Parking.

"Chief, I want to check this out," Clark told him. "This car has been here for over twenty-four hours, and not only is it parked illegally, but it's also a traffic hazard sticking out into the road inside a blind corner."

"I see the passenger-side door's ajar. Guess we could take a look," Silas agreed. "Sure this car has been here twenty-four hours, Clark?"

"Yes, I am. I noted the plate number yesterday. I'm going to run them now for anything outstanding."

Got some serious doubts this vehicle has been abandoned here for twenty-four hours.

While Clark ran the plates, Silas had a look around the vehicle and the surrounding area.

Clark returned. "Impound is on their way, Chief," he said with the pride of a can-do guy.

Oh, Christ. This kid's gonna be the death of me. "Hold up, now, Clark. Call 'em back and tell 'em to stand down for now. Need to talk about this for a minute."

"Respectfully, Chief, it's illegal, and it's a hazard. It's been here for a day—I think we need to get it moved before someone gets hurt," Clark insisted in a tone just shy of respectful.

"We can, and we will, if necessary, Clark. But first, let's take a walk. See if we can get a sense of the situation."

Clark shook his head in frustration, but he seemed to know better than to talk back or question the judgment of his new boss, odd as it might first appear. With a resigned look on his face, he got out his phone to call impound back.

Silas didn't want to undermine Clark's instincts; he wanted to refine them. *Maybe throw him a small bone.* "You are right about safety. Why not nip your cruiser in behind and leave some flashing lights on?"

Clark got the car set up and trudged after Silas. They crossed the road, ducked through dune grass, and skirted a split-rail fence into the far edge of the parking lot. The hot pavement radiated a smell like summer. Silas didn't yet know precisely where he was going, but he had a sense.

"Where are we going, Chief?" Clark asked over the sound of the surf coming from the beach.

"Gotta hunch. Follow me. Let's see how it plays out," Silas said as they headed down one of the pathways between sand fences. They came out on the end of the beach where the Hatches Harbor salt marsh met the ocean. The view was spectacular—wide, sandy beaches, rolling surf, and Race Point Light off to their right.

Silas peered down the shore, looking left and right. He chose to head right.

They trudged toward the mouth of the tidal river formed by the long, thin spit of sand stretching down from Race Point Light parallel to shore. The sand spit separated the water coming out of the marsh from the bay, forcing it to travel along the beach for a few hundred yards before it was able to turn and form a wide, shallow mouth in the surf.

Silas spotted the circling gulls first. Below them, a man stood on the beach casting a fishing line into the swift tidal current leaving the marsh on a falling tide.

When they got closer to him, the fisherman noticed Clark's uniform. "Afternoon, Officer. What brings you out here?"

Rather than answering the man, Clark looked at Silas with a face that said, *This is your show, so why don't you tell the man?*

"What's biting today?" Silas asked.

The man looked relieved it was just fishing talk. "Nothing so far today. Nothing yesterday, either. This can be a great spot—the blues and the stripers can poke up here at slack tide before the high water turns and heads back out of the marsh. Always assumed they're looking for easy meal targets—bunker hatchlings and smaller bait fish. This isn't the right time of year for hatchlings, though, which probably explains my bad luck."

Silas smiled and nodded before getting right to it. "That your Blazer parked out by the road?"

With a guilty look of realization, the man said, "Ah, yes . . . it is. Sorry about that. I can explain."

Silas stole a glance at Clark before giving the man an "I'm all ears" look.

"The last few years I've been coming out here, I haven't been laying out the cash for a national seashore pass—the ridiculous prices are kind of edging us locals out. So, in the high season, I can't park in the lot here without paying. Parking is the only thing they really care about. The rangers really don't mind the fishing—but even a day pass is a lot to pay for an hour of parking."

Silas nodded, but not as knowingly as Clark, who had a local's perspective.

"I'm off this week and trying to get a little fishing in before the week completely gets away from me."

"Well," Silas said, "I get that. Thing is, truck isn't in the safest spot on the corner there, is it?"

"Guess not," the man had to admit, eyes cast downward.

"So, we've got a situation here, but how 'bout we make a deal?" Silas said, and the fisherman's face brightened. "We agree not to ticket and tow the truck, and in exchange, maybe you'd be willing to walk up with us and get it out of the crook of that blind corner?"

The man wore oversize sunglasses, but it was plain to see relief wash over his face.

"Know it's a longer walk back out to this fine spot from the Hatches Harbor parking lot just over this hill, but it's the safe way to do things. Bike trail here"—Silas pointed toward the dunes behind them—"gives you the perfect route. Besides, little walking never killed a fit sportsman like yourself. And it's not my jurisdiction, but maybe next year you'll reconsider supporting the national seashore. Full week pass is a damn good deal, and they could sure use the money. Then you could park right next to the fish as often as you like."

"That's a fair exchange. I'm happy to move it, and I appreciate you coming out here before I had to spend an entire vacation day trying to get my car out of the impound lot. Fees would cost more than a lifetime pass."

"Exactly. I'm Chief Lopez, by the way," Silas said, extending a hand. "And this is Sergeant Kevin Clark. Bet he'd like to hear about some other good fishing spots you've found."

A few minutes later, Silas and Clark sat in the cruiser, watching the man drive off.

Silas was trying to think of the right way to explain things, draw the lessons from yesterday's stop and today's mistaken tow call. He needed to be gentle. He'd only come out today intending to talk about yesterday's fiasco, and they'd stumbled into another hiccup. Was Clark just trying too hard to impress him, or did he lack the steadiness to read situations? Before he'd decided, Clark interrupted Silas's thoughts.

"How did you know this time?" he said in a defeated tone.

Okay, so he knows he slipped. That's half the fight. Still, he needs to hear it straight.

"Well, Clark, if I'm bein' honest, it wasn't hard. Soon as we pulled up, I saw another set of the same tire tracks, making it almost guaranteed the truck had been parked twice, not left overnight—which meant the driver had to be nearby."

Clark nodded, turning the key in the ignition but keeping the cruiser parked.

"Then I saw a jumpin' fish sticker on the bumper and another fishing sticker on the rear window, and I figured, *Well, this one's gotta be a fisherman*. Walked up front, noticed rod holders for surf casting on the front bumper."

Silas looked to see Clark, who was continuing to nod.

"Looked in the window of that unlatched door, saw an open tackle box on the seat. Noticed we're near the end of the national seashore's parking lot at the last spot before the road starts to move away from the water. Figured we might have a small-time rustler lookin' to poach a few fish real quick, then be on his way."

"And I missed all that," Clark acknowledged.

"You did." Silas kept his voice neutral, as if commenting on the color of the sky. "And do you notice any pattern in that, Clark?"

Clark didn't answer right away. The way he clenched his jaw and stared forward—like a man on the edge of a bench warrant—told Silas he knew his credibility as sergeant was on the line. *Good. Means he's taking it seriously.*

"I missed some details," he began.

Yeah, you could say that.

"Yes," Silas confirmed. "You're routinely missing important details. Details, well . . ." He couldn't think of any other way to put it. "Details a five-year-old with a fever shouldn't miss."

"Sorry, Chief."

"Nah, buck up. This ain't a 'Sorry, Chief' situation. This is a learning situation. I know you're trying your best; can see the effort you're putting in. Mixed in might be a little, 'Impress the new boss; let's get shit done, lickety-split.' I appreciate that effort. I do," Silas said, trying to be as patient as he could while making it clear that this needed improvement.

No good in sugarcoating it. Could cost lives if Clark can't figure this out.

"Lickey-split's all fine and dandy, but son, bein' real fast at jumpin' onto the wrong solution ain't worth a bucket of spit. What you're lookin' for is the *right* solution, even if it takes a minute to get there."

How to lay this out proper?

"Your creator gave you pair of eyes, ears, perfectly good brain. Use 'em. Study the situation. Ask yourself what might be goin' on. Might be a bank robbery, sure. Might also be a customer just cashing a paycheck. Or a store clerk stocking shelves. Or a hard-of-hearing old-timer cruisin' around in his truck without a care in the world."

Was he getting through, or was Clark still blind with pride?

"For this job, most of the time, it's more important to be right than fast," he added, watching Clark's expression shift from something akin to bracing for impact to a softer, more malleable look of openness. *Great. Great sign.* "Don't want to misjudge a developing situation any more than you want to shoot the wrong person."

Clark visibly cringed. Silas was being hyperbolic, but it still cast a pall over the conversation—an effective pall, perhaps. That was the reality of police work. Unpredictable action demanding a reaction that could stand up in the court of law. Best way to inform one's reaction? Observation. And Clark's observation skills needed work. As far as deficits go, this was serious.

"You're right, Chief," Clark said, shoulders sagging, the fight gone out of him. "I guess I do need to slow it down and analyze situations more." Then, after pausing to think for a beat, he said, "But I'm not sure if I can ever do it as well as you do. I don't know how you stop to notice the things you notice right in the middle of a tense situation. Hell, you weren't even *at* that convenience store that night, and you *still* noticed things Byrne missed. Maybe I'm just not cut out for this kind of work."

This was the first sign of humility and honest vulnerability Clark had shown him. He felt a rush of relief and optimism. He could get Clark there. Clark wanted to learn.

Kid's green broke, but he'll settle.

"Hogwash," Silas replied. "Got the potential to be a great cop. Just gotta focus more on *becoming* a great one than being so intent on *proving* you already are."

"But how?" Clark asked.

Now you're tracking, son.

"Easier than you think. Starts with understanding the real goal—rest comes with practice."

Seeing the confused look on Clark's face, Silas realized he needed to give more. "Gotta go into every situation with the goal of *understanding what's goin' on*, not just slapping cuffs on a perp, writing a ticket, or balling somebody out. If you go in with a goal of understanding what's goin' on, next logical step's gonna be looking for details and clues that might explain it to you. Mix those observations with a little common sense, and soon you'll start being able to read, assess a situation. Once you get into that mindset, practice will make you better and better. Which is good, because you got no chance of handling a situation correctly if you don't know what the hell the situation is in the first place."

Clark was nodding again, like he was seeing the way forward.

"You were within your rights to tow that truck. Play it by the books, ruin that guy's week. Make him hate the Provincetown PD for the rest of his life. But once we knew he was just an ordinary guy, trying to save a buck and get a little time off, we were able to protect public safety and make the guy into a lifelong fan of the force."

"One thing I've noticed is you give people the benefit of the doubt," Clark said, and Silas had a hard time concealing a smile. *Now you're gettin' it.* "I identified a crime and kept it at that. I didn't care about extenuating circumstances."

"That's spot-on, Clark." Silas sat back, sighed. "Think you can train that head to look for the big picture, help you figure out what you're dealing with before you go off half-cocked?"

"Yes, sir," Clark said with a tone of dejection, humility, and cautious optimism.

"Makes you feel better, Clark, I believe you can too."

Silas let out a long, soft breath. With a bit of luck, Clark's next few days would go smoothly, and he could regain some of his confidence. *For now, best let him be. He'll steady up. I got other fires to tend.*

CHAPTER 35
Wednesday, September 24

Silas felt like a horse with a burr under its saddle.

He was a day late submitting a quarterly spending projection—*damn branding-iron work, but it won't do itself*—so he forced himself to stay put and plow through it. He didn't like sitting at a desk, didn't enjoy writing, and finance and numbers had never been a strong suit, but he snatched up the paperwork to get the damn thing done.

Oughta start farmin' this kinda thing out to Genny. But can't hand off what you don't rightly understand. Not yet.

After forty-five minutes of arithmetic, hunting and pecking, sighing and harrumphing, he had the ten-line report in hand.

Walk it upstairs myself. More than a victory lap; need to see and be seen around this building.

He disliked office politics even more than paperwork, but he wasn't naive enough to believe that perceptions didn't matter. Good working relationships were essential when doing his kind of work. So he made an effort to interact with his colleagues in town government.

Bandit had opened an eye when Silas stood to get the report off the printer. When Silas headed toward the door, Bandit rose and trotted out behind him.

The Finance Department was a pale-yellow room with everyone spread out along a single continuous work surface that ran along all four walls. Silas could smell someone had been sucking hard candy or a lollipop. *Sweet scent's a little bit sickening.*

"Well, if it isn't the chief of police and his owner, Silas Lopez!" one of the younger finance people joked, looking up at him with a smile.

Very funny. Guess someone has been making his rounds up here.

After overcoming the surprise of seeing the new chief walk in the door, the young team was friendly and professional. Silas had made some mistakes in classifying a couple of department expenses, but the finance manager was understanding. She crossed them out and said she would fix them when keying in the data. As they talked, Silas noticed Bandit wagging his tail as he completed his circuit of the room.

Yep. This team's got some pushovers who are regulars on Bandit's daily begging loop. Even this dog knows the value of relationships.

Silas had something he wanted Wren's input on, so he ducked into a back staircase to her office. Canted noticeably from level as they spiraled, the old, dark-wood steps were cupped from wear. Silas stooped with a twist of the shoulder to make his way up. The town's departments were busting out of the building. Silas knew it was because so much space was devoted to the large, ornate auditorium on the first floor—a town treasure for public gatherings, shows, and concerts. They were talking about a new building, but that thought gave him the shivers. This place had character. It was the heart of the town too. He couldn't see the department letting that go.

One floor up, he emerged near the offices of the Human Services team. Because all the office doors were open, he could hear Wren on the phone down the hall. He figured he'd stick his head in and give her the "call me" gesture.

But she was deep in the room, her back facing the door. Standing. Looking out the window, the old desk phone receiver to her ear, curly cord hugging her shapely torso. The bright sky silhouetted her tall, willowy frame, and Silas was struck anew by the grace of her proportions.

He waited a moment to see if she was going to turn around and couldn't help but overhear some of her call.

"Shawna, I appreciate how hard this is for you," Wren said. "But you can get through this. You've got the smarts and the capability to make changes and see the results."

He listened a little more. From what he could hear, it was a client. Wren was gentle but firm. Patient, even when she had to say it twice. *Would've lost my temper by now. She hasn't.*

"I know you're feeling down right now. But powerless isn't an accurate self-perception, nor is it a helpful one. Of course you feel overwhelmed. Anyone in your situation would feel challenged. Difficult things happen—we've all been there. But it's how you play the cards that matters. I believe in you, even if you don't right at the moment."

This might be a minute, Silas thought. He ducked into the empty office next door and grabbed a sticky note, scribbling, *Question for you. —Silas,* on it with an uncomfortably skinny little pen. He returned to the threshold of her office door, sticky note in hand.

She continued her call, tone never wavering in its kind, soft encouragement. "Like I said, you have the tools, the opportunity, and the capabilities to effect change in your life. I know you, and I'm certain you can do this. And you're not alone. I can help you if you commit to trying."

Despite having to repeat herself, there was no scolding or judgment, no detectable exasperation in her voice, just compassion and understanding. The client must have been pushing back against Wren's input, maybe searching for a different path forward or some external factor to blame, but Wren persisted and didn't patronize.

Hearing her in action was fascinating, but he was uncomfortable eavesdropping on her. So, he tiptoed into her office and put the sticky note in the center of her desk. Then he turned and headed back toward the staircase. Curled up in a ball outside Wren's office door, Bandit got up and loped after him. Descending the spiral, Silas mulled over what he'd heard.

As a somewhat impatient person with a bit of a temper, he thought about how much he admired Wren's discipline on that call. Here was a person from tremendous privilege, choosing to work with and respectfully relating to people in different, often dire circumstances. *Doesn't matter where she comes from—Wren knows people. Reads them. Can talk to folks without talking down to them. Natural people skills.*

By the time he was back in the basement, he'd realized she had to be a keen observer of people to do what she did. Besides the obvious parallels with the observation skills required in his work, he wondered if that ability to observe was also what made her a good photographer.

"There you are!" Genny said when he returned to the police offices.

"Had to turn in my quarterly spending report," he said.

"You did, huh? Is that right? And the chief had to walk all the way up there to do it in person?" she said in a chiding tone.

Silas heard his phone ring at his desk and Genny's. She picked it up and said, "Chief's office, how can I help you? Oh, hello, Wren." She paused, giving Silas a wink. He felt himself blush and went straight for his office. "Yes, in fact, he's standing right here. I'll transfer you."

Silas picked up the receiver in his office and said, "That was fast."

"Hello to you too, Silas," Wren said, teasing him. "I got your note. You had a question for me?"

"Two, actually."

"Sorry, the note only indicated one," Wren joked.

"Related. Call 'em *one a* and *one b*."

"Fair enough. Shoot," she said.

"Heard a rumor you know this town. You're good with people— know the town's population and their rhythms, especially the vulnerable and the working class. Wanted to get your take on a situation that might help me with my current case."

"Oh?" Wren said.

"Before you agree, gotta warn you. Need to keep it aboveboard, so it would mean you'd need to sign a confidentiality form and be officially listed as a volunteer civilian adviser."

"Wow, sounds impressive! Do I get a silver deputy badge? Just kidding. Sure. I'm happy to help. I'll run it past Roger, but I am sure he'll be fine with it. What was the second question?"

"Wondered if you wanted to get up early and discuss this situation with me and Bandit on our morning walk. Lately, we've been walking the back beach."

"Hmm. What's your definition of early?" she asked with some hesitation in her voice.

"Lotta coyotes out here, so usually wait till after first light—give 'em a fighting chance against Bandit." He chuckled to indicate he was joking. "Let's see. Sunup's around six right now. That too early?"

Wren laughed.

"Let me get this straight—you want me to get up at six in the morning on a weekday and brave the elements to go for a walk with you and talk work, Mr. Lopez?"

"That a problem? Could push it off till six thirty. Beach is still empty and quiet then," he said.

"Only you could make such a request in earnest. But you know what? I'm going to call your bluff and take you guys up on it. Early mornings are the best part of summertime, anyway."

"They are. Can pick you up if you tell me where you live."

"This will test your wayfinding skills. I'm up on the rise called Mayflower Heights. I look down on the dirt path called Mayflower Avenue. Technically, the road I'm on is Priscilla Road, but it's tiny and not marked. It's just past the Maple Grove Bird Sanctuary. If you get to Mayflower Avenue and the garage doors with the big murals of Marilyn Monroe's face, you've gone too far. My cottage is number fourteen."

"I'll find you," he said, before adding, "Meantime, Genny will stop by your office with the civilian adviser form for you and Roger to sign off on."

CHAPTER 36

Silas was packing it in for the day when Marsh shouted out from the briefing room. "Might have a license plate hit!"

He set down his canvas shoulder bag and dropped the evening work he'd been stuffing into it.

"Chief, I think I found something that fits. It's a silver GMC pickup, five years old, so it would look about the same as the one we saw on the video," Marsh said, wasting no time. "It has the Massachusetts license plate G53-R6Y. Address listed on the registration is down in New Bedford. The physical description on the owner's driver's license even works—lists him as male, five foot ten, age thirty, brown hair, brown eyes."

"Does sound like a possible hit," Silas said. "What else we know?"

Marsh continued, "Registration lists the owner as an Anthony Faria."

Anthony Faria. Silas tried the name on in his head. Faria? Could possibly be a Portuguese family name, in which case New Bedford would make sense. Name didn't ring any bells. But he liked the feel of this lead in his hand—*solid enough to heft*.

"I didn't want to get my hopes up too far, so I checked for trailer registrations under that name. There's nothing current, but up until a couple of years ago, he did maintain a registration for a heavy-duty, two-axle trailer. It may be the same trailer—he could have let the registration lapse, or he could have sold it to a buddy and occasionally borrowed it back."

Silas slapped the doorframe. "That's some top-notch police work," Silas said. "Perfect end to the day. Follow it up first thing tomorrow. You two sure have earned an early evening off. Get out of here. Hope you take some time to savor this find, catch up on your rest. First thing, I'll make some calls and head to New Bedford and see whether I can lay eyes on this Faria fella. Figure out if he could be our guy."

Then, turning to Genny at her desk behind him, he said, "You should head out too. Did you get that adviser form to Wren Bradford?"

"Yes, it is signed and in the files, Chief."

"Thanks. Why did I even ask? You're a model of efficiency. And you're free to go—almost. Got one last to-do item for you to jot down. Can I ask you to dig around and figure out who on the New Bedford force I should lob a courtesy call to? If I'm goin' to be wandering around their turf asking questions about a hit-and-run, it's good form to let 'em know."

Plus, if this New Bedford guy is our perp, might need their help before too long.

"Don't worry, I'm going home," Genny said, "but I'm making a note and will get you a name." She collected up her bag and waved. "See you then."

"You two scoot as well," he repeated to Marsh and Byrne. "Good work."

He looked around the quiet room. This time last week, they'd had little. Now, there was a name, a truck, and a town to visit. He could feel it—momentum. *Always darkest before the dawn.*

CHAPTER 37
Thursday, September 25

The dirt road was just a thin layer of hardpan over sandy soil. The Jeep bounced like it had no suspension. Silas slowed down for the potholes—with the doors off, last thing he needed was Wren getting doused in mud on her first ride out with him.

In the rearview mirror, he could see Bandit knew precisely where they were going. He whined softly, pacing excitedly in the back seat.

When they'd crossed the low bridge over the salt marsh, the remaining traces of dawn fog drifted between the reeds and out over the marsh's main channel. It filtered the gathering light and nearly obscured the doe crossing a tidal creek, knee-deep in brackish mud.

"Great blue heron!" Wren gasped. "Can you pull up for a second?"

As Wren readied her camera, the bird stood motionless on sticklike legs. There was a perfect upside-down reflection of the bird in the still water below. When her shutter clicked, a red-winged blackbird took flight. Silas watched as it deftly landed—somehow—on a vertical reed stem a short distance away.

The marsh was misty, quiet. It was so still that Silas couldn't help but sense a certain intimacy about the setting, the moment—as if he and Wren were the only people who existed in the world and were sharing something secret and special. Contentment welled up in him with such a rush, he was momentarily overwhelmed with emotion.

Acknowledging the bumps throwing them around, Silas said, "Sorry—not a great road."

"No, I love this. Thanks for dragging me out." Wren flashed him a smile.

"Big-sky day like this makes you forget your troubles," he said over the noise of the Jeep bouncing.

Wren let go of the roll bar and expertly folded a navy blue and white bandana into a long band to hold her hair back. With a side glance, Silas noticed her fingers working the knot under her still-damp coppery waves. He found himself more than a little distracted by the soft golden hairs the low morning sun highlighted at the nape of her long neck.

Funny thing about her—hair flared like wildfire, but she carried herself quiet, like she was used to being noticed but didn't care. He caught himself staring but looked away too late. She saw his eyes on her. He covered with a head gesture down the road.

"Sand road segment out to the beach is probably open, but if you don't mind, be my preference to walk out to the water from the turnaround instead," Silas said. "No air-up station out here. I'm on call. Don't want to air the tires down for drivin' in the sand then get caught with low tires in case I have to report somewhere in a hurry."

"That's fine, but I'm going to insist on a rain check for a ride in the dunes sometime."

"Be my pleasure," Silas said with a grin. *That's definitely going on the to-do list, not just for the dunes.*

They parked. Wren slung her camera bag across one shoulder, and Silas reached back and unclipped Bandit's harness. The dog lunged through the open doorframe, airborne for a beat before hitting the ground and tearing up the sand road. They followed, footfalls softly crunching in the dew-wet sand, amplified by the hush of the still morning. Silas detected the pleasant scent of coconut. *Gotta be sunblock. With that freckled skin, surely sunblock's a habit.*

The marshy brambles framing the road quickly gave way to an open clearing ringed by dunes dotted with lichen-covered shrubs and carpets of dark-green bearberry. Past the clearing, the path bisected a thick stand of weather-beaten pitch pines. Silas noticed Wren inhale the scent of the pines. More notable to him was that she sighed. *Seems content too.*

Just before they cleared the trees about halfway out, Wren stopped to capture some photographs of the low sun refracted in hundreds of water droplets hanging from pine needles.

"I have to admit, it's heavenly out here this time of day," she said, then laughed as Bandit appeared out of nowhere and blazed across the sand path ahead of them.

"Yep," Silas said.

Only thing better than a summer morning is a summer morning outdoors with this one. She's a trooper to get up and come out. Game for it. Nice quality in a person.

At the base of the high dune ridge before the beach, the sand rose steeply into a tall slope. The climb slowed, and their steps shortened as the narrow path pushed them closer together.

Pointing northwest, Wren stopped partway up and said, "See there? That's one of the famous dune shacks."

Silas scanned the far end of the low seagrass swale sweeping below them.

"Need the history on those," he said. Then, after a beat, he added, "Heard about 'em. Fuss with the park service trying to lease them or some such. Old shacks full of stories. Might make a good side trip one day."

They paused, hiking up the soft, steep sand that seemed to swallow half their shoes with every footstep. The silence was disrupted only by their heavy breathing until Silas asked, "Speaking of fuss, ready to tackle my question, Ms. Civilian Adviser?"

"Sure," Wren said, stopping at the crest of the dune and pulling a bottle of water from her bag.

"So, I'm dealing with a pedestrian hit-and-run," Silas began, surveying the three-hundred-sixty-degree view around them. "Can't make much sense of it yet. But the victim of this hit-and-run was fighting with his husband at the time of the incident. At the start, we were wondering if that could play into it."

"How do you know these hypothetical people were fighting?" Wren asked.

"Husband, eyewitnesses. Neighbors. Friend he'd confided in on the evening of the incident."

"And so, you were wondering if the husband ran him over in a fit of rage?" Wren asked, swiping a lock of hair out of her face, shielding her eyes from the sun. The question wasn't humorous. It was, surprisingly, entirely serious.

"Guess that's the horse I thought I was tryin' to rope. Certainly seen stranger things. But once I dug in proper, I quit likin' the husband for it. Car isn't right, sort of fightin; isn't right."

They crested the dune and headed down the gentle slope of the backshore toward the water. To their right, a fiery orange sun was rising out of the Atlantic. Its light on the water formed a dazzling, unbroken expanse, the horizon obscured by the wash of sparkling light. Deep blue ocean spread out before them, and wild, untamed beach stood empty for miles to either side. The breeze off the water carried nothing but the scent of salt.

"It would seem unlikely," Wren said. "But I guess it would depend on the nature of the argument they were having."

Yep, when you hear about the fight, you'll understand why we stepped off that trail.

"How do you figure?" Silas asked, curious about her thought process.

"Look, I am no criminal profiler, but my instinct is that with murder, you'd expect the kind of impulsive rage that comes from catching someone in bed with someone else, or an instant defensive impulse when faced with an attacker—an immediate reaction, not a premeditated one. But finding the car keys, going out to the car, getting behind the wheel, and hunting someone down would take a really atypical mix of cold premeditation and hot passion," Wren theorized. "You'd need to be mad enough to kill. Reckless enough to commit the crime in a hurry, without concern for the stupidity and traceability of your actions, but calm enough to drive around looking for your spouse to plow down. And that's assuming you would catch them on foot in the first place. I agree that's pretty far-fetched."

Silas felt a knot loosen in his chest as the tumbler clicked into place. He'd moved on already, but it was a comfort to get that outside read—someone with her sense. *Shuts that gate for good.*

"Yep. That's what my gut's tellin' me too," Silas said, stopping at the surf line. Turning toward her, he pointed an index finger in each direction with a questioning look, silently asking which way she'd like to go.

"No preference," Wren said, shrugging.

"West, then. By the time we turn around and go back, sun will be higher, easier on the eyes."

They walked on the broad, hard-packed sand.

"So if it's not the marital angle, how can I help you?" Wren asked.

"Vehicle that hit him was a work truck—pickup—pullin' a heavy trailer. Don't know this town, what makes it tick. Can't say who'd be rolling that kinda rig through town in a hurry, wee hours of the mornin'. You know the rhythms of this town, its workers. Figured you could help me sift it some, maybe whittle it down."

Wren blew out a breath and shook her head. "Silas, it could be almost anyone. Keeping the summer population fed, the houses cleaned, the hotel linens washed, the restaurants supplied—it takes an army of workers. Many struggling, working more than one job, working night shifts. I can think of at least half a dozen types of people who'd haul trailers at weird hours. In the summer, it's a town of gig workers and hustlers."

Silas glanced at her. "Dishwasher or housecleaner with a big trailer?"

"Contractors hauling heavy equipment, landscapers hauling terrace stones," Wren said. "Furniture movers, restaurant suppliers, fishermen hauling traps, antique shop owners, recreational boat haulers, gallery owners setting up an installation, real estate agents staging a property. You name it. And it's an invisible army. The streets are so crowded with pedestrians and tourists in the daytime, the nights can be when things need to happen."

Silas nodded thoughtfully. "Huh. Even accountin' for a flatbed trailer not being a fit for some of those jobs, still a whole barrelful left to chew through. 'Preciate it, though. Gets me thinkin' the right way about the nights around here." They walked in silence for a little while.

"Tide's low, so the surf's breaking offshore out on the sandbars," Silas said.

"Yes—look at you, picking up on the rhythms of coastal life. And speaking of coastal life, look at the sweet curiosity of those two!" Wren said, pointing to Bandit, standing in the backwash of a wave, having a stare-off with a juvenile seal bobbing in the surf.

The seal eventually dove under the waves with a tiny splash of its flipper.

"Many of them will be gone in a couple of months," Wren said.

"Seals? Where do they go?"

"Those bigger black ones with the longer heads mostly go down the coast and tend to winter over and breed on Monomoy Island here on the cape, south of Chatham. Those ones are called gray seals. You saw how Bandit's buddy was smaller, lighter, and spotted? He was a harbor seal. The harbor seals fluctuate. Some from farther up north in Maine winter here; others from around here go farther south into New Jersey, the mid-Atlantic coast."

"Good to know where their hideout is, in case one of 'em's ever a suspect," Silas said, winking.

Wren laughed. "Stolen fish for sure—drives the surf casters mad how much fish these guys eat." Then, looking at Bandit still in the surf line, she asked, "Does he like to swim?"

"Waded in a couple of times. Hotter than a branding iron when we first got here. But breed's not much for dog-paddling. Tell the truth, neither am I. Maybe over time," Silas said, watching Bandit turn and watch some terns skimming over the wave tops.

"So, you're back to square one?" Wren said. "I wish I could have narrowed it down for you more than I did, but at least we're getting a spectacular morning beach walk out of it." Holding up a smooth, round, frosted chunk of turquoise glass, she said, "And this one's a keeper."

"You shored up my instincts, gave me the lay of the land; that's a big deal. This is nice," he said, looking at the light dance in her green eyes for a long moment.

There's something in that look. Hooks in and tugs. Case didn't move much today, but something between us sure as hell did. Day's still young, and we've got this whole beach to ourselves. This sandy place does have its charms.

CHAPTER 38

Silas felt good—rested, focused, raring to go. When was the last time he had more than one good thing on the boil? Longer ago than he'd like.

He knew it'd be about a two-hour drive to New Bedford without traffic. After his walk with Wren, he'd prepared—put the doors back on the Jeep and consulted a map on his phone. Traffic was the big question mark. He'd been warned the traffic getting on and off the cape could be brutal, but he didn't yet have personal experience with that agony. He figured a weekday morning after rush hour was about as good as it was going to get.

For many officers, a two-hour drive to ID a single person would be considered a chore, but Silas didn't mind. Gave him a chance to see a bit more of his newly adopted region. He'd done some research on New Bedford and knew to expect a gritty old port town. He'd learned it used to be a whaling port—once the world's leading whaling port—and a big textile mill town. Thinking of the whaling history flooded him with memories of a thick, old paperback of *Moby-Dick*, the spine broken, corners curled and soft as felt from nonstop dust and jostling. He'd ridden with it for months, determined to make his way through it.

Now, New Bedford was home to a large commercial fishing fleet. Not a tourism hot spot like Provincetown, but so different from anything in his past that it promised to be interesting by contrast.

Genny had walked along next to him from his office to the door. She handed him slips of pink paper. "These are the calls you need to return from the car, and this is the number of the New Bedford police contact for the courtesy outreach. Call him first so you catch him before roll call—the others can wait."

"Perfect. Thanks, Genny. You're on fire watch. Hold the fort while I see if this Faria guy exists." He stepped out the side door, slung the list onto the passenger seat, wedged his coffee in the holder, and climbed in. Bandit rode shotgun, ears already perked for the mission.

When Silas was on the move, he placed his first call.

The gruff voice on the phone said something that Silas thought might be, "This is Camara," but he wasn't sure.

"Mornin'. Silas Lopez, chief of police in Provincetown, out on the cape. This Lieutenant Paul Camara?"

"Yeah. What can I do for you, Chief?"

"Courtesy call, let you know I'm tracking one of your citizens to ask some questions related to an incident up my way. Told you're the officer to speak to."

"Well, I'm the watch commander this morning, so I guess I am. You just letting me know, or are you looking for something from us?"

"Hoping I won't need help just yet. No warrant. Not planning any surveillance, just looking to get some answers on a voluntary basis, assuming he's willing," Silas explained.

"What's the name? What's he involved with?"

"Guy's name is Faria—Anthony Faria. Last-known address on Earle Street. He's the owner, and possibly driver, of vehicle involved in a fatal hit-and-run."

"Sorry to hear that, Chief," Camara said. "Earle Street's over in the North End; locals refer to that area as *the Ave*. That area is all residential—it's always been a quiet, mostly Portuguese neighborhood. Can't say the guy's on my radar, but doesn't mean he's not someone NBPD has ever dealt with." Then, after a pause, Camara said, "Well, if there's nothing else,

I've got to get roll call going. I appreciate the heads-up. Please keep me updated if this goes anywhere."

"Yep. Hey, before I lose you, can I get a mobile number? You bein' my point of contact, that might save us both time."

Camara hesitated, clearly not keen on giving out his personal mobile number, but he ultimately went ahead and agreed, anyway—perhaps out of gratitude for the courtesy call.

"I'm behind the wheel. Lemme give you my number, and you shoot me back a text?"

Silas heard a sigh, followed by an "Okay."

He confirmed the text had come in and got to work on his other calls as he made his way along the Mid-Cape Highway.

Earle Street was definitely residential. Streets lined on both sides by modest houses, almost shoulder to shoulder. As he pulled up to park, Silas noticed many were double- and triple-deckers—multifamily houses—most vinyl-sided with paint peeling away in flakes anywhere the old trim was exposed. The rest were sided with weather-beaten asphalt shingles. There were a few single-family houses mixed in.

Bandit needed a walk after their ride. Silas had no familiarity with this kind of old-fashioned multifamily housing, so he looked around with interest as they strolled. He noticed they all had plain, poured-concrete front steps and a lot of wrought-iron accents—fencing, fixtures, and even grates that covered first-story windows.

The look ended up somewhere between decoration and prison. *What's with all this metalwork?*

A few of the houses had chain-link fences around the front yard, which was a security measure familiar to Silas. Most of the concrete slab driveways along the street contained older cars or pickups. Not much greenery for Bandit to sniff.

It was a plain but tidy working-class neighborhood. He could tell owners were taking pride in keeping up their homes or rental properties. There was some grass, as expected in the wetter eastern climate, but no landscaping along the foundations, no trees.

It was stark. All function, no fashion—*no budget for flourishes.*

Silas secured Bandit in the Jeep and walked to the front of the two-family house located at Faria's last-known address. A wooden exterior staircase was the only way to the second-floor unit, so he headed up and knocked on the aluminum storm door. It rattled from top to bottom.

"Who's there?" a woman said, peeking through the door's glass.

Silas held his badge against the glass with a metallic tap and said, "Officer Silas Lopez, ma'am. Just have a few questions."

Silas omitted his rank as chief and, more importantly, the fact that he wasn't local. Guilt clawed at his gut. *A half-truth is a whole lie, but I can't have Faria getting a warning about a problem in Provincetown if it can be helped—so, I won't offer anything extra unless pressed.*

When the door opened, Silas stood on the stoop facing a woman he guessed was in her late fifties, at most early sixties. She wore a generous wraparound apron in a bright floral print over a simple housedress from another era. She had open-toed, slip-on terry-cloth slippers. Silas could smell traces of cumin and garlic in the apartment. She reached up and patted her curled gray hair in a few spots as she stepped out of the doorway to let Silas in.

"Thank you. Got a lovely home, ma'am," Silas said, noticing the traditional old-world feel of the decor. A crucifix hung prominently over the stove, along with an old-fashioned kitchen wall clock out of decorative hammered copper with a rooster illustration. Silas observed that the kitchen was tidy, with vinyl wallpaper at least forty years past its prime. The worn appliances were spotless but bore the battle scars of many home-cooked meals.

Old appliances with dated-lookin' colors, but still, a well-kept household with a matron who raised a family here.

"Lookin' for a gentleman named Anthony Faria," he began evenly. "Few routine questions for him. Guessing he'd be your son?"

"Tony? That's right, Officer, I'm his *mãezinha*, his mother. But Tony hasn't lived with me for five years. He works on the fishing boats, and since about a year before the baby came, he's been living with the baby's mother."

"I see. You have a name and address for her?" Silas asked.

"What's this about, Officer? Tony's not in any trouble, is he? He's a good boy, Tony is," she said, nodding.

"At the moment, just need his help clearing up some routine questions, ma'am. You have that name and address?"

"She's a Pacheco—Ana Sofia Pacheco. Their baby is Anthony Jr. She has an apartment all the way down in the South End. It's on Roosevelt Street, near the Cove Street end. I really don't know why they need to live so far away from me. This," she said, pointing at the floor, "is Tony's boyhood home and the neighborhood he grew up in. Right here in the Ave."

Tight-knit. Strong family ties. Provincetown's not the only place where the Portuguese community sticks together.

Silas got the address and said, "Mrs. Faria, you've been very helpful. Lemme get out of your hair. Thanks for your time."

He retraced his steps to the car, feeling a little relief at having gotten in and out without divulging any details about the case.

Let's put a leash on Bandit, get him some exercise. Chance to chew on my next move. This guy's real, and we've got a bead on him.

CHAPTER 40

Silas sat in the car and consulted his map to try to get himself oriented.

South End neighborhood's really more west than south from here. Looks like about a nine-minute drive, including stoplights. Not what most people would call far away. Guess for some mãezinha, *anything farther than inside a hug's too far.*

He picked his way across the unfamiliar old town, taking in the old brick cityscape. Turning onto Roosevelt Street, he noticed it was a little narrower than Earle. Aesthetically, it fit the same theme as the one Tony's mother resided in: an urban jungle of concrete, vinyl, and wrought-iron bars.

Adding to the similarities, Ana Sofia Pacheco's apartment was a walk-up too—at the top of a triple-decker. In her building, the staircase to the upper units was located on the inside.

Silas stopped one step short of the top.

Take some height off. Come across less imposing that way.

He reached up to knock softly on the thin, hollow-core door. Softly not because he could easily punch through a crappy door like this but because the apartment had to be small enough that a light knock could be heard from any room. No need to wake up a potentially cranky infant if it could be avoided. Experience had taught him crying babies shortened interviews.

Ana Sofia cracked open the door, still locked with a chain. "Who is it?"

"Officer Silas Lopez," Silas said, nodding at his badge.

"Officer?"

"Yes, police officer," he clarified. "Officer Silas Lopez."

After a few skeptical breaths, she eyed his badge and removed the chain, opening the door.

She was young, probably early twenties, with pleasant features. Shorts cut from gray sweatpants with the word *PINK* printed across the backside, a black T-shirt advertising a local pizza shop, and plastic slip-on Adidas slides with socks. Her shirt front was mottled with spots. *Guessing that's dried baby food. Worst case, dried baby spit-up.*

Silas stepped in and, using a soft voice, apologized for the disturbance. No sooner had he closed his mouth than the baby registered his voice, startled, and began to shriek. He saw a look of weary desperation settle over Ana Sofia's face and cloud her dark eyes. With a curt, firm tone, she told Silas to wait while she went to get the baby.

Silas looked around the room. The space was furnished, he supposed, in the sense that it had furnishings in it, but this wasn't what anyone would call homey or lived-in. *No curtains. No pictures. Just bare plaster walls. Feels like nobody had the time to settle in—or didn't plan to.*

Young couple, so of course, a large flat-screen TV. It stood on an old dark-wood table in front of a bricked-over fireplace. Silas could see crumbs and stains—the table was also used for eating. Old-world rug—looked handmade—threadbare in spots, too old to be anything but a hand-me-down, possibly a thrift store find. Opposite the TV sat a discolored, uncomfortable-looking beige velour couch. Capping off this odd mix was a coffee table constructed out of an old lobster trap.

Silas was sympathetic, remembering being young, just starting out. Not having much, not having the luxury of worrying what it looked like.

Ana Sofia returned with the baby. After rocking and gently jostling him on her hip for a moment, she laid him down carefully in a bouncy chair on the floor. She switched on the battery-operated vibration, and the motor's soft hum filled the room. Silas looked at the baby with concern; he wasn't crying, but Silas noted he wasn't asleep, either. *Don't have much time to work with here.*

Ana Sofia stood directly in front of him. It felt confrontational to Silas, and she didn't invite him to sit down. Silas showed her his badge and repeated his name. Ana Sofia waited, showing no reaction, while he explained he was looking for Tony Faria.

"Anthony isn't around right now. He's away a lot."

Guarded, not hostile. Careful with the police. She doesn't want any trouble, so figure she'll ultimately strike a somewhat cooperative tone.

Silas was preparing to ask where Anthony went, but Ana Sofia kept going.

If a witness wants to talk, you let 'em.

"Don't know what you want, but he's a good guy. He works hard and tries to help as much as he can with expenses."

Odd. Why'd she volunteer that? Was it pride? Makin' sure people know the baby's father was in the picture?

He sensed a hint of unease in her eyes. They were not quite meeting his, and he decided to start pressing on that pride a little.

"You sayin' he *does* help with expenses, or he says he *wants* to help with expenses?"

"He helps. But because his work's not real regular, it's not like clockwork with his money." Ana Sofia sounded a little defensive. "Sometimes when there are jobs on the boats and work's good, he's more flush with cash. Other times . . . Well, let's just say we get by. My family helps out. Tony's mom sometimes sends us a casserole when we're really stretched."

"What kind of work does he do?" Silas asked.

"He's a deckhand on the fishing boats, mostly, but I think he does other odd jobs too."

This doesn't make sense.

Silas nodded and asked, "Is it only when he's back from a fishing trip that he's, ah . . . flush?"

Ana Sofia gave a vague, back-and-forth wave of her hand. He could tell she was trying to look casual, but he could smell some kind of bubblegum scent intensifying off her as the heat of embarrassment built.

"Maybe? No. I'm not sure. I guess it seems more random than that. Actually, now that I think about it, he doesn't talk about the boats as much as he used to. But he mentioned catching work at the harbor and around town."

She covering for this guy, or is he keepin' her in the dark?

"Mind if I ask a dumb question?" Silas said. "These odd jobs around the harbor—that enough to keep a guy flush with cash?"

Ana Sofia's eyes narrowed, and her mouth tightened. Having already admitted Tony no longer seemed to have regular work on the fishing boats, she was boxed in, and Silas could tell she knew it. A flash of anger clouded her eyes, clearing as fast as it arrived. "I guess not," she agreed.

Time to change tactics. Surprise approach has done me no good, so let's go ahead 'n' see what she knows.

"Okay, he's not working fishing boats much anymore. So, I need to ask why a guy who doesn't work with boats would've been up the coast on my wharf in Provincetown, middle of the night, few weeks back?"

"I have no idea. I wouldn't know. Tony doesn't tell me every little detail of his days."

Silas nodded and pivoted back to Tony's current whereabouts. *Always keep a subject a little off-balance.*

"So, Tony's not around? He tell you where he was goin'?"

"No," Ana Sofia said. "He told me he was taking off for a job, or had to take care of a project or something, and wouldn't be back for a few days."

"Was it a *job* or a *project*?" Silas asked.

"I don't know!" Ana Sofia snapped, making the vague hand gesture again. The anger was back.

Fuse on this interview is burning down fast.

"I kinda got my hands full here, and when Tony's around, I'm not going to waste time nosing into his business. I'm gonna take some laundry down to the basement, take a shower, or go get some groceries if he's buying." She had a pissed-off look on her face, and Silas knew he had pushed this about as far as it was going to go.

"Like I said," Silas went on, keeping calm, "just have a few routine questions for him. He have a mobile number? I could just reach out to him that way."

"Yes, he has a mobile," Ana Sofia said, with a tone that implied only a moron would ask, "but he usually calls me, since his number changes."

"Number changes?" Silas clarified. "Why's that?"

"Tony uses prepaid phones," Ana Sofia explained.

Now we're getting into some interesting territory. What's a nice guy like this baby's dad need with burner phones?

"He prefer those?" Silas asked, hoping to hide his piqued interest.

"Why do you think?" Ana Sofia asked, her tone sarcastic. "He told me he doesn't have good credit to get a regular phone contract."

Silas felt a wave of guilt for assuming the only reason a person would use a burner was for nefarious purposes. This spitfire had him back on his heels for a split second until he remembered the comment about number changes.

"But why the number changes?" he asked, feigning confusion. *Just a simple moron who needs things explained to him.* "Can't he just add more minutes?"

Ana Sofia looked deflated. She seemed to appreciate the awkwardness of that point but rallied, offering, "He says he often loses or breaks the cheap prepaid ones he buys."

Right. And you believe him? Or just hoping I'm a moron, and I'll believe him?

"So, Tony calls you. When was the last time he called? You have the number from that call?" Silas asked.

Ana picked up her phone from the coffee table and showed the record of a late-night call several days earlier. Silas wrote the number in his notebook. *Don't know why I'm bothering—if I've got Tony pegged right, no chance that number is still in service.*

"Is there anything else, or can I get back to the baby's nap?" Ana Sofia asked.

Not gonna get more here today. She's hit her limit. Best to back away for now.

"Of course. Thanks for your time and help. Here's my card. You speak to Tony, can you ask him to give me a call?"

"Yeah, I guess, but don't hold your breath because I don't know when he'll be back."

"Understood. Thanks. I'll let myself out," Silas said.

He felt tired. Not from sparring with Ana Sofia so much as from the crushing sense that this young mother was in a dead-end relationship, with a dead-end, two-bit, no-account loser. She seemed like a bright kid with potential, and sooner or later, she and that baby were going to be visiting Daddy in jail.

He'd seen it countless times before, but it never got easier.

CHAPTER 41

He was technically zero for two, but Silas was not discouraged. The noose was tightening.

His more immediate problem was that he was hungry and thirsty. He'd forgotten to bring water for Bandit too. So, he found a parking space at a *mercearia* that offered homemade sandwiches, an assortment of groceries, and cold drinks.

After a look around, he concluded he should place his order over a tall, cluttered counter on top of the display cooler. A spicy smell drifted off the hot, greasy grill, and Silas's appetite surged. He asked for a sandwich made from marinated thin-sliced pork on a crusty *papo seco*, with a fried egg tucked in. He also ordered a pair of empadas—he figured the Portuguese version of empanadas—with different kinds of marinated meats. *When in Rome, eat Roman food,* he thought with a shrug.

He took his order slip and two ice-cold bottles of water to the register. After he'd paid, he told the clerk he'd be just outside. It felt cool enough in the shade of the building. He perched on a wire mesh chair next to a wobbly sidewalk table. The kitchen smells drifting out were rich and sharp—onions, grease, yeasty dough rising, spices.

Haven't forgotten you, buddy—just a second. Bandit sat. Silas opened a water bottle and quickly took a long pull on it. He capped it and laid the bottle on its side, then cut a strip down the length with his pocketknife, creating a makeshift water trough for Bandit.

Bandit was familiar with this drill and drank with enthusiasm, letting Silas know he was done by placing his sopping wet muzzle on Silas's thigh. Silas registered the pressure too late to prevent the soaking. When he looked down at the culprit, he could see expectation in his eyes, not remorse.

I know, right? Silas thought. *What's taking so long in there?*

The cashier stuck his head out and mumbled something when their order came up. Silas nodded his thanks, went in, and grabbed the to-go bag, returning to the table to eat and map out his approach to the commercial harbor.

The sandwich was salty and spicy, with the runny egg soaked into a roll that was about as fresh and delicious as any he'd ever eaten. To his dismay, it was somehow gone in an instant. Still starving, he broke the empadas open and stood them on their ends to cool. Once cooled, they turned out to have distinct flavors, also spicy and savory. He licked his fingers. Greasy. Good—even though they might weigh somebody down on a hot, early fall day. Bandit, however, had no such qualms and made quick work of his pieces.

When they were finished, Silas cleaned up his trash and waved a thank-you to the cook who'd taken his order. Then he and Bandit headed for the port.

Silas surveyed the area before pulling in. *This port's way bigger and more spread out than the one in Provincetown. Saw the ocean for the first time a few weeks ago. How would I have any idea how a commercial port like this works?*

He spotted a corrugated-steel building with a sign that read Harbormaster. Didn't take a genius to conclude that was as good a place to start as any. He made his way down, finding no obviously marked parking near the building's entrance. He pulled up at an angle and parked. Men mulled about, talking and largely ignoring his existence.

"Afternoon," Silas said, holding up his badge. "Name's Silas Lopez. Lookin' for a guy I'm told works on boats and around the harbor."

A middle-aged bald man with a gut pushing against the buttons of a stained white shirt sporting epaulettes on the shoulder and a loose tie around the unbuttoned neck looked up.

"Yeah? Who's that?"

"Name's Tony Faria. Five ten. Brown hair. Thirtyish."

"Faria?" the potbellied harbormaster repeated. "I might know who you mean, but I haven't seen him in a while."

"Anyone here who might have?" Silas asked.

"You're welcome to ask around. If anyone knows, it would probably be Gus, who captains the *Madalena*. Biggest boat and crew. He's been around forever. Knows everybody."

"Okay. Where can I find him?"

"If he's around, *Madalena* berths at dock two, out at the end." He pointed. "It's slip . . ." He paused to check the slip assignment map on the wall behind him. "Slip eighteen. Can't miss it."

Silas held up Bandit's leather leash, asking, "Okay?"

The harbormaster laughed and said, "Sure, but if he likes rat, you might want to hang on tight. Seen a dog chase one halfway up a bowline before falling in. Took the dog twenty minutes to swim all the way back to shore."

"Understood," Silas said, feeling a pang of concern at the idea of swimming to shore. He managed an appreciative nod and a wave. He parsed the guy's instructions, guessing a slip was the watery parking spot for a boat.

Walking out with a white-knuckled hold on Bandit's leash, Silas could smell the thin slick of oil and fuel shimmering on the stagnant seawater under the wharf. Several boats discharged streams of dirty-looking bilge water out their sides. *No swimming today, Bandit.*

Silas found slip eighteen easily enough. But it was empty.

"Charter fishing boats for the tourists are on the other side of the harbor," a man on the stern of the neighboring trawler said in an obnoxious tone.

"That so?" Silas said, holding up his badge. "Not lookin' for striped bass. Lookin' for a guy who's done some work around the harbor and on some of the boats."

The man looked a bit sheepish at the sight of the badge and said, "Which guy?"

Silas repeated the details he'd given the harbormaster.

"Faria? More than a few of that lot around this town. Still, I think I might know which one you mean. This one, he worked on the *SkipJack* a bit. That's Skip Jackson's boat."

"Okay. Know where I can find him?" Silas asked.

"You can't," he said.

Silas looked at him. *Dumb, unhelpful, or trying to be funny?*

"Not right now, I mean, unless you've got a boat of your own," the man added.

"*SkipJack*'s out workin'?" Silas clarified.

"Out on a haul."

Unnecessary fisherman talk for "out working," but okay.

"So, there's no way to contact Mr. Jackson?"

"Could probably raise him on the satellite ship-to-shore if it's an emergency."

"Not that kind of emergency," Silas said. "And sounds like it's a long shot he's even on board."

He was about to ask when the boat might be back, but the man interrupted him with, "Yeah, no reason to think he is. But even if you don't radio Skip, you'll find out soon enough."

"How's that?" Silas asked, growing weary of this back-and-forth.

"This time of year, *SkipJack*'s hauling bluefin, so he won't be gone long."

Okay, I'll take the bait. "Why's that?" Silas asked.

"Sushi fish," he said, with an implied *duh*, like it was the most obvious thing in the world.

Silas just looked up at him, squinting. Waited.

"People want to eat it raw. Don't want it cut up sloppy and frozen belowdecks. Get more for them whole when the brokers can inspect them. Boats come in and sell to the brokers every couple of days."

"Ah, got it," Silas said. "Then I'll just try an' leave him a message. Meantime, here, in case you see him before he gets it. Can you ask him to call me?" Silas said, reaching up to hand the man his card.

"Sure. You can probably get his number from the harbormaster."

"Will do, thanks," Silas said, relieved to be done with this tooth-pulling. Since he was already there, though, he decided to wander about a bit to see if anybody else might know Tony. He got some scraps, but interestingly, no one around this harbor had seen or heard from Tony in a while. Silas gave up and headed to the harbormaster's office. After securing the number, he and Bandit stretched their legs while he left a voicemail for Skip Jackson. Then they loaded up for the ride back to Provincetown.

Back in the Jeep, Silas let his hand rest on Bandit's back. The sun was just starting to lower behind him to the west. Oncoming vehicles had their sun visors down, but everything in front of him on his drive eastward was bathed in golden afternoon light. *Kinda light Wren would probably like.*

He thought about the case. Still no solid sighting of Faria. He felt like he was a couple of years behind the guy, chasing the old version of Tony. But the shape of the man was emerging—mainly in a negative way. It was coming in tiny increments, but Silas *was* making progress. It had been a long day, full of small, indirect insights, but when he assembled the mosaic, a picture of this guy was starting to form.

CHAPTER 42

"Hey, there! You boys heading out too?" Wren asked.

She and Silas had bumped into each other as they left through the Town Hall side door. He held it open for her, his hand across the top of the door, and they stepped onto the mossy old brick path. Around them, a low hedge of privet enclosed the building's grassy side courtyard, giving the public space a cozy, private feel. The late-afternoon air was warm but pleasant; the ancient maples around the building scattered dappled shade.

"Yep, sure are. Feels like I galloped a hundred miles since our beach walk last week. Been on the road all day. My colleague here needed a walk," he said, raising the leash. He swung a beaten canvas messenger bag. "Figure I can just as easily look at this stuff at home."

"Same," Wren said. "Not much summer left. I wanted to catch some light. I'm headed out to the wharf to watch the ferry come in. You boys want to keep me company?"

"Day's been like plowin' a field with the blade backward. Be bone-deep nice to walk and unwind," Silas said automatically, only to second-guess himself and ask, "You meetin' someone?" After he said it, a tinge of jealousy rushed over him at the thought, taking him by surprise.

"No, no. It's just for kicks. Boats won't be busy much longer. It's great people watching—which for me is code for *street photography*. Unlike the fishermen and charter operators, who are always heads-down busy when they're out on the wharf, most of the ferry passengers are excited to be here, full of wonder."

They crossed Commercial Street, Bandit sniffing the warm pavement while Silas caught the scent of steamed lobster and buttered rolls drifting from the takeout on the corner. *Gonna be ready for some dinner before long, this keeps up.*

At the kite store, they cut left and walked along the municipal parking lot toward Lopes Square and the wharf. The tide was dead low. As they got away from the buildings of town, the breeze picked up. The air smelled of seaweed and the roosting cormorants out on the breakwater.

"Ah, the peaceful silence of a conversation with Silas Lopez," she said with a laugh.

He cleared his throat. *Gloves are off. Can always count on this one to cut to the heart of it.*

"Don't say much as some," he allowed. "But I take things in. Notice a lot."

"Yeah? Like what? What have you noticed?" Wren asked over her shoulder as she stooped to compose a picture of a braided boat line coiled in a perfect spiral.

"Noticed we've worked in the same building a little while, never laid eyes on each other or spoken. Then all of a sudden, wind shifted, trail took a turn, and we've bumped into each other more than once lately," he said.

They walked down the rough timbers of the big wharf's sidewalk, a rusty, battered fishing fleet to their left, shiny charter and whale-watching boats on their right. The harbormaster's offices and the pirate museum loomed farther out. Beyond that, a turnaround circle and the passenger ferry kiosk. Silas liked the contrast—working boats on one side, tourists chasing whales on the other. Made him feel all right with being halfway between worlds himself.

"So, you never miss a trick, huh? You're sure we'd never laid eyes on each other?" she teased.

"Had we?" Silas asked. "Pretty sure I'd remember meeting the likes of you. Reckon I'd remember that a whole lifetime."

She blushed a little. "Aw. That's sweet. Never said we'd met, cowboy. Just saying, I might have noticed you and Bandit around Town Hall. Maybe been a little curious about such a fine dog. Wondered about the tall, quiet mystery man he keeps company with as well."

"That right?" he asked. "Which man we talkin' about?"

"The quiet one? Unusually tall, black hair, black eyes. You know the guy. Some might say handsome. Wears Western shirts. Even boots and a hat sometimes too. Definitely looks like a washashore."

Silas's brows furrowed. "A what now?"

"A washashore. Local term for people who are not from these parts," she explained.

Nodding, he paused to look at her with a shrug. "Guess maybe you notice things too."

"And maybe you don't notice as much as you think, big guy."

Oh, this one just keeps pressing. Never lets up with the teasing.

Wren stopped along the edge to compose a picture out across the harbor. "Ever cross your mind *why* we might have started running into each other?" she asked.

Suddenly not so sure where she's going here, but let's play along. See where this trail's leadin'.

"Small town?" he surmised.

Laughing softly to avoid being overheard by passersby, she said, "Nice try, Sherlock, but didn't it strike you as odd I was out messing with my camera in the middle of the day when you were on foot patrol?"

She stopped talking, and the implications of her comment bloomed in his head.

"Did you think it was a total coincidence," she went on, "that we came back with lunch at the same time that day? Me coming down for a tea bag? Both leaving work a smidge early tonight?"

"Detect a pattern," Silas said.

"And based on your extensive investigative training, do you have any theories or possible explanations for said pattern?"

"A few come to mind," he offered.

"Getting answers out of you is like pulling teeth," she said, grinning. "What are your theories, pray tell?"

"I suppose it's possible you have me under surveillance," he observed, trying and failing to keep a straight face.

Wren scoffed. "Yeah, that's your theory?"

"Well, maybe. My experience, private citizens don't usually surveil officers of the law," he said, stroking the five o'clock shadow on his chin with a calloused thumb and index finger.

"So, the other theory?"

"Stalker," he said.

Wren surprised him with the size of her laugh. "There *is* a sense of humor in there!" she exclaimed in triumph. After a beat, she added, "Could there be *any other possible* explanation for this so-called shift in the winds of fate?"

He took a few paces to gather himself. Felt the pull toward her—undeniable now. Quirky, sharp, beautiful. And he knew people. He couldn't be completely imagining the warmth coming back at him. Without really deciding to or consciously intending to, he stuck his neck out.

"Had a chance to think on it a stretch more now," he said, looking away from her, toward the breakwater. "Might be a third theory."

"Oh, yeah?" Wren said, mischief and expectation lightening her voice.

"Believe this pattern could also be explained by you wantin' to have dinner with me next week." He turned just in time to catch the way her eyes lit up. Freckles, laugh lines, and that wide, unguarded smile. It was precisely the reaction he was looking for.

"Aha," she said. "Is that what your training and experience tell you?"

"It is," Silas insisted. "At seven p.m., to be specific, on the day and at the chow hall of your choosing, since I've got no idea what's good around here."

The silence hung. Warm. Stretched. Uncertain.

"It's a date," she said with a grin, and a shoulder bump hard enough to wobble his stride.

Relief. Anticipation. Maybe even joy flooded into Silas's chest.

You're too old to feel like a schoolboy, Silas.

Don't care. Some things, you chase—frightenin' or not. This one feels like one of 'em.

CHAPTER 43
Friday, September 26

The team was gathered in the briefing room. Silas kept the rundown short.

"Me and Bandit took a ride yesterday . . . Well, more like got taken for a ride, you could say. Down to New Bedford. Most substantial thing I got all day was a decent sandwich."

The team was growing more comfortable with Silas, so a few acknowledged the levity with a small laugh. Silas noticed chief among them were Marsh, Byrne, Evans, and surprisingly, Clark. Burig released a full-blown guffaw.

"Faria's no longer at his last-known address—hasn't been for a couple of years, but his momma still lives there and wants us to know he's a good boy." A few members of the team snickered again, and Silas felt himself enjoying the mood of the meeting. "His girlfriend, who's the mother of his son, also wants us to know he's a stand-up guy—despite admitting some things that, well, wouldn't shine up with a gallon of polish."

"What'd ya mean, boss?" Evans prompted, eager for details.

Silas leaned against a side table, ticking off a list using his fingers. "Never around. Doesn't tell her when or where he's going. Often has nothin' to contribute to the household expenses, except every once in a while when he has wads of cash she can't account for. Calls her from burner phones; changes numbers as often as socks. Tells her he's a butterfingers who keeps losing or breaking his phones. No steady work. Top it all off, nobody around the dock—where he supposedly works—has seen him lately."

Some heads shook around the table, and Marsh asked, "Anything we can use to locate him?"

"Probably made it sound worse than it is. Did pick up a few scraps. Guy's a no-account bottom-feeder on extended leave from responsibility and honest work. Feel like this guy's just beyond the tip of my fingers. Most promising lead: trawler captain who might know something. Left him a message. Waitin' for him to return to shore."

Silas wrapped the briefing up by saying, "Meantime, I'm gonna work the knot from the other end of the rope—talk to folks at our docks here, see if anyone knows anything about what he could have been doing."

He gathered his things and left the room. He hoped he'd struck the right balance between recap, procedural logic, and next steps. This guy was proving harder to find than most suspects, whether by design or coincidence, which made him a pretty good teaching case for the squad.

The Provincetown harbormaster's office was smaller than New Bedford's and quite a bit more attractive—white-trimmed glass windows and silver cedar shingles. It had a pair of windowed cupolas, one large enough for the harbormaster to use as a lookout. Silas took the five concrete steps into the building.

"Melvin Miller?" he said, walking inside. "Silas Lopez, chief of police."

"Good to meet you, Chief," the harbormaster said, smelling of pipe smoke and body odor.

"Pleasure's mine. Late gettin' over here to introduce myself. No disrespect meant. It's no excuse, but this hit-and-run has us busy."

"I can imagine, Chief. How's that going, anyhow?" Looking at Bandit, Miller added, "He like biscuits? I keep a box here for some regulars I see."

"I think you could probably get him to take one," Silas said with a wink. "Making progress with the hit-and-run. Hoping for your help."

"Happy to try," Melvin said, puffing up a bit before leaning down to give the biscuit to Bandit. "What do you need?"

"Some advice. Tryin' to figure out why a truck and trailer might be out on your wharf middle of the night."

"What kind of truck and trailer?"

"Full-size pickup. Long, heavy-duty, two-axle flatbed trailer."

"Hell if I know, Chief. Honestly, that doesn't make any sense."

"How do you figure?"

"Look around this wharf. No place to maneuver a rig like that. Commercial boat traffic alone keeps the wharf jammed, but throw in foot traffic, ferry traffic—it's a circus most days and nights."

Now that Silas thought about that, the man had a point.

"No local'd pull a trailer like that out onto this wharf during normal hours, or even after sunset," Miller elaborated with a wave of his hand. "Just not worth the aggravation. Look for yourself. Locals don't run trailers. They convert pickups to flatbeds, haul right off the back. Might take more trips, but still easier than tryin' to operate out here with anything bigger."

"That tracks," Silas said. "Guy's not a local. He was on your wharf at about four a.m. Any chance he worked out of here? Name's Tony Faria."

"State doesn't require crew rosters, but I'd likely know. Same thirty-eight or so boats working out of here every day. I see the crews. Don't recognize that name."

"Okay. That's helpful. Sounds like we're looking at a transient visitor. Anybody around who might know more?"

Miller scanned both windows. "Curtis Berrick's probably your best bet—red-hulled trawler over there," he said, pointing at a large ship out the fleet-facing window. "Try him. He'd know anyone crewin' out of this harbor."

"Appreciate the help, Melvin. Pleased to meet you."

Silas continued down the wharf and approached the trawler. The twenty-questions drill with tight-lipped fishing types was getting repetitive. *Gotta run this Tony-as-a-deckhand lead to ground. Need at least a shred of useful information before I walk away from it.*

The rusty red trawler was rocking gently in the light breeze. Silas spotted the man Miller had pointed to only moments ago.

"Curtis Berrick? I'm Silas Lopez, chief of police," he said, stepping closer to the edge of the dock than he liked. The man stood up on the stern of the trawler, seemingly not feeling any need to come ashore to talk to Silas. "Hopin' you can help me find a guy."

"You are, huh?" Berrick said. He had a single tuft of white hair that looked sort of like a dollop of whipped cream, pushed awry by the wind. Was Berrick questioning whether he was the chief or whether he wanted help? Hard to tell. These fishermen made him look chatty.

Silas plowed ahead. "Few weeks ago, guy was seen in a full-size GMC pickup, haulin' a long flatbed off this wharf around four a.m. Tryin' to figure out why."

"And you want me to help?"

"I do," Silas said, mustering a tepid smile to mask his rising annoyance. "I'm told you know the score 'round here."

"Don't know 'bout that," Berrick said.

Unbelievable.

"But you're willin' to help?"

"Maybe so. What's your question?"

Silas looked at him long enough to signal just how much this dance irritated him. But he didn't let it affect his even, friendly tone. "Ever heard of Tony Faria? Any clue why he—or anyone—might be towin' a flatbed off this wharf in the middle of the night?"

"Never heard of him," Berrick said, apparently without giving it any real thought.

"Okay," Silas said. *Hold it together. Use the last reserves of patience you've got.* "Then, how about the second part? Any reason someone would be hauling something off this wharf at around three or four o'clock in the morning?"

"No idea. Wouldn't be hauling a catch. Maybe a couple of hand-caught squid—some folks use lights to grab a few at night right off the wharf—but nobody would be coming in with a catch."

That got Silas's attention. "Why's that?"

"Boats might head out around then, sure. But they don't come back then. Either they return before dark or stay out overnight—fish one more early morning—and haul back once there's daylight. Nobody hauls in at four a.m."

"You're sure?" Silas asked, out of reflex more than anything. He instantly regretted it.

"Fisherman all my life, trawler captain half that, and you're asking me if I know fishing? The hell you think I'm doing here?"

Had that coming. Think we're done here.

"Right. Didn't mean disrespect. Just checkin' facts. Appreciate the help," Silas said, turning with a wave, still cringing as he walked away and back down the wharf.

Silas didn't get far. Halfway down the wharf, his phone rang. It was an unknown number. Silas fumbled to swipe the answer button in the bright glare.

"Lopez."

"Chief, this is Skip Jackson from New Bedford. You asked me to call?"

Great. Another fisherman.

Silas ran through his spiel again, reminding himself that police work meant turning over lots of stones. You never knew when you'd uncover a good witness.

"Yeah, I know Faria," Jackson said, and Silas's pulse picked up. "Hasn't worked the *SkipJack* for a while. Don't miss him."

"That right? Why?"

"Something off. Shifty. Never loyal to a boat. Other crew didn't like him. Maybe just lazy, but always chasing a shortcut."

"Huh. Sounds like the guy in my sights."

"Heard he was dealing drugs. Small-time. Didn't want that poison on my boat. Risky enough without booze or drugs involved."

"Understand that," Silas said. He found himself liking this guy. *Straight shooter. Maybe came to fishing from another line of work.* "Any clue where I might find this prize of a guy?"

Silas heard a scratching sound like Jackson was rubbing the stubble on his jawline with his knuckles. "Don't have any idea where Faria is these days, and like I said, that's just fine by me."

"Any guesses at all? Any ideas you can give me about where to look would be a big leg up."

"Well, last year a cousin of mine told me he'd seen Faria in New Bedford, connected to an unfamiliar ship not on the harbormaster's rolls. A few people were wondering if he'd found a new boat to crew."

"Anything else? Any details he might've shared about his life?"

"Well, no idea if this is helpful, but I remember Faria had a friend in Carver who ran a big cranberry operation and gave him work from time to time. He used to ask me for time off during the harvest season."

"Thank you, Mr. Jackson. You've been a big help," Silas said, ending the call. This investigation was filled with setbacks and red herrings, but this felt like a genuine lead.

He headed off the wharf, toward Town Hall.

What had he learned? Faria's picture was getting clearer. Still possible that the fatality was a tragic mistake—and possible Tony didn't even know he'd hit someone. Had to keep that in mind. Just because he was shifty didn't mean he was malicious.

But even so, Tony wasn't the innocent angel his mama thought.

CHAPTER 44

After popping into his office briefly to check in with the team, Silas went straight to see Flood and provide an update on the Perkins case.

He poked his head around Flood's open door before giving a quick knock.

"Silas, what can I do for you?"

"Keepin' you up to date on the hit-and-run." Silas didn't bother to sit down—it wouldn't be a long update.

Flood brightened. "Great. Have you wrapped it up yet?"

"Not yet, but feels like we got rope around it. Damn near certain we know who owned, likely drove, the truck involved." Silas walked toward Flood's desk and rested a fist, knuckles down, on the tallest pile. "Been searchin' 'round New Bedford for the guy. Talked to family, folks who know him. Feel like I got him in my sights. Not clear if he knew he ran anybody over, but pretty sure he's a shitweasel either way."

Flood grinned. "That a legal term?"

"Sorry for the color. Long day. Anyway, we've got leads currently pointing to a cranberry operation in Carver. Let you know as soon as I have eyes on him."

Flood sagged a little. Silas figured he'd better keep managing expectations.

"Fair warning, though—as of yet, the evidence is thin, indirect. Likely need a confession, and gonna take some luck to get it."

"But you just said you know who did it!" Flood's voice rose in pitch.

"Knowing and proving are two different things. Law court means beyond a shadow of a doubt. And we don't have weight to lean on him yet. What I do have is a video of his truck leaving the wharf around the time of the incident. And another clip shows it turning the corner where the victim was hit."

Flood spread two hands open as if to say *What more do you need?* with a wide-eyed, questioning look on his upturned face.

Silas nodded to acknowledge the perspective. "It's a good start, but we can't prove for sure some other vehicle or some other driver wasn't responsible—and we need to know *for sure*. Know it sounds stranger than a two-headed calf to say so, but might be a lucky break if he didn't know he did it."

"How's that? Wouldn't that mean a lesser charge?" Flood asked.

"Depends on lots of factors, but I'm talking in terms of evidence. If he didn't know he hit something, he wouldn't realize there's forensic evidence on the trailer. If he knew, trailer'll be burned, sold to someone in another state by now."

Flood took off his glasses and rubbed his face.

Doesn't take a genius to see Flood's not pleased. Frustratin' not to have more to offer.

"Right. Well, shit," Flood said. "I appreciate the updates. This is proving to be quite the maze."

"Ain't wrong there," Silas said.

As Silas was turning to leave, Flood said, "I have to say I feel fortunate to have brought you on board before this mess happened, Silas."

"Honor to have your trust."

And it was. *Worked for far worse bosses than Flood. Not gonna rest until we get this sorted out for him.*

CHAPTER 45
Wednesday, October 1

The restaurant was in the center of town but hidden away, tucked above an enclosed courtyard of small boardwalk shops. Wren had led them through to the back of the courtyard and up the curved staircase to the entrance.

Silas gestured for Wren to walk ahead of him as the waiter escorted them through the restaurant. They wove through the main dining room to a balcony table facing the water.

Nice. Modern with those black walls and ceiling. Not exactly a grub tent.

As he walked behind her, he could catch her scent when she moved— clean and faintly floral. The hem of her dress brushed her calves as she walked. A couple of men noticed too, and their looks weren't what he'd call polite. One glare from him was all it took to make them remember their manners.

The indoor dining room tables were scattered around a large, dark, U-shaped bar. He caught the smell of lemon and orange peel. *Fresh. Good bartender, then. Nobody likes a brown slice of lime floating in their beer.*

Four-person tables filled the open space in the dining room and the prime spots along the floor-to-ceiling windows. Outside, two-person tables hugged the balcony railing. *Looks like one of those is ours. View's somethin' else.*

Silas pulled out a chair for Wren, then sat down himself, finding places to stash his bent legs before placing his napkin in his lap.

From the table, Silas could see the town's beaches and wharf, the marina full of boats resting at anchor, Long Point Lighthouse, and beyond it, across the bay, the hills of Truro and Wellfleet curving around the bay.

"I hope this isn't too fancy," Wren said quietly. "I picked it mostly for this view and because the menu has a lot to choose from. If I'm honest, I struggled a bit. This place is a little spendy, so I would go here only for special occasions. I didn't want to be presumptuous or put you in an uncomfortable position."

"Does have an air about it," Silas admitted, noticing Wren's eyes widen a fraction. "Looks real nice. Good choice. Already like it. Thank you."

"Well, okay," Wren said, settling in. Facing him now, she smiled. There was warmth in it. He watched her eyes take him in—a solid black dress shirt, clean jeans, and cowboy boots. "Now, look at you, all gussied up! You clean up real nice," she added, imitating a country accent as best she could.

"Well," Silas teased, rubbing the back of his neck in an exaggerated fashion, "I usually take a bucket from the stream to wash trail dust off before eatin'." He cut the act before adding, "Wasn't actually raised in a stable. Mama didn't have a lot, but she held me to high standards. Got no slack around her hacienda."

"Well, good. Glad to know you won't embarrass me."

"Didn't promise that." He grinned.

A waiter took their drink orders and left them with menus.

"Anyway, that'll be enough about me," Silas said, opening his menu. "Came here to learn about you. Tell me 'bout yourself, Wren Bradford. How'd you end up here?"

Wren took a deep breath. "Well, I spent every summer of my life here, so I've always had roots—and I've always loved it here. When I got out of grad school for social work, I started my career in Boston. I completed my internships and experienced classic big-city social work . . ." She trailed off a bit, frowning. "With all that entails."

"Sensing that was a mixed blessing," Silas said.

"Well, it was an invaluable experience," Wren reasoned, shifting slightly, as if she were still shedding the weight of those years. "I got to handle a lot of cases and had a varied and interesting mix of them, but I was part of a big bureaucratic system with lots of rules and paperwork. And cases rotated too often for anyone's good. It started to feel impersonal. I didn't have long enough to connect with my clients to make me feel like my work with them was impactful."

"Gotta be hard, being young and idealistic, frustrated that way," Silas said, watching her face.

She gave a rueful half smile, green eyes lowering briefly. "Yeah, I was a little lost—living up to other people's expectations, not my own. I'm not trying to sound ungrateful," she added quickly. "I was fortunate to have the opportunity to help and get training. But I knew I wanted something more, something for myself."

Wren leaned forward, stiff menu standing straight up in her lap, with her hands resting lightly on its top edge. Her gaze grew distant, almost like she was speaking half to herself. "I wanted to get out of the city, to be able to interact with nature, and to photograph real wild landscapes. I realized that in order to feel like I was making a difference, I had to become part of the community I was helping. The city was always going to be too big and too anonymous."

"Provincetown'd be a fit," Silas commented. He could see it clearly— why she'd come, why she'd stayed.

"I knew Provincetown had access to some private money that enabled their Human Services program to be bigger than it might otherwise have been." She smiled as she warmed to the memory. "And I knew that the seasonal nature of the town, the mix of old and new industries, like fishing and tourism," she said, gesturing out over the harbor and the town with one hand, "the LGBTQ+ community, the gentrification, the Portuguese traditions and heritage all made for some complex and, for a social worker, interesting dynamics."

Silas could see the appeal. Knew what that tug felt like himself.

"So, you put in your application?" he surmised.

Wren moved her menu to the corner of the table. Silas did the same.

"Well, that was the tricky part." She paused to sip from her sweating water glass, other hand cupped for drips, then glanced over the rim at him. "There wasn't a job yet, but my boss in Boston knew Roger Chandler, head of Human Services here, from way back. With some digging, I found out there was an opening being created in the next year's budget. She was willing to put in a word for me. She got the sense they were interested since I had a fancy degree and big-city training and experience."

"That tracks. Good to have friends. If there was no opening yet, could you apply?"

"Not exactly. I got word out that I was interested. I knew I'd be a far more credible candidate if I were already living in the community, so I reached out to my summer boss from the art gallery where I had worked and asked for any hours he could give me—hosting when it was busy; administrative work; helping frame, box, and ship prints in the offseason. I'd be lying if I didn't admit staying closer to my photography daydreams was part of the motivation there as well."

Their server came and took their orders, then set down a three-segment plate of bread, virgin olive oil, and shreds of Parmigiano Reggiano, as well as a separate little square bowl of green and black olives. *Not sure what all that's for, 'sides the bread, so maybe I'll hang back on it. See what she does.*

"Speaking of photography," he went on, watching Wren to gauge her reaction, "I stopped by the art gallery. Haven't met Deschamp but did meet Rafael. Wren, I gotta say, your pictures put a hitch in my step. Gave me a lot to think 'bout."

She blinked, then her eyes bounced open wide. "You've seen my work? When?"

He shrugged. "Like to know what I'm dealin' with. Might have poked my head in to size it up. Concerned I broke Rafael's heart, battin' for the other team and all."

Silas watched Wren dip a small piece of the bread into the olive oil, then into the shreds of cheese and pop it into her mouth. *Huh. Oil's for dippin'?*

"Ha! He's a doll. Loves to tease. I bet he had a ball with you."

You don't know the half of it. Still embarrassing just thinking about it now.

"Don't worry, I'm sure he'll bounce back." With a mock grimace on her face, she asked, "Dare I ask what you thought of the work?"

Silas didn't hesitate.

"Thought it was beautiful. Somethin' special. Not trained to judge these things, so I had to take my time and think hard about each one, but I could tell I was lookin' at special pictures. Got me thinking so much, I even came up with some theories."

Wren's eyebrows shot up to a comedic degree as she ducked her chin toward her collarbone and looked right at him with the brightest of eyes. "Theories? Do tell!"

He looked out at the harbor. *Daylight's gone, but still that glowing pink across boat hulls, rooftops, the lighthouse. Tar on a nearby roof's cooling—can smell it.*

"That's a long ramble for another time—but the short of it is . . . I started wonderin' if we look at the same scene but see different things."

"Hmm. Say more," she said, the stem of her pinot grigio in the slender fingers of her left hand, her right hand and wrist rotating in a "go on" motion.

"Guess, well, I see specifics . . . objects and items with names, people, motion, pieces of a connected system. I'm always lookin' at things objectively, assigning meaning to 'em, like a cop assessing a situation. Maybe a rancher deciding if a bull's fixin' to charge."

Wren nodded. He could tell she was fascinated.

"Have a hunch you may look at the same thing, see more like a slideshow of still images rather than the video or film I see. You see *moments*. Moments with textures, shapes, light, color."

He paused, unsure if he was getting himself into the weeds.

Then, he shrugged and added, "Workin' theory's all."

"Wow, that's pretty perceptive, Silas. I think you might be onto something there."

"Try not to act too surprised," he said with a wink.

Wren changed the subject to get herself out of the spotlight. "I've seen you looking at that lighthouse. Do you know the deal with that green light?"

"Can't say I do," he said, feeling relaxed, comfortable. He was eager to learn about the town through her eyes.

"So, this one's Long Point Light, with the green flash." She pointed over his shoulder. "Wood End Light, just around the bend there in the West End of town, blinks red." He looked, nodding. He was familiar. "And the final light out here in Provincetown, Race Point Light, blinks white."

"Now you mention it, seen that one too."

"So, what's neat is mariners and fishermen have always known about each light's color from their charts, tradition, whatever. They know which color is associated with which location. At night or in bad weather, they can use the relative position of the colors to figure out exactly where they are and which way they need to steer to reach the shelter of the harbor."

Silas was tickled by that bit of knowledge. "Huh. If only everythin' else in life were that clear." After a beat, he added, "Don't suppose you've got a favorite one?"

"Lighthouse? Huh, good question. Never actually thought about it. Race Point is way out there, all windswept and isolated. It takes a long hike or Jeep ride over sand to reach it, which makes it special. Plus, it's the only cylindrical one of the three, which also makes it unique. Casts gorgeous shadows across the cylinder's curve when the sun gets low. But white light is kinda boring, right?"

Silas jerked his head back in mock surprise. "Makin' a strong case for that one, till you pulled the rug out at the last minute."

Wren's eyes twinkled as she smiled. "Wood End is easy enough to walk to along the breakwater. We're going to need to do that with Bandit sometime soon, by the way."

We sure are.

"I like Wood End Light. I've gotten some good sunrise shots of it, timed perfectly so the red blink of the light blended into the reddish colors of dawn. There was coppery-colored sun reflected in the wavy old glass windows too. Very fun."

She's starting to take this analysis more seriously than expected. Winner's gonna be valid.

"But I think Long Point has to be considered my favorite. It's a familiar friend, blinking away, right here in the middle of a busy harbor. And it marks the absolute tip of the whole entire cape—'land's end,' as they say around here. Plus, it reminds me of a favorite book. The green light in the book became a symbol of dreams, yearning, and hope. Gives this light some heft."

Her obvious satisfaction was delightful.

Could watch her reason all day.

"Might need to reread that book. Been a while since I checked in on Daisy and Jay," Silas said with a grin. Wren seemed pleasantly surprised by this revelation.

"Ah, a reader, I see," she said with a smile.

"TV's a bit bulky to take with you on the horse to camp. Book tucks in the saddlebag real nice. Trade 'em with other ranchers for different ones when you're through reading 'em. Time I was done ranching, the readin' habit stuck."

They let a moment of silence pass, each sipping their drinks.

Then, Silas turned things back to Wren. "So, you were workin' at the gallery. What 'bout your living situation?"

"Well, the family summer place was too big and too stuffy—heavy with the family past—to live in year-round by myself. It had too many memories and was too much of a downtown location. Plus, it was in trust to both me and my older sister, Clare. For a lot of reasons, I wanted my own place. So I convinced my sister to buy out my interest, which she was happy to do. I used some of those proceeds to buy my cottage."

"Clever. Won't miss the old place?"

"Nah. Besides, I can visit her there anytime. I prefer having my own cozy nest."

This was nice, being with Wren. *Her cozy nest sounds nice too. Stormy night, or cold, it'd be good to have a cozy nest.*

"Imagine first winter for a summer person is eye-openin'. Been hearin' stories. Interested to experience it myself. Wind never quits blowing in Provincetown. Winter storms gotta get it going like a runaway freight train."

Gonna starve if they don't bring me some real food soon. Guess I'll break down and try this oil-bread-cheese contraption.

"It can be wild. You already know about the wind. Short days. Surprisingly, winter's not bad for photography," Wren said.

"Thought your ilk was after light above all else. Ain't there less of it in the winter?"

She gave him an assessing look. He was paying attention, interested.

"That's very true. There's less light, and further, it's often flat light, which is usually not what you want to photograph with."

"Flat?" Silas clarified.

"Diffused—no shadows, no contrast, filtered through clouds, fog. It seems to dull color so that nothing pops. No highlights, no depth, just dull . . . Do you ever ski?"

"Ah, no, I don't."

"Flat light, like you might get on a snowy or cloudy day, or in the late afternoon, in the mountain's shadow, can wipe a skier out—a fast-moving skier can't read the surface of the snow. There's not enough contrast. *That's* flat light."

"Can understand why photographers don't like it."

"But there are positives. The landscape looks so different, so barren, it can be like it's a whole new place. And what light there is is lower, more angled, more golden. When it's right, winter light is spectacular out here."

Silas held up a hand. "Whoa, now. Lower and angled? What's wrong with good, strong high-noon sun? Figured that'd be best," he commented, genuinely curious, dabbing another piece of bread into the pool of oil. *Oil bread's not bad. Cheese has a heck of a salty kick to it—little of that stuff goes a long way. Still, beats starvin'.*

"Actually, high-noon sun is bad for all the opposite reasons. It's harsh and too high-contrast and reliably unflattering. Makes subjects squint and look old. No subject wants that for their portrait. Throws dark shadows all over pictures. But with winter light, the sun is always lower in the sky. That can lend itself to capturing the moments you want."

"Photographers are fussy about their light. A lot more to it than just clickin' a button." He smiled at her.

Their food arrived. Corn and lobster chowder and a salad with salmon for Wren. New England clam chowder, a hanger steak, potatoes, and green beans for Silas.

Hot food—finally. Just in time.

As they began to eat, Silas realized just how famished he was. *Best eat up because you can tell she's fueling herself and gathering her strength for a prolonged assault. Gonna be some personal questions coming.*

Wren made quick work of the chowder with small talk. But as she tucked into her salad, she surprised no one by asking, "So, how did *you* end up here?"

Silas looked out across the harbor as daylight faded into evening.

Truth will eventually need to come out, so might as well make the best of it.

"Well, if I'm bein' honest . . ." He paused a beat. "Not entirely on purpose."

He looked at her as he pulled together the courage to tell the story.

"Fact is—and please keep this under your hat," he said with a wink, "I thought I was answering a job listing in the capital of Rhode Island. That place turns out not to be an island, by the way."

"What?" Wren blurted out, almost a spit-take, but quickly covered her mouth. "You got Providence, Rhode Island, and Provincetown, Massachusetts, confused? You have got to be kidding me! If that isn't proof you're not from around here, I don't know what would be!"

Silas put down his steak knife and fork and finished chewing.

"In fairness, now, me and Bandit were on the road cross-country, workin' out of the Jeep, just using my phone to try and do stuff."

He picked up his utensils and cut another piece of steak, then held it while he finished the thought.

"Jugglin' pit stops, finding places to bed down, grub to eat. At times, trip was a bit of a goat rodeo. You know, like the Bard says, misty mountains, crooked highways, sad forests," he said with a grin. "I skimmed a posting on a job board using my phone and, well, mighta let a few strays slip the fence. Not my finest moment."

Genuinely embarrassing now that I get the local perspective on my mistake. Hopefully, Wren has the decency not to mock me too fierce.

She looked delighted by his misadventure. "This is *so* much better than I expected! I have to know more. How did you realize your mistake?"

"Well, seemed odd—big-city police department reporting to a town manager. Figured maybe things worked different out East. But then Flood kept goin' on about 'the Bourne' versus 'the Sagamore'—turned out they were bridges. Bridges in a different damn state."

Wren's coming apart, laughing at me. Makin' a fool of myself, but at least she's happy. Actually, I can see the story's got humor potential, now I'm telling it for the first time. Besides, come this far, best see it through.

Wren's mirth appeared difficult for her to contain. The smile screwed her whole face into a picture of delight, laugh lines highlighting the timeless beauty of her spectacular eyes. She looked at the other tables to make sure she wasn't making a scene before quietly begging, "Please, go on."

Butt of this joke, but a grin like that makes it worthwhile. About as beautiful as it gets. All the reason needed to keep this epic tale of misadventure rolling.

"Thought that bridge stuff was odd, and the mystery deepened a bit until I got a map, studied it hard. Found a place not too far away called Provincetown."

Wren laughed, and it came out as somewhat of a snort.

"I admit, I still didn't realize quite what I'd done at that point. Couldn't find the original job listing, but I'm trained as a detective. I looked up the size and the type of town government. It fit. Then, I had Flood's number in my recent calls list—a quick check of the area code map told me I was on the track. All's left, a check of the town website for a manager named Flood. Clinched it. Rest is history," he said with a shrug and two raised palms before wiping his mouth with his napkin.

Wren was shaking her head in disbelief, her big, luminous eyes tearing from the laughter. "And you came here anyway?" she blurted.

He shrugged again, looking more serious.

"In the river awful deep to turn back at that point. I'd made a commitment to Mr. Flood. Plus, I liked his manner on the phone." His look became more wistful. After a pause to take in the twinkling mooring lights of the harbor, he added to the thought. "Had nowhere else I needed to be. I'd never seen the ocean. I was fixin' for some change, anyway."

Shaking her head in amazement, Wren said, "That's just remarkable!"

His shift in tone hung over the table between them. They'd both finished eating, and their plates had been cleared, so Wren put her elbows on the table, chin in her palms. "Meanwhile, why the need for change? You were already a police officer, weren't you?"

"Doin' your homework too. Yep, Salt Lake City. Sixteen years. Was done there," he said with distaste on his face.

Wren shrugged on a white cotton cardigan against the cool breeze— Silas did his damnedest not to look at the fabric of her dress accentuating her curves as her arms went back—then continued to untangle the story. "Why was that? Why did you want to leave?"

"Whole passel of things. Demanding job, big-city force. Made detective, good at cop work, but didn't have much truck with department politics. Had, ah . . . a bit of a scrape with a colleague. Never got much of a social life going. Salt Lake's in the West, but I always felt like an outsider in the city. With the police community, things revolved mostly around the Mormon church. I'm not Mormon."

"Did you like the city itself?"

He shrugged with a slight curl of the lip. "It was a city. Lake mud smelled something awful."

Wren chuckled at the inclusion of that detail. "Those mountains, though . . . You didn't like to snowboard, either?"

"Yeah, I did like the backcountry with a horse and a pair of snowshoes. Never saw any sense in cutting down all the trees on a mountain to slide down it on toys. Hiked a lot with Bandit the year before I left."

"Cannot say I'm surprised by that answer, Mr. Lopez. So, you had Bandit at that point?"

"He was one of the reasons I left. Came to me a year before I left Salt Lake. Was a litter down in Cortez when I was visiting my mama. Like I said before, rancher didn't want most of 'em, so Bandit was gonna be put down or maybe turned loose."

"That's just so awful," Wren said, brows furrowing.

"I think so. But lotta ranchers think of dogs as tools, not pets. Climate's tough out there, so life as a stray's nasty, brutish, and short, in the words of one philosopher."

Wren seemed to have a small involuntary shiver at the thought.

"Saw fine dogs perish like that; couldn't let it stand. Spent a little time among the litter. Kept the one that attached itself to me like a burr, and before I headed back up to Salt Lake, I took the rest to a ranch that shelters livestock dogs. Real nice animals. Damn lucky I walked away with only one. Even if it would be nice for him to have some company, Bandit's more than enough on his own. And the two of us are tighter than a cinch knot."

With a little laugh, Wren summarized her findings. "So, you weren't comfortable at work, not enamored with the city, and didn't have a social life, but otherwise, things were good?"

"Well, not all good. My superior got into some crooked doings. Took favors for lookin' the other way while thugs preyed on Hispanic neighborhoods, businesses. It was over the line." He shook his head. There was a rueful look in his eye. "I had a problem with that. If you don't stand up for the ones who can't, you don't stand for much. Wanted my partner to go call him out with me. Tried to make him understand justice that runs on favorites ain't justice. But my partner of nine years dug in. Family man. Couldn't risk a hit to his career. He sided with the sergeant, claimed it was a gray area."

Wren was listening, motionless with interest.

Uncomfortable memories. This story's goin' in a bad direction, but there's not much can be done to head it off at this point.

"It wasn't a gray area. You do right, or you don't. Ain't shades of it," he said firmly, thudding the heel of his fist on the edge of the table for emphasis. "Right's right, even when it ain't easy. His cowardly behavior really stuck in my craw."

Their server offered them coffee and dessert, which they declined.

"I'm happy here for longer if you want coffee," Wren said. "I just don't drink it in the evening. So, you and your partner disagreed?"

"Tried to let it go, but it wouldn't go away. Came to a head. Jackass threatened me if I spoke up."

"Isn't this always the way? I'm sorry, Silas. So, what did you do?"

"Tried to avoid him, but we eventually fought," Silas admitted, and Wren's eyes widened. "He'd gotten drunk and started to grind on the topic with me, actin' belligerent. Warned him he didn't want to go down that path, was gonna get himself hurt."

"What happened?"

In a soft, remorseful tone, he said, "Fool came at me." He snuck a glance before saying in a tiny voice, "I hurt him bad."

"Oh, Silas, that's not good. What happened?" Wren asked, her tone cold and serious, all traces of warmth in her eyes replaced with worry, disapproval.

"The doctors called it an orbital blowout fracture—smashed eye socket. Broke his cheekbone, forehead, some ribs, among other things. Didn't die, but got a case of double vision. A cop can't work with double vision."

Her face clouded. "Oh my God, Silas! What were you thinking?"

That landed hard. She looked scared now—of him.

Great job, Silas. Repercussions from this screwup are still playing out. Now she thinks you're a dangerous animal too.

"Guess I wasn't thinking is the point." He sighed. "I know it was wrong." He rubbed his chin nervously before adding, "Truth is, that's not the first time it ever happened. Like to think I learned my lesson now, though."

She was silent. Unconvinced.

"He did recover," he added feebly, but the damage was done. "Vision cleared up, and he was back on the job within a couple of months. They got him a new partner."

"What did they do to you?" Wren asked.

Not looking to have this shared. Haven't told anyone. But it feels like she deserves the whole story. And I feel like I can trust her.

"Do I have your word it stays between us?" Silas said in a somber tone.

"Of course, you have it," Wren said. "I'll keep it to myself."

Silas took a deep breath. "Obviously, it was gonna ruin my service record. Gettin' into a little beef with a colleague is one thing, but seriously hurting another cop like that is no small thing. Luckily, the chief knew me from my years of service and from something we'd worked on together. Liked me, knew that I was a decent man, done good work for him."

He risked a look at her eyes, which were still narrowed, betraying concern.

"More importantly, he understood I wouldn't do something like that without a damn good reason—a reason the size of Montana. I told him why, and that put him into a jam. He was up for reappointment and didn't want it all going public until he'd had at least a chance to clean it up."

"Way of the world . . ." Wren sighed.

Can't tell for sure, but doesn't look like she's blaming me totally. Maybe just the whole corrupt system.

Silas leaned back in his chair. Shrugging, nodding sadly, he said, "His jam was my lucky break. Chief offered me a deal. If I just left quietly, there'd be no investigation; department wouldn't press charges. He'd give me a personal letter of recommendation. He knew I had good reason. Knew I didn't start it. Knew he had some cleaning up to do. Be a lot easier without me around."

"Oh, Silas, that must have been difficult."

"You'd think so. But truth is, it wasn't. Felt like clouds finally parting. Realized with the suddenness of a thunderclap that Salt Lake had nothing left for me. Just wanted to get out." He leaned over the table on his forearms. "Lease was comin' up. Had vested a good pension. Sold—or donated— everything but the dog bowl, some clothes. Loaded the Jeep, headed out to see some other places, figured I could look for work somewhere on the way."

"You just picked up and left?" She blinked. "Was there someone in your life? A girlfriend?"

Oh, boy, out of the pan, into the fire. Goin' to this topic next?

He sighed again. "Never went too far down that road. Kept to myself mostly. Can't really say why. Never could date much while ranching. Long stretches, outside of towns, mostly. Didn't afford much opportunity to be around somebody special."

Wren's eyes quickly scanned his face, his muscular shoulders and chest and arms, with a look of unguarded disbelief on her face. She said nothing—and she didn't have to.

"Did have a gal in Salt Lake briefly, but if I'm bein' honest, it just felt too hard."

Wren's eyebrows shot up.

Their server arrived with the check, and they both reached for their credit cards.

Wanna pay, since I invited her. But I'm on the defensive here, already looking like a Neanderthal. Push the bill issue too hard, gonna confirm it.

He put his card down next to hers without comment.

When the bill was paid and tips calculated, they walked downstairs. To get outside, they had to pass through the rich scent of roasted nuts being candied in a corner shop. Silas felt sweat on his palms. *Can't get a read on this. Might've blown it. Wouldn't blame her if she chooses to bail now.*

Without a word, they both turned left and began to stroll west along Commercial Street. Strings of colorful lights pierced the warm darkness. Banners and flags hung over the street. Voices swirled and blended with the faint sounds of buskers playing up and down the length of the town.

"God, I love this town on a summer evening!" Wren said.

Tone of that didn't sound too bad. Is it possible things aren't completely ruined?

"Understand why," Silas said.

"You were talking about just picking up and leaving Salt Lake City. It sounded like it was more than just the mess at work . . ."

"Like I said, it was a bunch of reasons. One was that I wasn't spending enough time with Bandit. He was startin' to act out. Rough up—nip and herd—other dogs at camp, some twice his size."

Wren laughed so suddenly, she was unable to prevent another little snort. "Silas Lopez had a dog in doggie day care?"

"Didn't say that." His tone was flat. "Said *dog camp*."

A third little snort escaped from Wren.

Don't love her tone, even if she's just teasing. I'm no latte-drinking yuppie.

A few strides flowed beneath them.

Not a deal-breaker, but I'd prefer if she got this instead of thinking it's a joke.

"Make a commitment to somebody, you see it through. Bandit's life is my responsibility. He's been loyal to me from the second he attached himself. Besides, I liked him more than any single human being in all of Salt Lake. Maybe all of 'em put together."

"I get that. I didn't mean to make light of it. Sorry." She rubbed his upper arm gently as if to draw the issue to conclusion, like punctuation. "You said it felt 'too hard' with the girlfriend. Mind if I ask how?"

He paused to formulate his answer, wondering if it was worth the gamble of opening up more than he already had. At this point, what did he have to lose? Might as well be honest about everything, all at once. He wasn't the sort who hid skeletons in his closet.

After a few more paces, he took a stab. "Guess, nub of it, she was making assumptions about the future. I worried for her. Could tell she was leaning in. Deserved better than what I was ever goin' to be willin' to offer her. Besides," he added with a dismissive wave of the hand, "there was always some dust being kicked up about one thing or another. That woman could start a fight in an empty room. Talk the ear off a cornstalk too."

He adjusted his long stride so he didn't outpace Wren as they walked.

"Better to give her a fresh start, look for whatever she was searching for. Not right to let someone invest in a dead end."

"With you being the dead end in that scenario?" Wren clarified. "Sounds like maybe you didn't love her, huh?"

"No. Don't believe I ever did."

'Course, I didn't even try. Kept myself guarded. Easier, safer that way.

He paused again, looking into the distance.

We really gettin' into this? Not sure how the hell all this mess is leakin' out all over the place like a busted feed sack. Hell of a night for truth-tellin'. Suppose no point holdin' back now.

"If I'm honest, Wren, I'm unsure about the whole love process. Not sure I got all the tools for it. Feels like tryin' to read a map upside down."

"Which parts are hardest for you?" Wren asked. Her tone was gentle, delicate, genuine.

"Countin' on 'em," he said, voice soft. "Havin' 'em count on you. Things of that nature. How to act. Especially now, with the rules always changing."

She nodded but didn't interrupt.

"I believe I'm a good man, Wren. I really do."

Gettin' a little worked up, but it's important for her to hear, so I'll need to see this through.

"Damned determined to be on the right side of history, but a lotta the time, I feel like a draft horse in a dance hall."

A slight trace of a smile showed on her face.

"Hard to know what's right these days. Even pullin' out a lady's chair can get you sideways."

Wren nodded. "Okay. I see. This topic is a long story, probably for another day, but I think I'll be able to help you with it." Wren clasped his forearm with two hands. "The chair was a lovely gesture, by the way. Noted and appreciated."

Silas bowed his head in silent acknowledgement and made a mental note.

Their walk had brought them into the West End. Away from the lights and sounds of the center of town, a dark hush enveloped them, just the swish of small waves curling onto the shore drifting between houses. They turned and walked out to the town boat ramp. Wren looked out across the harbor. In the dim light from a nearby window, he could see her warm smile transition into a more thoughtful look.

"Let me see if I can boil this down quickly," Wren said, "just as a placeholder for now . . ."

"Okay."

"In a nutshell, if you think about our changing social norms as an entirely new, detailed rulebook you need to memorize, you're thinking about it wrong."

He paid close attention to her words.

"Instead, just think of it all as one simple framework in which you weigh every statement and every action through the lens of minimizing assumptions about a person. It's simpler than it seems most of the time."

"Put it that way," Silas said, "sounds somethin' like the golden rule."

"Exactly. It's just about doing the best you can to clear your mind of inherited—possibly outdated—instincts, and instead replace them with thoughts about what would make the other person feel okay about themselves."

She turned toward him.

"For example, you probably had an instinct to pay for all of tonight's dinner, and I'm going to tell you right now that I will always want to pay my half in situations like that."

Silas's pulse quickened.

"Will always want"? Huh. Could mean there's more dates coming? Or not. Don't overthink it—eyes front.

"Okay. Good to know. Appreciate having things clear as a stream. And this is helpful. There's things to ponder. Could be useful when interacting with this new community I'm in here. Gonna think some on it." Silas stuffed his hands into his pants pockets. "Meanwhile, feel like I talked more tonight than the whole last year. Except for the parts that made me look like an idiot—or a hothead—it was surprisingly delightful."

"Surprisingly?" Wren asked.

"The talking, not the company." He winked. "Knew the company was gonna be better than a winning poker hand." He nudged her shoulder, like she'd done to him.

"Is that right, cowboy?" Wren said with a smile. "I've had a nice time myself. Learned some things about a pretty interesting guy. Fascinating guy, if I'm honest. But I also have some things to think about."

"Yeah, maybe I didn't put myself in the best light," Silas said.

It occurred to him that he should clear the air now, while he still had the chance.

"Tempted to regret that. But I'm of no mind to lie to you, Wren. Fact is, I can lose my temper standing up for what I think is right. And when I do, lotta damage can get spread around in a hurry. Gotta be honest with myself about it if I am going to fix it, and I feel I should be honest with you too."

Wren nodded slowly, her eyes downcast. "I appreciate that. And I am not standing in judgment. It's just that violence, Silas, is against everything I stand for, everything I do, everything I think is right."

He was taken aback to hear her voice waver. She looked up at him, and he could see her eyes were watery with emotion.

"It's not okay, Silas. It scares me. I can barely stand the idea that you carry a gun. The times I've noticed it on you, I've involuntarily recoiled in horror. I don't want to be anywhere near one of those things."

"I guess I can understand that," Silas said—not really understanding but just to say something. He felt panic rising and the urge to recover, to explain. "I come from a different world, Wren. Ranch people are a rough bunch. Fighting happens—it's part of the way of life, establishing the pecking order. And out alone in the high mountains, if a grizzly's got a mind to have a meal, a gun's a damn handy tool to have. Here, this line of work, a gun's just part of the job. But it's a tool to keep people safe, not to harm them."

"I know that. I appreciate how different our worlds are," Wren said. "It just scares me. Really scares me. And I'm confused."

Felt that one in the gut. She isn't accusing me—she's scared. Of what I might be.

"Confused?" Silas said, wincing inside.

"Yeah. I mean, how could I feel so safe with, so drawn to, a man who almost killed someone with his bare hands? How does that make sense, Silas?"

"I know it was wrong. I'm determined to keep a handle on it, and I've been workin' hard to improve myself," Silas said. It came out with more pleading in his tone than he intended. He felt a flush at the thought of appearing desperate.

"I know," she said, but it didn't sound like she really did. "I appreciate it is some kind of honor-code thing with men in cultures like the one you come from—but Silas, a big part of my job is to help protect women and children from violence. Violence overwhelmingly perpetrated by men. It's my deepest calling, the deepest instinct I feel. To protect the vulnerable, to get them justice."

We've got that in common. Could be an opening there.

"Making sure justice is served is something we both focus on," Silas offered.

He was scrambling.

She can almost certainly smell my desperation here.

"Something we have in common." He kept going, trying to turn the tide. "And you said you feel safe with me, didn't you?" he asked tentatively, hopefully.

Wren turned to face him. She looked up at him with a softening expression. To Silas, it felt like she was looking at him anew. He knew the look on his face was pathetic, but he couldn't help it. He felt like he was slowly disqualifying himself from something important. Something wonderful . . . something essential.

She shocked him by taking his hands in hers. "Yes, I did say that. Not sure why, but I do." She paused, like she was thinking deeply about her gut instincts. "I really do." Her grin widened. "And I also admitted I was drawn to you too, if we are going to be sticklers about accuracy."

"Believe you did," Silas concurred, hope suddenly taking flight.

"What I need to work out is why, Mr. Lopez," she said, spreading their arms out wide, looking up into his face, and pressing her chest and body against him.

At the touch of her body, Silas felt like he'd just grabbed an electric fence in the rain. Her eyes had mischief in them.

"I can't deny it, and I'll admit it's a powerful feeling—this sense of safety, being drawn to you. Given what we've just discussed, I can't begin to explain why I feel it, and if I'm being honest with you, it does confuse me." Her tone was gentle and reassuring. "But if you'll be patient with me, and don't beat anyone up in the meantime, I'm willing to put in the time figuring it—*you*—out."

A cold splash of relief hit Silas. He felt the blood drain from his head so fast, it made his ears ring.

"Thank you. Can't say how much that means. Will say for you, Wren Bradford, I've got all the time in the world."

Feels like I've dodged a bullet, but it sure grazed close.

Their walk back was mostly silence. The good kind.

CHAPTER 46

After his dinner with Wren, Silas took Bandit around his neighborhood for his last stroll before bed. Bandit was thrilled. Simple, happy, uncomplicated. Returning, he attached the leash ends together and draped it over the inside doorknob. He bent to scratch Bandit behind the ears, and in return, Bandit gave him a look of devotion.

Silas was still restless, like a saddle horse too long in the stall. It wasn't the heavy meal—he'd had only one steak, after all, and not even a large one by his standards. This feeling was in the gut, just not related to food. No, this was something else entirely.

Wren had been drifting through his thoughts like a background hum—subtle, constant, impossible to miss. She'd burst into his consciousness only a short time ago, but the effect had been like the sudden warmth of a sunrise over the mountains.

Things had gotten a bit knotty tonight. Weighty, important, urgent.

He found himself sitting with his thoughts in the dark stillness, not bothering to flip on a light.

He hadn't had many relationships, so he didn't have much to compare this to. Yet he felt an intuitive nudge, persistent as a heartbeat, that something important was unfolding with Wren. She stirred something in him he hadn't felt before.

He might not be able to characterize it, but it was there—the way you know a fire's caught, not from the flame but from the smell of the smoke:

hot, clean, and right. Just like that, the pull between them had shifted—from something uncertain, thick and gray and opaque, drifting low—to something thinner, bluer, hotter. A fire that was burning now, starting to consume the fuel around it.

Whatever this was with Wren, it had taken hold. He was a little confused too. It scared him, this feeling of being caught in a strong current with snags lurking just below, and it confused him that he felt no instinct to fight it.

He was kicking himself for not making it clearer that he would, of course, never hurt her. That wasn't in his nature. He'd grown up with a mother who'd received that kind of treatment, and he'd never in a thousand lifetimes be found on the other end of that, perpetrating the same violence.

Either way, he sure hoped that went without saying. But then, in her work, she dealt with men who did. Was it a mistake not to say it?

His quiet brooding was interrupted by noise over the police radio. Of course, it was Clark. Who else?

"Chief, can you read me? This is Sergeant Clark. Do you copy? I answered a call about a possible prowler. Looks like it might be a break-in going down, but I didn't want to act without your advice. Do you copy?"

At least he'd thought to ask for input before jumping with both feet this time. Silas sighed and picked up the mike, trying to be patient. *If nothing else, the kid had learned not to go in half-cocked.*

"This is Lopez. I copy. What's the sitrep?"

"The house is completely dark and looks empty," Clark whispered. There was a rhythmic, scratching noise like he was running to a different location so he could talk. "The neighbor heard a suspicious noise. The guy's slowly trying to jimmy every door, window—even cellar windows. Right now, he's in a window well in the back, trying to jimmy the cellar window lock."

Silas asked where the callout location was, and when he realized it was just a block and a half away from his apartment, he told Clark to surveil from a distance and follow the prowler if he left but not to approach alone—to hold off until he got there.

Moments later, Silas said softly, "Sergeant Clark, it's Chief Lopez here, comin' up on your six."

Better to be careful than to get shot.

It was cloudy. With no moonlight to brighten it, the alley was as dark as a cave. Silas could barely make out Clark's silhouette, turning to acknowledge his arrival.

"Gimme the rundown. What're we lookin' at here, and what's your recommendation?" Silas whispered.

It was too dark to see Clark's face, but he could tell by the tone of his voice that the sergeant was as taut as a coiled spring. "He doesn't know we're here, so that gives us the drop on him. I guess the textbook would say we quietly approach from two angles, weapons ready, until we're close enough to get our lights on him, identify ourselves, and order him to freeze. Once he's secure and we're no longer in potential danger, we would question him and figure out what he's up to. That would be the safest way to do it."

"Well, definitely one way we could play it," Silas whispered. "Agree, it would have a low-risk profile for us. Is that what you're suggesting, Sergeant?"

"I have a feeling you'd approach it differently, and I want to go through it with you and figure out how."

"Okay. Before we make any decisions, lemme ask you some questions real quick, see if you can get the gist of how I'd think this through."

Clark nodded in the darkness.

"First, what's he wearing?"

"Red sweater, blue jeans," Clark said.

"So, not exactly burglar clothes. See any tools? He wearin' gloves?"

"Saw no tools, and I don't know about gloves . . ."

"Notice his car? What can you tell me 'bout it?" Silas asked.

"Wagon. New Hampshire plates. I wrote down the plate number."

"Good. But what else?" Silas asked.

"I don't know!" Clark said. It came out a little sharp. "I'm worried he's going to get away if we don't hurry this up."

Silas had to make an effort to keep the impatience out of his tone. "Appreciate the concern, but I'm not convinced we're in a rush. Picked up a few additional details when I looked at the car, Sergeant. Feel like now's a pretty good time to discuss them."

He could see Clark turning to look at him and felt the mix of frustration and dread.

"You notice it's a new luxury Audi wagon?" Silas let that sink in. "Because I did. I peeked with my light and noticed two nice-looking pieces of luggage in the back. I could hear the exhaust still ticking as it started to cool, like it was hot from a long drive. Also felt the hood and grille—both are still warm as a fresh-baked biscuit, Clark."

Clark's shoulders dropped, tactical readiness evaporating. He looked at Silas like a student realizing he'd skipped half the items on a checklist.

Silas gave a directional jerk of the head, and they stepped back out to where there was a dim orange wash from a distant streetlight. To Silas, it was obvious that one part of Clark was baffled about all this car stuff, and the other part of him was sure he'd missed an obvious clue.

"Clark, this isn't a burglar—" Silas began to explain, just as the prowler came around from the back of the house. Silas flicked on his light and pointed it at Clark, illuminating Clark's badge and uniform to identify them as cops.

The prowler came to a halt.

Silas said in a cheerful voice, "Evening. Can we help you with anything, sir?"

"Scared me there for a second, Officer. Yes, this is our summer and weekend house, and I stupidly came all the way down from Hanover without my house keys. I was hoping for an unlocked window. Rob Hatcher," he said, sticking out a hand and brushing off leaves with the other one.

Silas shook his hand, taking in the candy-sweet smell of vape fumes coming from the man.

"Chief Lopez. This is Sergeant Clark. Understand your predicament. Sorry for your trouble, but I think we can get this handled."

He glanced to make sure Clark was following his lead.

"Okay, great. How?" Hatcher asked.

"In this situation, you got two options, Mr. Hatcher," Silas began. "One option—which is the extra-cautious one—is we ask you to leave the property, come back in the mornin' with a locksmith."

"Wait, where am I supposed to sleep, Officer?" Hatcher asked with the sulk of someone used to getting their way. "I'm exhausted after a long day at work and a long drive all evening."

"Hear you. We could recommend some places to stay, if you need suggestions." He looked at Clark, and Clark nodded in agreement.

"You said there were two options. What's option two?" Hatcher asked.

"Safe to assume there are some photographs of you inside, bills with your name on them, other identifying paperwork? Something matching the name on the car registration and a good photo ID you can provide?" Silas asked.

"Of course. We have utility bills for the house here and pictures and other papers."

"Perfect. What I figured. Then, we can help you find an easily repairable windowpane, carefully break it for you to gain entrance, quickly verify you're the owner, and get everyone to bed," Silas offered.

"I'll take that option," Hatcher said, eagerly handing Silas his New Hampshire driver's license.

"Had a hunch you would. Let's find a good window," he said, turning to face Clark. "Sergeant Clark, while we're breakin' and entering over here, can you go next door and kindly tell the good neighbor who called that they're safe, that the possible prowler has been identified as the property owner?"

Clark broke character from the sidekick role. "Uh, shouldn't we compare his ID to some papers first?"

"No need to wait. It'll match. Trust me," Silas said.

Clark gave him a quizzical look and hesitated a beat before shrugging and walking next door with a shake of his head.

"Thanks," Hatcher said. "The back door is under a portico roof, so if we break a window under there, we've got some weather protection. There's a row of panes all up and down alongside the door, so we can easily break a pane near the knob to let ourselves in that way."

"Sounds like a plan. After you, sir," Silas said.

Silas squatted down and used the back of his elbow to shatter the windowpane, removed the remaining large shards, and reached in to unlock the door. After he was done confirming Hatcher was the owner, Silas apologized to him for the hassle.

"Sure you understand, though—as a homeowner and community member—cautious is best."

Since Hatcher couldn't really argue with that, he gratefully thanked Silas for the help.

Silas let himself out the back door and walked down the narrow gravel passageway along the side of the house. He was met in front by Clark, clearly illuminated by the living room light now pouring through the house's front windows.

Silas thought for a moment, then looked at him and said, "Why did I think it was okay to send you over to the neighbor's?"

Clark sighed, seeing it all clearly now. "Because a burglar would not opt to hang around with police and get proven guilty. He'd promise to come back in the morning and then hit the wind."

"You're getting it, Clark. What else did we learn tonight?"

"Details matter," Clark said. He sounded less glum than Silas expected.

"They do. Takeaways? Common sense often goes further than textbook protocols. Practical solutions land better than perfect ones every time. And if you can help instead of punish, then do it."

Clark was nodding, his face cast downward.

"Don't go glum on me. You handled yourself fine. Got some good learning out of it. I appreciate your efforts, your initiative. I appreciate your help on this one."

"Yeah, guess so."

"Night, Sergeant."

He walked back home, feeling a bit more like himself.

Silas made good time to Carver. After crossing the canal, the town was twenty or so miles west.

Small rural town, beautiful. We're definitely in a different part of the country now.

The area was dotted with white steepled churches, low colonial-style commercial buildings, and old farmhouses, all connected by narrow rural roads lined with pine trees. Most of the area was flat, with low-lying sandy soils and agricultural fields cut into the dense woodlands all around.

At first, these fields struck Silas as like any farming area, but then he noticed the elevated sandy dirt roads and the deep drainage ditches running between them. Ponds dotted all throughout. Scruffy, crimson ground cover in each of them. *Bogs. Cranberry bogs.*

From what he'd turned up with quick research, this town had long been a major player in cranberries. The place didn't seem large enough, but a fifth of all the cranberries in the United States came from this one town in around 1900.

The history might have fascinated him, but the navigation frustrated him. Byrne had given Silas a list of the growers to speak to, but finding and getting into the farms proved nearly impossible.

This place is nothing like the wide-open West, where you can see a road's dust plume from ten miles away. So many roads here, none of 'em straight, all hidden in trees.

Many of the farms were invisible to passersby, obscured behind a thick wall of white pines and understory scrub. Entrances hidden on unmarked dirt roads that notched through the tree line. Everything was poorly marked, no street numbers.

After stumbling around, overshooting, mistakenly entering the back side of farms, and doing multiple U-turns, Silas paused to regroup.

Crashing around here like a bull with a stone in his hoof. Gotta be a better way.

He tried looking at the satellite view of the map on his phone. The farms were now easy to spot. The aerial view showed the massive scale of the growing operations. Pinching and zooming, he was able to locate the main entrances to the farms on Byrne's list.

Shoulda used this approach from the start, Silas.

The first two farms he stopped at were a waste of time. One was occupied only by a work crew repairing a dyke between fields. No one had heard of anyone named Tony Faria. The other had a reasonably helpful shift manager, but he didn't know anyone by that name, either.

When Silas's cruiser approached the third farm on his list, his mind's radar went off immediately. The foreman caught sight of him and turned on his heel, as if in retreat from the devil himself. *Something's off. This guy doesn't want to talk to me.*

The man couldn't evade Silas forever, though. After a "Police here; need to speak with you" and a semicomical "Sir, I can see your feet standing behind there," the foreman eventually gave up, stomping out from the dim barn to where Silas stood in the daylight.

"I need to ask you about a Mr. Tony Faria," Silas said. "You know him?"

There was surprise, maybe some fear in his small eyes. "Yeah, I know him," the foreman admitted—but it was grudging. The man's eyes darted anywhere but Silas's face. His receding hairline exposed a high forehead with thinning strands of sun-bleached hair parted on the side. Weathered, leathery, tanned face and neck. *Difficult to guess his age.*

"Know where he's at?"

"No, I haven't seen him in months."

Blurted that a little too quickly. Takin' an instant dislike to this guy. Then again, liars are never likable.

"That right?" Silas said. "Because I heard you give him work. This being harvest season, figured I could find him here. Got a couple of basic questions—traffic incident—I need his help with."

At the mention of police questions, some of the foreman's color drained, and his eyes took on a look of mild panic. *It's not hot. So, why the beads of sweat on this guy's upper lip? That sour body odor suddenly gettin' the best of him too.*

"Well, sorry I couldn't be more help," the foreman said, starting back toward Silas's cruiser as if to escort Silas off his property.

He hadn't noticed Silas wasn't following when he said, "The way you came in is the best way out. Should I call you if I happen to hear from Tony?"

Dripping with insincerity.

"Don't believe I've given you my number yet," Silas said, walking up and looking down to study his face. "Besides, drove two hours to come see you. Surely you wouldn't mind if I let the dog stretch his legs, have myself a look around before I leave?"

The man was looking behind him and sidestepping.

Tryin' to block my view of whatever's behind him.

"Ah, well," the foreman said, stalling. Then, after a beat, he added, "We're an organic farm. Can't have a dog relieving itself in our fields."

"Okay. I'll be sure he doesn't," Silas said with a smile before turning to the car to get Bandit.

"Wait!" the foreman said, running to catch up and confront Silas. "Don't you need a warrant to search a place of business?"

"Who said anything about a search? Just said I wanted to stretch my legs, find a stalk of grass to chew, and enjoy the fine view." *Hit him with the friendly, innocent face.* "Don't need a warrant for that, since I'll be doin' it with your permission."

Silas donned his most disarming smile, patting him a couple of times on the top of the shoulder.

"I prefer you don't. There's nothing here for you to see. I've got to get back to work. Why would I give you permission to look around? I have things I need to finish while there's still daylight."

Silas stepped in front of him and leaned toward his face until he was uncomfortably close.

"Because sooner I have a gander 'round here, sooner I mosey off this property into yonder sunset. Right, partner?"

The foreman nodded, resignation slumping his shoulders.

"Thank you. Appreciate your hospitality."

Silas put his forearm in front of the foreman and stepped past him, heading directly toward the gap between a large shed and a smaller outbuilding. The man stood with his hands on his hips, mouth open, watching Silas go.

Silas found exactly what he thought he'd spotted—the drooping ramp-style tail end of a black trailer. A large, two-axle flatbed trailer. With a half-length shipping container on it. The angle improved as he stepped through the gap between the farm's outbuildings. Silas felt a rush of adrenaline—it was hitched to a silver GMC truck with the license plate G53-R6Y.

At once, Silas grabbed his phone to call Evans to request backup from the local force. As soon as he'd hung up to text Evans a pin of his exact location, the foreman approached him from the side.

Silas casually tucked the phone into his pocket and pivoted instantaneously, moving improbably quickly for his size. He shocked the foreman by grabbing the front of his shirt with both hands and slamming him into the side of the shed. Silas knew from experience that catching suspects off guard with a sudden, unexpected show of force could encourage what his partner used to call "extreme candor."

The metal wall of the shed was still ringing as Silas hissed through clenched teeth, "Thought you said you hadn't seen Faria?"

The foreman's surprised eyes were as big as pie plates.

"Lyin' to me, you just drew yourself a bad hand. Don't like bein' lied to. Makes me real irritable, prone to grabbin' shirtfronts." Silas pressed his knuckles in a little to underscore his point. "Best tell me where your buddy is now before I get every state and federal agency in existence to come down, inspect your operation, tie you up in paperwork till birds eat every last berry."

The foreman was shaking his head wildly and waving both hands outside Silas's bent elbows.

Silas roughly pulled him forward and up by the shirtfront until he was right in his face. "Was it that you didn't understand the question? I need to know where Faria is right now, or you're 'bout to regret some of your life choices deeply."

"Look, man," the foreman said in a high-pitched, panicked voice, "I don't want any trouble here, all right? This isn't my farm. I'm just the foreman. I'm sorry I misspoke. Tony's just an old friend. He's no part of this operation. I just didn't want the farm mixed up in anything."

"Like what?" Silas asked.

"Like what, what?" the foreman said, appearing confused.

"Operation mixed up in *what*?" Silas said.

The foreman's eyes betrayed his realization, and he scrambled to recover. "You know, like whatever you're looking for Tony about?"

Credit for the attempt at a save, buddy, but not buyin' it.

"Said I needed Tony's help with couple of routine questions related to a traffic incident. How's that got anything to do with your farmin'?" Silas put his free hand on his chin and scrunched up his face in mock concentration. "I just said *questions*. You're the one talkin' about searches, tryin' to give me the bum's rush, lyin' to a police officer."

Silas stared at the sweaty, sun-creased, dirt-streaked face before him. The foreman looked miserable.

"Thing is, more I sit with it, worse it looks for you. I'm gettin' real curious about what kind of pebble might be in your shoe."

"Look, man, I'm sorry. *Really* sorry," he said, and he looked it, but it was too late for all of this backtracking now. "Like I said, I don't want trouble. I need this job. I got a young family. I swear, Tony's not a part of this operation. I know him from high school and occasionally give him some hourly work. I really need my job. I don't need any trouble from the police. *Please*."

Silas wasn't inclined to back off even an inch, despite this guy's smell.

"Sorry don't cut it. You already lost my trust. Faria's truck, trailer, and container are parked in the shade of your barn, and you expect me to believe he's not parta this operation?"

"Yes, sir, I swear."

"Well, can't take your word for it. Which's why you're gonna tell me where Tony is, so I can ask him 'bout it directly. Make me wait another second, that's a decision you'll sorely regret."

The foreman nodded vigorously, tripping over his tongue to say, "Buck's! Probably playing pool at the taproom. Buck's Taproom and Grill in town. That's probably where Tony is."

When Silas released the shirt, he didn't just let go. He flicked the shirt and its contents away with a shove, and the man stumbled back and crashed into the metal wall with a clatter, slumping down it a few inches.

Silas started back toward his cruiser. The Carver patrol unit had arrived. Sergeant Evans had called it in at Silas's request.

Silas introduced himself and explained what he needed done with the foreman.

"Keep him off his phone—no calls or texts warning his buddy, who I'm going to brace now. Secure the truck and trailer until a forensic team can collect them—the vehicle is a crime scene. This is my card, cell number. Appreciate the help. Gotta jackrabbit after the truck's owner."

Some gravel sprayed as he and Bandit headed back toward town. Daylight was burning, and Tony's trail could easily go cold.

CHAPTER 48

Buck's Taproom and Grill had seen better days.

Silas pulled past a rough-looking letter-board sign missing one wheel. The fluorescent bulb inside it blinked and flickered. He noticed the irregularly spaced letters advertised $1 Draft Beer Happy Hr. but didn't mention anything about what time happy hour was.

Silas pulled into the gravel lot, navigating among a series of large, dirty puddles. He parked far from the building in a quiet, shady spot for Bandit. After switching off the ignition, he sat to collect himself before going inside.

Now's the time to confront Faria—only way to get an unrehearsed reaction. Catch him off guard now, or he learns about the impoundment of his truck some other way. Need to see his eyes.

Satisfied he was making the right move, Silas got out.

The building was low. It had clearly once been a single-story house before it was bastardized by sprawling ramshackle additions and converted into a bar. The peeling paint bore discolorations and construction scars from an old porch that had been ripped away.

Drawing close, he could smell the stale beer pooled around the dumpster. Muffled music thumped through the wall.

Silas rolled his shoulders and grabbed the handle of a rusted steel door with an oval window. Fake diamond panes molded into the glass caught the light.

His eye caught bits of a faded "Visa/Mastercard Accepted Here" sticker clinging to the window. *Why let it fade and get ragged? Don't they give those to you for free? Some establishments have just given up hope. Quit trying.*

Silas's eyes adjusted to the gloom as he headed into the bar. He had no interest in the nonalcoholic beer, but he needed it to blend in. Elbows on the high bar, he began to look around. His eyes quickly settled on the group of sorry-looking men playing pool at the one table in the room.

Look at this crew. Seen cleaner dogs in a rainstorm.

He waited and watched. The pool game inched along slowly and chaotically. As the players took turns missing, they slowed and distracted one another with inane conversation.

Silas was dying to stick fingers in his ears when someone pointed to a player and said, "Tony, you're up."

The man he pointed to looked passably close to the dark-haired driver in the video from the wharf. Five foot ten or so and skinny as a stick. Twitchy, nervous. Eyes darting about. Rubbing at his nose. Pupils looked dilated even under the glare of the pool table's hanging Budweiser light.

Silas could see his pointy sternum bulging slightly through the sleeveless undershirt he wore. Over it, he wore a ratty flannel shirt with sleeves chopped off at midbicep.

Those sleeves cut by someone wearing a blindfold? Maybe Tony was wearing a blindfold when he got dressed. Still, there's a little lean muscle in the forearms and biceps, like you see on someone who used to work with a rake, shovel, maybe a paintbrush. No power in the twitchy shoulders.

Silas's first drink was gone, and the brown glass bottle of the second beer had grown warm in his hand. He'd been sitting there long enough to be certain which one was Tony and also to hopefully start sticking out among the small number of patrons.

Tony was trying to look cool and ignore the giant stranger staring at him, but Silas clocked him glancing his way now and again—aware and suspicious, but not enough to leave. In fact, Tony stopped looking weary and started looking irritated.

Scowl and nervous eyes say Tony doesn't like being watched. Little paranoid. Twitchy. Tremors in the fingers. Talkin' fast. Eyes a little too wide for the bright light over the table. A total cokehead.

The game broke up, and the players wandered off to the men's room, the bar for refills, and to tables across the room. Some watched with smirks as Tony decided to swagger up to Silas and said rapid-fire, "You got some kind of a problem, cowboy? This ain't no gay bar, you know."

"Need to talk to you, Tony," Silas said, standing from his barstool.

"The fuck you know my name?" Tony's head swiveled as he looked around frantically. Seeing nothing, he said, "What if I don't want to talk to you? Ever think of that?"

Silas looked down at him and said matter-of-factly, "Said I need to speak to you, Tony."

"And I said I didn't want to, so fuck off before me and my buddies make you."

Silas had a bored expression on his face. He stepped closer to Faria, leaned down, and said softly, "What you want don't enter into the equation. Just question of where we talk, and whether I'm pushing the soft part of your throat here," Silas said, jabbing Faria's Adam's apple with an index finger, "hard against the edge of my car's roof while we're talking."

Tony's red-rimmed eyes flashed with anger. The expression on his face looked like a bulldog chewing a wasp. Silas held up his badge.

Tony's anger gave way to a flash of concern before he held up both hands. "Okay, okay. You don't need to be an asshole. And you could have mentioned you were a cop, pig."

Silas said, "Let's go," and effortlessly shoved him with one arm toward the door. The motion was quick and economical, but it imparted enough force that Tony stumbled five steps before regaining his balance.

When Tony stopped near the door, Silas pushed him again and said, "Keep goin', you maggot. We're talking outside, so none of your friends are tempted to get themselves hurt."

Faria stumbled out the front door into the early-afternoon light, and they both blinked while their eyes adjusted. Birds chirped, and the air was fresh, with a light touch of autumn. It didn't fit at all with the hostile tension between the two men.

Silas wasted no time. "What were you doin' on Macmillan Wharf in Provincetown, middle of the night on September 2?"

Faria's eyes said it all in the split second before he recovered. "What? Why would I go there? I wasn't there. Who says I was?" Faria blurted.

"Good reason to believe otherwise—that reason bein' video footage that includes your license plates." Silas let that sink in. "So, cut the shit, genius. I'm not a guy who likes bein' lied to. Already well above quota today. Means my blood's all stirred up, and there's not a lotta leeway left for you to get creative."

"Bullshit," Faria said, trying to bluster his way out of the conversation. Silas was ready to concede this guy had nerve before he added, "Fuck off, buddy. There are no cameras on that dock. Besides, there's no law against driving on a public dock."

Silas nodded, then said, "But there is a law against running over people and fleeing the scene."

Tony froze, a scowl spreading like a rash. "Wait! What are you talking about? I've never run anyone over."

"But you were at the dock that night?" Silas asked.

"I didn't say that. And even if I was, I've never run anybody over." Silas noticed Faria had a new thought—one that gave him newfound confidence. "See for yourself. You can look at my truck. It's parked down at one of the bogs right here in town."

"I didn't say your truck ran anyone over. I'm sayin' your trailer did," Silas clarified, and Faria's reaction shifted again. Now, his confidence was gone. "That's why the state police are collecting it—and your truck—for forensic analysis. Inspection's gonna find some real serious problems for you, Tony. My guess? Worst problems be located on the trailer's right side."

Faria looked like a rat scrambling under a switched-on porch light. Silas could see the gears turn in the powder hound's scrambled brain. Someone in Faria's position should know with certainty he hadn't hit anyone with his truck, but the trailer would give him pause. Silas knew anyone who'd pulled a long, heavy trailer like that wouldn't be able to rule out the possibility categorically.

Still, Faria tried to stick with the false confidence. He let loose another torrent. "You're fucking crazy, man. I didn't do anything wrong. I never hit anybody. I'm a safe driver 'cause I can't afford to lose my license, man. I haven't been in any accident, but if I was, it'd be exactly that—an accident."

"So, you're sayin' there could've been an accident when you were driving in Provincetown that night?"

"No! I'm not saying I had an accident. Or drove in Provincetown! Something wrong with you, idiot? You got no right to take my truck. I need that truck—I got debt. I need it for work."

"Tony, didn't I tell you I didn't want to be lied to? Lyin' dirtbags make me madder than a cat in a mailbox." Silas grabbed his layered shirtfronts with both hands and said flatly, "You don't want them cat claws."

Faria squirmed against the hold on his shirts. "What's your problem? Got me constitutional rights as an American!"

His courage was failing him, and the bravado was faltering, so the civics lesson didn't land.

"You know what's buildin' around you? Clear picture of a lying, shirking, lowlife junkie in way over his head with debt to the wrong people. I already know you were on that dock. Left a dead man in your tracks."

Now he's rattled. Can see it in the eyes.

"Let's try it a different way. Exactly where were you that night? Ana Sofia already told me you weren't around, meaning you got some explaining to do."

Faria erupted. "You *went* there? This is police harassment! How the hell would I know where I was September 2? I'm gonna have to ask my fucking secretary and get back to you! What's it matter? I didn't do anything wrong. That means it's impossible for you to prove I did. If you could, you'd be taking me in right now!" Faria said with a stupid, smug look of satisfaction on his face.

This nostril jockey's set on stonewalling. Thinks this is just about a traffic accident. Got what I need for now.

Tony squirmed, and Silas kept the pressure on him while he decided.

Guy had any brains, he'd hit the wind. Plain to see Tony isn't smart enough to be a flight risk. Either that, or he can't afford to run without uprooting his baby and its mama or putting them at risk.

He shrugged at Faria and said, "May haul you in yet, Tony . . ." Then he let go and smoothed out the wrinkles in Faria's sweaty shirts in an exaggerated manner before walking away.

Silas rolled his window all the way down and stuck an elbow out as he wound his way back to the main road. *Found my guy. Got the trailer into the lab. Got a look of dead certain confirmation off his face and found a cranberry farm of interest. Not a bad haul for one day's work, Bandit.*

CHAPTER 49
Friday, October 3

Silas was heading out the side door when he bumped into Wren. He wondered if his face lit up as obviously as hers did. *Way I feel when I see her? Has to show.*

"Oh, hey there," she said. "Heading out? What are you two boys up to this evening?"

Her tone was so casual that Silas didn't pick up the hint right away.

"Stakeout, of sorts," he said on impulse. But that word hitched, and he had a different instinct. It had been a long day, and he wanted to spend some time with her, so he added, "Well, that's not right, not a stakeout—more of what I call a POP—parkin', observin', ponderin'."

Sometimes you need to sit still. Let a place, and a case, talk to you.

She looked confused. *You haven't given her an opening, blockhead.*

"Case I'm workin', something's not sitting right. Need to have a ponder." He looked her right in the eye and added with a grin, "What I'm drivin' at is thinkin' is hard, lonely work. Could use some company while I'm doin' it."

"You romantic fool. Inviting a girl to go on a police stakeout." Wren raised her brows with a smile, then splayed the back of a hand across her forehead theatrically. "Give me a moment while I recover from my swoon."

"Like I said, it's truly not a stakeout. Can't bring a civilian date to a police operation, much as that'd be nice, given the length of some stakeouts."

She chuckled.

"This is closer to a picnic. Just going to sit and think. Moon's pretty full tonight. Bright out there. Havin' a lady friend with me gives a good cover story," he said, winking. He hoped his eyes had the mischievous twinkle he wanted them to.

"It gets better! Now I'm a *lady friend* and an undercover decoy on a police stakeout!"

"No decoyin'. Promise. No stampedin' or crossfire, either. Just gonna sit there, let the place show me what I missed, have a think about what might be goin' on with my suspect."

Sounds flaky, now I'm sayin' it. But sittin' quiet works.

He turned toward her and cupped a hand around his mouth like he was about to impart a big truth. "Ya know, I can let you in on a secret: Herdin' criminals isn't that different from herding cattle. You spend a lot of your time watching and thinking to yourself, *Now why 'n hell are they doin' that?*"

Her laugh was instantaneous. It gave him a jolt of heat.

"Anyway, understand it's not much of an offer. Be a couple of hours, most."

"I'm too tired to work tonight, anyway. Sitting and taking in the view might be just my speed. If I decided to join you, what time would this not-a-date, not-a-stakeout be taking place?"

"Dark's best, so maybe pick you up around seven p.m.? Be fully dark by the time we're parked up back in town."

"See you then, partner," Wren said, cocking two index fingers, gunslinger style, and mock shooting him with a big grin.

CHAPTER 50

The moon was bright once the last of the clouds moved out to sea. Its rippling reflection dwarfed the pale ribbons of light from town.

From their perch, they could see nearly the full length of the wharf. The fleet rocked slowly on the rising tide. Low white dock service pedestals interrupted the wharf's dark walkway every few feet, casting small, warm pools of light in circles around their bases. The wind was still, and a growing chill had settled into the damp air.

Where we're at right now on this case, it feels like driftin' on slack water before a storm hits.

Silas had thought to bring Wren a thermos of chamomile tea, which she sipped silently. Bandit slept on the back seat, curled tightly into a ball against the cool air. To prevent fogging, Silas had the windows cracked open an inch. Occasionally, a soft sound from town would reverberate across the water. Silas stared into the middle distance, going ten or more minutes at a time without twitching a single muscle.

"I don't know much about stakeout etiquette," Wren whispered, "so I'm just going to come right out and say it: I'm a little cold. I think I underdressed for this night op."

"Top's canvas," Silas said, closing the cracked windows. "Let's the cold right in."

She doesn't need an explanation, dumbass. She needs a fix.

"Tea help at all? Chamomile felt like a safe bet."

"It's very good, and warm, and it was incredibly thoughtful of you, Silas. I appreciate it. Thank you." *There's more coming. Can feel it.* "However, as a heads-up for future stakeouts, you might want a separate thermos. The taste of coffee can linger. Overwhelms milder teas."

"Darn it! My apologies. That thermos got more miles on it than most old trucks. Might be time to add a new one to the stable." He turned toward her. "Appreciate the honesty. Hate the idea of fallin' short and you not sayin' so. Makes life easier when I don't have to read minds to get things *just so.*"

"Ha! How likely is that to happen, in your experience, Mr. Lopez? Don't think you need to worry about me not speaking up."

"That's true. And I'm glad of it. Like things running slick as new rope when you're around. Matters to me that you're comfortable."

He couldn't see Wren's blush in the dark, but he felt it just the same.

She took his hand and said, "I know you do. I can feel it. That means a great deal to me. Now, in the hopes of guaranteeing you a five-star review for this experience, any chance you have a blanket or something warm I could borrow?"

"Right! Forgot for a second. Think I do," Silas said before creeping around to the tailgate and rummaging to find a soft, worn, gray wool blanket. It had a broad black stripe at each end.

After getting back into the front seat and closing the door quietly, he laid it over her, spreading it smooth over her lap, taking care to reach across and tuck it snugly into the gap between her body and the seat, then up around her shoulders.

Wren sniffed the blanket once, then again, then leaned back. "Mmm. Thank you."

"Uh-oh. Smell okay?" Silas asked. He felt a little nervous.

"Better than okay," she murmured. "Heaven." Another sniff. "Woodsmoke . . . wet horse . . . juniper . . . and I think maybe . . ." she smiled. "Is that starlight I smell?"

Silas smiled. A wistfulness descended on him, and he stayed quiet for a long time. Finally, he said softly, "Imagine it is."

Wren didn't answer, though, because she'd fallen fast asleep.

He looked back at the water.

Heaven is right, he thought.

Silas had just asked Genny to team up with Clark to figure out what state prosecutor would be assigned to their hit-and-run case. He was in the middle of telling her to set up a call so he could brief the prosecutor and discuss the next steps when the phone rang.

Genny answered. "Hang on, Dr. Reynolds, I've got him right here." She put her on hold, still cupping the receiver in her hand.

"Chief, this is the medical examiner in Sandwich."

Silas nodded toward his office and headed in, Bandit trotting along behind him.

"Hang on, I'll transfer you now," Genny said, and Silas's phone rang a second later.

"Hey, Tammy," he said, sitting back in his desk chair. "Silas here. What you got?"

"Hey, Chief. I'm here with senior forensic analyst Neel Bhatt. He and I work closely together. We aren't done with the analysis yet, but I wanted to get you some preliminary info because this one's a doozy."

At once, his adrenaline kicked into high gear. Silas sat up, snatched the nearest pad of paper and a pencil. "Shoot."

"Neel, here, Chief. Good to meet you. Again, we're not one hundred percent sure yet until the labs are back and I can chemically confirm blood, fiber, and paint matches, but this trailer ran over something big, warm-blooded, and wearing clothing. Likely a human. I've got blood traces on the frame, leaf springs, tire sidewalls, fender, and the rusty bolt holding the license plate on. Plate's expired too, by the way."

Silas laughed, but Bhatt continued.

"I have a whole mess of blood and tissue traces on the ramp end of the trailer where it droops lower. Chief, this trailer ran somebody over, dragged them, cut them up for sure."

Knew it. Good thing. Been trusting that hunch since the first video.

"The forensic traces are a good fit for the injuries we saw on our victim. And just based on an informal visual fiber match from some fabric snagged and left behind, I'd bet my lunch it's your victim."

"Buyin' you two a lunch either way. Dealt with lotta MEs and forensic analysts in my time. You know your work. Learned a lot watchin' you. And appreciate the call for an early take too."

"There's no need for that. We're happy to help; it's our job," Reynolds said.

"Well, you did right by this case. And by me. Won't forget it," Silas said.

"Don't thank me yet. There's more . . . a *lot* more," Bhatt said.

"Oh yeah?" Silas asked, hit with another jolt of adrenaline. "Got my attention. What else?"

"We found a gun, some coke, and some oxy in the cab of the truck. It was in an insulated square, zip-up lunch bag under the passenger seat. The weapon was a cheap, nasty street gun—a Hi-Point C9 that looked like it had never been cleaned, with two extra clips sitting next to fifteen small bags of oxy. Just a couple of vials of coke, indicating it might have been a personal stash—but if I'm not mistaken, the small bags and total quantity are more than enough in Massachusetts for intent to distribute."

"Believe you're correct," Silas said, "but I'll confirm—have a call in to a prosecutor already."

Silas heard paper rustling on Tammy's end of the phone.

"The gun's listed as stolen, so ballistics will probably show it's been used in the commission of other crimes, but I haven't tested ballistics yet," Bhatt said.

"That's a haul. Sounds like our guy's been up to no good," Silas said.

"Wait. You still don't know the half of it, Chief," Tammy Reynolds said.

Just keeps gettin' deeper. Like diggin' in mud.

"There's more?" he asked.

Bhatt sighed and blew out a breath. "Chief, there are signs that people have been living in or at least riding in that cargo box on the trailer. When we cut the lock and opened it up, we found urine in water bottles, vomit, cigarette butts, a broken flip-flop, a sweatshirt, and wrappers from some kind of protein bar."

"Been wonderin' what that maggot was doing lugging that crate around," Silas said. "Now you've got me real worried."

"Exactly. Here's the weird thing, Chief. Those cigarette butts? Not a brand I recognize. And the wrappers—protein bars or energy bars—they weren't in English. I thought maybe Spanish at first, but I've seen enough of that to know that's not it."

Silas's mind reeled. *Sounds like foreign migrants.*

"One of our analysts did a quick web search and determined the brand of energy bar is sold in Latin America. Brazil, Venezuela, Colombia, Argentina," Bhatt said. "Turns out the label is in Portuguese, suggesting it's from Brazil."

Silas felt a chill ripple up his spine. *Looks like we've got our felony if we can prove it—but got a sinkin' feeling this might be bigger than we thought.*

"Startin' to get a hunch 'bout what this parasite's been up to," he said, sighing. "Thanks so much for the quick outreach. Lemme know when testing's complete. And no need to do ballistics just yet. With everything else here, an unlicensed firearm would be plenty to hold him."

"You got it, Chief."

Silas hung up, stunned.

What foul wind's blowin' through this town? And how the hell was he going to drag the bastard behind it into the light?

CHAPTER 52
Wednesday, October 8

Silas had to double-check the address. This old colonial-style shingled house on a beautiful village street with brick sidewalks and shade trees all around could not possibly be a DA's office. But the number matched what Genny had given him, and she never made mistakes. Plus, the sign said Cape and Islands District Attorney's Office Main Entrance.

I'll be damned. Things are a little different out here, that's for sure.

He stepped into the reception area. It was a small, stuffy old building, and the lobby had an uncomfortably low ceiling that hovered not more than six or seven inches above his head. A receptionist took his name, confirmed his appointment, and then told him to have a seat. Hat in hand, Silas ran through what he'd say.

The prosecutor's name was Mike Deegan. Silas had looked him up—liked to know what he was dealing with. Deegan was a senior assistant district attorney out of Barnstable. Early to midfifties, Silas guessed, which meant he was a lifer—a prosecutor who had stuck with public service rather than moving on to other, better-paying things.

With these guys, that usually meant one of two things: either Deegan had a genuine passion for public service, a desire to help the community, or he was a burned-out nine-to-fiver lacking the ambition and skill necessary to escape this role, just looking to get through the caseload.

Deegan had grown up and gone to high school in Hyannis before heading to UMass and Suffolk Law School. *Local—at least maybe he cares about the community. But no sense lettin' foolish hope run wild.*

Silas had dealt with prosecutors plenty of times. To the last one, they were overworked, hard to impress, and eager to move things along quickly.

More concerning, Silas had learned Deegan's office handled all felony prosecutions for three areas: Barnstable County, which covered the entire cape; Dukes County, which was the island of Martha's Vineyard; and Nantucket County, the island of Nantucket. Given how much ground that was, Silas assumed the office would be large. But the short list of employees his research turned up surprised him. And this small building wasn't exactly bustling. *Hopin' the short staffing is just a quirk of cape life, but this Deegan's almost sure to brush me off. Of course, showing in person ups my chances.*

Silas was shown into a cramped office lined with bookshelves and dominated by an old metal desk. It was buried under stacks of expanding folders, manila files, and more half-used yellow legal pads than Silas had ever seen. He had to step over and navigate around some additional piles on the floor to sit down. There was a notch between piles in front of the guest chair that Silas could peer through.

Deegan's voice and smile were warmer than expected. After a quick handshake, Deegan said, "I look forward to working with Provincetown's new chief of police."

"Pleasure's mine. Could use some help, bein' new to these parts. Got a tough case—felony murder, I think—and I'm lookin' for some direction," Silas said.

"Okay, sketch it out for me," Deegan said, picking up the yellow pad closest to him.

Silas leaned back, the chair creaking ominously under his weight. He'd done many case overviews. He quickly explained that a pedestrian was killed by someone pulling a trailer, how he'd tracked the driver down, and what evidence he had. He concluded with a mention of possible international human smuggling but admitted it hadn't been verified yet.

"Hmm. Not yet a rock-solid foundation, if I'm honest," Deegan said. "Good police work—great, actually. I'm not knocking that, but there are some complications."

Silas braced himself.

Prosecutors always want more. They want convictions too. Gotta remember we're on the same side.

Deegan went on. "For starters, the smuggling raises serious jurisdictional issues—the feds could take over a case like that. I'd steer clear of that part. Also, towing a big trailer has inherent blind spots. That lends itself to the defense arguing this wasn't an intentional hit-and-run. Could even suggest it wasn't especially negligent."

Silas's stomach churned.

Deegan continued. "Lastly, while it sounds like we've got the vehicle dead to rights between the video and the forensics, the case against your driver is circumstantial. The video ID is weak, and due to the burner phone, we have no trace to link him to the location. There's a commonsense presumption he'd be driving his own truck, but without more, any defense lawyer would have a field day with the lack of direct evidence."

Silas leaned forward again, chair groaning under him. He didn't say a word.

"I think you've got something here, but to be blunt, you haven't brought me enough to get a felony murder charge to stick."

Deegan paused, looking out his window to gather his thoughts.

"The unlicensed gun's illegal, and the drug quantity is enough to charge intent to distribute, but we can't link either to this death," Deegan added. "To get a felony murder in a case like this, we'd need to prove the collision occurred during an inherently dangerous felony, or the victim was struck during the immediate flight from one."

Silas was disappointed but not surprised. "Mike, you're circlin'. Land the plane. What's it boil down to, as of now?"

"Chief, without a confession, ironclad proof he was driving, or solid evidence this happened during a crime or right after or during a flight from, I could try and charge felony murder and tack on gun and drug enhancements, but I'd be pleading him out to negligent operation, possibly vehicular manslaughter. With negligent operation, he'd do some jail time. Probably a year. Lose his license for a long time too. If you're done gathering, that's what I would recommend you do."

Silas stared down at the tips of some winter boots sticking out from under the desk, summer's office dust on their toes. *Just one year of jail time? After all this? Feels like being told to turn a stampede into a parking ticket.*

"Mike, the problem is you're latched onto the wrong felony. I'm not trying to prove anything with the gun and drugs—it's the smuggling I'm trying to center this on," Silas said, and Deegan drew a horizontal line across his page and started scribbling. "That's my felony. He was hustlin' those migrants away from that wharf when he ran my guy over. That's the during-commission-fleeing-dangerous angle I'm working. I know the feds are handsy, but that's the needle I'm lookin' to thread."

"And you think these are internationally smuggled migrants?"

"Forensics found solid evidence the trailer was moving people, most likely Brazilians. Still trying to understand the to-and-fros, but likely brought in from a bigger ship in international waters."

"See, I wouldn't touch that if I were you. You don't have the resources to investigate, let alone stop, something like that. Once you ask for help, this thing gets taken out of your hands—your guy with it. If you want to get this guy, smarter just to pick him up and charge him with negligent operation. With what you have and a little more legwork, we can make that stick. Do a year, lose his license for a long spell. Don't get greedy. Take the win."

Deegan had the tired finality of someone who had struck ten thousand plea deals—seen it all, no longer surprised or impressed by anything.

Silas looked him in the eye. "To be clear, you're saying I might want to back away, not that I *have* to back away, right? I'm allowed to investigate this local crime even if there's some possible federal gray area, aren't I?"

"Well, yes. Local PD can investigate local crimes, even if they overlap with federal cases—so long as they're not obstructing federal operations," Deegan admitted.

"I'm not obstructing anything. I'm just chasin' a runaway truck."

Deegan shook his head. "Well, it's complicated. Where it gets murky is when local action interferes with an ongoing federal investigation. Like causing a suspect to flee or evidence to disappear."

Silas leaned forward in his chair for emphasis. "But if I'm not doing that, I'm okay, right?"

Deegan sighed. "Look, Chief, I am not here to bless your approach or give you permission, you understand? You asked me a question of law, and I'm explaining that legal point. We clear?"

Silas leaned back, a little annoyed. "Appreciate the help."

"Here's what the law says: if you have probable cause to pursue your driver for a local felony—your fatal hit-and-run would qualify—and the feds haven't deputized you or embedded you in their investigation, then your pursuit is technically justifiable."

Silas nodded. "Lines right up with my gut, Mike."

Deegan held both hands up, palms forward. "Just because it is allowed doesn't mean it's a good idea or that you should do it. Messing around where you don't belong is risky if it steps on federal toes. I've seen careers hurt by this stuff, Chief. Don't be a cowboy."

Deegan looked at Silas's shirt and the wide-brimmed hat on the chair next to him. His color went deep red, and he swallowed awkwardly at his choice of words.

Silas grinned. *This guy doesn't know the half of it. Be funny when he finds out he's talking to an actual cowboy, let alone a lawman as stubborn and determined as me.*

Silas stood. "Well, appreciate the advice and concern—real solid and practical. Need to let it percolate. If I'm honest, I might poke at it some more. See what's under the next stone or two. Can I circle back to you?"

Deegan stood too and extended a hand. "Sure. Fine. You've been warned," he said with a smile. "And, you know, it's not all bad, Chief. It's kind of amazing that you found this guy. Who knows? Maybe you can jam him up enough to get a clean confession about being the driver."

"Hear you. It's a fallback, but I'm hungrier than that—I want this roach for felony murder, so I wanna prove he was up to no good on that wharf. I'm mule-stubborn like that, always have been. But thanks for your help. Back to you before long."

Silas tapped the door twice with his palm as he showed himself out.

He got back into the car and ruffled Bandit's fur for a long while, thinking hard on what to do next.

Could close the books. Got enough to lock him up. Should feel like a finish. But it doesn't. Not when folks are being hauled through my harbor like livestock. Not when the man drivin' that truck don't give a damn who he runs over. That's not just a crime—it's rot. And if it's touchin' my town, I'm gonna cut it out at the root.

Don't much care if the law says quit while I'm ahead. Feels like leavin' a fire smolderin' just 'cause it ain't jumped the fence yet.

Ain't how I was raised. Ain't how I do things. So, no. I'm not done.

CHAPTER 53
Friday, October 10

A small throng of people had gathered to watch a street performer in front of Town Hall on this cool but surprisingly bright day. Silas rushed down the steps and wove through the knot of people, anxious to get where he was going. He caught a glimpse of Wren coming the other way, arms full of papers, bag strap slipping, frustration on her face—but couldn't afford to stop.

Can't ask after her right now. Deal with that later.

He brushed past her with urgency, but with his width, he was unable to avoid bumping her on his way by.

"Hey, where's the fire, Officer?" she blurted, swiveling to see where he was going.

Without turning around, he lifted a hand in passing—just enough to register her voice, not enough to make it friendly. He didn't slow, didn't speak, didn't look back.

He was rushing to the scene of a single-car wreck in which a teenager had been hurt.

The injured teen and a buddy had swiped a police cruiser for a joyride, wrecking it. A couple of complaints about reckless driving had barely come in before they'd lost control on a sharp bend on a forest road out near the campground. The car blew wide and stuffed itself into a pitch pine.

Arriving on scene, Silas noticed the ambulance was blocking one lane on the steep uphill corner and immediately called for one of the patrol officers to come out and manage any traffic flow. He got out and approached the paramedic in charge, nodding toward the ambulance. "One of those kids looks rough. Airbag fail to spark?"

The paramedic shook his head, saying, "Oh, it lit off all right. The kid just wasn't wearing a seat belt and was closer to the center of the car, so he went face-first into the console and your police computer equipment."

"Injured bad?" Silas asked.

"He'll live, but he might have a scar or two on his face, depending on whether anybody gets a plastic surgeon involved. Gotta ask—how the hell did these kids get into this car in the first place?" the paramedic demanded, a scowl on his face.

"I aim to find out," Silas said, walking in the direction of Sergeant Clark, who stood behind a cruiser in the shade at the side of the road with a pale and drawn-looking expression. "What kind of goat rope is this here, Sergeant?"

Don't wanna come down too hard—he's been showin' effort. But Jesus, what kind of circus is this?

His pudgy cheeks flushed, Clark said, "Domestic call out up behind the high school. Wasn't planning to leave the vehicle, but I heard shouting, and no one answered when I called out. Stepped away from the vehicle momentarily, and then the husband and wife burst out of the door, slapping each other. Got dragged into refereeing and separating them, making sure she wasn't hurt. When I turned around, the car was gone."

Silas nodded, then scuffed the roadside grass with the toe of his boot. "Seen barn fires go better, Sergeant. Kid got hurt. Worse, people out on the roads could have got killed."

"I know, Chief," Clark said. "I screwed up bad. I get that. I'll try to make this right."

"Time for talking later," Silas said. "For now, I've sent for a patrol officer to come down here and manage traffic. You finish processing this scene and get this cow patty cleaned up. If the parents don't come here to the scene, get a hold of them and talk to them on your way back to the office."

Silas surveyed the wreckage. "Don't see how we can avoid pressing charges here, do you?"

"No," Clark said with a shake of the head. "Some of the blame's definitely on me for creating the opportunity, but those kids broke all kinds of laws here. They are going to need to answer for that."

"Expect so," Silas said, nodding as a feeling of sadness and frustration overtook him.

CHAPTER 54

When Silas returned to the office, a note was taped to the screen of his computer. He pulled it off and opened it. The handwriting was neat and scrawled in blue ink. *Private school handwriting.*

It read: *You seemed preoccupied this morning. Heard it's already been a challenging day. How would you like something home-cooked for dinner? Maybe chili? Email or call me before five if you're up for it, and I'll hit the market on the way home. You could swing by around seven? —Wren*

Nearly trample her, and this is the response? Offers to feed me. Like some kind of angel. I don't deserve it.

Silas was still studying the note when he smelled lavender. Genny leaned in his doorway, arms crossed, giving him the look.

"You found it," she said.

"You know about this?" Silas asked, raising the note slightly.

"She stopped by earlier. Said you nearly knocked her down rushing out this morning, then didn't wave, apologize, or even speak to her. She wanted my take on whether you were mad at her or just being you."

Silas winced. "Wasn't intentional. You saw how things got sideways around here today."

"She figured that out before I told her. Smart girl, Wren Bradford. But you don't exactly make things easy for people," she added, raising her brows.

He glanced up, confused. He took in the scowl on her face. "What's that supposed to mean?"

"That means you're about as readable as a fence post. Not just today. She spent twenty minutes fussing over that note. Wren's sharp, and she's patient, but she deserves better than guesswork and crossed signals."

Silas flushed. Cleared his throat. She was taking him out behind the woodshed.

"Wasn't lookin' to cause trouble."

Genny raised an eyebrow. "Yeah, yeah. You always mean well. And I didn't say trouble, Chief. I'm just reminding you that Wren's no fool. She sees through the quiet cowboy routine and wants to figure out what's underneath it. She's reaching out because that poor dear thinks you're worth the effort for some reason. It might be decent of you to meet her halfway."

Silas glanced down at the note again, feeling something shift inside him. "She spent twenty minutes on this?"

Genny cracked a small smile. "She went back and forth—envelope, no envelope, envelope again—paperweight, tape, paperweight. Finally, just taped it on your screen. If it didn't break my heart to see her struggle, I'd say it was the cutest thing I've ever seen."

"Breaks your heart how?"

"She's good with people. But she's struggling with you. You're inconsistent. You have a good time together, then she doesn't hear from you. She never knows what's going on, where things stand. Heaven help her. But she won't put up with it forever if you don't get your head in the game."

Silas shifted uneasily, giving Genny a helpless look.

She picked up on it and spelled it out.

"That note? She's put herself out on a limb, Silas. That's big. She's a special one. This town's lucky to have her. And I swear, if you let her fall off that limb because you can't get out of your own way, I'll climb a step stool and wring your neck myself."

"My neck—" he started, then stopped when he saw the set of Genny's jaw. "Wait, you sayin' she's . . . ? Me . . . ? Feeling serious?"

Embarrassing to be discussing this with Genny, but not as bad as it might be. And we're up to our necks in it, so guess we'll see it through.

"Yes, she's getting some feelings for you somehow," Genny said, and Silas winced at her use of the word *somehow*. "And after the brush-off, she was worried she'd upset you."

Silas rubbed the back of his neck, throat too tight to swallow. "Didn't mean to stir dust. Was a mess around here. Reckon she does deserve better'n that." He glanced at his watchless wrist. "Damn. What time is it? Gotta email her before five."

Genny grinned, backing away. "Relax, Chief, it's three thirty. Plenty of time to get back to her."

Dumbass. Rushing around for no good reason. Some things matter more than bein' first on scene. Don't get many second chances with someone like Wren. Better use this one wisely. Already on thin ice over the temper stuff. Get it together. Don't screw this up, Silas.

CHAPTER 55

The team assembled in the briefing room that afternoon. Silas had calmed down somewhat about the wrecked cruiser. They had a lot to catch up on—Clark's patrol car was just one topic. *Take no joy in singling him out, and I don't want to spook him back into his shell, but we've gotta face this issue head-on. Too serious, too good of a learning opportunity.*

"Afternoon, everyone. Learnin' day today," he said as his team funneled into the room. "Grab a seat; get real comfortable. Lotta miles to ride, so let's get after it."

Officers settled into their usual places, setting water bottles down, pens and pads at the ready.

"No sense beatin' 'round the bush," Silas began. "Sergeant Clark slipped up this mornin'. Might seem like a small thing—could've been any of us—but this slipup hits hard. And bad as it was, we're lucky it wasn't a fair sight worse."

Everyone looked uncomfortable—none more than Clark, whose beet-red cheeks and downcast eyes were locked on the floor in front of his feet.

"First, you should know, I don't bring this up to single the sergeant out. We all know he's a fine officer, me included. Valuable member of this team." Silas gave Clark a reassuring nod, and Clark returned it with a wan smile of appreciation. "And I mean it when I say it was the kinda oversight that could happen to any cop rushing too fast. That's why it's so scary.

Only a liar would claim he's never forgotten to latch a corral gate once or twice in his time."

He received nods from several of the team, and Clark's shoulders relaxed a bit.

"Reason I bring this up is 'cause there's lessons we gotta learn. Got lemons, gonna use 'em for lemonade." Silas scanned their faces. "Cops have procedures and checklists for a reason. We do dangerous things, do 'em fast, sometimes with a lot of force. Drive at high speed, carry firearms, rush into dangerous situations. Takes half a second for a situation to go sideways."

He paused to make sure everyone was paying attention. The room was tense with a stretched silence, all eyes on him.

"Cops have learned a lot of lessons the hard way through time, and we've got the gravestones and folded flags to prove it." Many of those eyes previously on him dropped to the floor. Somehow, the room felt even quieter than before. "So, we've taken those lessons, whittled them down, carved 'em into smarter ways of doing things. We teach those smart ways as procedures, checklists, and steadfast rules. One of my old instructors said it best: 'Standardize, memorize.'"

Silas walked over to pick up his water before continuing.

"Reason being, you always do the same thing, same way, and so does everyone around you—it becomes second nature. Habit." He scanned their faces, nodding slowly, then added, "Guess what? Habits save lives. *They do.* Situation can spiral outta control faster than a rattlesnake strike, so you cut one little corner, step away from the script for one second, let your attention get pulled away—you can quickly find yourself miles from where you need to be."

Heads nodded; a couple of pens scribbled. Silas took another sip of water.

"Wanna bullet in your foot? Get outta the habit of throwing the safety on your service weapon. Wanna chair smashed over your head? Skip the handcuffs just one time when breakin' up a bar fight. Cause the death of an innocent child? Skip the siren at an intersection; place your weapon somewhere other than your holster; leave a patrol car running, unattended, with the door open."

And there it was.

Clark's cheeks were back to being the deep-red flush of embarrassment. His colleagues averted their eyes and looked like they were thanking their higher powers they weren't in his shoes right now.

"Yeah, we lost our newest patrol car, a vehicle we can't afford to replace until I take time away from police work to help sort the insurance claim." Disappointment, frustration, definitely. But it was pure fear and the shakiness of a too-close call that was animating him right now. "Losin' a new car is bad, sure, but at the same time, it's nothin' compared to what it could've been."

He slapped the table, which thundered under the blow, and everyone around it jumped.

"*Damn it*, kids could've been killed, or could've killed somebody!" Silas boomed, blowing off some steam and letting his anger and fright show a little. "This ain't about a car, ain't about some kids doing something wrong. Kids'll always do dumb shit—young brains just don't fire right. Never did. Never will."

He could tell people wanted to laugh at that just to relieve some tension, but they didn't. They looked cowed.

"It's about the fact that those kids could've badly hurt someone and *used our patrol unit to do it*! How's that likely to sit with the community we've been hired to keep safe?"

Let that sink in for a moment.

"Lemme repeat myself, make sure nobody mistakes me. Incident this morning wasn't a story 'bout bad kids stealin' our car. It's a story about *us*. Us failing to secure a dangerous vehicle properly, even though we had all the time in the world to do it."

Most eyes were cast downward. Marsh and Byrne, however, kept their heads up, eyes alert, and nodded to indicate they were listening.

"What's next? Gonna fail to secure a firearm, get somebody shot? No, we are not! Not on my watch." He took a deep breath. "Hope I'm making myself 'bout as clear as a slap in the face. Do any of you need me to elaborate?"

His eyes scanned every single face in attendance. Each officer nodded—all silently, solemnly, and it felt like he'd made his point well enough. Sergeant Clark looked about ready to leap out of the nearest open window.

"All right, I've said enough for now, but we're going to come back to this. Figure out the right way to review checklists and procedures—and hold ourselves and each other strictly accountable for following them."

Silas looked pointedly at his two sergeants and Genny. Even she looked solemn in light of the day's events. He turned to put his water down, gathered his thoughts to change channels mentally, and faced the room again.

"Next item," he went on, clearing his throat. "We've got developments on the Perkins case. Situation there brings us to a fork in the trail, and how your gut reacts to that fork tells a lot about the kinda cop you might wanna be. Like I said, this here's a learnin' day. We're gonna use this opportunity to talk about career paths a bit too."

Silas saw a few confused looks in the group.

"But first, an update on the Perkins case. Had to beat some brush to find the GMC pickup, but we finally tracked it down at a cranberry bog in Carver. I found the owner attempting to play pool at a taproom not far away. Long story short—impounded the vehicle, and the forensics say that sure enough, it looks like our truck and trailer."

There were a few whoops of approval in the crowd. Silas noticed Marsh and Byrne side-eyed each other with excited, satisfied looks.

He raised his palms, calming them down. "Official confirmation is still in the wind, mind you, but I'd say it's sure to come. The forensic team also found a stolen nine-millimeter firearm and enough bags of oxy for a charge of intent to distribute. Looks like our guy is a cokehead too."

The crowd began murmuring. Evans piped in with, "This is a huge development, sir."

Silas scoffed, shaking his head. "That's just the front porch. House runs way back."

"There's more?" Marsh asked.

"A lot more," Silas replied, exhaling. "Lowlife also looks to have been haulin' human beings in the container on that trailer."

Gasps of shock escaped the team.

"That's right. Lookin' at a god-awful, sorry mess here."

Just arrived in this town, already up to my neck in a cesspool.

"But snag is, we got no ironclad proof he was the driver—or he was even here in town."

Gotta slow it down to make sure people understand how this works.

"Got a brief, grainy shot of his profile, other circumstantial points, sure, but with no phone trace, no eyewitness. What we got, prosecutor says he can probably toss him in jail for a year—at most two, with aggravating factors. The DA would throw the full book at him, then deal it down to negligent operation."

The team made sounds of anger and disappointment, shifting in their seats, their faces spotlit by the warm afternoon light.

Silas took a deep breath and watched some dust motes drift through the light for a moment as he thought.

"Now, bad as that sits, where it stinks like a buzzard's breakfast is there's a felony murder charge, with big run in the joint attached, sitting just beyond our grasp."

Who's got the look? Who among them is hungry for that?

"Fact is, if we could prove Faria caused the crash while fleeing from the scene of a violent felony, well . . . we could throw away the key. And that brings us to the career-day bit of this meeting," he added with an upbeat tone.

Mouths gaped. Everybody in the room, including Genny, looked at him like he'd lost his mind.

He scanned their faces before continuing, undeterred.

"See, there's two ways to look at a pickle like this one. One person might look and say, 'Caught that shitbird who ran our victim down, and he's goin' to pay the price for negligently operating his vehicle, as he should. Punishment fits the crime we got, so this is a job well done.'"

Clark and Burig nodded at this logic.

"Another person might look at this mess and say, 'This maggot was up to something far worse than just driving like an idiot, and I'm not goin' to rest—not gonna think about anything else—until I figure out what it was, pin it on him, and punish him for every damn bit of it and then some.'"

He noticed Marsh, Byrne, and Evans nodded at this while Clark's and Burig's brows furrowed with disapproval. Silas made a mental note of their reactions before he continued his lesson.

"Now, neither of those views is wrong. Police work's about facts—the kind you can weigh in your hand. Not flights of speculation, running around like a hawk on a windy day. Truth is, cops have limited time and even more limited resources."

Silas gestured, both hands to his left, setting up a comparison.

"Some officers look at a rodeo like this one and think pragmatically. Gotta do most you can with what you've got. Recognize you can't always get every last drop. World keeps churnin' out new criminals and fresh trouble. Perfect is the enemy of good enough."

Out of the corner of his eye, he saw Clark and Burig still nodding, and Genny caught his eye, clearly noticing him cataloging reactions.

Then, Silas gestured to his right.

"Other officers hit a milepost like this and get fixated—obsessed with getting to the next one. Solving the full mystery, getting to the bottom of the big picture, making sure the bad guy's exposed and punished, fullest possible measure of justice served."

The energy in the room was restless, uneasy. He could feel it. People were struggling with the conflict between opposing viewpoints, and it looked like several were starting to wonder where this was going and where they stood in the scope of it.

Silas plowed ahead, knowing it would all become clear soon enough. "Two basic career tracks in police work, and everyone who stays in policin' will figure out they're more suited for, and drawn to, one over the other."

Marsh, Evans, and Byrne were all paying rapt attention, like this was clicking. *Some are starting to understand now.*

"One's a patrol officer and managerial type of role," Silas clarified. "Other's a detective. Now, detective work—that seems sexy. They make TV shows about it, after all."

After a pause, during which he caught Clark's and Burig's eyes, he warned, "But don't be too quick to draw a bead. Being a uniformed officer is nowhere near as mundane as you might imagine. It pays the same pension but has regular, family-friendly hours—what some might call a work–life balance. Generally, you can leave your work problems at the office at day's end."

He could tell that people were weighing the trade-offs in their minds, and he kept the list going.

"You can schedule—and actually take—a vacation." He pointed out the window toward the center of town. "You can work regularly with members of the public. Get to take leadership positions, become a manager of other members of the force. Hell, a good administrator runs the whole operation on some level."

Clark and Burig are getting it, but some of the others are also starting to relate to the trade-off.

"If you're someone who likes to organize, keep order, get trains running, it's just the ticket. Get to go home every night knowing in your gut that the job is done, and done well."

Silas paused to let it sink in for a beat. The room, filled just moments ago with confused faces, was now a circle of rapt attention.

He switched to an expressive, booming, low-toned voice. "Being a detective, on the other hand, has some serious downsides. You'll work all the time, day or night, but for the same pay. You'll get up before the sun, go out in a cold, driving rain, and deal with grisly crime scenes, look unspeakable tragedies right in the eye."

He noticed Marsh, Byrne, and Evans were still nodding, albeit somewhat more reservedly.

"When a case lands, your plans—family or otherwise—scatter like quail in a mesquite thicket." He looked around at the sober faces and made a dismissive hand gesture before saying in a loud voice, "Hell, that's the easy part."

He let some suspense build, turning his head and sneaking a wink to Genny, who beamed.

"Worst part of it all is, unlike a uniformed officer who regularly feels a measure of completion, feels satisfaction of job done right, on the detective track, you are going to your grave with open cases that've nagged at you your whole professional life. Hell, that alone drives some to crawl into a bottle."

Silas looked around. Folks were finally starting to get it.

He caught Genny's eye, and she winked back at him and grinned with obvious approval. It was clear she cared about this team and was thrilled to see him methodically investing in their development. *Truly appreciate her. Good soul.*

Silas walked closer to the table and leaned on it with his two hands, spread apart enough to lower him down a bit, signaling a new phase of the conversation.

"Now, we can take our time with this, let it simmer for a spell. But that choice is in the path of every cop, like a low-hanging branch over the trail. Like it or not, you're gonna need to contend with it, or hit your head."

He pointed a finger toward his forehead for emphasis before moving it down to his abdomen.

"Sooner you figure what's in your gut, sooner I can grab a spade and help you dig in that direction."

People are smilin' for a change, but I don't want anyone gettin' too loose—have to ground us back in the here and now.

"I should also point out, this outfit ain't big, and our seasonal swing's wild, so complete specialization just ain't on the menu at this particular eating establishment. Everyone'll learn from each other's work at case meetings, lend a hand when needed. And there's gonna be times—Fourth of July fireworks and whatnot—when everybody's pullin' traffic duty."

Silas heard some soft groans but ignored them as he brought the speech to its conclusion. "But to the extent you like a track, I'm happy to put you on it, make sure you're successful at it."

He stood quickly and clapped his hands together in a way that made a couple of people start.

"All right, meetin's over. Time to get back to it," he said, circling a hand and forearm in a helicopter motion. "Let's go catch bad guys. Meantime, you have any questions about this stuff, big or small, you come see me. Get every single one of you sorted out and on the track that works best for you and the department."

People started to get up.

Over the murmuring din, Silas said, "Clark, you're ridin' with me."

CHAPTER 56

Silas closed the door to his office after Clark stepped in. "Sergeant, hope you realize I didn't enjoy singling you out. Meant what I said about you bein' a good officer. And I'm damn proud of the progress you've been making. Perhaps most important, your attitude has gone from a thorn in my side to a workin' gear in this here gearbox."

He reinforced the point with eye contact.

"But, son, a grizzly bear of a mistake's a terrible thing to waste. If we've gotta go through it, might as well spread the lesson around. Burden shared, burden halved, and all that." He slapped Clark firmly on the back and said, "Think you can forgive me for making you an example, shake it off?"

"Yeah," Clark said, expression fragile. "Could've been worse. I royally screwed up, and instead of punishing me, you used it as a teachable moment. And I guess you did it in the kindest way you could've. I get it."

After a pause, he looked around and said, "Is that all? That what you called me in here for?"

You wish, buddy.

"No, we got a few chores need doin'. One of them will make muckin' stables look fun; others aren't too bad," Silas said with a grin.

"Oh, man. Don't love the sound of that," Clark muttered.

"You and me are gonna go see Mr. Flood."

Clark's eyes widened, and he froze.

Silas ignored the balk and steamrolled ahead. "No, no. Gonna be productive. Visit's gonna bag us three birds with one stone." He looked at Clark. "First, you're gonna explain to him about the patrol car before he hears it from someone else. Gonna tell him how it happened, what we learned, why it won't happen again, why he needs to keep it in perspective."

The look of horror on this kid's face is as plain as the stripes on a flag. But we'll steer him through it.

"Calm yourself, son. This gives him a chance to see you grow, take responsibility, handle a bad situation well, show leadership . . ."

"Aw, hell," Clark said. "What are the other things?"

"Attaboy. Next, you're going to help me give him an update on our Perkins case by standing there and quietly lending support to my, ah, recommendation on next steps. You will be nodding in agreement at all the right places," Silas said with a sly grin.

"Okay, I can do that," Clark said. "Is that it?"

"Third item happens all by itself," Silas said.

"Oh, yeah? How so?"

"It's us showing Mr. Flood that you and I were able to wrestle your head unstuck from your ass, and we're now working well together."

Silas had a big smile and a mischievous look in his eye that conveyed he was joking around with Clark.

Hope he knows that was a joke. From that nod, it looks like it.

CHAPTER 57

Upstairs, they settled into Flood's guest chairs. Clark did a solid job walking him through the theft of the cruiser. As Silas had suggested, Clark stated that the department took it seriously, was using it as a training exercise, and would initiate a review and conduct drills to ensure adherence to procedures. Clark said the department would be getting reimbursed by insurance.

Went a bit light on his own culpability, Silas thought.

He also glossed over how close we came to a full-blown disaster. And if we're pickin' nits, he padded it a little with that story about how we hated to lose the car, how most police cars had short, rough lives, and how our department did far better than most in terms of average service life of its vehicles. Could have lived without all that, but gotta admit, it was almost certainly factually correct and pretty fast thinking.

When Flood looked over for confirmation of the tale, Silas gave him a curt nod.

Overall, Silas was relieved. Flood took it all pretty well. *And the way his eyes are zipping between me and Clark . . . Looks like satisfaction with us working well together. That's the two easy items down.*

"Okay, we'll file that under *S* for *shit happens,*" Flood said. "But one more dumpster fire like this, and heads'll roll." He paused. "What else have you got? Please tell me we can finally put this hit-and-run to bed?"

"Found our man," Silas said, "and spoke to the Barnstable prosecutor, Mike Deegan. Know him?"

Flood shook his head.

"Ran what I've got past him. Deegan says if we charge now, he'll get at least a year for negligent operation, at most two, if we pile on aggravating factors—illegal gun, some drugs. Also looking at license suspension, mandatory minimum of fifteen years. And yes, I said years, not months."

"Wow. Fifteen-year suspension is actually pretty stiff," Flood remarked, brows raised. Then, he squinted at Silas, face growing visibly skeptical. "So, why don't you look happier? What aren't you telling me?"

There was apprehension on Flood's face as he glanced at Clark, who, up until then, had been nodding along.

"Well, if we left it at that—fifteen-year suspension—I'd be glad to know he'd likely never run another one of our people over," Silas said. Then, shaking his head, he added, "But it don't sit right."

Flood sighed lavishly. "Okay, I'll bite. What in particular doesn't *sit right*, Silas?"

"We aren't done," he said with a shrug. "'Turns out this crime's a hell of a lot bigger than a fatal hit-and-run—which is sayin' something. Got more victims than just Perkins."

Flood's eyebrows went up. "Go on."

"Based on what I've learned, the reason this guy was on our wharf—the reason he ran Timothy Perkins down—was because he's smuggling migrants into the country." Flood's jaw dropped in open shock and horror. "Desperate people from Brazil. Lot of 'em. When he hit Perkins, we believe he had a container full of undocumented migrants on his trailer and was rushing to get them off our wharf and out of town."

"Holy shit," Flood said, taking it in. He looked like he was about to be sick.

Hard to tell if it's the human tragedy or worry about the kind of bad press that ruins summer tourism, but I'll give him the benefit of the doubt.

Flood struggled to regain his footing. "Okay, okay . . . so . . . well, that's an even bigger crime, isn't it? Why don't we charge him for that too, and put him away for even longer?"

"Wait now, hold up. You're dead-on. It's a bigger crime—*way* bigger."

Now's when we sell him on felony murder.

"If we pin that on him, Perkins's death becomes felony murder—first degree in Massachusetts. That means life without parole."

"Great, so let's charge him for that," Flood said simply, with absolutely no conviction.

Silas shook his head. "Prosecutor won't go for it. Not until we've gathered evidence that will prove beyond a shadow of a doubt this guy's guilty of what we think he is—and we're close, but not quite there yet. Like I said, we're not done. I need a little more time and some slack in the rope to jam this guy up good with a felony murder charge that sticks."

"Why wait, though, Silas? I want to wrap this up—tell the husband, the town board, the media we've arrested our guy."

Silas shook his head.

"What's the problem with that?" Flood asked.

"Ain't right, lettin' a maggot like this off with a suspended license. He's victimized others, not just Timothy Perkins. This is a bigger crime— right here in our town."

Flood pinched that spot on the bridge of his nose, sighing. "What's it going to take in terms of time and effort to get the felony murder to stick?" he asked, frustration and impatience creeping into his tone.

"Here's where we're short. We can't yet prove he was the one driving when Perkins got hit. And we can't yet show he was fleeing a violent felony."

Flood looked glum.

"But we're as close as a boot to dirt. I know I'll get there and do it before long," Silas said.

"What's *before long* mean, Silas?" Flood asked. His voice was weary, downcast, and he had an apprehensive look on his face.

"End of this week, maybe middle of next—I'll have him nailed," Silas said, solid as stone.

A silence settled in.

Fork in the road, Flood. Chance to do the right thing. You do it, and we'll be fine working together. Jerk my rope now, this relationship's headed downhill fast.

Flood looked at him and had to see the sheer determination burning in those eyes. Clark looked fired up too.

Shown this guy I know my job. Finding Faria was damn near a miracle. Be poor form to second-guess your new chief now, worse still to try and force his hand.

Flood said, "The hit-and-run's faded from the news these past couple of weeks. A few more days won't make much of a difference. And I can't exactly ignore human smuggling in my town—even if I'm dreading the press and worried we're more than just a one-off pass-through."

Flood sat with it for a breath.

He locked eyes with Silas. After a long beat, he said, "Do it."

Silas gave a slow nod. *Right answer, Patrick.*

Gonna get this bastard—put a stop to this trade.

CHAPTER 58

Silas pulled up the dirt road that led to Wren's cottage. He parked under an old oak as dust he'd kicked up settled behind him like a cape. It was autumn, but the air was warm and still and carried the pitch-and-vanilla scent of the forest. He saw a white beehive at the edge of the clearing.

He hopped out of his Jeep and knocked on the front door, holding a small bouquet of flowers to his chest.

"These're for you," Silas said, extending the flowers when she answered. He also handed her a little bear silhouette carved from elk antler with the other hand. While Wren took them, Silas ducked down to step through the old cottage's rough-sawn doorframe.

"Zinnias! Thank you!" Wren said, her smile flickering with a little thrill. "You didn't have to."

Silas met her eyes. "Know that. Felt bad for earlier."

"You did?"

A pause. "Genny might've helped me . . . parse it some."

"Parse?" she said, with a widening smile. "Well, I . . . might have spoken to her too. Heard it was a rough morning. I'm sorry. It's why I thought some home cooking would help."

"You know at least some of the story, then." He sighed. "Newest car. Kevin Clark." He shook his head. "Well, we'll get it handled. Insurance should cover it."

Wren turned the bear over in her hand. "And who's this little guy? Looks like a bear, doesn't he?"

"Bear fetish. Zuni tradition. From back home. I carve them when I'm thinking. Keep 'em in an old wooden box, sometimes give one away—for luck, protection."

"It's exquisite! Looks just like the traditional fetishes I've seen with its arched back and head down. So smooth. And it feels cool to the touch. What's it carved out of?"

"Elk antler," he said with a shrug. "Dogs chew 'em. Used to collect antler sheds in the mountains when I was a kid. Carved 'em up. Now, I swipe 'em from Bandit's supply. Most days, I have a chunk in my pocket. Carve and fiddle while I'm thinking or waiting."

He pulled out a battered old pocketknife, handle worn nearly smooth. Its old steel blade was visibly narrowed from repeated sharpening.

"Use this. Uncle gave it to me, fifth birthday." He shrugged again, head drooped bashfully, and added, "Wanted you to have one. Maybe keep you safe."

"That is so thoughtful of you. I will treasure it. Truly," Wren said, holding it over her heart with crossed arms, looking at him with visible emotion—maybe a little watery around the eyes.

Silas swiped his hands down his thighs nervously and looked around the interior of the rustic hilltop cottage nestled among the oaks. It was the first time he'd seen the inside, and he was momentarily transfixed. Bright, airy, all worn shades of white, pale gray, faded turquoise. He'd never seen anything quite like it. Rough exposed beams; wide, pale old pine floorboards scrubbed soft by generations of sandy feet.

There was a tiny dining table with mismatched chairs brightly painted in different colors, paint worn and patinaed at every edge and corner. Simple built-in plank shelves on the walls groaning with books, worn old white paint, seashore jetsam, framed photographs . . .

In the living room, he noticed a pale-gray potbellied stove standing on bright-blue, white, and yellow nautical tiles. A tidy crib stack of firewood sat next to it. There was white wicker furniture worn down to wood on all the corners; incandescent copper lanterns, wooden pulleys, and other remnants of ancient hemp rope rigging hung from the rafters; old glass fishing net floats; and photographs hung in frames all over the walls—professional photographs, which Silas had to assume she'd taken herself.

Never seen anything like it. Feels like another world. But at the same time, comfortable, like home.

While taking in the cottage, his eye turned to the ingredients on the wooden countertop. He gave them a dubious gaze.

"This all for chili?"

"Yes!" she said, then registered his look. "Red meat isn't the only food group, Silas."

"What's this?" he said, gesturing toward a package of pale meat.

"Ground turkey. Here, brown it for me? Chop as you go."

"Okay." He took it, hesitated. "Skillet?"

"Skillet?" she repeated, amused.

He gave her a look.

She smiled, eyes catching the cottage's warm light, green with flecks of gold. "We usually call them frying pans in these parts, cowboy." She pointed. "Under the microwave."

Skillet food's good enough for me.

He set the meat sizzling, breaking it down with a wooden spoon. He had to admit, it smelled okay now that it was browning. His gaze drifted to the counter. "This?" he asked.

"Bulgur. It's a cracked wheat. Bulks up the chili, adds nutrition."

"Nutrition?"

"Yes. Chili can be good for you if it's made with some care."

"I've read bison's healthy for you," he said with a tinge of hope.

"This is too. And delicious." She paused her measuring. "I do large batches and bring it in for my lunches. Play your cards right, maybe I'll pack a lunch you can take home for later in the week."

Not sure if that's a promise or a threat.

"It will have three kinds of beans. Lentils. Tofu. Bone broth for collagen and gut health. Fire-roasted tomatoes and green chiles."

"Fire roasted?" he asked, looking around.

"Yes, you can do them next, when your meat's brown. You hold them directly over the burner flame with a long fork. Takes practice, but someone who's used to cooking over a campfire can surely figure it out."

Brown freckles dotted the soft laugh lines around her eyes and the scrunch of her nose. Her bright-green eyes glittered. She tipped her head toward the ingredients. "That's almond butter for creaminess and good fats. Cocoa powder too—think Mexican mole kinds of flavor. And my secret? You can't tell a soul." She paused, smiling. "*Cinnamon*."

Silas gave her a slow blink.

She bit back a grin, hurrying to add, "And of course, my extra-spicy, extra-strong chili powder. A custom mix."

His shoulders relaxed slightly.

"Why the hangdog face?"

"No face," Silas said.

She paused, looking skeptical, and waited.

"Lot of—uh—city food goin' into this chili is all. New experience for me. Lookin' forward to it."

"Surely the promise of some good heat reassures you?" she said, touching the tip of her pinky finger to her tongue, then to the surface of the chili powder mix. She moved to him, told him to open up, and dabbed the dusted finger onto his tongue.

He felt the warmth of her body before the warmth of the spice hit.

"Spice fixes a lot. Maybe bison next time?" he said. "You know, for its health benefits?"

"Next time, huh? So, you're not worried this chili is going to kill you?"

He met her gaze, unwavering. "Stuff I've eaten, would take a lot to put me down."

Her laugh was soft and generous. "Fine. Next time, some bison."

An hour later, they'd eaten, and the big three-wick candle in the storm glass had burned down a half inch. They sat on either side of the table's corner, elbows almost touching in the loftlike space.

Two large bowls sat before them. He'd filled his twice. Silas pushed his chair back an inch. "That there's good eatin'. Had more supper than you can say grace over. I'm full as a goat." He was unsure what to do with the cloth napkin in his lap. It was too nice to actually use.

"Ha! I knew you'd like it," she teased, punching him in the arm, then looking a little startled at how abruptly it stopped her hand.

He gazed at her, taking in all the bits of driftwood and shells on the windowsills behind her.

"Where'd you learn to cook like that?" he asked.

"I've always loved to cook. I taught myself. Guess you could say I was motivated."

"How so?"

After reflecting on that for a moment, she said, "It was just part of trying to separate myself, I suppose . . . Well, maybe *distinguish from* is more accurate."

"From what?" he asked.

She paused, hesitant. Rising to move to the white pillows of the slat-back wood-framed couch, she said, "Well, from a rather suffocating family."

"How so?" he said, following her to the couch.

"Are we going to do this?" she said with a smile.

"You got my backstory last time," he wagered, brows raised. "Your turn, way I see it."

"I don't want to dwell—or sound like an ungrateful brat." She sighed, seemingly trying to select her words carefully. "Let's just say my family is, how should I say this . . . from a certain social stratum."

Silas caught her drift immediately, having already been tipped off by Genny. "You sayin' your family's posh?"

Wren balked, then nodded, as if surprised that word was part of his vocabulary. "Right. Yeah, they're posh—like, people-with-domestic-help posh. People who live in historically significant houses. Silver utensils and good china for regular meals. Always horrible, traditional food too. Overcooked meat, mashed potatoes, and boiled vegetables. We were expected to sit up straight. Wait to speak until spoken to."

"Tough on a kid."

"Yes. But a privileged life, to be sure, full of opportunities. I'm not ungrateful. But all those opportunities came with . . . expectations."

"Expectations?"

"The proper schools, friends, degrees, clothes, boyfriends," she said, fingers fidgeting with a single bead on her string bracelet. "Never bought into any of it. The older I got, the more repelled I felt. I didn't see the point. It's not like I ever saw any happy people in that world."

"Uh-huh."

"Bradford's an old family name," she said. "Comes with a lot."

"Spotted Bradford Street," he remarked, and she nodded, mouth falling into a slant.

"Good eye. Provincetown's main thoroughfare—believe it or not, named for an ancestor, William Bradford, second governor of the Plimoth, with an *i*, Colony in 1621. They landed here in Provincetown first, you know. Then went across the bay to what's now called Plymouth with a *y*. It's the same family—my family."

"Lot for a kid to carry."

"Like I said—suffocating. Even my hair color has family weight. My mother calls it *Bradford copper*, says it skips generations, so in her mind, I am a special one with extra responsibility to the family traditions."

Wren shrugged, looking off in the distance.

"The minute I could make choices, I did. The highly selective but not Ivy League college I chose was barely acceptable to them, but they stopped short of refusing to pay. Adding insult to their injury, I chose to study art history, a subject not considered appropriate. And minored in public health, fine arts, and photography. Not appropriate at all."

"Explains the job," he said. "And the pictures."

"Photography is my passion. Public health–oriented social work is my calling."

"Noticed." Small nod. "Good at both."

Her milky skin blushing, she waved him off, fixing her fiery rust hair up into a loose knot and dispersing the scent of her warm neck. Silas felt so intoxicated by it, he had to take a moment to gather his wits.

"Enough about me!" she said, uncomfortable. "Your turn. Tell me something about you, Silas Lopez."

"Not much to tell."

"Start with the name."

"Can do that. Grandfather was a near-giant named Silas. Lopez is my mother's family name."

When he offered nothing more, she smiled. "And? That's a start . . ."

Guess we're not off the hook yet.

He reflected before continuing, "Old family too. Around Cortez, Colorado. Spanish colonists. Roughly same period as your kin—mine were 1590s. Originally settled in Santa Fe. Taos later. Did badly by the Pueblo people."

She winced slightly. Waited him out.

"Eventually, some settled north, into what's now Colorado. My people were among them."

"Fascinating. This is your mother's family?"

"Yes. Spanish."

"Who was your father?"

He shrugged. "Never met him."

"You never met your dad?" she asked, visibly surprised. She pinched a full and freckled upper lip with two fingers, thinking it over. "In a million years, I would never have guessed you grew up without a fatherly role model."

"Uncles. Cousins. Other ranch hands . . ." He shrugged. "Grew up around men."

"So, who was he, this father?"

"White. Also a mountain of a man. Descended from prospectors, exploiters. My mother's family land probably caught his eye. Back in the day, land was prized for prospecting. Now, it's grazing, water rights, other mineral rights."

"So, your mom still owns land out there?"

"Good chunk of the original holdings. Still owns about one hundred twenty thousand acres or so. Scrubland. Grassland. Some stands of pinyon. Few year-round creeks, two with native cutthroat trout. She supports herself and pays the taxes with grazing fees, gas leases, some water rights. Also, a wireless company put a rig on the ridgeline. Wind developers probably next."

"Wow. I bet it's beautiful," she said.

Silas nodded with a faraway look. "It's what I know."

"Can I ask what happened with your father?"

He shrugged, unable to wrestle the contempt out of his face. "One of many deadbeats she couldn't say no to. Heard she was pregnant and vanished. Never saw him again."

"I'm sorry," Wren said, momentarily placing her hand on his.

"Don't be. She's proud. Gave me her family name—Lopez—on the birth certificate." He looked off. "But she was also sentimental. Gave me his father's first name, Silas." *Not used to talking this much about myself, but notice things've been different lately. She draws me out.*

Looking through the cottage's wavy old single-pane glass, he could see even the last traces of evening light had faded.

She let the quiet stretch, left him alone with the weight of it. Then stood and uncorked a wine bottle by the white porcelain sink. She came back with two jelly jars, setting them on the battered wicker coffee table.

He looked at the garnet liquid. "Don't know 'bout wine," he said.

"Don't know if you want any?" she asked, clarifying.

"Don't mind a sip. Sayin' don't know good from bad."

"Me, neither," she said with a laugh of relief. "And you know what—who cares? I know what I like. They call this table wine, and I think it's decent."

Silas sipped, nodding his agreement. "Yep."

"So, your mom never married?" Wren went on, not letting it go. "By choice?"

"Choice? Huh! I guess."

She tilted her head, both reddish-blonde brows rising.

"Seemed like all she had to choose from were bad guys," he said. "Bad guys you wouldn't wanna marry. Lookin' to take, not to give. Certainly not to commit."

Echoes of distant pain were evident in his tone, despite his best efforts. Perhaps sensing them, Wren changed the subject. "What's she like?"

He watched the candlelight flickering in its storm glass on the table, eyes soft with memories.

"People say she's beautiful . . ."

"What do you say?"

"I'd allow people are right about that. Tough as sagebrush too. Raised me single-handedly."

"What was your childhood like?"

"On horseback, mainly. From earliest I can remember."

"You and your mom would ride?"

"Yes. I always rode a pinto—a painted pony. They've got large spots of white against color—maybe that's why I like spotted dogs," he said, smiling.

"Did she teach you to work with horses?"

"She was good with them, sure. But I don't recall lessons. I can't recall a time I didn't already know how to ride. Grew up that way. It was second nature to me. Guess I probably know horses better than people."

"Today's hiccup aside, you do all right with people, Mr. Lopez."

"Don't always hit my mark when I'm interactin'. Lotta talk, dealin' with people. For me, it's an effort," he said, giving her a quick side-eye to make sure he wasn't giving any offense.

She squinted. He could tell she was uncertain of his meaning.

Yep, like I feared. Gotta bundle this up better.

"Horses take a gentle nudge. Bit of pressure. Maybe a whisper or a spur if a storm's coming. People? Lot messier."

"People aren't your thing? Yet you find yourself in police work, serving the community?"

She's not wrong.

"Well, I am curious about people. And I do notice things. Helps me to think of it like a challenge, like solving a puzzle." He chanced some eye contact. "I'm told I can be rigid, though. I've got a sense of justice and don't like people breaking the rules, treating other people badly."

"I get that," Wren said.

"But a day with a lotta talk—sometimes I feel like I wrestled a mountain."

"So, you might not always like lots of talking, but you'll admit you've found some effective ways of dealing with people?" she pounced.

He shrugged, palms skimming his jeans. "Just tryin' not to overstate my ability. Or my appetite for it."

"Would it shock you to hear that some people think you've got a way with people? That some even find you . . . occasionally charming?"

Wouldn't raise it to the level of a skill or any such thing. More like gettin' through the day without sayin' somethin' dumb.

"I guess a bit surprised," he paused, suppressing a slight grin. "And happy too." Then, with a widening grin full of all the charm he could muster, he winked and said. "As long as one of 'em is you."

She laughed. "It's true, I do," she said. She stood, kissed the top of his forehead, and tugged him up by his hand.

"C'mon," she said. "Let's check the back deck, see if the owl's out tonight."

Can't tell what's burnin' hotter—my forehead or my cheeks. Feel a little lightheaded from that kiss. Just focus. Big man in a small room. Thread the needle, make it to the deck. Get out into that cool open air with her without knocking somethin' over.

They settled on the weathered bench outside, backs against the close-set balusters and faces tilted toward the dark sky. The sun-warmed wood gave off the scent of cedar as it cooled. A breeze from the east carried the smell of the ocean and the distant rumble of Atlantic surf.

Silas breathed in deeply, feeling contented—by the food, the company, the wine, and of course, the embrace of the outdoors. He was more comfortable outside.

Perhaps Wren picked up on that, because she risked a nudge for more biography.

"So, you were an only child. And you left?"

He thought before answering. "Had to. Still feel guilty. Wonder if I could have done more. But truth is, I didn't have a choice."

"Why? What happened?" she asked.

Silas's head hung low, and he rotated it to look at her sidelong with an expression of reluctance. After a second, he said, with bitterness in his voice, "A guy crossed the line. Hit her."

"Oh, Silas, I'm so sorry. That's awful. What did you do?"

Really don't want to go here, but probably best to get it all out, get it over with. Earlier it comes out, sooner it's hopefully behind us.

There was a long pause before Silas spoke. His voice came out soft, hushed, tentative.

"You're not gonna like this."

Wren's voice hardened slightly. "What did you do, Silas?"

"Remember, it was a really long time ago. I was just a kid."

"You are making this worse. What did you do?"

"Gave him a beatin' he wouldn't forget. Went too far. I was just eighteen. He was older—but I was a big, strong kid. Grew up fighting . . ." He looked at her. "Wren, I recognize now I'm lucky he didn't die."

"Wait—you almost beat him to death too? That's horrible. You're scaring me again, Silas."

"I know. Like I said, I'm ashamed, not proud. That fight, the mess in Salt Lake . . . they're the worst but not the only close calls I've had with rough stuff. Felt justified at the time, but I see the bigger picture now. I'm workin' on it, workin' on findin' other ways."

Wren looked alarmed, her eyes squinting, expression sour. There was an awkward silence.

Shaking her head, she asked in a curt, perfunctory way, "Was your mom okay? Was she angry? Is that why you left?"

"No. Asshole got the wires out of his jaw and swore I'd pay."

"So, you were scared and had to leave town?"

A flare of heat rose in his chest—the old instinct to bristle. He hated that she might think he ran out of fear. *Coward. That word never sat easy. Careful now, Silas. That's not what she meant. Don't go twisting her meaning. Show her a toxic reaction like that, it's gonna make things worse.*

He reined it in and shook his head gently.

"No, I wasn't scared, Wren. I was just roped in tight."

He didn't know if she'd understand what that meant—but it was the closest he could get to saying he'd felt cornered, out of options.

"How so?" she asked, sitting forward, gauzy blouse sleeves on her thighs. A bat fluttered silently over the treehouse-like deck.

"Guy was a biker. Rode with a crew. Put the word out. Had to go at another of his boys not long after. Just made it worse. After that, I was always lookin' over my shoulder—"

"That cycle of violence, Silas—it pulls people under. You were only eighteen. That must have been terrifying," she interrupted.

"I see it now. At the time, I didn't think about it as scary. Probably should have. I was a kid. I just looked at it like more of a straight-up problem. Just saw it as simple math—sooner or later, I was gonna get cornered by more of them than I could handle alone."

"Jesus, Silas! This is terrible! So, you left town?"

"I did. I hoped Mama had finally learned to pick 'em better."

Even saying it feels like betrayal. But it's the truth.

"Fact is, I didn't want to stay and see otherwise—see her make the same mistake again. It would've been too heartbreaking. By then, the ranch I worked had been selling off, like most others. Shrinking pool of work for ranch hands."

"So, what did you do?"

"Knew a guy in the state police. He encouraged me—said it might be a good path forward for someone like me. I already had a two-year degree, so I lay low. Bunked with a buddy outside of town. Figured big cities would have more openings, so I applied to all the big-city forces in the Southwest. While I waited, I hiked. Fished. Rode my horse in the mountains. First one to take me was Salt Lake."

Wren sat in silence. She looked stunned. That worried him more than he'd expected. He needed her to say something—anything. Words might not be Silas's tool of choice, but he needed to bridge this gulf to her.

"Put myself in a bad light again," he said, mostly to himself.

Wren was quiet, lost in thought.

Silas tried again to redeem himself. "I was young . . . I understand it was wrong. In fairness, though, I didn't have the easiest life growing up. For as long as I can remember, I felt responsible for protecting my mama. For paying her back—for feeding me, raising me, keeping me alive. Maybe grew up too fast."

He paused.

Not sure where I stand. Best stop digging.

After a moment, he said, "Wren? You okay? Did I upset you?"

Her voice was choked with emotion. "Yes, I'm fine. Just . . . sad. Life can be so unfair. How does a kid end up feeling like he has to beat a man nearly to death to protect his mom? And then have to leave his hometown—and her—just to stay alive?"

"You're making it sound bad, but it didn't feel that bad at the time. It was what I was used to. Knew it was probably time to be movin' on, anyway."

"Silas, at that age, I was riding horses in shows as a hobby, not as a job! They gave me ribbons. I was serving tea and cucumber sandwiches with no crusts at a country club and resentful of how hard I had to work. I was picking out gowns and going to debutante balls!"

Debbie-taunt? Not gettin' all of this. Not sure whether it's important, but best play it safe.

"Um, guessing those were some kinda fancy thing?" Silas interrupted.

Despite the seriousness of the moment, a little spurt of laughter escaped from Wren. "Yes, Silas, debutante balls are fancy. One of the fanciest of things."

"So, we grew up different," Silas said. "That's okay. I'm not sore about how I grew up. Guess I'm learnin' it left me a little thick-skinned. Thickheaded too when it comes to fists and temper. But in the scheme of things, I got no complaints about how the blanket unrolled."

Wren seemed to still be composing herself.

He chanced a peek at her, meeting her eyes in the darkness. "Brought me to this place. This moment. This person . . . In my scorebook? That's a huge win."

Silas was shocked when Wren grabbed his hand and squeezed tight. She leaned her shoulder against his bicep, inhaled the salty night air in a big breath, then let it out slowly.

Hand is a good sign, but best to sit still and keep the trap shut.

Shaking her head, she said, "My thickheaded, thick-skinned, cowboy poet philosopher." She thumped their intertwined hands on his thigh. "I want to be mad at you for being so scary and violent, but I can't make myself. It feels like being mad at a trapped animal for trying to fight its way out."

Her voice sounds close to teary. Careful now. Easy does it.

"Instead, I feel sad for that young man looking out for his mom." She leaned her head back and looked up at the stars through the canopy of oaks, still holding his hand. "Why did the universe drop you at my feet—make you so complicated? What am I supposed to do with you?"

She raised the back of his giant hand and studied it for a long time. Scars, callouses, wrinkles, coarse hairs, enlarged crooked knuckles that had hit too hard. With the tips of his long fingers, he felt the cool smoothness of the carved bear in her palm—she'd picked it up and brought it out with her.

It was as if he were facing a judge or jury. Then, some catch deep inside her seemed to release. He could feel the change in the energy all around her. She pulled his hand the last few inches to her mouth and gently kissed each of the giant, rough-skinned knuckles.

A flood of relief swamped Silas, leaving him spinning, dizzy. He needed to say something.

"Well, that's nice. It's certainly one thing you can always do with your cowboy poet philosopher," he said.

Good place to quit talkin' for a spell. Let her settle with it some. Better to clear out 'fore I go and tangle it up.

"Another is, tell me where the soap is so I can clean up that kitchen for you," he said with a warm smile. "I'm hopin' it'll increase my chances of gettin' invited back sometime. Would dish duty be okay?"

"That would be wonderful, cowboy. Thank you. Under the sink. I'll join you before too long. I just need a minute to sit with this."

He went back inside, flexing the tingling hand she'd kissed. He was grateful for something mindless to do. Needed time to process all the water that passed under the bridge tonight. His hands knew what to do, even if his head didn't yet. Wreck pan duty. He'd scrub until the rest of him caught up.

CHAPTER 59

Silas left Wren's cottage feeling tired but energized—like he'd grabbed a cattle prod by the wrong end. He'd been running on too little sleep, but he was humming from his evening. And it was crunch time on the Perkins case—or, as he thought of it, the Faria case. The additional runway Flood had given him was like a battery swap.

He'd be itching for days from all the mosquito bites he'd collected on Wren's deck, but it was worth it. He'd hated to pull himself away and sensed she wasn't eager to see him go, either. But the well-mannered thing to do was to excuse himself.

Bandit was ecstatic to see him return. He still hated being left behind and was adjusting to the new place. Silas bent down on one knee and hugged the leaping dog as tightly as he dared, burying his face in the warm, coarse, gray-and-black speckled coat.

He breathed in his earthy, yeasty dog scent. *Thank heaven for animals like this.*

Silas was so keyed up, he decided to give Bandit a special middle-of-the-night walk—he'd been on his own for hours and resisted any urges he might have had to eat the couch. He more than deserved it.

The cool night air made Silas more awake and alert, so the two of them wandered around outside for a long time. Silas let Bandit lead. They traced narrow streets. Picket-fenced flower gardens encircled immaculate yards. Bandit's nose pulled them down grass alleys lined by trumpet vines, drooping under the weight of apricot-colored blossoms. He had to admit it was magical, even as he ducked his shoulders to avoid getting soaked by night dewdrops.

They made their way along tiny connecting lanes lined by walls of climbing beach roses and down sandy, single-file walking paths.

Warm, humid air carried the sweet fragrance of beach rose mixed with the spicy vanilla scent of autumn clematis clinging to fences and sheds. Silas's soft footfalls and the click of Bandit's claws were barely perceptible.

He noticed raccoons were still busy working, and some of the earliest-rising foxes were already moving around, so he could sense the tension pulsing up the leash when Bandit regularly stopped and alerted. Brief flashes of movement and quiet rustles inevitably followed, but Bandit didn't bark or give chase. He was leashed, and besides, tracking and herding Silas was his top priority.

After wending their way home and falling into bed, thoughts of Wren still raced through Silas's head. He tossed and turned, restless, like he was sleeping on uneven ground.

Giving up, he rose, threw on jeans and a sweatshirt, and took a tumbler of water and his laptop to his front room. There, he forced himself to think about the case.

He'd been through it over and over again. The only plausible explanation that fit all the facts was that this former fishing boat deckhand was bringing migrants into the country illegally, and likely doing it on a local trawler. Why else would someone not from around Provincetown, and not connected with any local boats, possibly be racing off the wharf in the dead of night with a large mystery shipping container full of people?

Silas didn't know for certain where the migrants were coming from or where they were going after Faria picked them up. He researched oceanic migration routes out of Latin America and learned about the economics of the trade. Migrants had to pay a lot of money for transport. Money they didn't have—which meant they were indentured to their smugglers and vulnerable to horrible exploitation. Indentured migrants owed whoever had possession of them. Whether in the form of cash or free labor, they were worth real money.

If he assumed these migrants were Brazilian—which was a good bet, given the food wrappers found—his research told him they were probably being bundled in Porto de Belém. There, they were packed onto big cargo ships bound for the North Atlantic.

Silas had learned that Belém was the largest commercial port in northern Brazil—it was situated near the mouth of the Amazon River and had deep-water access to the Atlantic. Its large-vessel capacity made it a busy hub for trade—vast quantities of soybeans, minerals, ore, timber, and other agricultural products from the Amazon basin passed through Belém every year. This kind of activity was the perfect cover for hiding a few migrants in the bustle. Which was why, he'd learned, it was a key point of departure in regional smuggling networks.

Best he could figure—and he'd need to prove it—was some large operation was smuggling big groups of migrants to international waters at various places off the Atlantic shore of the United States. Independent operators like Faria were paid to meet them and sneak the migrants into smaller ports.

These independents were locals who would have access to boats that wouldn't raise an eyebrow at the smaller ports. Assuming Faria was playing this game, Silas wasn't sure what he did after he got them onto his trailer, but temporary work in the cranberry harvest seemed like one answer, based on what he'd seen.

A problem nagging at Silas was that he didn't understand how such an arrangement could pay enough to possibly be worth it to Faria, given the risks involved.

As the first, almost invisible hints of light diluted the inky darkness to the east, Silas concluded his next step was going to require him to head out to New Bedford and see what more he could learn about Faria, then to Carver to see who was picking the cranberries.

No sooner had he decided than he realized this late-night timing was an opportunity. If he left now, he might be able to catch Faria leaving the apartment in the morning.

The more he hefted it, the more he knew this was a good idea and a solid plan. *Enough thinking—time to put it into motion.*

His fatigue receded as the plan started to form, but Silas still needed coffee for the road. Cowboy coffee was fastest and his favorite. Easier than detouring to find an open shop. He worked fast in the dark. Inch and a half of water in a pot. Couple of big fistfuls of grounds dumped in. Burner on high. While it boiled, he dressed and fed his puzzled dog.

Silas had recently cut Bandit's meal size back slightly to compensate for his many office snacks. The dog was grateful for the bowl—he just wasn't sure what he did to earn breakfast so early. He wolfed it down quickly while Silas shoved into his boots, then grabbed his keys, gun, badge, phone, two different-colored baseball caps, and two different-colored pullovers before finishing making the coffee.

It wasn't pretty—Silas poured the scalding, roiling sludge from his stove through a sheet of paper towel tucked into his battle-scarred travel mug. Suspended above the mug, the paper towel drained slowly, and he felt the coffee's heat creep up the fibers.

Hot! All this damn office work is making the calluses thin.

When the dripping slowed, he tossed the towel and grinds back into the pot, threw the pot in the sink, and bolted out the door with Bandit and his stuff.

Clean it up when I get back. Right now, no time to waste.

The morning air was cool and dark as he loaded Bandit and his gear. This time of year, the cape was still lush, living, and green, but the foliage had long since lost the freshness of spring. Drier, a little faded, dusty from a long summer of heat and sun.

After stopping by the office to pick up the department's camera, he hit the highway. He pushed his speed but only so far. The badge might get him out of a ticket but not out of wasting time with the whole song and dance.

With school back in session, the summer crowds and traffic had thinned. Still, most of it was heading onto the cape on a Saturday morning. Just he and a few tradespeople—restaurant delivery trucks, landscapers, and the like—shared the dark, predawn road to the mainland.

He got himself posted in a spot on Roosevelt Street across from Ana Sofia's apartment by 5:55 a.m.—a good forty minutes before sunrise. That would give him time to settle in nice and quiet.

He pulled a recently adopted Red Sox ball cap down low over his forehead, leaned back, and settled in to watch. With luck, he'd catch this lowlife heading out and learn some more about what he was up to. But first, he'd have to wait.

Turned out Tony wasn't an early riser. Silas had taken Bandit on two walks—in two hats and pullovers—snuck a guilty leak between parked cars, and nearly given up hope before Faria came out at around 9:30 a.m. He had a jangly, bouncy gait. *Looks like a string puppet run by someone sneezing.*

By this time, Silas was hungry enough to eat the paint off a barn door, but he followed Faria anyway. Faria bounced into a beat-up Hyundai sedan with dull, sun-faded silver paint. The rear window had a sparkly "Princess on Board" decal; the bumper had one that said "Bad Girl" in hot-pink block letters.

Don't need to look it up to know this has to be Ana Sofia's car.

Faria pulled away. As Silas left his spot to follow, he noticed a lowered Honda Accord with a wide stance pull out of a slot a dozen cars back.

At Tony's first stop, Silas watched closely. It looked like Tony was working out a truck to borrow from a friend. From the vantage point Silas found, he could see they talked casually and at length with friendly body language. No money changed hands before Faria was given the keys, but something small, like a tiny plastic baggie, was pulled from Tony's pocket and passed palm to palm. Faria started the truck and parked it just outside the lot's chain-link fence. *Planning ahead—after-hours pickup when the gate's locked.*

Silas made a note of the license plate in case he needed to speak to the owner later.

Looked like Tony's next move was to get himself a trailer to match the truck. Faria spent a moment at a heavy-equipment rental site, looking at trailers. Beat-up trenching and earthmoving equipment was strewn around the lot. Silas could smell the hydraulic oil soaked into the dirt through the thin layer of gravel.

After zeroing in on a flatbed similar to the one Silas had impounded, Faria handed over some bills he'd peeled off a roll and signed paperwork at a shallow counter in a grubby little glass-front office with a dirty window. Tony walked out first, followed by the rental guy, who hung a Reserved sign on the trailer's neck.

Guess Faria'll be back for that with the borrowed truck. Impounding his truck and trailer definitely ruined his weekend.

They drove some more. Before long, Faria was down at the docks. As he pulled in to watch Tony from a distance, Silas saw a car full of teenagers go by him in the opposite direction in a lowered, wide-stance Honda Accord. Same color and look as the one he'd seen pulling out before. The teen at the back-seat window stole a glance at Silas.

Not much for coincidences. Looks like we've got some company. But why does this gang have a tail on Tony and now me?

As he watched Tony, Silas thought about the angles.

Unless they had a good reason, they'd just cut Tony loose if they thought he was hot.

Then, it hit him. There was always someone higher on the totem pole.

If these New Bedford boys owe their bosses in New York a steady stream of folks they've trapped into work, well . . . that'd be a reason. Tony's a dirtbag, but he's got specialized skills and connections. Until they find another guy to replace him who can handle the boat end of things, they might be stuck with him.

Tony had come out of a building with somebody who looked like the manager of a cargo area or loading dock. The man was in a hard hat, work pants with boots, and a shirt open at the neck, with an ID badge hanging on a chain around his neck. He was gesturing at a selection of worn, faded cargo containers. Faria pointed at the lone half-length container. The manager checked his watch and nodded. Faria peeled more bills off that same fat roll. The dock manager spray-painted a black "SOLD/Private" on the gray container.

At least that rusted-out box would let some air in its holes, so people inside could breathe.

While Faria zigzagged across town, Silas hung back—just in case the guy had the sense to check his mirrors. Silas was probably being too careful. *This guy moves like he's never heard of surveillance.*

Where to now, Tony? Let's see what you're fixing to haul.

Silas was relieved when, a little past noon, Faria parked on a side street and stepped into a dive bar offering a four-dollar basket of buffalo wings with the purchase of any beer. Lunch and televised sports looked like Faria's next to-do list item, so Silas parked a little farther down the street's first block, walked Bandit quickly, then took a chance. He ran up to the head of the street, ducked into a deli to grab two giant Italian subs, and used the bathroom. When he got back to his Jeep a few minutes later, Faria's car was still there, and Silas could make out his profile in the same spot at the bar.

Silas greedily devoured the cold sandwiches with some help from Bandit, then rehydrated them both and awaited Faria's next move. After nearly two hours, Faria bounced out of the bar with the slightly clumsy gait of a day drinker who'd just taken a bump of coke. Instead of walking back toward his car, Faria turned down the street in the other direction, ambling with a loose-limbed sway along the sidewalk. *Had he just been passing time before his next stop?* Silas quietly stepped out of his Jeep and tracked him from the other side of the street.

On the next block, Faria glanced up at the sign of the Golden Dragon Chinese restaurant. Then, he glanced a second time, as if to double-check he was in the right place, before sending a text. After a minute of standing around and looking fidgety, he read something on his phone and headed down a shoulder-width alley along the restaurant's left side. Silas could see Faria standing and waiting in a large alley behind the restaurant, illuminated by the bright high-noon sunlight. There was a dirt parking lot on the right side of the restaurant, so Silas jogged across the street and into the lot, wondering if he should have brought Bandit for a plausible dog-walking cover story.

He crept to the back corner of the building and got down on his knees behind a stack of empty pallets. They'd hide him from passersby out on the street. The steamy, greasy smell of fried dumplings wafted from the back of the restaurant. From his low position, Silas snuck a quick peek around the corner to assess the situation. Faria was talking to an Asian man who looked to be about the same age. The man was wearing the white double-breasted shirt of a kitchen worker and the black-and-white checkered chef pants to go with it. He had oily black rubber clogs on and a rolled red bandana tied around his head.

Silas pulled back and pressed his forehead against the last brick of the building wall and got his ear as close to the corner as he could. When he still couldn't hear clearly, he used one end of his flat smartphone to cup his ear forward while extending the other end out around the corner of the building at an angle. The flat glass surface reflected just enough sound to make a difference. It was a trick he'd learned on the Salt Lake force to allow you to listen around corners in urban environments. It wasn't foolproof, but it was almost undetectable compared to sticking a head around the corner, and it often made a difference in what you could pick up.

Silas heard the Asian man say one word—*weekend*—followed by more murmurs he couldn't make out. Then, he heard, "Bring them here after we close and the kitchen crew's gone. Let's say one."

One o'clock?

"I can do that. It's two thousand a head," Faria said. His voice was fidgety, staccato. "Like we agreed, with a five-hundred-per-head down payment now. You got the down payment money with you? With my truck nabbed, I already got extra transport expenses to cover."

"What do you think? I don't have the fucking money? Duh. Here." Silas heard the crunch of a paper bag changing hands. "It's all there," the Asian man said. "Twenty-three, you said, right? So, this is eleven and a half g's."

"Make sure you have the rest, then," Faria said.

"No shit, dickhead. Don't worry about the money—worry about a nice, clean transfer. Make sure nobody bolts, you're not seen or followed, nothing goes wrong. I was promised twenty-three; I've made commitments for twenty-three. You fuck this up, bring attention—or worse, *heat*—here to our place of business, you're not only done doing business with us. You're a dead man. You understand?"

"Yeah, yeah," Faria said.

Damn. If they'd said what day the meetup was, Silas had missed it. But he did know one o'clock—sometime this weekend, it seemed—and that there were twenty-three people involved.

Silas quickly retraced his steps across the street and toward the Jeep so that he wouldn't be visible on the near sidewalk when Faria emerged from the alley. From a block away, he could hear Bandit barking in a frenzy. As he drew closer, he could see people clustered next to the vehicle. Four young Asian teens were talking and laughing.

Looks a lot like the Honda crew.

The oldest couldn't have been more than eighteen. Two were leaning on his Jeep, and two were facing the others from the sidewalk. Bandit was leaping from the front seat to the rear inside, snarling uncharacteristically. His teeth were bared to reveal traces of foam, and a ridge of fur along his spine stood on end.

"Move along, boys," Silas said, holding up his badge from ten feet away.

Silas saw two of them steal a glance at the oldest one leaning against his Jeep's front passenger door, clearly in search of direction. *Now I know who the leader of this posse is.* When the leader ignored his instruction, Silas stepped in front of him, with his hand on his hip above his service weapon. He was careful to keep the other three in his peripheral vision.

"Said outta my fucking way," he said quite plainly. "You're upsettin' my dog, which is pissin' me off. Neither of those outcomes is good for you."

"Free country," the leader said with a shrug. "Besides, this is our neighborhood, and your dog is breaching the peace with all that noise."

"He hunts vermin by smell. Makes you the problem here, not him," Silas said.

"Nice pooch," the leader said, lifting his shirt to reveal a gun tucked into his pants. "It would be a shame if he ended up in the wrong place at the wrong time and something happened to him. The same goes for your family. It might be best if you kept them out of our neighborhood. And kept your nose out of our business. Are you catching my drift, *gweilo*—"

Before the last word was out of his mouth, Silas had his hip pressing against the kid's abdomen, blocking his access to his waist, and the barrel of his gun pushed so hard under the kid's chin, it made his skull thud loudly against the window glass. Bandit went still. The leader put his hands up against the car, palms toward Silas. Using his left hand, Silas took the gun off the kid, released the magazine onto the ground, and tossed the weapon underneath the car parked behind his. He moved his left forearm across the kid's throat in order to free his gun and allow him to rotate his body.

Silas could see one of the other kids had a switchblade in his hand but hadn't opened it. Silas looked the knife guy in the eye, and the knife hand stealthily moved out of sight behind him.

"I think I caught your drift. Believe we're communicating clearly. But I got a drift for you too. And I'll say it plain. Don't know who sent you flunkies on this suicide mission, but I don't like to be threatened. Understand?"

Silas was shoving the forearm harder across the windpipe and keeping the gun hand free in case it was needed for the others.

"Understand?"

The leader's face was tingeing toward purple, and he couldn't nod with the arm pushed into the soft flesh under his chin, so he blinked.

"One additional thing we need to be clear on: you and your playmates here fuckin' with me, my dog, or anybody else I care about, be a mistake with life-altering consequences. You catching that drift?"

The guy with the knife released the blade with a metallic snap and started to bring it forward. With explosive swiftness, Silas rammed a knee into the crotch of the guy he was pinning. It hit hard enough to raise the kid off the ground and rock the entire Jeep on its suspension. The leader doubled over with a groan, eyes rolled back into his head, and slid down the car door to his knees before crumpling into a fetal position.

Before he'd hit the ground, Silas had rolled away and snatched the knife arm of the other kid by the wrist, twisting it so far up the kid's back that his knuckles almost touched the base of his neck. The kid squealed in pain as the knife clattered into the gutter. Silas kicked the knife under the Jeep and slammed him face-first against its side, intentionally hard enough to leave a shiner. He gave the other two kids a look that said, *You still paying attention? Wanna be next?*

The remaining kids took a step back. The knife kid snarled, "Fuck you!" through closed teeth.

"Yeah, kid? You really in a position to be dealin' out tough-guy insults?" Silas asked.

The kid turned his head and spat on the Jeep. "You're a dead man, *gweilo.*"

"That right?" Silas said, tightening the grip on his twisted arm. "This the arm that's coming for me?"

This isn't personal for them. These kids were sent to do a job—a job way bigger than they could handle. And they are in danger from their bosses if they don't do it, or prove they got hurt trying.

"You bet your life!" the kid said, spitting again.

"No, I don't think so. Gonna do you a favor by putting this arm outta commission for a while," Silas said, twisting the arm hard enough to dislocate the shoulder with a pop before the forearm bones gave way to a spiral fracture. The two kids watching gave a start when they heard the bone crack over the sound of the kid's gurgling squeal. With queasy looks on their faces, they instinctively stepped back and out of reach.

The knife kid went instantly pale as he went into shock. Silas let him drop to the gutter. He stepped over to the leader, who had gotten onto his hands and knees and was trying to stand. Silas gave the leader a swift boot kick to the ribs, lifting him off the ground, with the ragged sound of bones crunching and air rushing out of him, then a softer kick with the arch of his boot to the eye and nose to make sure he had something visible on his face to show for his effort.

"You kids got yourself mixed up with the wrong situation. A person threatens me, my dog, or my people, they're damn lucky if the damage can be mended with just a plaster cast. Took it easy on you young squirts 'cause anyone can see you're not the brains of this operation. But next time, I won't be so gentle."

He surveyed the scene.

"You two chickenshits," he said, pointing at the two who had backed away. "Over here. Get this garbage out of the gutter before I run it over leavin'." Nodding at the knife kid, he said, "Suggest you move Mr. Switchblade by the ankles, not the arms, unless you want the right one coming off in your hand."

From the ground, Silas heard a quiet, breathless, "Tough guy with a gun right now, but better be careful, *gweilo*."

It was the leader speaking. How he found the nerve was beyond Silas.

"This octopus has eyes and ears everywhere," he said. "Long arms that can reach out and find you where you live. We're movin' along for now, but you'd be smart to do the same. You're not welcome here, and next time won't be just a warning."

"Right. Well, I guess everybody got a warning today," Silas said.

He looked at them with the sound of blood pounding in his ears for a few seconds, tempted to do more, leave a more lasting impact—but he thought better of it. He'd done enough for now.

He walked around, got in his Jeep, and started it as the two smaller kids scrambled to help the injured pair away from the vehicle's tires.

Silas swung out and heard the knife handle crunch under his wheel as he moved down the street.

After a couple of blocks, he pulled over to check his navigation and soothe Bandit, who was still in a state, white froth beaded at the corners of his mouth, having been unable to assist with an obvious threat. Stroking his thick fur helped Silas calm down a bit too, and after a moment, he put the Jeep in gear and took off.

These were tough kids, getting in my face like that. Or scared. Silas thought about their calculus. If coming after him in a suicidal way like that was their best alternative, he'd hate to see the shot caller these kids were afraid of. He regretted having to put them down so forcefully, but they'd threatened him, his dog, and maybe Wren. It was not only necessary; it was safer for the kids that way. He needed to send a message that these kids hadn't chickened out and backed away—they had been forced to step back. Only way their superiors were going to respect their effort.

He picked his way through the grubby surface roads and onto the highway, thinking about this spiraling mess. First thing pressing into his mind? It had been less than twenty-four hours since he'd promised Wren he was working on his tendency toward violence, and he'd just put two kids in the hospital. He'd had ample justification, and ultimately, it was the right thing to do, but he needed to sit with that a bit. *Maybe some way I could have handled it differently, but I don't see it at the moment.*

This logic of rough justice was not something that would be easy to explain to Wren if he ever decided to try, but that was for another day. Right now, he needed to set that question aside to revisit later. He had bigger problems closing in at the moment. Chief among them: favor to those kids or not, his message came with a downside.

Gang knows they need to bring more power next time if they want to scare me off. Now they know four gangbangers isn't enough. Next time, it'll be a more serious crew. Would rather they hadn't figured that out just yet.

But they had, which meant two things.

First, case is now on a short fuse. When it goes, it's gonna scatter wreckage.

Second, gotta admit the feds belong in this. They're better equipped to clean up this gang mess. They're going to be stomping all over this case if they aren't already, and they'll want no interference from a small-town local. Textbook approach? Refer this to the feds, give them everything we've got— evidence, hunches, everything—and let it play out. In other words, trust the process.

But trusting the process wasn't an option. He'd had too much experience playing that game. The feds' priorities never overlapped square, if they overlapped at all. They'd be interested in the gang end of this, the smuggling aspects of it, any organized crime implications.

Faria and his New Bedford sideshow could easily slip through the cracks. Even if he got swept up, he could strike a plea deal and be set loose with a wrist slap in exchange for a few bits of information, leaving no closure for Stevenson, the team, or the town.

He didn't need to step on the feds' turf. He hoped they nailed the whole crew, every last one who came after him. But that wasn't his problem. His job was Faria. If he didn't stay locked on that, the bastard might walk.

With the resolve that follows from a moment of clarity, Silas decided he needed to grab his guy, get him charged for felony murder, and get the hell away from this gang and this town. He'd happily leave the rest of this mess to the New Bedford police force and the feds, but only after he'd snagged his perp.

Feds might be pissed, but when aren't they? Let the chips fall. There's a dead victim in Provincetown Faria needs to answer for. Only question is where and when to grab Faria. Need to think on that.

Silas had no idea what time of day people started picking cranberries. So, he set out toward Carver while it was still dark as tar.

He didn't mind the drive; he needed some windshield time to think about this brewing tussle with the feds and how to wind up this case. If he could pick up any more intel on Faria's operation with these migrants, that'd be a bonus.

As the light came up over the crimson patches of low cranberry bushes, he could see from the notch he'd parked in that some bogs already looked harvested. Combed clean and drained. There was no one around any of the bogs near the barn. He set out on foot along the hedgerow and found them farther out in some of the smaller bogs scattered around the area. The hedgerow provided him enough cover to observe without being spotted, and small holding ponds gave him some distance to survey the scene.

Over half these bogs are picked. If we're going to gather evidence of this operation, need to do it soon.

Is that something Clark might be ready for? If instructions were clear, he could probably get some photographs. Better him than risk the manager seeing me again. Put on some tourist clothes, bring another officer, maybe a female one to look the part, and claim to be interested in the history of the cranberry industry. Could work.

Meantime, Silas needed to get back to Provincetown and talk to Camara about the Golden Dragon on the way. Camara picked up on the third ring.

"Lieutenant, Chief Silas Lopez from Provincetown callin'."

"What's up, Chief? Is this another courtesy call? I'm kinda in the middle of something here."

"Only need you for one shake of a lamb's tail but can try you back later, need be."

"No, if it's short, shoot. Easier than phone tag." Silas overheard him say in a quiet voice to someone else, "Gimme a moment for this—circle back in five? Thanks." Then, back to Silas, he said, "Okay, what is it?"

"Still workin' my Provincetown hit-and-run. Guy we talked about, Tony Faria, is the perp. Found the truck and trailer up in Carver, mess of forensics all over it," Silas said. "Also a dirty gun, a bit of coke, and a bunch of small bags of oxy too, FYI."

"Well done. You need backup in town when you arrest him?"

Silas checked his mirrors before overtaking a slow truck in the right lane.

"Not just yet. This thing's growin' antlers like an eight-point buck," Silas said. "Got reason to believe this guy was in Provincetown pickin' up a load of undocumented Brazilians. Likely was rushin' from an initial drop point with 'em in a shipping container on his trailer when he hit my pedestrian."

"Holy shit, Chief. That's a mess. Okay, so, what do you need from me?" Camara asked.

"Suspect your town might be the next transfer point for the Brazilians. Think this scumbag's worked out a deal to rent these migrants out before turning them over to bigger players. Pretty sure he's using 'em for seasonal work harvesting cranberries in Carver, then plans to sell them to somebody down here," Silas said.

"Wait—you're here in New Bedford right now?" Camara asked.

"No, I'm in Carver and headin' out. If the clock wasn't chewin' on me, I'd have come by with donuts and coffee for your team, but the town manager has a noose 'round my neck, and this thing's unfoldin' faster than a tent in the wind."

Silas changed the subject. "Before I go, is a Chinese restaurant called Golden Dragon on your radar? Gangs, drugs, vice? Anything like that?"

"I know of it. It's not on my radar beyond being told to avoid the owners, but . . ." Camara paused, sighed, and said, "Let me see if I can patch in our head of vice. She'll know more. Hang on."

The line went silent, and Silas waited as he drove.

"From Provincetown on the line," Camara said. "Chief Silas Lopez. Silas, you on? Marcia, have I still got you?"

Silas and Marcia both confirmed they were on.

"Go ahead, Lieutenant Dawood," Camara said.

"Chief Lopez, Marcia Dawood with NBPD vice and gangs squad. Good to meet you. Paul tells me you're asking about the Golden Dragon."

"Thanks, Lieutenant. Yeah, potentially got some human smuggling mixed up in a hit-and-run I'm working out in Provincetown. Believe there could be a transfer of undocumented Brazilians fixin' to go down at Golden Dragon at some point. New in these parts, so just checkin' to see if that's plausible or I'm breathin' my own trail dust."

"Ha! Yes, I know the place. Wouldn't recommend their kung pao chicken—or anything else, for that matter. The owner of the restaurant has known ties to Asian gangs in New York City. It seems he employs undocumented migrants and dips a toe into a variety of other illicit activities in town. Frankly, I wouldn't be surprised if he bribes the health inspector too."

"Might've had a tussle with some of his junior foot soldiers the other day. Doubt they'll file a crime report, but if they do, I'm happy to answer questions," Silas said.

"Interesting," Camara said. "Here in town?"

"Yeah, near the restaurant."

Marcia interrupted, "But anyway, so yeah, I'd say your scenario's plausible. But undocumented people fall under Homeland Security, not NBPD. If you tell me there's drugs, criminal activity, or prostitutes, you'd be in my jurisdiction. But if it is just gang stuff, you'd best stay away from the feds' turf. We've been warned to steer clear of that until further notice because of, ah . . . um . . . an interagency situation. They don't take it lightly if state and town folk get underfoot."

"Understood," Silas said. "Thanks very much, Lieutenant. Like you, my primary focus isn't on the migrants—beyond wanting to keep 'em safe. It's the dirtbag selling 'em like cattle I'm lookin' to get off the streets, and he's my target only because he fatally ran someone down in my town while doin' it."

Camara cut in at that point. "Chief, two things. First, if the streets in question are in my town, you should know I don't like surprises. Is there anything I need to be aware of right now?"

"Not at the moment. Crime was out my way, and I braced the guy in Carver, just with some pointed questions for now. Only came to New Bedford because I followed him here to his girlfriend's place the other day. At this point, I don't know when or where an arrest will make sense. Right now, just searchin' for evidence on the smuggling because I talked to a prosecutor. Gotta get proof of the migrants—only way we can kick him up to murder on the hit-and-run."

"Uh-huh," Camara said. "Second thing. This gang situation Lieutenant Dawood is bringing into this? Let me be a bit more direct and explicit. My chief here at NBPD has been in touch with the feds in recent months. I can't confirm or deny whether there is an active investigation or operation ongoing at the moment, but let's just say he has been crystal clear that our people are to stay the hell away from this gang and these known gang areas. If we trip over something, we are supposed to refer it up to our chief."

"Hear you," Silas said.

"Not sure you do," Camara said honestly. "What I am saying is, the same extends to you. Now that you've gotten me involved as your liaison at NBPD, it's gonna be on me to make sure you don't go stomping around where you're not supposed to. Sounds like you've already done that with some foot soldiers. So, let me spell it out for you: stay away from the gang shit, and leave it to the feds."

"Understand what you are saying, Lieutenant Camara. I've got no interest in the gang. Happy as a pig in shit to stay away from it. Believe me. Just need to get my guy and enough proof for a felony murder wrap, and I'll be moseyin' on down the trail. Appreciate your help and the cooperative spirit, especially since I'm new around here. Got my word, I'll give you as much of a heads-up as I can if my chase takes a turn toward your patch."

"Thanks, Chief."

"And thanks to you, Lieutenant Dawood. Hope we have a chance to work together again sometime. Kung pao chicken's on me," Silas said. He heard her laugh before hanging up.

Messy. Hate to keep Camara in the dark, but if he knew I was thinking about the Golden Dragon as a possible arrest point for Faria, he'd have to tell his chief, and the shit would rain down on both of us. Don't want the feds messing my case up any more than they want me messing up theirs— especially now that Dawood says this gang is based in New York City. All the more reason to fear they'd cut or trade a local like Faria loose with some kind of blanket immunity if they had their eyes on a bigger prize.

This way's better. Camara can tell the boss he warned me off and has no reason to believe there will be any issue. Deal with the question of updating him when there's a solid plan.

Meantime, need to shore up my proof before all those berries are picked.

CHAPTER 63

Silas was lost in thought on his drive back to Provincetown. He wasn't usually an air-conditioning guy, but it was unseasonably warm and humid, not to mention on the highway, the Jeep was less noisy with the windows up—still noisy, but not tornado level. So, he'd made concessions in the last couple of months. If pressed, he'd have to say the fancy method wasn't half-bad—especially with this coastal humidity. Nothing near as fine as a mountain breeze, but the AC dried a sticky shirt out just about as well.

Not long after he'd crossed the Bourne Bridge and passed the *Cape Cod* lettering sculpted out of evergreen yew bushes in the rotary, his phone rang, and the dashboard of his Jeep showed it was the office. He was glad the windows were up.

"Lopez."

"Chief, it's Genny here. Are you somewhere you can talk? Someone from Homeland Security called looking for you, and Anna Marsh has a question for you. Of course, I couldn't tell her when you might be back since you don't tell me where you are going like you should."

"Know it, Genny. Got me dead to rights. In all fairness, it was quarter till the crack of dawn when I took off, but I'm tryin' to get better about that before you take me out to the stockade and lock me up. I'm a bit less than an hour out, headed back. What's Marsh want?"

"She didn't say. She just went through me because she wasn't sure what your preference was, specifically, whether it was okay for her to call you directly on your cell phone."

"Hell, she's got something going on, she should call. I'm a resource for everyone on this team, all the time. If I'm in the middle of a saloon brawl or a shootout and can't talk, I won't pick up. That goes for you too, Genny. I want you to make sure everybody on the team knows, understand?"

"Yes, Chief. Right answer, by the way."

Spunky. Lucked out with this one.

"Meanwhile, can you patch her through?" he asked.

"She's here with me now, but she's going to go back to her desk to call you directly."

"Okay. Did the Homeland Security person say what it was about?"

"No, just that it was important and to call them back."

Silas felt a prick of apprehension about that. "I will, but just not right now, Genny. Keep the message slip for me for when I get back. Thanks."

Silas hung up, put his turn signal on, and moved over to the right lane closest to the canal, where he could slow down and pay attention to his phone call. As expected, his phone rang just a few seconds later, the office's number bright on his dashboard.

"Marsh, what can I do for you?"

"Chief, I've got a guy here I think you might want to talk to. It's about the Perkins case, and he might have information for us as a potential eyewitness."

"Listenin'."

"Well, he's a biologist from the Institute for Coastal Research—it's a nonprofit organization here in town. I'm not sure how much substantive information he has, but I know we need to run every lead to the ground. It's a long story how I tracked him down, but when we got to the specifics, I realized what area he was working in and what time of day. I immediately jumped to the possibility of eyewitness evidence. He may have some for us. I didn't say anything to him because, well . . . I didn't want to screw it up or plant any ideas in his head."

"Understand, Marsh, and I appreciate the smarts you're usin' there. We can interview him together. I can put the spurs to the horse and get there as fast as possible. You think you can hold him for forty-five minutes or so? Get him something to sip and maybe some vending machine grub? I can head straight to you."

"I dunno, but I can ask him."

"If that seems like too big of an ask, figure out where he'll be rest of the day, and make an appointment for us to come see him later."

"Got it, Chief."

"Good work, Marsh. Thanks."

CHAPTER 64

When Silas returned, Genny told him Homeland Security had called again. This time, it was a Special Agent Donna Calkins who'd asked for him.

"See if she's legit and whether she swings a big stick," Silas said, walking straight for Marsh's desk in the bullpen. "I'm going to see Marsh about her witness."

As he walked over to Marsh's workstation, he noticed she was sitting there alone.

"Marsh, we set up to talk to the wildlife guy?" he asked.

"Yes and no, Chief. We have an appointment to see him but not until Thursday. He had to run down to the Woods Hole Oceanographic Institution for a two-day conference. Says he's happy to help, but his grant funding and livelihood rely on him delivering a research paper there, and he can't miss it."

"Is he bringing a damn phone with him?"

"I am sure he is, but we want to see him in person. I got into it a little bit more with him, and he thinks he might have useful information. Long story, but he has some night-vision thing he uses for his research and thinks he could have some useful images for us."

"Fine, Thursday it is. But if he's not helpful, we put him in jail for making us wait."

Marsh laughed. "Not sure that's legal, Chief," she said.

As he walked away, Silas looked back over his shoulder. "Kinda state is this? Should've never left the Wild West."

CHAPTER 65

Genny followed him into his office. "Chief, I have some information about Special Agent Calkins."

"Yeah? What are her particulars?"

"She is with HSI, Homeland Security Investigations, which is a division of ICE."

"New names for old departments. Waste of perfectly good stationery."

"Well, here's what I learned. The reason you're dealing with her is because HSI is the principal investigative arm of DHS—the Department of Homeland Security." She checked the scrap of paper with her notes on it. "HSI has jurisdiction over human smuggling and trafficking, international criminal organizations, maritime smuggling, and immigration-related crimes tied to criminal enterprise."

Silas looked at her. She raised her eyebrows and nodded.

Uh-oh. Guess we know why she's trying to get in touch with us.

"Chief, these operations are big. They often work with the Coast Guard Investigative Service for maritime enforcement and Customs and Border Protection. So, yes, I think she has clout—or as you so eloquently put it, she swings a big stick."

"Damn," he said, sighing. "All right, gimme her number, then. Might as well try to get points for calling her back before she calls again."

Silas trudged into his office. He asked Genny to close the door behind her before he picked up his phone and dialed the number she'd left him.

"Chief of Police Silas Lopez from Provincetown returning Special Agent Calkins's call."

Will I hold? 'Course, I'll hold. Do I have a choice?

After a long wait, a gruff and impatient female voice came on the line. "This is Special Agent Calkins. To whom am I speaking?"

"Silas Lopez, chief of Provincetown Police."

"Right. Chief, I hear from NBPD that you are messing around with the Asian gang in New Bedford. I need you to knock it off, right now, and stay the fuck away."

Silas blinked, taken aback by how abruptly she'd gotten to the point. He couldn't tell if he was impressed or intimidated.

Well, that's a hell of an opener. Suppose it's one way to kindle interdepartmental cooperation.

"No, ma'am, I'm not." He kept his voice level.

"Not going to stay the fuck away?" she retorted, words clipped.

"No, I'm not messin' around with the Asian gang," he clarified, and she sighed audibly.

"That is not what I've been informed by the chief in New Bedford, who has been speaking with a Lieutenant Camara," Calkins said.

"I'm working a felony murder out in Provincetown. Guy from New Bedford ran somebody over with a trailer coming off our wharf. Killed him. I've got him for negligent operation, but I believe the hit-and-run occurred as part of the immediate flight from the commission of a felony inherently dangerous to human life."

Or some such—think I'm quoting Deegan right.

"Stop, Lopez. I have no time for you citing Mass state law to me, nor do I care. I need you to stay away from this gang smuggling thing. Why are you anywhere near it?"

Well, isn't this one high-and-mighty.

"That's what I'm tryin' to explain. I'm not trying to get near it," he said, keeping his voice as flat and firm as possible. "As I said, I'm after my hit-and-run perp. Now, I'm pretty sure the dangerous felony he was fleein' was pickin' up smuggled undocumented migrants on my wharf in downtown Provincetown. That's what was on the trailer that ran my vic over." He stood up, began pacing behind his desk, the curly phone cord pulling taut. "I'm not interested in your gang or your smuggling. I am just trying to tie up this local who killed my victim fleeing from my wharf. That's it."

"That is not the information I have received."

"Well, then, the information you received is *wrong*." His voice cracked like a whip now, louder than before, with a little more edge.

"Why were you involved in a confrontation with gang members near the Golden Dragon in New Bedford? We've got sources that say there are two foot soldiers in the hospital in serious condition, and you are the one who put them there."

She knows about them? That was fast.

"I'm telling you right now," she said, not mincing words. "I will have your badge if you don't stay away from this thing. This is a multistate, multiagency operation that has been ongoing for a year. Let me be clear: I need you to stay the fuck away. Do you hear me?"

"Hear you." He gathered hold of his anger, forced his voice low again. "Rest easy, I'm not steppin' on your case or lookin' to step anywhere near it. I was keeping an eye on my lowlife driver in New Bedford when those gangbangers braced me as I was just trying to get into my car. I warned them to move along, and I would have moved along too, no feathers ruffled, but one flashed a gun, and another pulled a knife. They threatened me. My dog. People I care about. I warned 'em off again. Pesky brats wouldn't back down, so I took their toys away and left 'em with enough bruises to sell the story to their shot caller."

Silas took a breath.

There was silence on the other end, which he took as an invitation to finish.

"That's it. They came to me, not the other way 'round. Guessin' it was because my lowlife might've told somebody he had some heat from Provincetown. I want nothing to do with your case. It's the lowlife I am after."

"Goddamn it, Lopez!" she exploded. Silas held the phone a bit farther from his ear to cushion the impact of her volume. "You still had contact with our gang! You are jeopardizing a massive federal operation! You need to stand down—*now*!"

She ain't listening. Just steamrolling. Fine. New tactic.

"All right. Then who's gonna round up my guy and hold him accountable for the felony murder in Provincetown?"

"We might as part of our operation, if we have proof he's an important player, but that is for us to decide, not you. You are officially relieved of responsibility for this case from this point forward."

Silas gritted his teeth. "When are you going to pick him up?"

"I am not at liberty to disclose that information," Calkins said, "but not until we are good and goddamn ready."

"What are you going to charge him with?"

"I am not at liberty to disclose that information, or any other information about this operation." Her voice was growing curter by the second.

"What guarantee do I have, does my boss have, does my victim's surviving spouse have, does my town have," he said, his hand clenching into a painfully tight fist, "that you are not just going to trade my guy out on blanket immunity for some small scrap of information?"

"None! Absolutely none. You have no guarantee. And frankly, I don't give a shit about any of those people. It is not in my job description. I'm after a much bigger fish, and you're wasting my time having to chase you down, leave messages, and warn you myself. I expect you to back the fuck off and to do so immediately."

Silas thumped his tight fist abruptly on his desk. He took a breath. "Don't care for your callous tone, Special Agent."

"Go to hell, Chief. I've got better things to do than babysit the likes of you."

The line went dead. Silas looked at the receiver for a long moment, shaking his head, before hanging it up. *Well, that went 'bout as well as expected. Rather hug a cactus than deal with a federal agent. It's like they don't know we're on the same damn team.*

He walked to the high window in his basement office, jaw flexing, and looked up at the light coming through the branches of the trees outside. He was more than happy to steer clear of her gang, sure. *But that call changes nothing. Not one damn thing. Faria's mine to bring in.* He could try to make it a clean pull, with as little splash as possible, but Silas was getting him. The only question was where and when.

Need airtight proof too, if I'm going to get out of this mess with my skin.

Yes, he would get Clark to take a ride to Carver. If there was proof in those fields, he wanted it on camera before it was gone. *I'll send Burig too—make sure Clark comes back in one piece.*

CHAPTER 66
Wednesday, October 15

Silas smelled lavender, then heard Genny arriving at her desk. He gave her a second to put down her things before saying, "Genny, get me Clark and Burig. Got something for 'em. Gonna take 'em off the board tomorrow, half a day or so."

"You have something for them, huh?" Genny said with a smile. "I'll send them in."

She looks pleased—happy to see me and Clark workin' together. She gives a damn about this team, even when they drive her nuts.

Burig came into the office and sat in Silas's guest chair, notepad at the ready. Clark followed shortly after her, carrying a second chair, which he placed next to Burig before sitting down and pulling out his own notes.

"Got something important for you two," Silas said. "Trust you'll do it well. Need you to put on some Hawaiian shirts and flip-flops first thing tomorrow and go to Carver with a camera."

Burig and Clark snatched quick looks at each other with expressions approaching shock before swiveling back at Silas.

Even by my standards, they probably think that sounded crazy. Better spell it out.

"Before we nail Faria for felony murder, we need airtight and irrefutable evidence that he was fleein' a dangerous felony. I think he's workin' the smuggled Brazilians on the cranberry harvest before he sells them on. That's the dangerous felony." He eyed the pair of them. "Need proof of this, of course, because it all comes down to whether he was fleein' a felony on the dock before he ran over our vic and killed him."

"You comin' with us, boss?" Clark asked, and Silas shook his head.

"The foreman of the farm has seen me, and based on our run-in," he added, pausing to recall the satisfaction of picking up the weasel by his shirtfront, "I suspect he'll remember me."

They nodded in unison.

"Now, like I said, I need you to throw on a Cape Cod T-shirt or something else that's touristy. Walk the edges of that farm, get a few shots of what's happening in the bogs."

Clark cleared his throat. "Chief, what exactly are we trying to capture in pictures?"

"Anything backs up our theory that it's the same Brazilians as in the crate. Anything that looks outta place. Improvise. Harvest's almost done. Clock's ticking. Need photos to lock down this part of it. Get whatever you can."

"Hawaiian shirts, Chief?" Burig teased.

Silas waved his hand back and forth in a gesture of indifference. "Whatever tourists wear. You're undercover. You're a couple from Toledo on vacation in New England interested in the history of the cranberry industry and the beautiful harvest. Carver is the cranberry capital of the world. Bogs as far as the eye can see, bushes as red as a flock of cardinals, and whatnot. Look it up so you can tell the story if you have to talk to anyone."

They looked at each other again, this time with wide eyes.

"Take the department's camera with the telephoto. And no trespassing. Unless someone invites you in, stay on public ways around the edges. Lotta the bogs are already done. I can show you on a map exactly where to go."

"Okay," Clark said, placing a hand on each chunky thigh. "And you want us both to go?"

"Yep. Safer with two. Better story if it looks like a pair of tourists. Besides, you've both earned some fieldwork. Now, go get me some proof that Faria was smugglin' Brazilians."

Plus, Burig can keep an eye on you. Be sure you don't get too clever or start bitin' off more'n you can chew.

They stood. Burig looked deeply uncertain. Clark looked proud, maybe a little too proud. They would either balance each other out, or this mission would implode like a dying star. He'd just have to wait and see which outcome came to be.

Hope I don't come to regret this.

Clark bent to pick up his chair.

"Clark, no—leave that chair in here. Don't know why they only gave me one guest chair, but two's better."

This pair gets something useful, and the biologist pans out, we'll have just about all we're gonna get. Then we'll see if Faria's reference to "the weekend" means what I think it means.

Gettin' closer. Can taste it.

CHAPTER 67
Thursday, October 16

Their biologist witness was back, so Silas and Marsh walked over to see him late Thursday morning. The Institute for Coastal Research was eight blocks from Town Hall, mostly uphill. They decided to go on foot since Silas and Bandit needed to walk off all the recent driving.

"It always this hot in October around here?" Silas asked.

"This is slightly warmer than normal, but fall is generally mild because the ocean stays warm for so long," Marsh said.

A thick blanket of humidity made it uncomfortable, but Marsh distracted Silas with the story of tracking down the biologist.

"I met a wildlife conservation friend of a friend and got talking to her. I learned there are quite a few people conducting fieldwork out here in connection with the research on the national seashore and private organizations, such as the institute. On a whim, I asked her if there might be someone doing any kind of night work anywhere near the point," Marsh explained. "She said sure, and she told me there was a biologist at the institute doing a study on the newly returned river otters. I used the info she could remember to track him down."

They'd climbed the first steep hill, and Silas felt some sweat on his neck. "Dog with a bone, Marsh. That's good police work. You've got the instincts. That's what's important. Rest is just miles."

Once they reached the top of the hill and passed the overflow parking lots near the monument, a nice breeze and a gentle slope down a tree-lined street with white picket fences and manicured gardens greeted them. There were pink and white crape myrtle trees and purple rose of Sharon bushes in bloom all along the way.

Outside the large building, Silas knotted Bandit's leash to a shady bike rack and gave the dog a quiet command to wait. Bandit obediently sat on his haunches. *Hmm. Wide tongue hanging to the side. Warm today, and a quick walk up the hill.*

He motioned for Marsh to stay put and said, "Be right back," before ducking into the building.

Silas got a cup of water from the lobby fountain. He held it low, and Bandit lapped thirstily.

Back inside, they were ushered into a small, cluttered office that smelled like rubber and damp canvas. *Yep, tall pair of waders on the back of the door.* The biologist introduced himself as Dr. Dexter Tilghman and told them to have a seat in his guest chairs. Silas pegged him at about fifty. Felt himself relax when the man said to call him Dex.

Silas introduced himself and said, "Dex, appreciate your time. Have a few quick follow-up questions branching off from your earlier conversation with Officer Marsh."

Tilghman nodded. "What's this all about? Those kids out at the point making the illegal fires and leaving trash all over the place?"

"Not exactly. As it happens, we're investigatin' a crime in the early mornin' hours in the area around the point and the town wharf. We're lookin' for anything you might have seen or heard early on September 2. What can you tell us?"

"Well, yes. My work is currently focused on river otters. They sound like a freshwater species, but they're highly adaptable, and they've been making a comeback in the saltwater marshes in our part of the world."

Silas shifted in his chair. *Should've known better than to go open-ended.*

"There's a breeding pair in the salt marsh in the West End of town—out by the breakwater and Wood End Light. River otters are primarily crepuscular, which means they're active at dawn and dusk, but in hotter weather, they can be active for much of the night, especially at certain times in the monthly tide cycle."

Running on fumes. Long days, little sleep. Maybe nudge the guy along.

"And how do these critters hitch into what we're dealin' with on September 2, Dex?"

"Right. I've been conducting a ninety-day study of the hunting behavior of these two mates. It's turned me into a regular night owl. But it is catching up with me. You're my last meeting before an early dinner and bed."

"So, you're sayin' you're out there in the wee hours?" Silas redirected.

"Yes, every night starting July first and running through the end of this month, I'm out along the strip that runs from Wood End Light to Long Point Light by about three in the morning, trying to observe them. They move all over the marsh, the stone breakwater, and up and down the beach out to the end of the point. They do go after fish, but shallow-water crabs and sea clams at low tide are among their favorite easy meals. Once the sun comes up, they become inactive, and so do I, usually taking a nap before going into the office from about nine thirty until, well . . ." He looked at his watch. "Until about ten minutes ago, most days."

"So, you're out on the point and . . . ?" Silas prompted. *Steer this conversation away from the sleeping habits of river otters and the biologists who love them.*

"I document them—field notes and pictures. For this study, I got the funds necessary to acquire some wonderful night-vision binoculars that have a camera built into them."

Now we're talkin'.

"They allow me to observe and photograph at night, even record video if there's enough memory."

Silas shifted in his seat again and looked at the wall clock.

Tilghman caught the hint.

"Anyway, I can observe them from a distance without disturbing them." Then, making the connection, he added, "Speaking of disturbing, that's why I mentioned those kids. They come out to the point late at night, drink and smoke and make noise, and leave trash. Once, they even made a bonfire, which is strictly prohibited. Their noise disturbs the otters' patterns and drives me crazy. The litter's just plain wrong, and I have to spend time picking it up each morning."

Silas glanced at Marsh, then back at Tilghman.

Tilman nodded and held up a hand with a sigh. "But Officer Marsh reminded me that Long Point and the surrounding dunes fall under the national seashore's jurisdiction, so I plan to speak to them."

"Right. So, let's get back to what you saw," Silas said.

This guy wanders off like a coonhound on a scent trail.

"Well, when I mentioned to your officer that I'm out there long before dawn every day, she asked me if I was there the morning of September 2. Of course I was, and I remember specifically. It was a stormy night due to the remnants of a hurricane that had passed out at sea. The otters were nowhere to be found in the chop."

Sounds like our night—and this is a helpful, cooperative witness—but at this pace, another hurricane could pass before this guy gets to any key information.

"I remembered I had seen something odd one day in early September. I went back and looked at my pictures to refresh my memory. A boat came fast along the outer side of the point. It was loud, even over the wind, like it was at full power. It was pitching and rolling pretty hard."

That explains the vomit forensics found. Poor, terrified people, probably still motion sick from the boat ride when they got in that cargo container.

"I went to the top of the dune to watch because until the otters turned up, I had nothing better to do. When the boat approached the end of the point, it went completely dark. All the running lights and all the lights inside the boat went out, and it cut back its throttle as it rounded the tip."

"You get a good look at it? Do you remember how big it was? The color, any special equipment on board, or any other identifying details?" Silas asked, voice hopeful.

"I don't need to remember because I took pictures with the night-vision binoculars, Chief," the biologist said with obvious satisfaction.

"The binoculars were still new to me, and I thought they were pretty nifty, so it was a good excuse to try them out on a different subject. After Officer Marsh mentioned the importance of the date to me, I came back here and looked at my image files."

This is startin' to look promising—so where's the catch? Every lead has one.

"I meant to throw the boat pictures away, along with any other useless field study pictures, but I haven't gotten around to culling my digital files yet. That's the problem with studies involving a prodigious amount of fieldwork—your office starts to look like this," he said, gesturing to his cluttered desk with a chuckle. "And you get behind on things like cleaning up your field notes and pictures."

"Can we see those pictures?" Silas asked, excitement cutting through his fatigue.

"Yes. If you want to come around to this side, I can show you." He waved them over to his side of the desk. "I took several of just the silhouette as it headed into the harbor, one of the stern as it was moving in, a few while it was idling, and one last one of the front as it headed back out."

Silas and Marsh exchanged glances as they came around the desk. He could sense her hope rising too. They bent toward the dusty old flat-screen monitor to take a look at the grid of green images on the biologist's screen. Mostly river otters, shore birds, and marsh grass, but it was the row in the center of the screen Silas cared about, where he could already see the black outline of a trawler—bright-green spots representing the white foam and spray off its bow. In one of the pictures, the binoculars were zoomed way in on the wide stern of the boat. Even in the grainy, low-light image, with the ship canted in the swell between the point and the breakwater, the block letters were clear across the stern. They read *SEREIA*.

Gotcha! Silas's pulse quickened as he scanned the rest of the shots. There was one other useful image. A long-range picture of the boat at the wharf. Its lights were still off, but there was some light cast on the dock from the street poles, and Silas could make out a group of people standing on the wharf above the boat. Then, his heart skipped. There it was. The square outline of the container on the trailer behind them.

"Dex, this is powerfully helpful stuff. Very grateful for your assistance. We're gonna need copies of these," Silas said, looking at Marsh, who handed him a memory stick.

As Tilghman copied the photos, Silas's mind reeled at what they'd found. *Got the boat. Got the migrants. Got the cargo box. Got the time stamp.*

And Faria's got a noose around his neck, gettin' tighter by the minute.

At this rate, Marsh is running away with case MVP too.

CHAPTER 68

"Log the copies of these photos into the case file, and get an affidavit from Dex authenticating them—but first, coordinate with Byrne," Silas instructed Marsh on their walk back to the office. "One of you get ahold of the harbormaster in New Bedford. See if they have any records on the *Sereia* or any footage on the harbor's cameras. Shots of it coming or going anywhere during September."

Marsh nodded. *Don't have to explain twice with this one.*

"Cast a wide net," he added. "As today shows, anything can turn into a lead. Again, great work finding Tilghman. Plugs up a big hole in our case."

Marsh nodded silently, but Silas could see by the twinkle in her eyes that she was pleased.

It was warmer now, and the walk back felt twice as long. They passed by people window-shopping in town, and Silas caught a glimpse of his reflection in a shop window. The Silas looking back at him had drawn features and bags under his eyes. This case was wringing him out. The sustained effort was a lot, but the weight of being in charge and responsible for the outcome, and being under Flood's thumb for a fast wrap-up, was also a lot of pressure. He wanted nothing more than to go home and sleep, but tomorrow was Friday, and he would be working most of the weekend.

Need to see Wren again. Left things kinda delicate.

Bandit sniffed while they plodded along.

Wouldn't mind seeing that smile. Be nice to cross paths before the weekend. Maybe a quick lunch. Could make it a dune ride, like I promised.

Silas trudged another couple of paces.

Could text her—if I had her damn number. Guess we never needed it, being in the same building. Hell with it. Go in person. She knows I'm sweet on her. No point getting cute or outthinking myself . . .

Back at Town Hall, he stopped by his desk for a fortifying gulp of room-temperature coffee, then plodded up the stairs to knock on Wren's office door.

"Hey!" she said. "Oh, man, I thought I was dragging a little today, but you might have me beat! You look rough."

"Thanks for noticin'," he said wryly. "Case's at full gallop right now, and I'm puttin' in long stretches in the saddle. Speakin' of that, gonna have to work through the weekend too, but couldn't sit with the thought of disappearin' without so much as a *caw*!"

Wren made a sad frown about the weekend, but her laugh at his crow sound wiped the frown away.

"Had an idea. Wonderin' if you're free tomorrow around midday—maybe sneak off for a picnic lunch. Thinkin' maybe go for a ride over the dunes, end with a picnic on the beach out by Race Point Light. You could check the cylindrical lighthouse for curvy, photo-worthy shadows; maybe I could catch my civilian adviser up on the case."

Wren's eyes lit up. "Ooh. You are selling this well. Tomorrow's supposed to be nice weather. That might be fun. What time are you thinking about?"

"Work around your schedule, but maybe eleven thirty?"

She looked at her computer screen. "I can do that. I have a meeting at ten thirty a.m. that should finish right around then." She moved her fingers on the trackpad and typed, maybe to block the time out on her calendar. "This will be fun! Do you need help with the food?"

"No, I'll take care of everything. You have a favorite sandwich from Farland?"

"Well, you know, they do have one very appropriately called the Race Point. It's roast beef and horseradish, which might interest you. But for me, hmm . . . the Ballston with the apple slices is my favorite. Marble rye. And you know, if you've never tried their strawberry oat bars, you owe it to yourself . . ."

"To myself, huh? That's solid advice you're giving me. It's a plan. Come downstairs around eleven thirty—or whenever you're finished—and we'll head out."

"Can't wait."

"Me, neither. Woulda missed talkin' to you all weekend, since the lady hasn't seen fit to give the gentleman her phone number."

Her eyes widened with surprise when she realized that might be true. "How is that possible?"

"You're the one keepin' the gate shut, so you tell me. Guess you've gotten away with it because we work in the same building, talk on work lines, email. Of course, now's your chance to make it right, if you've a mind to do so."

She gave him a wicked smile. "We'll see how this goes. If I have a nice time, maybe you'll get that number."

"Sure like to have it, so I'll give it my best."

He rapped on her door twice to signal the end of the discussion, turned on his heel, and headed for the staircase with a stupid grin on his face. Bandit clicked along behind him.

If she's wavering on me, she's hidin' it pretty well. Still, it's an undeniable fact that I don't actually have her number, so best bring the A game tomorrow.

CHAPTER 69
Friday, October 17

Silas had been up early, taking the doors and top off the Jeep. He didn't have a vacuum—one of many things left behind in Salt Lake City—but he used his apartment's little whisk broom and pan to tidy the sand in the footwells and brush off the seats. He also ran a damp cloth around the dash for good measure. Then, he headed into the office.

When Clark knocked on his office door, Genny was showing Silas how to order things from Farland using the shop's phone app.

"Clark, come in," Silas said, noticing Burig behind him. "Morning, Burig. Gimme a second—Genny's givin' me a tune-up on my phone skills."

Clark and Burig sat down in Silas's mismatched guest chairs. Burig was holding an iPad.

"There, that's the big items taken care of," Genny said, gesturing at the phone. "Just specify when you want to pick it up here, and then press this checkout button here. Don't worry about any of this small stuff—you can add chips and drinks or whatever in person when you go to pick it up."

Silas tapped at the phone like a bear trying to thread a sewing needle— big hands moving with surprising gentleness, but still making the thing wobble like it was trying to get away. After a final, delicate jab, he set it down with quiet triumph.

"Genny, you work miracles. Couldn't make it a day without you."

Genny paused with a hand on his doorframe before leaving. "Happy to help. And I am jealous of your outing. If you don't send me at least one picture from out there, you are in trouble."

Silas smiled at her, but she'd turned to go and didn't see it.

"Sergeant, Officer, you're both wearin' that cat-who-got-the-canary look," he said, turning to Clark and Burig at last. "What'd you pull off down there?"

"Chief, I think we got some useful evidence," Clark said. His face portrayed a mixture of pride and relief that the assignment had gone well. It was clear that he was trying hard and cared about the outcome of this assignment. *All good things.*

"I brought this bigger screen so we can show you," Burig added, holding up the iPad.

"Okay, bring it around. Anybody see you or ask any questions?"

Clark said, "We were out in the more remote bogs like you said, and it was mostly quiet except for the workers and a couple of supervisors. The department's lens is not as powerful as some, so we had to make ourselves visible to a supervisor so we could get closer and get enough detail."

"Uh-oh. Hopin' you didn't have to shoot him," Silas said with a grin.

Clark gave a half smile. It was genuine but reserved, like he didn't want to be teased in front of Marsh. *That's fair. My mistake.* "No, we did the tourist thing—said the red bog and all the fruit was beautiful. Burig deserves at least an Emmy, if not an Oscar. The manager said it was private property and asked us to move along. Burig chatted him up about the art of growing cranberries while I stole a few close shots, and then we ambled out of there."

Burig beamed. She was nodding along at the retelling, clearly grateful that Clark was being so generous with the credit.

"Well done," Silas said. "Let's see what came through."

"We got some useful ones. It's migrants, like you thought. Burig looked up some information while we drove back. More on that in a second—but Chief, we also learned something about the timing of the harvest."

Silas raised his eyebrows. This was good intel.

"Burig asked when they'd be done and whether we could photograph the very end part—you know, the millions of floating berries making the whole pond pink. He said, 'No, no pictures,' which seems a little odd for a law-abiding farm. However, he also said the harvest was essentially complete, anyway. They said it'd been a really dry season, so they harvested early. They were working on some of the last bogs to be flooded. Said they'd finish the last fields in a day and a half, maybe less."

"That's helpful for me to know. Got good intel. Means we don't have a lot of time to play around with, so it's a relief you got some pictures." Silas tapped both palms on his desk. "Okay. Migrants. Let's look at the photos and see what you got, Ansel Adams."

Clark said, "The workers seemed nervous—heads down, no eye contact, not even a nod, wave, or smile, as if they wanted nothing to do with me. I thought that was notable."

He's pickin' up some details. That's progress.

They looked through the photos, and Silas saw things they could use almost at once. The faces of the workers looked unmistakably Latin American and could be Brazilian—but their clothing was most definitive.

Burig said, "See, most are in plain, drab-looking clothes . . ."

Silas noticed mostly long sleeves for sun protection and pant legs rolled up in the water but soaking wet, anyway.

"But not everyone was in drab clothing," Burig said. "See here, one of the younger male workers has a bright-yellow shirt with green trim that has the letters *CBF* with a crest on the front and the word *Brasil* across the back."

Silas leaned in and looked closer, but Burig took two fingers and pinched out to make the center of the image fill the screen.

"And see here, an older worker has a baseball hat with a red and blue Skol Ultra logo surrounded by this swooping yellow arrow." She swiped quickly through a few photos. "And see, this third man sticks out because he's in a white jersey with a horizontal red and black stripe and the letters *SPFC* and a crest emblazoned across the front."

Silas nodded. *Got questions, but let them tell the story their way.*

Burig continued, "On the way back, I used my phone to search the web for these words and logos. Chief, it took no time to figure out that *CBF* is Brazil's national football league. Skol Ultra turns out to be pretty much the Budweiser of Brazil, and *SPFC* stands for"—she checked her notes—"São Paulo FC, the big football club of São Paulo, Brazil's largest city."

Burig swiped to images of the various logos and crests to show Silas her findings. She'd been thorough. Silas took in each one, more convinced with every swipe. They weren't trying to blend in—some part of them still carried pride for home on their backs.

This is gold. Can do something with this for sure.

"Well done. These pictures will help our case. Ain't proof, but they sure as heck back my hunch up strong." He looked up at Clark and Burig. "One of you go get Marsh; have her bring the shots from the biologist. Let's see if any of these striped shirts show up in that wharf photo. If they do, we're cinching the knot a bit tighter." He nodded at the iPad. "These the clearest ones you got of those logo shirts?"

"Yes, and we had to get too close to get them. Chief, not sure what the budget priorities are, but I think we need a better camera for long-distance surveillance," Clark said.

"From what I understand about photography, a bigger sensor and a brighter, longer lens would have allowed us to get better shots from farther away," Burig said.

"Good thinking. Happens I know a photographer who might be able to give us some advice on that. Might even be able to loan us something in the meantime," Silas noted. Burig and Clark exchanged quick glances, but not quick enough—Silas caught them, and the smirks that followed.

He didn't even try to keep up the act.

"Yeah, yeah—Wren Bradford from upstairs," Silas admitted. "I saw those looks. Knock it off, you two. Gonna jinx me. Besides, none of your damn beeswax. Get out of here before I put you two undercover agents on permanent desk duty. Great work, Officers."

They got up to leave, shuffling toward the door.

Before they left, he added, "Hey, not quite done here. This assignment was out of the ordinary for you two. Bit of a stretch. But I knew I could count on you with it. You done good. Those pictures are a big contribution to our case. Hope you know how much I appreciate it."

Burig and Clark nodded bashfully, clearly thrilled by the praise and flush with success.

Times like this, feels like things are on the right track around here.

Meanwhile, case is coming to a head.

Timing's primed to blow. No way Faria's feeding twenty-three workers multiple meals a day much past harvest time. No way he's keeping that rented trailer longer than he needs to. These migrants could be back on the move again in the next day or two. Gotta get some eyes on tomorrow. See what I can learn.

CHAPTER 70

Wren was talking to Genny when Silas returned to the office to meet her.

"Everything go okay with the order?" Genny asked him.

"Buttoned up fine," he reported, giving Wren a smile. "Got the fixin's. Now just need someone to split it with. Shame to eat it solo."

Wren raised a hand and gave a small wave. "I'll go," she said with a smile.

"Don't mind if we do," Silas said, holding out an elbow for her to grab.

Can feel Burig and Marsh staring at my back, but not gonna let that shake me off the job.

"Feel bad duckin' out when things are hoppin', Genny, but a man's gotta eat. Rover and cell phone should both work out there, so holler if you need anything. Back before too long."

A few minutes later, they cut through the brown, summer-burned swales of the cemetery before crossing the highway and picking up Race Point Road out to the back beach. The road through Beech Forest was a tunnel of green and gold, with layers of leaves scattering dappled light that danced all around them as the cool scent of the forest swirled in through the roll bars.

Wren pushed her sunglasses up onto her head—*like some kinda movie star.* "This is heavenly!"

Silas was wearing a faded red cotton ballcap, sun-bleached along the crown, softer at the brim edges where time and weather had chewed it down. Blocky white stitched letters read "TAOS FEED & GRAIN Since 1948," with a tiny embroidered steer head below the lettering, thread fraying on one horn. From under its brim Silas looked at her with a smile, nodding three times.

He pulled up next to a weathered old shed nestled against a dune and got out. Old country classics played quietly through the speakers. "Gonna be a minute while I air these tires down soft enough for the sand, but there's a breeze, so shouldn't be any mosquitoes. Pesky critters stick around late into the season here."

"They do," Wren said, watching him work on a front tire through the open side of the Jeep. Then, turning to look around the interior, she added, "This thing's called a Wrangler, right? I confess, I looked it up."

"Yep. This is an Unlimited, I think, as it's a four-door."

"Kinda fits you. Always been a Jeep guy?"

He nodded.

"Grew up 'round 'em. Always driven 'em. Old CJs back in the day." He shrugged. "Tough. Can get up narrow, twisty trails a pickup's too big for. Go like a bighorn sheep through mountain snow when it hits. Seats slide way back, so I can fit. American-made, so parts are easy to find; can fix 'em most places." Silas warmed to the topic. "Unless you're haulin' heavy loads everywhere, just more all-around useful than a pickup."

He got lost in the memories for a moment. Wren sat, turned in her seat with a look of curious interest on her face.

"Kept with 'em when I moved to the city. Easier to fit in parking spaces than a truck. Warm weather, top 'n doors off is nice. And you can hose 'em out, so no fuss if Bandit gets filthy and wet."

He looked around, pulling back to the present moment.

"Bonus that they're good on the dunes out here."

He stopped, flushing slightly.

Might've gone a bit overboard there. Hope she doesn't think I'm pitching a car commercial.

He changed the subject. "Now that the piping plovers are fledged and summer sands have built up, most of the beach is open. Figured we could take the Pole Line route along the dunes to the light station, then cut out onto the spit across Hatches Harbor. Wind today should be just right. Enough breeze. Not too much."

"Sounds perfect." She looked all around, took a long inhale of the scent through her nose. "Can't remember the last time I rode out here. When I was a kid, my family used to have a big International Harvester Travelall. Adirondack green with wood-panel decals." Then, syncing with the theme of their truck talk, she added, "I think it was a '69."

Don't know if she's a car person, but like that she asks, remembers details. That's people skills. Kind and considerate. Gotta repay that effort wherever I can.

Wren's voice softened, sifting through memories, as Silas finished up with the tires. "My dad loved that thing. He'd load the whole family— my mom, grandparents, and my sister and me in the way back. We'd roam dunes, beaches. Sometimes fish and picnic out here. Good memories. Time spent outdoors, and on the cape in general, took them away from being so stiff and proper. They could just . . . be." She chuckled ruefully. "Even laugh once in a while, if no one was looking."

Can picture a miniature freckled version of Wren bouncing up and down in the back row of that old truck.

Different from what I'm used to, but family memories, traditions, same as any.

Tires deflated, Silas put the now squishy-riding Jeep in 4-Low and turned onto the sand road. The road scrub of the soft tires went silent except for the muted churn and crunch of sand. Gears from the transfer case whined softly under them as the view changed to an otherworldly landscape.

"Not likely to get used to a view like this," Silas said.

Layers and layers of wind-driven sand hills surrounded them, most covered by waves of pale-green dune grass, some dotted with beach plum shrubs, poison ivy at their bases. The road over the dunes was nothing more than a wide path zigzagging between dunes, grooved by overlapping tire tracks.

Leaving nothing to chance, Silas had reviewed the route carefully in advance, so he navigated with ease and managed the deep sand well, pulling over for an oncoming vehicle at one point when he reached a suitable wide spot. The breeze through the Jeep alternated between warm and cool—one gust heated by sunbaked sand, the next sweeping in off the cooler water. Bandit's fur blew back and forth as his head swiveled to follow a red-tailed hawk hunting for its lunch.

Wren was quiet at first, taking in her surroundings, not feeling any need to fill the silence.

Like that about her.

After a while, he said, "Penny for your thoughts."

"Just enjoying the ride." She grabbed the passenger bar in front of her, leveraging it to turn and give him an appraising look. "It's odd to see you in a new context, doing something different, out in the real world. Never really thought about you as a good driver, confident navigator, or road trip partner."

"Figure I always relied on my horse to navigate?" He grinned. "Had plenty of time off-road and backcountry like this, but done my time in cities too. Found my footing in the 'real world.' Learned I don't mind some modern conveniences. Computers, for one. Hard to do my job without 'em. Smartphones, too."

"So, you're fully modernized, huh? And yet, at the stoplight on our way out, I saw you jot something into that ancient little pocket notebook in the center console. What's that about? No Siri in this car?" Wren teased, a wide grin lighting up her face.

"Old-school scribbling's quicker. Makin' note of a song title."

"Writing a book?" Wren asked with a laugh.

"Nothin' like that. Tryin' to teach myself about music. Older country songs, in particular."

"Oh, that sounds interesting. Why?" Wren asked, her head cocked to the side.

"Uh-oh, stepped in a cow pie now," he said, chuckling. "Gonna have to explain this. Okay, lemme see if I can . . . I get comfort from old country songs. Had an uncle who played what he liked to call 'the classics.' Those old country standards remind me of home. Truth is, I regret not payin' more attention when he taught me, 'cause now those songs give me some solace when I find 'em."

Wren nodded encouragingly. "I get that. Makes sense. But how does the notepad fit in?"

"Helps tryin' to track 'em down. Use satellite radio for hearin' the old stuff. Something familiar or good comes along, note the title and musician. Look it up later when I have time. Try to learn more, find connections—other songs by them, similar artists. Want to be able to find my way around on my own. Learn the deepest old roots of country music. Know what I like. Find things reliably."

"That's neat. Interesting." They came around a bend into a flat area. "There's the lighthouse ahead."

Wren held her phone out her side of the vehicle at arm's length and pointed it in through the open doorframe to take a picture of the two of them. "Smile for Genny! We promised."

Silas made the best smile his face could before turning at a rough fork in the trail marked by a sand fence. He went left and crossed a pebbly area, then past the giant rusty anchor outside the lightkeeper's house. The path turned sharply at the base of the conical lighthouse, and they slipped through a narrow spot in some flowering scrub before popping out through a dune cut onto the sparkling beach. Another sharp turn to the left allowed the sea breeze to pass through the vehicle, blowing Wren's wavy hair across her face.

She worked on tying it back with her rolled-up bandana headband, and Silas steered them down the long, narrow sand spit that ran between the bay on their right and the vast salt marsh to their left.

When the spit had tapered to almost nothing, Silas said, "Set up here?" before letting off and allowing the Jeep to roll to a short stop in the deep sand. He unhitched Bandit, who leaped out to explore while they spread out Silas's gray blanket and Wren began unpacking lunch.

"Wow, you outdid yourself with this spread, cowboy," she said as she unpacked the brown paper bag. "Sides, chips, drinks. Thank you! Hope you're hungry." She pulled out the last items from the bag and peeked into some white deli paper. A smile bloomed across her face. "And I see strawberry oat squares too! You're in for a treat."

He grinned. "That's right. Got those *just* for me."

Wren punched his arm. "Here, before we eat, move in close. Let's get one more for Genny," she said as they put their heads together. After the click, he caught a glimpse of the photo on the screen. It was a timeless image. Two happy people, relaxed and warm, sitting on a picnic blanket spread on a windswept spot. Looking at it gave Silas a quiet glow. He wondered if Wren felt the same.

"Speaking of pictures," he said, "I sent Kevin Clark and Laura Burig on a photo job this week. Case has developed since our morning walk on the beach. Migrant smugglin' is the working theory now. Believe victim got hit by a long trailer full of Brazilian migrants being hustled off the wharf. Pictures from the photo job were to help prove my theory that those same smuggled Brazilians work some cranberry bogs over in Carver."

"Oh, really? That sounds quite a bit more complicated. Smuggling? In Provincetown? And you sent Sergeant Clark to get pictures?" she asked, brows raised skeptically.

"He's makin' good progress," Silas informed her. "Wanted to give him a chance to shine after some of his recent troubles. Burig was my insurance policy—keep him on track."

Wren laughed.

"Got the pictures we needed, but they had to get so close, they nearly joined in on the harvest. Was looking for surveillance, not day labor. Think the department's camera gear's not up to the job—lens doesn't reach." He gave her a mock-quizzical look. "Wondered if you knew anybody who knows about that sort of thing?"

"It just so happens I do, you goof," she said with a grin. "For that kind of work, you need a big lens and a camera with a large sensor for sensitivity to light. I can help you find the right gear. Meanwhile, if you need something for this case, I have a setup you can borrow."

"Thank you. Could use the leg up."

Wren put her arms around her knees and looked out at the water.

"You know, since we are talking tech, I had a thought about your music project. Your method works, but it might take a while, just waiting and hoping they play something you like. I could give you a shortcut if you're curious?"

She looked at him, eyes inquisitive.

"Worse things than listenin' to some country while you wait."

"That's true," she said, grinning, holding both palms up. "No pressure. Just an idea."

"Hold your horses, missy. I'm not shuttin' ideas down. Whole point's to learn. Sounds like somethin' is up your sleeve. Like the balladeer says, 'I don't believe in criticizing what I don't understand.' Tell me what I'm missin'."

Wren, four years younger but at least two tech generations ahead, rotated on the blanket to face him and explained with enthusiasm how the subscription music services on his phone had nearly infinite back catalogs and could learn what he liked, recommending similar songs.

As Wren talked, Silas looked down past the end of the sand spit. His mind spun a little, taking it all in. But her method sounded like a fastball right over home plate, so he tried to keep up. She even showed him how to have his phone listen and identify songs playing in public places around him. By the time she finished, he was blown away with excitement, admiration, and gratitude.

"You amaze me, Wren Bradford. Could get used to havin' a brain like yours around." Then, wary of where he might be heading, he added, holding up a palm, "And, 'fore you say it—no, not just the big brain. Like the sum of the parts. With you, it all comes together real nice. Can't think of a thing I'd change. Nobody me and Bandit would rather picnic with."

He winked, then deftly changed the subject. "Fact, let's get after those sandwiches."

"Nice save," she said, and they ate.

As they finished and crumpled their sandwich wrappers, a large pod of seals swam by. Bandit alerted and ran to the surf line. Seals bobbed up to look at him, and Wren grabbed her phone and crept toward the shore.

When she sat back down on the blanket, she said, "I got some adorable shots of him and that small one looking at each other. I have to get you copies."

"Got service. You could text 'em to me now, if you like," Silas suggested.

Wren's head swiveled. "You sneaky devil!" she said. "I am a virtuous woman, and here you are trying to use your dog to help you swindle my phone number early! Did you concoct this whole thing just to get it?"

Silas laughed. "Makes you feel better, you'd be sneakin' my number too. And I might have earned it. Picnic's not over, but it's been smooth as calm water so far. Got out here without rolling the Jeep or gettin' us lost. Ate well; gave you a chance to show how smart you are. If I don't deserve the lady's number, who does?" he said with what he hoped was his best twinkle in his eyes.

"All right, I'll give it to you, but only because you're my ride back to the office."

Silas dictated his number, which still had an 801 area code, and Wren finished sending him the pictures.

Silas admired them. The pair fell into a comfortable silence. It was broken by Wren coming back to Silas's case. "So, you were saying your current theory for your case is migrants? How did you arrive there from a seemingly simple hit-and-run?"

Silas thought for a moment before answering. "We had to put a lot of work into identifying the vehicle. In the end, the only way we could do it was to trace the likely route to find any video of it we could. Left us wondering about a long trailer coming off the wharf in the middle of the night. Did enough digging to confirm our hunch that a big trailer, that time of night, didn't make a lot of sense comin' from out on the wharf itself, so we circled and stalked around it. Eventually, we had enough details all pointing in the same direction, and our hunch became the leadin' theory."

"It's interesting to watch the way you work, Silas. There's more intuition and guesswork than one might expect. It strikes me that some of the same is true in my work."

"Can't know what's in a person's head or heart," Silas said, "even when they tell you. Can only read what's in front of you and hazard guesses."

Wren shook her head and looked out at the horizon where the bright water met the clear blue sky. "Those poor migrants. Some people are capable of unspeakable cruelty, which, sadly, is something we also both see in our work."

"Yep. You get to protect victims, which has some weight. I like that I get to go further, see to it that bad actors are punished. I like having a hand in making sure justice is meted out. Satisfying part of the work for me."

"Speaking of work, we probably can't stay out here forever, even if it is a Friday," Wren said.

"Sadly not, but I'm awful glad we got to come out. With luck, I'll get this case wrapped up soon, release some of the pressure clampin' down on me. Meantime, it's back to the coal mine."

As they picked up their picnic and loaded it into the back of Silas's Jeep, Bandit jumped in. Wren looked Silas in the eye, her face wearing an irresistible look. "This was lovely. Thank you. I think you did earn that number, and I hope you use it."

"Was fixin' to," Silas said with a grin. "I hope you don't regret givin' it to me. Find myself with a powerful urge to talk to you when I haven't seen you. Now, I got the means. Better watch out."

Wren laughed and grabbed the windshield frame as Silas swung the Jeep around and headed back up the narrow sand spit.

CHAPTER 71
Saturday, October 18

Silas spent most of Saturday in the office, reviewing the case file and organizing the materials they had. He planned to head to Carver to have another look around and get more pictures later in the day. Before he went, he wanted to get his horses in the corral, review his process notes, eyewitness reports, and evidence lists—and most importantly, identify any gaps.

He worked slow and steady, sorting and cataloging what they'd gathered. Broke only to walk Bandit and grab three slices of pizza from the Greek place across the street.

Get this case done, gotta do better on meals. Can't run an engine on bad fuel. Gettin' close. Can feel things circling around.

When he was sure things were in order, he checked for gaps the best way he knew how—he forced himself to write a summary of his theory of the case, referencing all the evidence backing up each assumption. Any critical assumption not backed up by solid evidence was a hole.

His handwriting was rough but legible. He wrote in big block letters as he always did, and the wide, flat pencil left deep grooves on the pad each time he flipped a page. He stopped now and then to sharpen it with his pocketknife, and by the end, his hand ached enough that half his notes had slid into chicken scratch.

Need to ask Genny for carpenter's pencils for my office—something with some meat to grip instead of those cheap, skinny Provincetown Police Department pens all over the place.

When he finished his summary, he was satisfied they had what they needed. Ultimately, it would be up to Deegan, the prosecutor. Still, Silas was confident they had done all they could do to document that Faria had been fleeing an inherently dangerous felony when he hit Timothy Perkins.

All's left in this case is to figure out how best to pick up this lowlife and turn him in. That's going to take some thought. Need one more trip to Carver, look around, scope it out proper, have a think about the geography of this case. Figure out the where and the when of picking up Tony. Safest, cleanest way's always best.

He decided to arrive at the farm around dusk so he could move around more easily among the deepening shadows. He thought about the case and the best approach to the takedown while he worked his way along the now-too-familiar route. When he arrived, he tucked the Jeep in the trees down a sandy little dirt turnoff. It was cool enough to leave Bandit, but Bandit wasn't having it.

"Gotta stay here, buddy—can't take you with me."

Look at those pleading eyes. All this driving's been rough on him. This dog needs to stretch his legs.

"You can't come, buddy, but I'll give you a walk before I go."

Once leashed, Bandit launched out and spun like he'd just won the lottery.

It's only a walk, boy, sorry.

When they returned to the Jeep, Bandit curled up on the driver's seat, and Silas walked along the narrow roadway to a thin spot in the tree line nearest the barns. He walked through the underbrush to access a break between trees, his footfalls crunching against dead leaves. He still couldn't see or hear much. He took some pictures, but they came out dim and grainy. *Useless.*

He moved farther down, crossing the mouth of the farm's main driveway. The look-through spots on the other side were a little more open but still not good. The farmyard was empty and silent. There was dim light in the small windows high along one big metal shed, but he didn't hear or see anything. He tried some more pictures. Same result, only now with a blotch of light in the center of the frame from the shed's windows.

He retraced his steps and decided to chance a peek from partway down the driveway. Silas came around a bend and got a good view of the farmyard—still nothing. The farm was quiet. If the migrants were here, they were on lockdown somewhere and not making themselves seen or heard. Saturday night, end of a long harvest . . . *The managers and supervisors are probably home with their families or out blowing off some steam.*

No noise, no activity, no trucks. An icy stab of a thought occurred to him. Was he too late? Had they come and gone, and he'd missed his chance? His pulse kicked up. Jaw clenched. All this, and he might've missed it by a day. He was seized by this uncomfortable thought. He turned back fast—quiet but quick. Retraced his steps to the Jeep.

He needed to know. Could they be done with this harvest and gone?

He started the Jeep and put on the parking lights. Dusk had almost faded, but he didn't want to use his headlights—make him too visible and cut his night vision.

After a short drive around the perimeter, he was relieved to find a few bogs way down at the end of the main clearing that were surrounded by beat-up harvesting equipment. One bog was still flooded; a harvesting boom made of rope through floats was cutting across the water. Inside the broad curve of the floating boom was a carpet of pinkish-red fruit.

Relief coursed through him. Chances were good they'd finish up tomorrow. He was still in the game.

From this distant vantage point, he could see a hilltop silhouetted against the denim-blue sky. It was on the far side of the barnyard from him. He spotted a cell tower poking up through its tree canopy, blinking lights on its mast.

Maybe there's a way up there. He drove around the big clearing full of bogs and eventually found a rough-looking, two-track dirt road going up the back side of the hill. If he could get up there quietly and find some cover, he'd be able to see the farmyard.

That's the spot for tomorrow when the harvest is done. Tonight, this place is dead. Time to get the dog home. Get some sleep. If I'm right—and I sure hope I am—tomorrow night will be a long one.

CHAPTER 72
Sunday, October 19

Silas was increasingly certain the transfer would go down this weekend. The farm being dead on Saturday night meant Sunday was likely the day. To be in the best position possible, he planned to head back to the bog late that afternoon, hoping to catch Faria gathering the migrant workers and get that on film.

His gut told him the man would show. Even with Clark's pictures the other day, Silas figured more pictures only could help—especially if Faria was present. But it was going to be dark, and the department's camera wasn't going to cut it for clear, detailed images. If there was a day to borrow that camera from Wren, it was today.

Padding around the house in old socks he'd mended several times, he texted Wren from the couch and asked if he could borrow "that camera with the big lens."

When he stopped by her house to pick it up later that afternoon, she opened the door in an oversize white button-down shirt knotted at the waist, cutoff jean shorts, and bare feet. She was holding a book with her thumb, marking the spot.

The scent of fresh-baked cornbread rushed out around her. Silas blinked.

Know that smell anywhere.

The sun coming through the house blazed behind her, igniting an orange halo around her hair. The light caught the fine golden hairs on her arms, setting them aglow. He could glimpse some skin above her hip bones and a thin strip of pale, faintly freckled stomach. It socked him hard, and he was speechless for a moment, taking her in. His hungry stare must've been obvious—he could plainly see her blush.

Flustered, she bent down to pat Bandit.

Think you're flustered? Live a thousand years, and never get used to the sight of you.

Silas recovered, blowing out a deep breath, and said, "Sorry. Only time I borrow your camera; got my word. If I can find one like this without hockin' the town silver, I'll get us our own."

"I can help you source something decent and affordable. I can also help you sell the existing one if you want—there are sites for that," Wren said.

Of course there are.

"Here, let me show you how to work it," she said. "Let's go out on the front balcony."

Wren showed him how to turn it on, how to put it in a mode for night shots, how to work the zoom. To properly demonstrate each feature, it was necessary to stand close to Silas, which made it nearly impossible for him to concentrate. But he got the gist, and he took it in when she warned him the autofocus would hunt a bit in the dark before locking onto its target. Finally, she let him look through the camera at the harbor.

"Whoa, now! Like being right there," he said, impressed. He could see every detail—the shiny black feathers on the row of cormorants across the breakwater, the rust on the hulls of the trawlers. "This thing could spot a tick on a bull at a mile!"

"Good gear doesn't make you a photographer, but it sure doesn't hurt."

He kept his eye peering through the viewfinder, panning across the horizon. "Damn thing's like some kinda space telescope that makes evidence! Thank you for loaning it."

"My pleasure. For my kind of photography, it is one of my least-used lenses, and that's a spare camera body, so it's really no trouble."

Silas looked down at Bandit quietly. "Hate to drag this guy all the way down there again. I like him by my side, but he's done more Jeep time to Carver and back than's fair for an active breed like him."

"Actually, I'm glad you brought that subject up. I agree he's been a good sport, but it has been a lot. In fact, I was just thinking about him earlier this afternoon. If you'd be comfortable with the idea, he could keep me company tonight instead of having to haul him all the way to Carver again. I would love it—I'd be happy to take him for a walk or two."

"Well, I'd hate to impose. Was gonna let him snooze in the Jeep and hoof it in . . ."

Shaking her head, Wren said, "It's really no trouble, Silas. I promise."

"Hate being a burden, but if I'm honest, the offer is tempting. Can't argue with your plan—it's got a lot goin' for it."

He looked down at Bandit.

"Hours and hours cramped up in the dark just to watch me watch nothin' is a grind on him." Silas thought some more. "Plus, there's a risk he barks and draws searchlights and snipers right down on me," he said, grinning to make sure she knew he was joking about the snipers.

Then, Silas second-guessed himself.

"But no—it'd be too late. Don't want to bother you comin' by to pick him up."

"Silas, I'm not offering just to be polite. I'm fond of him, and I think he might enjoy a change of pace instead of another car ride. Might even be healthy for him to broaden his horizons a little, realize there are other people in the world besides you."

Wren looked at him with a reassuring smile.

"How about we try it just this once as an experiment? I'm up early too, and you can just come by first thing in the morning and pick him up before his breakfast. I promise to tell you honestly how he does." She put a light hand on his arm. "It really would be my pleasure."

"He's had a long week," Silas admitted. "You're sure? Could be good for him, remind him I'm not the only source of regular meals and company . . ."

"It's settled. Leave him with me—we'll paint the town red."

"I keep a stash of dry food for him in the Jeep; I'll leave it with you. But this is a slippery slope," Silas mused. "Owe you two favors now. Piling up debt like a busted gambler."

"Nonsense. You're two guys I enjoy helping out. Don't give it a second thought, Silas."

Gonna be hard not to. First night we've been apart. But he likes her, and she might be warmin' to him—that's where I want their relationship headed. Guess I ride solo tonight, for everyone's sake.

CHAPTER 73

Silas had been driving for the last few minutes with his headlights off. He paused to drop the Jeep into four-wheel drive before creeping up the steep track to the cell tower. If he could get up there without attracting attention, it would be a good vantage point without the risk of being seen.

The road was rough and rutted, but the Jeep quietly and easily crawled up it. He steadily crept up the narrow track to the top.

Sunset was already pretty early this time of year, so by 8:00 p.m., it had been completely dark for over an hour. Luckily, a waning moon and a cloudless sky provided him with just enough light to navigate by. Some trees were starting to pick up tinges of the earliest fall colors, but the forest still had all its leaves to muffle the sound of his movements and give his approach some cover. At the top of the rise, before parking, he turned the Jeep so it was facing back downhill in case he needed to retreat in a hurry. He grabbed Wren's camera, his tumbler full of hot coffee, and the blanket they'd used for their picnic and walked to the far side of the chain-link fence around the cell tower.

Silas spread out the blanket at the edge of the clearing and lay out like a sniper, looking for a gap with a good view of the barnyard. He set up the camera. Wren had given him a small tripod he could use to keep things steady.

She was right—the autofocus searched before finding a fix in the low light. But the barn had a gooseneck lamp with a wide galvanized metal shade. Whenever he trained the camera on the area illuminated by its yellow cone of light, it focused immediately and sharply.

Ready now, he sipped his coffee, looked at the stars and out across the quiet bogs, listened to the woods, and thought about how an echo of Wren's scent had been mixed into the others on his blanket. He smiled. Then, he settled in to wait.

The barnyard was quiet. Every once in a while, Silas wondered if he had heard a faint, muffled voice, but the only thing he saw was a coyote loping along one of the field roads. His patience was rewarded at 11:30 p.m. when he heard the sound of an engine approaching. He switched on the camera and readied himself.

As the sound grew louder, he also heard metallic clanging. *Like the sound of trailer ramps rattling in their trays.* His pulse quickened. Then, the dim sweep of distant headlights came into view. He fired a burst of pictures of the front of the truck as it pulled into the pool of light. He could tell from the license plate it was the same truck Faria had borrowed. *He's here.* Through the open driver's window, he got another shot of Faria driving—the green glow from the dash lights eerily illuminating his face— and got a third shot of him stepping out of the truck.

You're in my crosshairs now, you lowlife.

A man emerged from the barn office. Through the lens, Silas recognized him as the foreman he'd dealt with. He was followed by two other men who hung back at the large barn door. The foreman exchanged words with Faria, then began counting off bills, placing each atop a stack growing in Faria's palm. Silas took pictures of the handoff, but he wasn't sure how much detail would be visible.

If this guy's giving Faria money, they must have cut a deal where the foreman got cheap labor and gave Faria a chunk of the wages that should have gone to the workers.

That would add a tidy profit on top of the money Faria got for delivering the migrants to the buyer at the Golden Dragon.

These people just want a better life. And they are being rented out like oxen.

While the foreman pushed the large barn door open, the two men stood on either side of the gap. Faria climbed onto the trailer and worked on releasing the latches on the shipping container. Through the lens, Silas could make out the "SOLD/Private" marking painted on the side. Out from the shadows inside the dark barn, people began to emerge—the workers Clark had photographed in the bog. Silas could pick out the two with filthy soccer jerseys among the small crowd as they moved in a single-file line between the two men and toward the trailer. His pulse raced, and he steadied himself to catch pictures of them. Most carried a small, soft-sided bag—*their worldly possessions*. Silas counted twenty-three people, the number Faria had confirmed with the man behind the Golden Dragon.

When the first of the migrants began to climb onto the trailer and file into the storage container, Silas knew for certain this was the weekend he'd overheard Faria talking about. His hunch had been right. Tonight was the night. This transfer was definitely happening, and happening now.

The ramifications lined up in his mind. In just an hour or two, Tony would make the drop and hit the wind.

If Tony bolted, Silas knew he ought to be able to find him again eventually—but with the burner phones, the boats, the borrowed vehicles, and the long stretch of New England coast dotted with a hundred small ports and marinas, it could take weeks. He was already at the end of Flood's extension window, and he'd given his word he'd wrap this up.

Silas formed a tentative plan to pick Tony up after the drop. At least with the trailer empty, there would be fewer lives at risk and less of a chance of stepping on the feds' toes. He wished he had backup for the arrest, but if he did it as a traffic stop, he should be able to get by without it. The truck and trailer would be a cinch to follow. He'd find a quiet spot, throw the blue lights on the dash, and make it go down like any routine traffic stop.

With that cumbersome rig, Faria could neither commit to a car chase nor lose him and park someplace discreetly without his rig being easy to spot.

Silas took a few more pictures before packing up his belongings. He needed to drive all the way around the edge of the farm if he was going to be in a position to follow Faria when he came out on the farm's main road.

He opened the driver's door quietly and tossed the blanket onto the passenger side with the camera nestled on top of it and the empty mug on the floor. He reached into the back seat for the portable police light bar and placed it on the dash, cigarette lighter plug dangling at the ready. He didn't close his door or start his engine. He released the emergency brake, put the clutch to the floor, and let the Jeep gather momentum as it began to roll silently back down the road.

At the base of the hill, Silas closed his door and let out the clutch in second gear to quietly start the rolling Jeep and drove away from the farm to circle back around. He left his headlights off, as well as the lights on his dash, and carefully made his way to a dirt road about a hundred yards from the main farm road. Then he backed in and reluctantly dialed Lieutenant Camara in New Bedford.

"It's late, Lopez. This had better be important," Camara said.

"Thanks for pickin' up. Guessin' you'll think it's important. I'm in Carver and pretty sure my perp's 'bout to drive a trailer-load of migrants to the Golden Dragon in New Bedford."

"You're certain?" Camara asked.

"Still puttin' two and two together, but I just watched him load 'em up. Put that together with what I overheard that day at the Golden Dragon, and I think it's going down."

"You're just mentioning this intel now?" Camara growled. "What did you hear?"

"Didn't catch enough to make any sense out of it until I watched them load just now. Caught the word *weekend* at one point, and I heard something about late at night after the dishwashers went home."

"Shit."

"Right. Just made the connection now while I was watchin' 'em load up," Silas said. He froze as he spotted Faria's truck. "Here they come now. Pullin' out of the farm road and comin' by me. Hang on, gotta lower my phone for a second."

Silas put the phone face down on his thigh to obscure the light from the screen, waiting for their vehicle to pass. As soon as it did, he brought the phone back up to his cheek.

"Okay, I'm pullin' out to follow. Guess we're 'bout thirty-five minutes out this time a' night, maybe a scootch more since he's haulin' a big trailer."

"How many people are in the container?" Camara asked.

"Twenty-three," Silas said definitively.

"Fuck! What exactly do you expect me to do, Lopez? This sounds like a shit show. It's the middle of the night. We don't have the manpower, firepower, or time to organize a raid, and this smuggling isn't even our jurisdiction. We've been told to stay away from this. You're talking about taking on an Asian gang, for Christ's sake."

"Don't do anything if you don't want to. Not interested in tangling with the gang or the migrants. Strictly an observer while that trailer's full. After he drops them, I am going to follow him to somewhere quiet, pull him over, and haul him in."

"By yourself?"

"Routine traffic stop. Consider this a courtesy call in case it's inside city limits."

"Lopez, this is crazy," Camara cautioned. "You should have backup! Why couldn't you have given me some warning, dammit?"

"Sorry. Things escalated quicker than a pot boils over. Wasn't expecting the cavalry."

"For fuck's sake. Lemme get some pants, make some calls, and see what I can do. Why don't you see if you can get here ahead of him, and I'll meet you at the street corner just northwest of the Golden Dragon? We can watch safely from there. If I can bring help, I will."

"Thanks. Didn't mean to put you in this situation. Fast-movin' storm."

CHAPTER 74

Once Faria hit the interstate, Silas could glide past him and get to New Bedford first. He pushed his speed on the dark, empty highway, silently thanking Wren for keeping Bandit. Last thing he needed while improvising on the fly was a dog underfoot.

Downtown, he circled the block and found a parking spot where he could liaise with Camara. Ducking low in his seat, he cracked the windows and used the door to block the light while texting his location, vehicle, color, and plates to Camara.

Minutes ticked by. Faria would arrive momentarily. *Where is Camara?*

Silas was still slumped over, staying out of sight, when a light metallic tap on the passenger-side rear window startled him. Camara's thick class ring clinked against the glass. "Lieutenant Camara here," he said, voice muffled through the closed window.

Silas responded by unlocking the doors.

Camara opened the rear door and kept himself low in the back seat. "What's going on?"

Headlights washed the street and slowly rounded the corner.

"Just in time," Silas said. "That's Faria now. Once he pulls into the lot and starts to unload, I'm going to try for a picture or two. Tryin' to gather photographic evidence of this. You keep your eyes peeled and cover me."

"Okay. And I've got a plainclothes coming too."

Silas nodded in the darkness. "A couple of pictures of the transfer, then we'll pull back, wait for him to finish. After that, we let him leave, tail him, and either pull him over together, or I'll do it myself—like I'd do a regular traffic stop, a little farther out."

They heard the trailer jounce and rattle as Faria pulled over the apron into the parking area, carving a big half circle around the dirt lot to pull up alongside the restaurant. When Faria killed the lights, Silas slipped out and crept across the dark street, crouching behind parked cars. Camara crouched a few cars down. Blood pounded in Silas's ears, sharpening his senses. He listened intently and pushed his vision to the edge, trying to make out details in the shadows. His angle was good. With the big lens, he should be able to get a couple of pictures and creep back without drawing attention to himself.

Faria worked the container's creaking latches before a door moved. Silas could hear the hinges groaning in the stillness. A migrant walked down the ramp slowly while a second tentatively crouched and jumped down from the trailer's side. Faria stood next to the trailer, waving them along—janky, fidgety, impatient as always.

More people shuffled off the trailer. Silas thought they looked worse for wear after the wet fields and the ride in the dirty, rusty shipping container. The knot of them was herded into the alley, then through the restaurant's back door. Silas saw a dim light come on through a filthy casement window at ground level.

They're going to hold them in the basement for the next transfer.

Enough light leaked from the back alley for Silas to get some grainy but usable pictures. He worried about the shutter's click, so after getting what he needed, he put the camera down quietly at the base of the parked car's windshield, resting against the wipers, and watched a moment longer.

No one spoke as the migrants shuffled out. A silent despair pressed down on the scene.

Suddenly, a loud squawk from NBPD's dispatch blasted out on a police radio and reverberated into the night. Faria spun, looking down the gap between the building and the trailer. Silas ducked, but Faria caught the blur of his movement. In a panic, he pushed someone and ran toward Silas, firing a poorly aimed shot from what looked like a 9mm handgun as he went.

Silas flinched. The shot fired was loud against the night. He flinched a second time when he heard the report from a second gun—this time, the gunshot of a high-caliber rifle ringing out from somewhere above and behind him.

What the hell?

He spun to see a muzzle pulling back into a second-story window across the street.

Sniper? Gang members providing cover? His instincts screamed, *This is bad.*

He unholstered his weapon and released the safety.

Faria shot again, and after a moment, Silas heard the report of another high-powered rifle. This one was coming from a different elevated point, somewhere up above the dirt parking lot. A swirl of dust kicked up in the dim light where the bullet hit the ground behind Faria.

Who the hell is shooting long guns down at this lot from distant vantage points? Feels like cover fire—somebody's herdin' 'em. But who?

Then, it hit him like a cracked whip. *Shit. Has to be feds! They're already watching the place.*

The alley behind the Golden Dragon was chaos. Migrants screamed and scattered—some took cover under the trailer; others went back into the container. Silas heard footsteps running up the alley behind the restaurant and saw the beams of tactical flashlights bouncing off the wall. To his right, Camara and the cop he'd brought still squatted behind a parked car—Camara berating him for the radio squawk.

Silas holstered his weapon, ducking down to crawl into a gap between parked cars—then, after glancing both ways, he scrambled through the gap and jogged low across the sidewalk toward the passage between Faria's truck and the building.

He stopped short. Faria had come down the slot from the other direction. He didn't see Silas down low, but Silas caught a glimpse of him ducking between the truck and trailer. A few seconds later, his head and shoulders began to bob, a rhythmic squeak drifting out. He was turning a crank furiously. Faria was lowering the trailer's caster wheel.

He's trying to unhitch the truck from the trailer so he can bolt.

Silas crept closer and unholstered his weapon. The light beyond him silhouetted Faria. Silas yelled, "Freeze, Faria! You're under arrest!"

Faria rose slightly and sent another wild shot over the truck bed. Silas ducked as chips of brick and mortar rained down on him from the shot. After a second, the truck's far taillight exploded, followed a split second later by the sound of another booming shot ringing out from the same high point on the far side of the dirt lot. Faria flinched and ducked down.

The smell of gun smoke hung in the air. Silas got down on his knees, bracing with his free hand, and peered under the truck.

There are four legs. Shit.

His heart sank. *Faria has grabbed a migrant. He's going to use them as a shield.*

Silas saw the trailer's caster wheel reach the ground and heard the mechanism groan as it started to take the trailer's load, lifting the tongue off the truck's hitch. He heard the rattle as Faria released the safety chains.

He's making a break for it. Thinks he can get away.

Not on my watch.

Silas pulled out his pocketknife and stabbed it into the sidewall of the truck's passenger-side front tire with a small pop, resulting in a soft, steady hiss of air. He put the knife back in his pocket before scrambling around the front of the pickup truck, palm on the bumper as he rose through a crouch, ready to stop Faria.

Faria stepped out from between trailer and truck, sweaty and wild-eyed. He had a girl—*can't be more than seventeen*—held in front of him. She shook visibly, back arched, a whimper escaping as her feet shuffled and dragged. Faria's left arm was locked around her throat, his pistol pressed against her temple.

Silas stepped out from the front of the truck to face him, hands relaxed, gun steady. Guy was a powder keg. *Time to talk him down before someone gets killed.*

"Told you to freeze, Tony. You're coming in. This ends here," Silas said, voice firm.

"Back off!" Faria shouted, voice cracking. "You come any closer, and she dies!"

Camara and the feds held their positions.

Faria took a step toward Silas, pushing his hostage forward with a thrust of his hips. The girl whimpered.

Silas still didn't move his weapon. Not yet. Didn't shout. Just looked. *Calm as sunrise. Talk him through it.*

"Ain't your day, Tony," Silas said—his voice steady. Final.

The girl struggled against Faria's grip. He raised his elbow higher, pushing his gun harder against her temple, giving no ground.

"Give her up, Tony. Make it easier on yourself by doing the right thing. Go down this trail, and you're done."

Faria staggered forward another step, pushing the terrified girl.

Without breaking his stare, Silas raised his gun and sighted down the barrel. The gun was steady. He stood comfortably with a two-handed grip. Guns were tools—familiar, reliable, accurate.

"Final warning. Put that gun down, Tony," he said, thumb easing back the hammer, "or I'll put *you* down."

No one moved. Silas felt the tension frozen all around him, but he was entirely focused.

Faria still didn't yield.

Silas concentrated on Faria's gun hand. There was a twitch. The muzzle shifted, just enough.

Silas didn't hesitate.

One shot.

Boom.

Faria jerked backward with a grunt, his pistol clattering to the dirt as he crumpled sideways, clutching his shoulder. The stunned girl stood motionless for a second, trying to comprehend what had just happened, before scrambling clear.

Silas held his firing position a moment longer, eyes on Faria writhing on the ground. When it was certain Faria was no longer a threat, he lowered his weapon.

A Homeland Security truck roared up the alley behind the restaurant, tight to the back door. Its lights flooded out into the parking lot, illuminating the dust from Tony's fall. Another pulled in front of the dark restaurant, filling the street behind Silas with light. Camara and the other NBPD officer ran to Faria at the rear of his truck, kicking his gun out of reach.

"What the fuck, Lopez?" Camara said. "You took that shot?"

Silas shrugged. "Faria made the call."

"But the hostage was right there!" Camara pressed.

"Had plenty of shoulder showing for a clean takedown."

A Homeland Security agent wearing body armor with the letters *HSI* across the front jogged from the building across the street, long gun on his back, pistol in one hand. "Brock, HSI. What's the status of our runner?"

Silas looked at the scene, then at Faria writhing in the dust, then back at the agent.

"He'll live."

Silas engaged the safety and holstered his gun. "So, I guess someone oughta cuff him."

He went to retrieve Wren's camera from the windshield of the parked car. When he reached the car and looked down the alley, he saw the girl standing there, looking at him, wide-eyed.

He held her gaze for a moment, finally giving her a nod. The nod she returned was almost imperceptible.

He headed across the street to put the camera away and grab a water bottle from the back of the Jeep. It was going to be a long night sorting out this tire fire. As he worked the cap off the bottle with his fingers, he felt the shakiness creeping in—adrenaline ebbing.

Did what I came here to do. So, bring on the fuss.

CHAPTER 75
Monday, October 20

They spent the next several hours on debriefs, statements, walk-throughs, shouting matches, turf battles, and recriminations. It turned out HSI already had the place under surveillance, with orders not to engage. Crews were positioned in second-story windows to observe and document. Camara's backup officer hadn't remembered to turn his rover down, so when NBPD dispatch reached out to him, it was like a megaphone exploding in the stillness.

When Faria's shots rang out, HSI wasn't sure what was going on and laid down some suppressing fire to try to drive people into the building or back into the container so no one would try to bolt. None of the law officers had prior awareness of one another, and there was no radio communication, so as far as Silas was concerned, it was a miracle only one person got shot—the *right* person at that.

Exactly what you get when the feds play it close and don't clue anybody in. If they hadn't been here and Camara and his guy hadn't been here, I'd be driving a handcuffed Tony Faria in for booking. Now, it's gonna be a mountain of paperwork and a tornado of blame.

Silas didn't care, though. He worked a piece of elk antler with his pocketknife and let the hours of administrative bullshit wash over him. He had the thing he cared about, the thing he'd come for. He had his man—the one who'd haunted every waking thought of his for weeks. Handcuffed to a hospital bed wasn't a holding cell, but it'd do just fine.

When the brass woke up, there would be a lot of heat directed at him, but he wasn't worried. He held a lot of cards he could trade in terms of useful evidence. So, Silas kept his head down, answered what he had to, and waited for the fuss to blow over.

Still, he had to wait for the firestorm to burn itself out, and that took several hours. When he wasn't answering questions or repeating the same sequence over and over, he waited and worked on his elk bone bear. He wasn't back on the road until 4:00 a.m.

The whole drive back, his thoughts raced—the girl's shaking, the shooting, her dark eyes, the successful end to his case, her look at him down the side of the building.

He pulled into the parking space next to his apartment just before 6:00 a.m., predawn stillness still cloaking the town. He stripped off, took a fast shower—rinsing away dust, sweat, snap decisions, and gunshot residue—and threw on clean clothes before starting another strong batch of coffee.

He didn't have much food in the apartment, but he put his last five slices of bacon into his cast-iron skillet. The old skillet—one of the few things he'd brought with him—was black and slick with years of careful seasoning.

When the sizzling slowed and the scent was perfect, he dropped the crispy strips onto a large tortilla he'd warmed over a burner's flame and set out on a plate. He cracked three eggs into the hot bacon grease, ground pepper from a disposable clear-plastic grocery store mill, flipped each egg at the last second, and brought the runny yolks just shy of solid.

With breakfast taken care of, he texted Wren to see if she was up, then slid the eggs onto the bacon on his plate and gave them a good shake of Cholula. *Not Hatch chiles, but good enough.* Best he'd found out East. He wrapped the tortilla, taking care to tuck the end so the slightly runny yolks wouldn't make a mess. The burrito vanished instantly, even with no help from Bandit.

As he put his plate into the dishwasher, he grabbed Bandit's vest and threw it over his shoulder. That would allow him to go straight to the office.

A text pinged his phone: Yes, we're up. Bandit has been a good guest. C'mon over. Haven't eaten. Can I make you some breakfast?

Just ate, but thank you. I'll be right over—bringing Bandit's vest so I can go straight in.

When Silas arrived ten minutes later, it was cool outside and still dim, but the dawn light was growing—the sun was getting ready to rise.

When the door opened, all four of Bandit's feet lifted into the air with joy, and Wren smiled.

Not sure who's happier—me seeing the two of them or Bandit seeing me.

He gave Bandit a rough bear hug and took the complete lick treatment—ears, neck, face. He buried his nose in Bandit's deep neck fur, and the warm, yeasty dog smell hit him hard. So did the feeling of holding him.

Mornings like this, after nights like that, just feels good to be alive.

When he stood, he took Wren gently by both hands and looked her in the eye. She was fresh and radiant from a recent shower. Her hair was damp and smelled like orange blossoms. She looked luminous in a flowy printed skirt and a white blouse—work clothes—but the blouse cuffs hadn't been buttoned, and her feet were bare. Silas was tired, but looking at her gave him a rush of energy.

"Thank you," he said from the bottom of his heart. "Never spent a night away from me. Much as it was hard not to be sleeping with him on my ankles last night, it sure made me happy to know he was on yours."

"He was! At first, he wandered. Wouldn't settle. But after the lights had been out about twenty minutes, he jumped up and curled next to me, chin right on my ankles."

Silas used the grip on her hands to pull her toward him and into a hug. He bent his head down, buried his nose, and smelled her hair, saying nothing. He was exhausted, so the sense of gratitude was overwhelming him. It must have been obvious because Wren was quiet and just hugged him back. They stood that way until Bandit barked. Still holding her tight, Silas turned his head, put his lips to her ear, and softly whispered, "You have a bowl? I should feed him."

"You romantic fool," Wren whispered back. "Yes, I have a bowl."

They both laughed, and before letting go, Silas kissed the top of her head.

Not sure I've ever put so much feeling through a kiss as that. Tired, still shaky from all the adrenaline, sure. But I know how I feel, and I ain't gonna back down from it or apologize to anyone for it. Gonna make this one mine if it's the last thing I do.

Wren broke away, studying Silas's face for a moment. Warmth and affection saturated her expression. She gave his thick forearm a squeeze. Silas returned her look. He said nothing because he had nothing to say. Nothing really needed to be said.

Wren went to finish getting ready, and Silas dished out the food for Bandit. Then, he stepped out on the balcony to look at the bay and sip his coffee as Bandit ate.

Be a tongue-lashing soon, but today's gonna be a good day. I can feel it. First of many, if luck holds and things line up right.

CHAPTER 76

"He lives!" Genny said at the sight of Silas in the office. She dropped her bag and draped her jacket over the back of her chair. The scent of lavender caught up with her a second later. "But just barely, by the look of you. What happened, Chief?"

Silas stopped in front of her desk. "Long story, for later. Main part is, I've been runnin' hard. I'm dog-tired and flea-bit. Catch me up?" He nodded, indicating she should follow him into his office.

Genny sat and looked at her notes. "Officers Marsh and Byrne have an update for you on the port in New Bedford, and Sergeant Clark has something he wanted to talk to you about. He's here already. Officer Marsh said she'd be along shortly. Everything else can wait for now."

"Roger that. Send Clark to my office."

"Will do," she said over her shoulder as she headed out. A moment later, Clark walked in.

"Mornin', Sergeant," Silas said, exhaustion evident in his voice. "How can I help you?"

Clark was beaming. Kid had a good smile—first time Silas had seen it.

"No help needed, Chief. That's kinda the point of this story," Clark said, sitting in the guest chair closer to the door. "Wanted to tell you about a call I handled over the weekend."

"Oh, yeah? We down one on the town population sign out at the edge of town?" Silas asked, grinning.

Clark gave him a small courtesy laugh.

He's out of the woods—time to retire those jokes with him.

"You'll be pleased to know I didn't shoot anyone. What happened was, I fielded a call that came to the switchboard about a suspicious person in the East End taking photos and lurking around an expensive house that's closed up for the season."

Silas nodded for him to go on.

"Of course, my first instinct was that this could be a burglary in progress or someone casing the house to come back later. A complicating factor was that the caller made a big point of the fact that the man was Black."

"Gettin' a bad feelin' about where this's headin'," Silas admitted. "Feels like you're leadin' me toward something I'd rather not step in . . ."

"Right?" Clark said, sitting up straight, excitement obvious. "I had the same thought. Last thing I needed was some racial-profiling incident where somebody gets unfairly stereotyped."

"So, what happened?" Silas asked, furrows of concern on his brow.

"I went to see him—slow and quiet, lights off. On my way, I thought about all the legitimate things he might be doing. An insurance adjuster looking at damage. Roofing or siding or painting contractor taking measurements for an estimate. Real estate agent preparing to take on a listing."

"Smart, Clark. Smart as a spare tire. Maybe there's something inside that hat rack of yours after all."

"Exactly. I parked a ways down so I wouldn't come off as threatening, like you taught me. I just strolled up casually and watched him for a couple of minutes, hands on my hips, like I was killing time on traffic duty at a construction site or something. Gave him a friendly wave when he saw me."

"Lemme guess—he didn't drop the camera, pull two pearl-handled silver revolvers, and start shootin' up the place?"

Clark's smile was wide. "Nope. Came down the side of the building, introduced himself, and said he was a contractor working up an estimate.

Handed me a card to back it up, without me even asking. The card matched the truck lettering, by the way."

"Look at you, Sergeant," Silas said, giving him an appraising look and nod.

Clark held up a hand. "Gets better, Chief. Card said he wasn't local, so I offered him a lunch rec."

Silas broke into a satisfied grin. "You're learnin', Clark. Gonna make a great cop outta you yet," he said with a wink. "Good work. And thanks for sharing that story."

Silas chuckled to himself as Clark left, the door swinging shut behind him.

Feels like we're over the hump with that one. Attitude's better. We can get him the rest of the way. Nice to see it—especially a local kid. And just like I promised Flood.

CHAPTER 77

Silas went to refill his coffee and find Marsh and Byrne. Marsh was at her desk, and when she saw him approaching, she stood, shuffled folders, and reached for one from the top of the pile at the edge of her desk. The bun in her hair was still snug and orderly, and she was crisply turned out in pressed blues.

"Morning, Chief," she said, holding an organized set of typed notes. "Lemme grab Byrne. Meet you in your office?"

Silas nodded, and Marsh turned toward the break room to find Byrne.

When she and Byrne sat in Silas's guest chairs a moment later, Marsh got right to the point.

"So, the harbormaster did have video of the *Sereia* leaving port on the afternoon of August 31 and returning the afternoon of September 2. He also had video footage of Faria approaching the slip and boarding the boat."

Byrne nodded and added, "The harbormaster gave us the name of the owner of the *Sereia*. We got in touch with the owner, who confirmed that he has been renting it to Tony Faria occasionally for the last few years. He admitted it was an off-the-books cash deal, so he didn't have substantiating records, but the guy was very concerned to have the police calling about his boat. He was upset by the implication that his boat might have been involved in criminal activity."

Silas's eyebrows went up. *Hope they didn't leak anything about an ongoing investigation.*

Byrne read the concern in his expression and put up a reassuring hand. "We told him it was an ongoing investigation, so we couldn't divulge any details."

Nice work. These two are on the ball. Solid.

"Sounds like our man Tony is still winnin' friends and influencin' people everywhere he goes," Silas said wryly.

"Yeah, the owner was pissed, Chief," Byrne said, tapping the edge of Silas's desk. "Says he'll gladly give a statement."

"Good work. How'd you find all that video so fast?" Silas asked.

Marsh sat up a little straighter. "So, that's the interesting thing," she said. "When I asked the harbormaster about the boat's comings and goings, he didn't go *straight to the video*." She paused for extra emphasis. "Instead, he told me he'd look at something he called his AIS logs. That's the acronym for"—she checked her notes—"the Automated Identification System. It's like air-traffic control for boats. There are specialized applications for accessing it, but it's essentially publicly available data. He found the records of the *Sereia* and saw it heading way offshore to a point in international waters, which starts at twelve nautical miles from shore."

"Tracks my hunch like a bloodhound," Silas said.

"Right," Byrne said, chiming in. "With a record of the key times like that, it was a cinch for him to locate the video."

With excitement and suspense in her voice, Marsh added, "The New Bedford harbormaster's use of the AIS gave me an idea. So, I reached out to our harbormaster here in town and asked him to look at his AIS logs."

"Good thinking," Silas commented, seeing where this was going.

She nodded as if to say, *I know, right?* before saying, "And guess what? He has the *Sereia* coming into Provincetown at three thirty a.m. on September 2 and leaving again at four twenty a.m. Despite the stormy weather, these guys turned their running lights off, but they either forgot or didn't bother to turn off the boat's AIS transponder. Of course, no video, but the AIS log data is almost as good."

She sat back in satisfaction.

"Outstanding initiative, Officers. Findin' all that—an' faster than a jackrabbit too. Real fine work there. Thank you. Got more than enough to impound and search that boat. Bet my best horse they're gonna find hairs, fibers, and DNA on the boat that matches the traces in the two shippin' containers Faria used. Could be a break for us."

Silas thought about the implications of that for a beat before speaking.

"Call that harbormaster in New Bedford back, and tell him that the boat is a crime scene and not to let it go anywhere," he said. "I'll risk my skin to call New Bedford PD and at least get it wrapped in crime scene tape, if not under watch, until a forensic team can get there."

Still in hot water, but getting enough bulletproof evidence that I might come out with my skin. If I do, credit goes to this team.

Fact is, whole team's worked hard, done good. Already come a long way. Clark the farthest. Got a couple of stars in the making with Marsh, maybe Byrne or Burig. Time'll tell. Big cases have a way of bringing teams together, showin' who's inventin' and who's copyin'. If I get outta all this with my badge, need to make sure they know it.

CHAPTER 78

Report finished, Marsh and Byrne packed up and left Silas to call Camara. It was still early, so he hoped to catch him at a time when they could talk privately. Camara picked up on the first ring.

"Chief," he said, with no enthusiasm whatsoever.

Not showin' his hand. Could take a swing at him for that radio screwup, but the trail's long, and you pass the same folks comin' and goin'. Bridges are easy to burn but hard to build.

"Lieutenant," Silas said, resting his head on his fist. "Calling to ask your team to mark a crime scene, and also to thank you for coming out for that mess at the restaurant."

There was a short silence during which Silas could hear the soft static of the line. "Not sure thanks are in order. My guy's radio was the match that lit the gasoline. Rookie mistake, and I apologize for the way it went down."

"Well, not sure about apologies, either," Silas said, waving his other hand in dismissal, even though he was alone in the room and Camara couldn't see it over the phone. "The situation we were dealin' with put you and your team in a bind—not sure anybody could have done any better. Grateful as hell to have backup when the match did get struck. Besides, perp was a coked-up tinderbox, waiting to combust. If it hadn't been your radio, would have been something else. Firefly could have set that guy off."

Silas leaned back in his chair with a creak.

"Appreciate you saying that. Wish my chief saw it the same way," Camara admitted, his voice edged with exhaustion. "He's getting hammered by HSI, and you know how that goes."

"Pain like that's always gonna be shared. Plenty to go around." Silas shook his head ruefully. "Sure they're gunnin' for me too. First call after this is to Special Agent Calkins—already gave me a tongue-lashing even before I did anything wrong. I suspect she's swinging her arm, winding up as we speak. Hopin' when she realizes how much work I can save her, she can put her pride aside and go easy on me."

"Maybe. What's this crime scene you're calling about?"

Silas sat back up and put his elbows on his desk. "Boat Faria used for transport is in New Bedford Harbor—called the *Sereia*. Harbormaster's already roped it off and keeping an eye on it, but I need one of your team to at least go tape it off and preserve the evidence. Gonna be fibers, DNA, what have you all over that boat. Can you keep it off-limits for me until somebody, probably HSI, sends a forensics unit down?"

"Sure. I'll send a patrol car over right away. Boat, huh?"

"Sounds like my smugglin' theory was spot-on," Silas said, picking up a ballpoint pen and clicking it in and out several times before twirling it on his thumb knuckle. "Last few days, my team's pieced together some of the links in this chain. Looks like Brazilians comin' up on big boats, gettin' transferred out in international waters to local trawlers, and being brought into smaller ports below everyone's radar. Migrants owe lots of money for their transport, so they get bought and sold because they'll work for pennies to get free of the debt."

"That fits," Camara said.

"Faria picked the wrong day to double-time it through my town with a trailer full of misery. Had a good thing goin'. He'd have been gettin' a transport fee, then sellin' these migrants onward to the Asian gang. But he figured out a way to rent 'em to his buddy's seasonal harvest in the meantime, skimmin' a chunk of their wages while he was at it. Just happened to drag his trailer across a pedestrian while double-timin' it off my wharf." Silas grinned widely, shaking his head. "Karma don't knock. She just kicks the damn door in."

"This job'll show you things you can't unsee," Camara said. "Hell of a life for those migrants. Something tells me they pay a lot more than they owe."

"Grim business," Silas said, looking toward the ceiling. "Sufferin' like that hurts to watch. You and I can't put a stop to it, but we helped drive it out of our towns—and whether they admit it or not, we helped the feds lock up some bigger players. It's something."

"It is. It definitely is."

Silas put a palm on the desk, as if ready to stand. "Well, thanks again, Lieutenant. I look forward to crossing paths again. *Vaya con Dios.*"

He hung up, eyes on the ceiling, hand still splayed over the cool surface of his desk, waiting for the weight of it all to shift. There was a lot to process. He got up and switched off his office light, then sat back down and looked at the blank wall for a few minutes. From the lavender scent, he could tell Genny had come by to hover once or twice, but since she'd figured out not to bother him when he was recharging his people battery, he knew she'd hold off till he was ready. When he felt some equilibrium, he stood up.

Maybe take Bandit for a walk, clear my head before Calkins calls back. Best to have my wits about me for that one.

CHAPTER 79

He didn't plan on it, but as he walked Bandit, Silas found himself tracing backward along the route Faria took in the final moments of Timothy Perkins's life. He and Bandit strolled down Ryder toward the municipal lot, smelling the scent of freshly made taffy from the vent fan in the wall of the sweet shop.

They walked along the lot to the wharf beyond. The streets were much quieter on weekdays now, and he enjoyed the slower pace. But he'd been warned the occasional fall weekend could be busy with tourists and shoppers looking for end-of-year closeouts on the summer's leftovers, plus seasonal people closing down their places for winter.

At the wharf's end, he looked out across the bay.

A lot's happened in a couple of months. Feels different. Like a lifetime's passed somehow.

His mind ran through all the steps he'd taken to track Faria down and all the things he'd learned about the town, his new team, and himself. As he looked out toward the point and the water beyond, he was overtaken with sadness for the awful journey those migrants took on their way to Provincetown. He silently thanked a higher power for his good fortune, his own arrival here. By the standards of people dreaming of a fresh start, Silas knew just how lucky he'd been to wash up in this unusual little town.

He was still standing and quietly taking in the scene when his phone rang with a call from a blocked number. He had a suspicion about who it was, so he answered.

"This is HSI Special Agent Donna Calkins. Who am I speaking with?"

Silas knew she'd call back fast. He'd left a message that he had information highly relevant to Faria's interrogation. Faria was still in serious condition, so he'd figured he'd get to Calkins before she conducted it.

The sun felt good on his face—the breeze had picked up, and Bandit had curled at his feet. Silas decided to sit on the wharf's low wall and take his medicine there with the cormorants on the nearby breakwater.

"Mornin', Agent Calkins. Provincetown Police Chief Silas Lopez here."

"Don't you dare *good morning* me, Lopez. There aren't enough shovels in the world for the shit I'm dealing with right now. I told you to back off, and you deliberately disobeyed me. There will be consequences—count on it. But that's a different discussion for a different day. Right now, I'm scrambling to get this case under control since some reckless two-bit cowboy unilaterally forced my timeline by months."

Two-bit? She's never met me, so I'm not gonna take that personally.

"Wasn't trying to disobey or trample timelines," he said apologetically. "Just takin' pictures from a distance. I'm sure you've heard it was NBPD's radio that triggered the stampede. Your boys shootin' up the place were part of the circus, by the way."

He braced himself for her renewed assault, but she didn't reply.

"Real sorry about all that," he went on. "But once the bulls were on the move, they had to be rounded up. Assure you, I wasn't planning to have any contact with Faria at that restaurant location. Lieutenant Camara will back me up on that—I planned to pull him over down the road, after he was done with the migrant drop."

"Save it. Not interested in your bullshit right now," she replied brusquely. "I'm calling because I'm told you may have information relevant to my interrogation of Faria?"

"Believe I do."

"What is it? And hurry up, because I'm under extreme time pressure here," Calkins said.

Real polite. Must take a whole training course on it.

Silas efficiently recounted his story of the hit-and-run incident and his hunch that there was more to it than met the eye.

Outside of a curt "uh-huh," she didn't say a word.

Hard to read someone over the phone, but guess I'll press ahead till she stops me.

He provided a concise recap of the challenges involved in tracking Faria down by license plate and how the shipping container and agricultural connection kept surfacing during his investigation.

She listened silently, so he kept going. But he could tell from the surging and then falling of the background noise that somewhere during his summary, she had put him on a speakerphone and then muted her end. He assumed it was either to take notes, share the conversation, or both.

Either way, means I have her attention.

Silas told her he had impounded the original truck and trailer, and in addition to finding ample forensic proof of the hit-and-run, and proof humans had been transported in the storage box, he found leverage Calkins could use in the form of an illegal gun and enough drugs for intent to distribute.

Calkins interrupted to ask where the trailer and crate were now, and Silas could tell from the background noise she'd come off mute to do it.

"Mass State Police have the truck and trailer at their crime lab," Silas explained. "Also gonna be useful DNA evidence on a boat called the *Sereia*, which transported the migrants in from international waters."

"Where's this boat?"

"Docked in New Bedford, wrapped in crime scene tape."

She's tryin' to poke holes, but I've done the legwork, have the answers.

Calkins and, he assumed, members of her team continued to listen quietly, so Silas began a crisp rundown of the mountain of digital evidence he'd collected. The videos of Faria seconds before the accident, the AIS data tracking the ship from New Bedford to the rendezvous offshore to Provincetown, and heaps of photographs documenting every step in the chain, including night vision and money changing hands.

When Silas laid it all out, even he had to admit—it was Sunday-best impressive. He could feel the mood of the call shift.

He stopped. There was silence on the line for a long moment before the speakerphone came off mute with a hiss.

"Chief Lopez, some of my colleagues are here with me and have heard most of this. Let me start by saying this . . ." She sighed. "This is good police work." Silas grinned, knowing that had to be a lot, coming from her. "I almost didn't make this call because I'm up to my ass in alligators today, but something told me to call your stubborn ass back. I'm glad I did."

Silas heard some noise, possibly a little laughter in the background.

"We've been focused on the Asian gang and the downstream end of this smuggling operation in New York City. This load of migrants we've just been forced to take into custody was looking to be a mountain of work for our team to trace because, frankly, we weren't ready."

"I just happened to be workin' from the other end of the rope," Silas said.

"Indeed. It pains me deeply to say it, but you have done one hell of a job here, Chief. To be blunt, it's been our experience that local cops just tend to get underfoot, so this is a pleasant surprise."

You don't say, Special Agent. Never would have guessed from your attitude that you lack respect for local cops.

"You've wrapped this piece of our investigation up with a bow. And you did it on a shoestring. I'm impressed with what you and your lean team accomplished. It shows the kind of determination and efficiency we need at HIS. If the small-town life wears thin, I could probably be convinced to find a place for your skills on my team."

"Mighty kind, ma'am, but I was just chasin' down my hit-and-run."

"Well, as of right this moment, I have three agents assigned to work with you to get all this evidence documented and transferred over to my team. We'll pick up where you're leaving off. An agent named Roland McCord will be in touch with you later today."

"Not so fast, Special Agent," Silas said flatly.

"Excuse me?" Calkins said.

"Can't let go without assurances."

"What are you talking about, Chief?"

"Need assurances Faria doesn't walk. You ain't gettin' a scrap of evidence till I got your word Faria faces felony murder. No deals. No trades." Silas couldn't be sure, but he thought he heard a sharp intake of breath somewhere in the background noise behind Calkins.

"Chief, I am not going to make promises I can't keep. And by law, you have to turn over that evidence, so cut the posturing."

"Oh, you can send your three agents here, and we'll see if we can pull it together. But we're just hayseed locals—as likely to get underfoot as anything. I'm not great with computers or backups, and I've never been organized with paperwork. If your agents are patient, I am sure we can pull together a few scraps of what we've found."

"Do *not* fuck with me, Lopez! You are back to impeding a federal investigation. I will have your goddamn badge."

Silas shrugged and calmly looked out at the breakwater. *Tables turn, Donna. You need me more than I need you. Probably not too comfortable for you. Cryin' shame.*

"Easy problem to fix, Special Agent. Talk about badges—if yours is worth anything, means you've got the authority to refuse to sign off on any deal for Faria. Give me your word, and I'll tag all the evidence, box it up, and hand deliver it to you wearin' a carnation."

Silas paused to let that sink in. The line was silent.

"But you try to trade my guy out," he went on, "and I'll make sure three of your agents spend at least a month out here by the beach, drinking horrible coffee and lookin' through video footage of coyotes and parades."

There was a stir in the background on her end. Was it a snicker?

She's not sayin' anything, but I know she's thinking. Wants this evidence. One more nudge oughta do it.

"Dead serious. Snakebite serious. You want the easy way or hard?"

There was a long silence during which Silas heard the background noise come and go on her line as they muted, debated, and unmuted.

Finally, her voice came on, sullen. "Fine. No deals for Faria."

"Goin' to walk my dog. Have that sent to me in writing, and I'll start organizing and working with your agents as soon as my dog's lightened his load. No letter, no organizing. We clear?"

"Yes, we're clear, Lopez." After a pause, she said, "I wish I could say it has been a pleasure working with you, but that's not the word. You are a stubborn pain in the ass, and your disregard for the needs of your federal government has been contemptuous."

Nickel word. Been called worse before. Go ahead and get it out of your system, Calkins.

"But as a professional, and a fellow officer of the law . . ." There was a pause. Calkins's voice had dropped half an inch. "I feel obligated, on behalf of ICE and Homeland, to acknowledge your efforts here. The reality is that your diligent police work and evidence-gathering have saved us a mountain of work."

Could say a lotta things right now. Point out how rough she made the road. Ask if treating folks decent ever crossed her mind. But not my style. Not today.

"Just doin' my job, ma'am. Look forward to your letter and working with Agent McCord. Best of luck to you, and thank you for your service."

The line clicked off on her end.

Feds. Always a stone in your boot. Never gonna change.

But we hounded our guy to the end of the trail, and his time is up. All I ever cared about in the first place.

Silas looked down at the dog near his feet. He was lying on his back, all four feet in the air, cooling his belly in the wind off the water. "Bandit, we've got more in common than you realize. We keep our heads down, do the job, don't complain—things have a way of shaking out."

He gave the dog a pat on the rib cage.

"Ain't just us anymore, is it?"

Bandit wagged once, his upside-down tail making a muted thump on the wharf.

"Still, not a bad morning for a walk. What's say we go finish ours before the next fire starts?"

CHAPTER 80
Tuesday, October 21

"Got him," Silas said before he'd even finished knocking on Patrick Flood's doorframe.

Flood looked up with a surprised expression.

Silas said, "He's in federal custody. Whole smuggling ring's goin' down, including an Asian gang runnin' it out of New York City, the guys in New Bedford. Even the guy renting the workers in Carver has been picked up and referred to the DA's office. With gun and drug enhancements, our perp'll be put away forever, plus a day—no chance for parole."

Flood beamed at him. "And you did it when you said you would. Nice work, Silas. That's a hell of a job. What a tangled mess this turned out to be. I got a call from a feisty Homeland Security agent. She was bouncing between furious and grateful. Seems you've got a gift for stirring up trouble and results at the same time."

"Did what needed doin'. You want a diplomat or a bureaucrat, hire one." Silas smiled to soften the point just a hair. "I wasn't the one who brought those feds in. Tried to steer clear of 'em. Turns out, they already had their eye on the buyer our perp was delivering the migrants to."

Flood looked interested, so Silas told the whole story of how the exploitation of the migrants worked, from Brazil to Carver, then New Bedford to New York City.

"Those poor people," Flood said.

"Clever scam for a dirtbag. I think he originally ran it out of New Bedford, but he'd annoyed people there and worn out his welcome. Also, harbormaster upgraded their security and video. So, he's been using Provincetown for the last few runs. Might've stayed below our radar for a while if he hadn't cut that corner too hard and run over Mr. Perkins."

"Hell of a job, Silas. I've been so impressed watching you work this case while simultaneously changing the tone and morale of the entire department. You have completely turned things around. The feedback from around Town Hall and the community has been stellar as well. So . . ."

He paused, glancing at Silas.

"I've been thinking over the last couple of days, and I've made a decision. I've spoken with all of the town's board. One abstained, but everyone else enthusiastically wants me to make your position permanent."

"Dog's permanent too?" Silas clarified.

Flood laughed, obviously not expecting that response. "I've gotten fewer complaints. Keep him under control, find something useful for him to do—like we agreed—and he's hired. Damn odd way to run a department, but I'll allow it."

"Had a hunch you'd go that way," Silas said with something of a smirk.

"Why's that?" Flood asked, surprised by his impertinence.

"Clues," Silas said with a grin. "Bowl of Milk-Bone biscuits on the shelf behind you being one."

Flood looked indignant, as if he'd been framed. "Wait now—my executive assistant put those Milk-Bones there!"

"Uh-huh," Silas said, nodding with a knowing grin.

"What's so funny?"

"Noticed bowl's mostly empty," he said. "Your assistant comin' in here to feed Bandit while you're working, or—"

"You're dismissed, Chief Lopez!" Flood said, though he was holding back a laugh.

"Appreciate your offer to stay on long term." Silas tipped his hat. "It's a vote of confidence. Lemme have a think on it, an' get back to you quick as a wink."

If Flood was surprised that Silas wanted to think, he didn't let on, so Silas ducked out of the room with two palm taps on the door.

Stuck the neck out pretty good on this one. Could've blown up in my face easy. But looks like this gamble paid out.

Feels good to have Flood's support. Didn't think I'd care so much, but I do.

This place . . . Well, it's starting to feel something like home.

"Wore clean through," Silas told Genny as he stood in front of her desk. "Figured I'd take the rest of the afternoon off, unless something urgent crops up. You can always call me. With most things, stitch in time saves nine, so call."

"Sounds good, Chief. I'll hold down the fort," Genny said, and he knew she'd do just that.

After leashing Bandit and returning to Genny's desk outside his office, he said, "Also, can you schedule a team case conference for first thing in the morning, and if you're willing, maybe pick up some of that tasty Portuguese bakery firepower? My treat."

"Great idea. Will do." Genny jotted down a note for herself. "Glad to see you taking care of yourself with a little time off for a change."

With a wave, he and Bandit started the long climb up the building's back staircase, heading for Wren's office. He arrived there only moments later, knocking softly on her door and meeting her with a tired smile.

He held up both hands. He said, "No pressure. I know you've got important work to do, but I hit my limit on badge work for now and was thinking a walk would be the ticket. Here because I'm hopin' for a partner in crime."

"Your case is wrapped up?" Wren said. Silas thought she sounded excited about that.

"That guy's days as a free man are over. He's in the cage, and the door's stayin' shut. Tell you the story sometime, just not now—please, Lord, not now," he added with a mirthless laugh, thinking of just how many times he'd discussed it in the last twenty-four hours. "Anyway . . . how's the load on your plate right this second?"

"Well, no more appointments this afternoon. Just paperwork. Lots of it. But you know what? It can wait till later. Why don't we head out across that stone breakwater in the West End like we talked about? It's a bit of a stroll from here. Have you got the steam?"

Silas's gaze rested on her face for a moment before he said, "Got the strength to follow you anywhere, Wren Bradford."

The air outside was perfect. As they walked west through town, the late-afternoon sunlight flashed on the slices of harbor they glimpsed between the surrounding old, tightly packed houses. Wren took Silas's hand with a smile and swung it forward and back as they made their way down the narrow, crooked strip of Commercial Street, through the West End, and toward the breakwater.

"So, I looked up that bear fetish you made me," Wren said. "Pretty neat symbol. Fits you, I think."

Silas nodded. "Zuni tradition. Pueblo people. Bear marks west on the compass. It symbolizes strength, healing, protection, survival, and wisdom. Hard to find fault with any of that, but what's special to me is, it also stands for looking inward, sittin' with something, workin' it out. What I try to do when I think."

Wren squeezed his hand.

"Mainly, bringing you good luck and protection is my aim."

"That's sweet. Thank you," Wren said. Then, after a few moments of companionable silence, she pointed to a house, saying, "See that blue enamel plaque there?" The plaque featured a pictograph of a small white cottage riding on waves composed of squiggly white lines.

"I do. And I'm guessing you're about to tell me what it means," Silas said, lifting her hand contentedly and kissing the back of it.

"It means that's one of the floated houses," Wren said. "If you look around town, you'll see a little over two dozen historic houses with that plaque."

"Floated?" *What'll these Easterners think of next?*

"There was a very early settlement out on Long Point near the site of the current lighthouse. The main part of town began to develop faster on this side of the water, and eventually, the settlers on the point decided to come over here and join the growing town. They floated many of the houses over."

"Lotta effort to float a house. Why'd they need to move so bad?"

"It was crowded out there, not enough fresh water, and the point is very exposed to storms—the sand can shift around. In addition, they wanted better access to the schools, churches, and work over here in town."

"Water gave 'em options, I guess. Out West, you'd just pack up and leave a ghost town behind."

Having reached the circle at the end of Commercial, they headed out along the breakwater. As they began to work their way across the massive stones of the breakwater, they found their rhythms with the long strides needed to bridge the deep, jagged gaps. Bandit was off leash, sure-footed as ever, leaping from stone to stone, scrambling down the sloped sides to investigate the waterline, then bounding back up.

As he walked, Silas listened to the rushing sounds of the rising tide as it poured between the causeway's stones, refilling the salt marsh. Birds swooped above them and paddled below, tempting Bandit to jump into the water.

Not like any place I've ever walked. Tides comin' in too, so all this water around us is only getting deeper. Best watch my step.

They made their way farther out, and their angle back toward town widened. A look over his left shoulder revealed a view of the town Silas had never seen. A long necklace of buildings—mostly white clapboard or weathered silver shingles—nestled against the water, with the steeples of several landmarks easily recognizable. The harbor and marinas were less crowded now, but a few pleasure boats were still rocking in the chop at their moorings. Up ahead and to his right, he could make out Wood End Light, and out to his left, the light and sandy tip of Long Point.

The inert mass of the giant stones was reassuring to Silas, whose slight discomfort was growing slowly as they walked farther out into the bay on the tiny strip of rock. He could swim if he had to but just barely—and he sure wouldn't want Wren seeing him thrash like a raccoon in a feed sack.

The uneven footing forced him to watch his step, just enough to keep the busy part of his brain occupied. That left the quiet part free to take stock of a bone-deep feeling of contentment he'd felt rising in him.

He hadn't set out to fall for Provincetown. He'd never really experienced a place like this. A tourist town, a vacation spot, a place where frivolous, flamboyant fun was had, just for fun's sake. In his mind, towns and settlements were primarily places to gather for work, trade, and survival. He was raised to believe the only legitimate way to earn attention and prove your worth was with your rope- and horse-handling skills, letting your competence speak for itself. And yet somehow, he'd been won over by folks just glad to be alive, happy to celebrate being somewhere they could breathe easy and be themselves.

Stepping across the deep gaps between stones, Silas had a realization. Even as an outlier—a big, uncommonly tall, funny-sounding cowboy far from home—he'd been met with acceptance at every turn. No one here had asked him to explain himself. Nobody here had questioned or judged him. Compared to the tight-laced social order back in Salt Lake, this place felt like breathing room. And he liked it. Sure, Wren was part of it. But what he felt for her wasn't contentment. More like the opposite. It was a steady ache of curiosity, fascination—and a hunger to know her better, be near her, hold her tight.

She caught him looking at her. "What?" she asked, smiling.

"Sorry. Didn't realize I was staring. Lost in thought."

"Penny for them?" she said, flipping his expression back at him.

He blew out a breath. "Wouldn't know where to start."

A long sequence of strides passed before he was ready to speak.

"Guess, I'm feelin' a powerful sense of home right here, right now," he said. *But that's just part of it, Silas. Gotta stick the neck out and own up to the rest. Overdue, and no better time than now.* "And a powerful sense of being with the person I most want to be with."

Wren grinned. Gentle, incandescent. "Is that right, Mr. Lopez?"

"Afraid so, if you can stand the idea."

She didn't answer that, choosing her own confession instead. "I've been thinking too. I like our time together—a lot. When we aren't together, I miss it. I feel a little stressed about missing it. I think that's because I never know when I'm going to see you next."

"Don't like to think of you being stressed, me being the cause of it. Something I could be doing differently? You say it, I'll do it."

"I guess what I am saying is that it feels like everything's been relying on chance, mostly last-minute, on-the-fly stuff. I can try to make something happen, but with you, it can be like trying to . . . how would you put it? *Lasso the wind.*"

"Tried to make as much time as I could, this case at full boil."

"No, what I'm trying to get at is that right now, somebody has to do the work to make time together happen. I did a lot of it in the beginning— well, all of it, really. You've done a bit more lately," she acknowledged with a smile.

"What do you mean by *do the work*?" Silas asked, sensing he needed to get this right.

"I am talking about taking initiative," Wren explained.

"What does that mean?"

"You don't know what *initiative* means?" she teased.

"Know what the word means. Don't know what you mean by it. There's a difference," Silas said with some apprehension.

Wren groaned. "You're not going to make this easy, are you?"

"Sure ain't trying to make it difficult."

"No, I don't think you are," Wren clarified with warmth. "I've known from the start you're well-meaning. I'm just beginning to suspect you don't have much experience with this stuff."

"What stuff?" Silas said.

Need to tread extremely carefully now. This is suddenly gettin' dicey as a busted saddle cinch midgallop.

"I rest my case!" Wren shouted, laughing.

Silas stumbled along the rocks, feeling bewildered and uncertain. *Not wild about being laughed at. Kinda outta rations, mentally speaking, and wasn't looking to find myself wading into deep water.*

"Si, look, I admire the very direct and straightforward way you conduct yourself with people, so in that spirit, I'll spell this out for you in the plainest way I know how, okay?"

"Be a powerful mercy if you did," he said, hit by a mix of relief to be out of the dark on the one hand and fear he was about to get dumped on the other hand.

"I've been attracted to you from the first time I saw you," Wren said. "Not physically—well, yes, physically, but also not physically. I want . . . I think we should . . ."

She trailed off.

An awkward pause yawned between them. *Is she finished? Because that didn't help.*

He couldn't wait.

"Thank you kindly. That's much clearer," Silas joked, relieved by the sense this might not be a disaster unfolding after all.

"Don't be a smartass," Wren said, nudging him in the side. "This mess is your fault because you appear to possess no social skills whatsoever."

"Oof. That drew blood!" Silas said, clutching his heart.

"No, that's not what I mean—I mean skills with women. Dating choreography."

"Okay, this is gettin' deep fast. You're sayin' I'm not only in the middle of doing something—which is news to me—but I'm also not doing it right?" Silas inquired.

"No. Well, yes, sort of. I'm saying you're doing things right and in your own special way, which I love. You're just not doing enough of it. Well, no, that's not it. Argh! Here goes nothing."

Wren stopped suddenly on a large flat rock, surrounded by the sea on both sides. She stood on her tippy-toes, grabbed Silas's jaw with both hands, and pulled him down into a long, hard kiss. For Silas, it was a kiss that had built layer by layer out of weeks and weeks of attraction, frustration, longing, uncertainty, desire, near misses, fears, hopes, and dreams.

"Well . . . that was . . . somethin' . . ." Silas choked out, breathless.

Wren searched his eyes with a frantic look of uncertainty before he realized he needed to be more specific.

"Real nice. Can't say I've ever had better," Silas said, still looking a little shell-shocked.

Wren laughed. "Yes! It was! And that's my point—I want to do this more often!"

"Kissing? Could get used to that," Silas agreed.

"Well, yeah, kissing's nice," Wren said, "but what I want is more time. Us time. Built-in time." Her words rushed faster than the noisy tide beneath their feet. "I'm saying I want to know now when's the next time I'm going to spend time with you. I want spending time together to be a thing we do regularly. Are you getting this?"

His arms were still around her, but he relaxed them so he could look down at her face.

"So, wait—you want to hit pause on the kissin' and schedule our next date? My schedule's unpredictable. I work a lot." Up until that moment, Silas had thought he understood what was going on. Now, he was adrift again, confused.

"Oh, my heavens. If I didn't already assume you were going to be a hard case, I would suspect you're doing this on purpose!" Then, after a moment, she jolted, as if a terrible thought had struck her. "Wait, is that your way of saying you don't want to see more of me?"

"No, it's me sayin' I don't know how to arrange it."

"Okay," Wren said, reclaiming her footing. "Let's back up and try this from a different angle."

She thought for a moment.

"I realize you really may not have much of an idea about matters of the heart, and I recognize you are exhausted and out of resources," Wren said, taking his hand. "I'm grabbing your hand so you don't spontaneously start crying, which it kind of looks like you're about to do. And now I am going to take a new tack."

Silas clung to her hand like a drowning man grabs a flotation ring.

"Si, have you ever heard the term *implied Saturday date*?" Wren asked, speaking very slowly.

"Implied date, not a real one? You're losin' me again."

"No, the *date* isn't implied, the *person* is implied." She rolled her eyes. "I underestimated how hard it'd be to tease a little commitment out of you. I'm trying really hard not to spook you—like a wild horse, right?"

She glanced at him, brows knitting with worry.

She's probably afraid I'm offended—might be, if I knew what the hell she was on about.

"It's implied by the context between two people that they'll be together on any given Saturday night."

A realization hit Silas swift and sharp as the kick of a mule. All the frustration and worry started to drain from his face.

"Aah, I get you now," he said, nodding.

"So, Silas Lopez . . . can I be your implied Saturday date?" she asked with a sigh of relief.

He looked into the depths of her vulnerable, uncertain green eyes, warmth swelling in his chest.

"I'd sure like that."

She pulled him into a tight hug, and he held on to her for a few moments, savoring the feeling.

As they started rock hopping again, Silas played the tape back in his head.

Not sure I'm totally understanding an implied Saturday date, but I've followed along enough to get the sense that maybe some sliver of Wren's heart might belong to me. Guess I'll figure out the rest come Saturday.

He stopped and threw an arm around her shoulder, squeezing her tight again before putting his chin on her head.

Did this mean he was staying here? It sure felt like that's what it meant, but when had he decided? When had this place become home to him?

He guessed his heart had decided somewhere along the way and just hadn't told him until now.

CHAPTER 82
Thursday, October 23

Silas took in the moment as he looked around the room. All the same faces from that first all-hands case conference. The same bakery boxes and heavenly scent. The same low ceiling and slightly worn surroundings. And yet everything felt different, as if a lifetime had passed.

He looked at the people around him—same crew, but no longer strangers. That ragtag bunch he'd inherited? Felt like a team now. They'd walked into that first meeting wary, uncertain what their future held, and justifiably so. Now, they were reinvigorated, optimistic, engaged, even *committed*. All of them had shown Silas good work. Many had shown flashes of real potential.

This once-unfamiliar room, with its fluorescent lights and banged-up furnishings, now felt like *his* place. The place where this team gathered to unite around a shared purpose. The nervous edge was gone, the original frowns and worried faces replaced now with comfortable premeeting banter—even a little laughter.

There was enough here for him to work with. He was sure he could build a top-notch department out of this crew.

"Round up, people! Think I got all day?" Silas said with a smile, indicating he was kidding a little.

Chairs scraped as people entered and sat.

"Most of you know all the details by now. Got our man. Federal custody, throw away the key. This team dug him up like a pack of bloodhounds sniffin' out the last sandwich on Earth. Takes determination and good police work to do what you people did, and I'm proud as hell of every one of you."

A ripple of chuckles moved through the group. Silas let the warmth of it settle before continuing.

"Started with a traffic issue. Ended up bringing down an international smuggling ring that was hurtin' a lot of people. Those smugglers had no business being in our town."

The room was quiet.

"You people held a bad guy accountable for bad things. For the kind of pain that don't go away easy. Got Blake Stevenson some answers, maybe a small measure of peace. Made citizens of this town feel just a little better about a senseless tragedy that happened under their noses."

The light changed, and Silas glanced up at the window to see a cloud scurry across the sun.

"That's called making a difference—and you did it," he said proudly, stepping to the side, eyes scanning the room, taking in the mix of familiar faces and tentative pride.

"On a more personal note—been an honor, and a pleasure, to do it with you." He cleared his throat to give his emotion a chance to subside. "I'm getting to know each of you better. Not as well as I'd like. A big case like this tossed all my plans for workin' with each of you in the early days right down the well. Hopin' to get back to that sometime soon here."

He paused, watching their faces again: Burig's tight blonde bun and bright-blue eyes; the upward tilt of Clark's chin bracketed by those rosy, pudgy cheeks, proud as he was; Marsh with her dark, intensely curious eyes, hair featuring the usual knot with the yellow Ticonderoga pencil; Byrne, with his carefully trimmed goatee, sitting by her side, always attentive. Evans up at the head near Genny, his ebony handsomeness and tall, athletic build contrasting her shorter, slightly frumpy but always crisp and professional demeanor. There was no doubt this group had the makings of a world-beating crew.

Eventually, he cleared his throat and added, "Which brings me to the next topic."

A hush fell, everyone sensing a shift, suddenly alert. He glanced toward the window, where the cloud had passed and bright light filtered through the blinds in fractured slices.

"I'm currently acting chief of police. Yesterday, Patrick Flood told me he'd like to make it permanent, earlier than scheduled." A few murmurs broke out. Silas turned to face them fully and noticed the surprise, the tilt of heads, the exchange of glances. "Now, before you go cussin' your bad luck, you should know I didn't say yes."

Shocked expressions swept across people's faces.

Genny, Clark, and Marsh looked downright dejected.

"Told him I needed time to think. Big commitment. Silas Lopez says he's gonna do something, he does it right or dies tryin'. But that ain't the whole of it." He let his voice drop, drawing them in. "Fact is, I don't need to think on it. I like it here, believe I could make a difference."

Confused faces surrounded him.

He placed both hands on the back of a chair and leaned in.

"The people who need to think about it are in this group right here," he said, wagging an index finger back and forth to encompass everyone in the room. "You want me to stick around? I will. I'll sign the papers and give you everything I got. You believe I can be an effective leader of this team, build each and every one of you into the best cop you could possibly be, then better believe I'll be here and do that." He took a breath, heart ticking a little faster now. "But if you got concerns about some tumbleweed cowboy blown into your town an' want a more conventional chief, maybe someone from around these parts . . . then I'll understand."

He stood up from the back of the chair, let it hang for just a second.

"I'll stay on as interim, help with finding my replacement, no hard feelin's. The choice is, and should be, yours."

He stopped there, put his hands on his hips. He met their eyes, steady and open.

He said nothing more. He'd ended so abruptly that the room was silent for an uncomfortably long time. Eventually, they broke eye contact and started to look around at each other, uncertain. Some furrowed their brows, like they didn't quite believe what he'd just said.

Silas had given them no specific call to action. He hadn't asked anybody for a yes or no or a show of hands; he'd just stopped talking. From the startled looks, it was clear no one knew what to do with that.

Just the way Silas wanted it. *Leave 'em stunned. Let it hang. See what bubbles up when you don't steer it.*

The silence held for a few seconds longer. Then, out of nowhere, Byrne began to clap—slow, quiet, steady. Marsh and Genny were quick to follow with a little more intensity. Evans, Clark, and Burig joined enthusiastically, and the room grew louder. Broad smiles spread as people stood and joined in, some clapping while others cheered.

Silas leaned against the wall, hands clasped behind him, nodding slowly as the room rose to its feet. As the clapping rolled on, he met each person's eyes and gave a nod that said, plain as day, *You have my word—I'll do right by you.*

When he'd made eye contact with every person in the room, Silas waved everyone downward with two hands and called for quiet. The room slowly came back to order. People looked at Silas in the sudden silence, expectantly waiting for him to give some kind of acceptance speech.

Instead, he picked up his mug. "Settled, then. Appreciate your trust. Proud to be your chief. Meeting's over. Let's get after it!"

Then, he and Bandit walked out of the room.

CHAPTER 83
Saturday, October 25

It was raining outside, and Wren's cottage windows had fogged. Silas's scratchy recording of Jimmie Rodgers played softly from the living room. Bandit twitched and let out soft little barks as he dreamed on the rug.

Wren's home was filled to the rafters with food smells—rich garlic, pork, chiles, oregano, and vinegar of *carne adovada*. The dark-red sauce bubbled languidly as it slow-cooked in a blue enameled pot on her stove. Elbow to elbow, Wren and Silas worked together in her small kitchen. To Silas, the small bumps and brushes felt just as good as the smells.

Wren's knife *thunked* against the cutting board as she chopped onion, zucchini, and green chiles for *calabacitas*. Silas was stooped, working on kneading the dough for the tortillas. He'd come clean and admitted to Wren that he preferred tortillas to silverware and always had.

It was the first Saturday evening they'd spent together, but they had big plans for more. Whenever they could, they promised each other they'd use Saturdays to cook one of the traditional Spanish New Mexican dishes Silas was homesick for.

It wasn't just Silas lobbying. The flavors, ingredients, techniques, and traditions fascinated Wren. Silas was delighted she wanted to learn more about his food and culture. When he arrived at her house that evening, he had brought her an enormous, gift-wrapped coffee table book for them to page through together. It was all about traditional Southwestern Spanish food, featuring a wealth of recipes, history, and reproductions of ancient sepia-toned photographs from the area. "Just arrived today," Silas had said as Wren tore the paper off with obvious delight.

While they were cooking, Wren reminded Silas he'd yet to tell her the story and details of how the Timothy Perkins case had played out in the end. When Silas finished narrating the final days, the final steps, and his interactions with Lieutenant Camara from New Bedford and Special Agent Calkins from Homeland Security, Wren was amazed—concerned, too.

"So, you just shot him? Silas, that's horrifying. An actual gunfight. I don't like—correction, I hate—to think of you in danger like that."

"He was pointing at his hostage. No danger to me. He painted the bull's-eye on himself."

"Still. Will you ever stop shocking me? I've got the shivers."

He wrapped his flour-covered arms around her and squeezed tight.

"I know. I'm so sorry. I don't want you to be shocked or scared. Gotta understand, I take every precaution." He held her upper arms and looked deeply into her eyes. "Nobody in the history of this world has ever had more to live for than me. Plus, I can still plug a silver dollar thrown twenty feet in the air. You should pity the fool who brings a gun into a conversation with me."

"Not sure that last part helps your case." She sighed. "Anyway, was your team pleased and satisfied in the end?"

"Believe they were, believe they were . . . That meeting felt different, like something had shifted. Like we were finally coming together as a team. It's why I felt comfortable putting the final decision in their hands," Silas said.

"What decision?" Wren asked casually, unsure what he was referring to.

"After we talked about the case, I told them about how, you know, Flood offered to make my position permanent. How I'd told him I needed to think about it. Of course, what I was really saying was that they were the ones who needed to be thinkin'. I knew I was ready to commit to staying, but only if the team really wanted me to, so I put it to them. Sure felt a measure of relief when they told me they wanted me to be their chief."

Silas happened to glance at Wren with a reflective smile, remembering the warmth of that moment with his team. But Wren had grown quiet. Her face had clouded over with a furrowed brow and a troubled look.

Silas picked up on the mood shift immediately, saying, "Wait, what made you sad? It was a nice moment—everybody clapping and whatnot."

Wren deflected, avoiding his question. "What do you mean, they applauded?"

"Told 'em I could stay or go, depending on if they thought I'd be a good leader. Let 'em stew a minute. They didn't know what to say, so they clapped. Nice moment is all I'm saying," Silas said with a nervous, solicitous tone in his voice.

Wren said nothing, but her gaze had gone a million miles away, so Silas said, "They clapped, stood up, and I said, 'That settles it. Now y'all get back to work.'"

Wren looked sick. Pale. Silas reached for her, concerned something was amiss. "What's wrong, my *pajarita*? Thought you'd think it was a nice story. But even someone as dense as me can tell you don't."

A single tear escaped Wren's eye.

A slow panic squeezed his chest.

"Talk to me, Wren. Did I do something wrong?" Silas asked.

Wren just shook her head, raising a hand to indicate she needed a moment to think and compose herself. Instead, Silas's impulse was to envelop her in a giant hug and hold her in his arms, leaning back for a moment to wipe away a tear with the rough pad of his large thumb. Cold fear was gripping him.

"What's wrong, Little Bird? Talk to me," Silas whispered into her hair.

Wren stepped back from his embrace—gently but with resolve.

Then, she spun, looking a little angry.

"You really would've left?" she asked, her voice incredulous. "I thought we had a real bond."

"We do have a real bond," Silas said. "Like nothing I've ever felt."

"But if they hadn't wanted you to stay, you would've just picked up and left?" Wren said, disappointment and a little anger tingeing her voice.

"The department? Sure. I like police work, but I'm not gonna stick around where I'm not wanted. Can't lead folks who ain't behind you. You get that, right?"

"And so you would've just left town?" Wren asked, too loudly for Silas's comfort.

"What?" Silas said, laughing nervously. "Who said anything about leaving town? I just got here. Unless you've got plans to move I don't know about, I ain't goin' anywhere."

Wren's face was a bunched-up ball of confusion. "But you said you'd quit as chief . . ."

"So what? What's that got to do with Provincetown? This is where *you* are. There's other kinds of work. I like being a cop, but if I needed to, I'd sweep streets. I'd do it happily if they were the streets you walked on." Silas looked at her. "That's what all this fuss is about? You got it in your bonehead I'd leave town that easily?"

Wren let out a small laugh, but waves of emotion and relief almost choked it. She blew and then wiped her nose with a piece of paper towel she'd yanked off the roll by the sink.

"You hear yourself just now? Ain't seen anything so sideways in a long while," Silas said.

"But you'd have to support yourself," Wren pointed out.

"I don't care 'bout money. Got more than enough. Never spent a dime I earned other than what I needed to keep clothes on my back, Bandit fed, and a roof over our heads. Got plenty of acorns stashed away. Plus, a solid pension from Utah. And ever stop to think what Mama's land might be worth? I'm an only child, Wren. Let's just say I'm not the least bit worried about that kinda stuff, and leave it there. I just figured I'd find some other way to contribute, to make a difference, make myself useful around here."

He smiled at her, and she smiled back, and he felt a wash of relief overtake him.

"Be your personal chef, way I'm pickin' up these advanced kitchen skills. Maybe carry a tripod and lights, do personal security work for a famous photographer I know," he added, joking.

Wren's tear-stained face brightened, and an involuntary snort escaped through her nose. A broad smile broke through, unstoppable.

"Oh, Silas!" she said, blowing her red nose again, then grabbed him and hugged him so hard, he could feel it flexing his ribs.

He hugged her back. Hugged like he had never hugged anything in his life.

"You're going to be the death of me, you knuckleheaded lug," Wren said. She softly pounded the heel of her fist on his chest. "This is embarrassing. I'm not like this. I've had a level head about relationships my entire life. I'm single at age thirty-three because I don't suffer fools. I've never been willing to date just anyone for the sake of dating."

She reflected for a second.

"Since I met you, I don't know what the hell is the matter with me. The intensity of these feelings has caught me completely off guard. It's turned me into somebody I don't recognize. Someone who would fall for a dangerous, violent man like Silas Lopez."

She looked up at him with a look of mock seriousness, mock concern.

Something told him that issue hadn't been put to bed yet. *But first, we deal with these other feelings.*

"Wren, you ain't alone in this. In case you haven't figured it out, this is . . . new territory for me, too. Been off my bearings. Truth is, I ain't found north since you walked up to me an' Bandit holdin' that camera. You saying you're struggling just a bit makes me feel a little less lost, if I'm honest."

Wren pushed her head under Silas's chin, and they held each other, Jimmie Rodgers yodeling softly behind them, their traditional Southwestern meal ingredients spread across the kitchen of this tiny East Coast seaside cottage in some kind of crude, mixed-up melding of cultures.

"Whippin' That Old TB" came on, and Jimmie crooned while Silas hummed along to the story about the guy who'd been all over but learned that there was no place he'd rather be than where she was.

They swayed a bit and held on for dear life. Eventually, Wren's head swiveled toward the kitchen. Silas cleared his throat.

"We got a lot of eating and cleaning up to do," he said. "What d'you say we get after it, *pajarita*?"

"What's that you're calling me, cowboy?" Wren asked.

"You know a wren is a type of little bird, right? I like to think of you as my *pajarita*, my little bird."

"Ah. That's sweet," Wren said with a blush. "You know, I've been wondering. Is there any chance the little bird could convince the big bird to nest here tonight?"

She asked this with an utterly irresistible look on her face.

Silas's reaction must've betrayed him.

He attempted to feign a completely indifferent shrug while saying, "Bandit invited? He and I always drop our bedrolls down next to each other, you know."

"Of course, you fool!"

"Then, yes, you could convince me," Silas said.

"Good. 'Cause I'm not letting you fly off tonight."